PENGUIN BOOKS

THE WITCHES OF EASTWICK

John Updike was born in 1932, in Shillington, Pennsylvania. He
attended the public schools of that town, Harvard College and
the Ruskin School of Drawing and Fine Art at Oxford, where he
spent a year on a Knox Fellowship. From 1955 to 1957 he was a
member of the staff of the *New Yorker*, to which he has contributed short stories, essays and poems. His novels include *The
Poorhouse Fair*, *Rabbit, Run*, *Couples*, *The Centaur*, *Of the
Farm*, *Rabbit Redux*, *Bech: A Book*, *A Month of Sundays*, *Marry
Me*, *The Coup*, *Rabbit is Rich*, winner of the 1982 Pulitzer Prize
for Fiction, *Bech is Back* and *Roger's Version*. He has also pub-
lished several volumes of short stories – *The Same Door*, *Pigeon
Feathers*, *The Music School*, *Museums and Women*, *Your Lover
Just Called* (published in America as *Too Far To Go*) and *Prob-
lems*; a children's book: *The Magic Flute*; books of poetry in-
cluding *Hoping for a Hoopoe*, *Telephone Poles*, *Tossing and
Turning* and the Penguin selection of his poetry entitled *Seventy
Poems*; plus two collections of essays and criticism – *Picked up
Pieces* and *Assorted Prose*. Many of John Updike's books are
published in Penguins.

D0551038

JOHN UPDIKE

THE WITCHES OF EASTWICK

PENGUIN BOOKS

Penguin Books Ltd, Harmondsworth, Middlesex, England
Viking Penguin Inc., 40 West 23rd Street, New York, New York 10010, U.S.A.
Penguin Books Australia Ltd, Ringwood, Victoria, Australia
Penguin Books Canada Ltd, 2801 John Street, Markham, Ontario, Canada L3R 1B4
Penguin Books (N.Z.) Ltd, 182–190 Wairau Road, Auckland 10, New Zealand

First published in the U.S.A. 1984
First trade edition published in Great Britain by André Deutsch 1984
Published in Penguin Books 1985
Reprinted 1985, 1987

Made and printed in Great Britain by
Richard Clay Ltd, Bungay, Suffolk
Typeset in Sabon

Chapters

i *The Coven*

"He was a meikle blak roch man, werie cold."
—*Isobel Gowdie, in 1662*

"Now efter that the deuell had endit his admonitions, he
cam down out of the pupit, and caused all the company to
com and kiss his ers, quhilk they said was cauld lyk yce; his
body was hard lyk yrn, as they thocht that handled him."
—*Agnes Sampson, in 1590*

"AND OH YES," Jane Smart said in her hasty yet
purposeful way; each *s* seemed the black tip of a
just-extinguished match held in playful hurt, as children do,
against the skin. "Sukie said a man has bought the Lenox
mansion."

"A man?" Alexandra Spofford asked, feeling off-center,
her peaceful aura that morning splayed by the assertive word.

"From New York," Jane hurried on, the last syllable
almost barked, its *r* dropped in Massachusetts style. "No wife
and family, evidently."

"Oh. One of those." Hearing Jane's northern voice bring
her this rumor of a homosexual come up from Manhattan to
invade them, Alexandra felt intersected where she was, in this
mysterious crabbed state of Rhode Island. She had been born
in the West, where white and violet mountains lift in pursuit
of the delicate tall clouds, and tumbleweed rolls in pursuit of
the horizon.

"Sukie wasn't so sure," Jane said swiftly, her *s*'s chastening.
"He appeared quite burly. She was struck by how hairy the

: 3 :

backs of his hands were. He told the people at Perley Realty he needed all that space because he was an inventor with a lab. And he owns a number of pianos."

Alexandra giggled; the noise, little changed since her Colorado girlhood, seemed produced not out of her throat but by a birdlike familiar perched on her shoulder. In fact the telephone was aching at her ear. And her forearm tingled, going numb. "How many pianos can a man have?"

This seemed to offend Jane. Her voice bristled like a black cat's fur, iridescent. She said defensively, "Well Sukie's only going by what Marge Perley told her at last night's meeting of the Horse Trough Committee." This committee supervised the planting and, after vandalism, the replanting of a big blue marble trough for watering horses that historically stood at the center of Eastwick, where the two main streets met; the town was shaped like an L, fitted around its ragged bit of Narragansett Bay. Dock Street held the downtown businesses, and Oak Street at right angles to it was where the lovely big old homes were. Marge Perley, whose horrid canary-yellow For Sale signs leaped up and down on trees and fences as on the tides of economics and fashion (Eastwick had for decades been semi-depressed and semi-fashionable) people moved in and out of the town, was a heavily made-up, go-getting woman who, if one at all, was a witch on a different wavelength from Jane, Alexandra, and Sukie. There was a husband, a tiny fussy Homer Perley always trimming their forsythia hedge back to stubble, and this made a difference. "The papers were passed in Providence," Jane explained, pressing the *nce* hard into Alexandra's ear.

"And with hairy backs to his hands," Alexandra mused. Near her face floated the faintly scratched and flecked and often repainted blankness of a wooden kitchen-cabinet door; she was conscious of the atomic fury spinning and skidding beneath such a surface, like an eddy of weary eyesight. As if in a crystal ball she saw that she would meet and fall in love with this man and that little good would come of it. "Didn't he have a name?" she asked.

"That's the stupidest thing," Jane Smart said. "Marge told Sukie and Sukie told me but something's scared it right out of my head. One of those names with a 'van' or a 'von' or a 'de' in it."

"How very swell," Alexandra answered, already dilating, diffusing herself to be invaded. A tall dark European, ousted from his ancient heraldic inheritance, travelling under a curse . . . "When is he supposed to move in?"

"She said he said soon. He could be in there now!" Jane sounded alarmed. Alexandra pictured the other woman's rather too full (for the rest of her pinched face) eyebrows lifting to make half-circles above her dark resentful eyes, whose brown was always a shade paler than one's memory of it. If Alexandra was the large, drifting style of witch, always spreading herself thin to invite impressions and merge with the landscape, and in her heart rather lazy and entropically cool, Jane was hot, short, concentrated like a pencil point, and Sukie Rougemont, busy downtown all day long gathering news and smiling hello, had an oscillating essence. So Alexandra reflected, hanging up. Things fall into threes. And magic occurs all around us as nature seeks and finds the inevitable forms, things crystalline and organic falling together at angles of sixty degrees, the isosceles triangle being the mother of structure.

She returned to putting up Mason jars of spaghetti sauce, sauce for more spaghetti than she and her children could consume even if bewitched for a hundred years in an Italian fairy tale, jar upon jar lifted steaming from the white-speckled blue boiler on the trembling, singing round wire rack. It was, she dimly perceived, some kind of ridiculous tribute to her present lover, a plumber of Italian ancestry. Her recipe called for no onions, two cloves of garlic minced and sautéed for three minutes (no more, no less; that was the magic) in heated oil, plenty of sugar to counteract acidity, a single grated carrot, more pepper than salt; but the teaspoon of crumbled basil is what catered to virility, and the dash of belladonna provided the release without which virility is merely a murderous congestion. All this must be added to her own tomatoes, picked and stored on every window sill these weeks past and now sliced and fed to the blender: ever since, two summers ago, Joe Marino had begun to come into her bed, a preposterous fecundity had overtaken the staked plants, out in the side garden where the southwestern sun slanted in through the line of willows each long afternoon. The crooked little tomato branches, pulpy and pale as if made of cheap green paper, broke under the weight of so much fruit; there was something frantic in such fertility, a crying-out like that of children frantic to please. Of plants tomatoes seemed the most human, eager and fragile and prone to rot. Picking the watery orange-red orbs, Alexandra felt she was cupping a giant lover's testicles in her hand. She recognized as she labored in her kitchen the something sadly menstrual in all this, the bloodlike sauce to be ladled upon the white spaghetti. The fat white strings would become her own white fat. This female struggle of hers against her own weight: at the age of thirty-eight she found it increasingly unnatural. In order to attract love must she deny her own body, like a neurotic saint of old? Nature is the index and context of all health and if we have an appetite it is there to be satisfied, satisfying thereby the cosmic order. Yet she sometimes despised herself as lazy, in taking a lover of a race so notoriously tolerant of corpulence.

Alexandra's lovers in the handful of years since her divorce had tended to be odd husbands let stray by the women who owned them. Her own former husband, Oswald Spofford, rested on a high kitchen shelf in a jar, reduced to multi-colored dust, the cap screwed on tight. Thus she had reduced him as her powers unfolded after their move to Eastwick from Norwich, Connecticut. Ozzie had known all about chrome and had transferred from a fixture factory in that hilly city with its too many peeling white churches to a rival manufacturer in a half-mile-long cinder-block plant south of Providence, amid the strange industrial vastness of this small state. They had moved seven years ago. Here in Rhode Island her powers had expanded like gas in a vacuum and she had reduced dear Ozzie as he made his daily trek to work and back along Route 4 first to the size of a mere man, the armor of patriarchal protector falling from him in the corrosive salt air of Eastwick's maternal beauty, and then to the size of a child as his chronic needs and equally chronic acceptance of her solutions to them made him appear pitiful, manipulable. He quite lost touch with the expanding universe within her. He had become much involved with their sons' Little League activities, and with the fixture company's bowling team. As Alexandra accepted first one and then several lovers, her cuckolded husband shrank to the dimensions and dryness of a doll, lying beside her in her great wide receptive bed at night like a painted log picked up at a roadside stand, or a stuffed baby alligator. By the time of their actual divorce her former lord and master had become mere dirt—matter in the wrong place, as her mother had briskly defined it long ago—some polychrome dust she swept up and kept in a jar as a souvenir.

The other witches had experienced similar transformations in their marriages; Jane Smart's ex, Sam, hung in the cellar of her ranch house among the dried herbs and simples and was occasionally sprinkled, a pinch at a time, into a philtre, for piquancy; and Sukie Rougemont had permanized hers in plastic and used him as a place mat. This last had happened rather recently; Alexandra could still picture Monty standing at cocktail parties in his Madras jacket and parsley-green slacks, braying out the details of the day's golf round and inveighing against the slow feminine foursome that had held them up all day and never invited them to play through. He had hated uppity women—female governors, hysterical war protesters, "lady" doctors, Lady Bird Johnson, even Lynda Bird and Luci Baines. He had thought them all butch. Monty had had wonderful teeth when he brayed, long and very even but not false, and, undressed, rather touching, thin bluish legs, much less muscular than his brown golfer's forearms. And with that puckered droop to his buttocks common to the softening flesh of middle-aged women. He had been one of Alexandra's first lovers. Now, it felt queer and queerly satisfying to set a mug of Sukie's tarry coffee upon a glossy plastic Madras, leaving a gritty ring.

This air of Eastwick empowered women. Alexandra had never tasted anything like it, except perhaps a corner of Wyoming she had driven through with her parents when she was about eleven. They had let her out of the car to pee beside some sagebrush and she had thought, seeing the altitudinous dry earth for the moment dampened in a dark splotch, *It doesn't matter. It will evaporate.* Nature absorbs all. This girlhood perception had stayed forever with her, along with the sweet sage taste of that roadside moment. Eastwick in its turn was at every moment kissed by the sea. Dock Street, its trendy shops with their perfumed candles and stained-glass shade-pulls aimed at the summer tourists and its old-style aluminum diner next to a bakery and its barber's next to a framer's and its little clattering newspaper office and long dark hardware store run by Armenians, was intertwined with saltwater as it slipped and slapped and slopped against the culverts and pilings the street in part was built upon, so that an unsteady veiny aqua sea-glare shimmered and shuddered on the faces of the local matrons as they carried orange juice and low-fat milk, luncheon meat and whole-wheat bread and filtered cigarettes out of the Bay Superette. The real supermarket, where one did a week's shopping, lay inland, in the part of Eastwick that had been farmland; here, in the eighteenth century, aristocratic planters, rich in slaves and cattle, had paid social calls on horseback, a slave galloping ahead of them to open the fence gates one after the other. Now, above the asphalted acres of the shopping-mall parking lot, exhaust fumes dyed with leaden vapors air within memory oxygenated by fields of cabbages and potatoes. Where corn, that remarkable agricultural artifact of the Indians, had flourished for generations, windowless little plants with names like Dataprobe and Computech manufactured mysteries, components so fine the workers wore plastic caps to keep dandruff from falling into the tiny electro-mechanical works.

Rhode Island, though famously the smallest of the fifty states, yet contains odd American vastnesses, tracts scarcely explored amid industrial sprawl, abandoned homesteads and forsaken mansions, vacant hinterlands hastily traversed by straight black roads, heathlike marshes and desolate shores on either side of the Bay, that great wedge of water driven like a stake clean to the state's heart, its trustfully named capital. "The fag end of creation" and "the sewer of New England," Cotton Mather called the region. Never meant to be a separate polity, settled by outcasts like the bewitching, soon-to-die Anne Hutchinson, this land holds manifold warps and wrinkles. Its favorite road sign is a pair of arrows pointing either way. Swampy poor in spots, elsewhere it became a playground of the exceedingly rich. Refuge of Quakers and antinomians, those final distillates of Puritanism, it is run by Catholics, whose ruddy Victorian churches loom like freighters in the sea of bastard architecture. There is a kind of metallic green stain, bitten deep into Depression-era shingles, that exists nowhere else. Once you cross the state line, whether at Pawtucket or Westerly, a subtle change occurs, a cheerful dishevelment, a contempt for appearances, a chimerical uncaring. Beyond the clapboard slums yawn lunar stretches where only an abandoned roadside stand offering the ghost of last summer's CUKES betrays the yearning, disruptive presence of man.

Through such a stretch Alexandra now drove to steal a new look at the old Lenox mansion. She took with her, in her pumpkin-colored Subaru station wagon, her black Labrador, Coal. She had left the last of the sterilized jars of sauce to cool on the kitchen counter and with a magnet shaped like Snoopy had pinned a note to the refrigerator door for her four children to find: MILK IN FRIG, OREOS IN BREADBOX, BACK IN ONE HOUR, LOVE.

The Lenox family in the days when Roger Williams was still alive had cozened the sachems of the Narragansett tribe out of land enough to form a European barony, and though a certain Major Lenox had heroically fallen in the Great Swamp Fight in King Philip's War, and his great-great-great-grandson Emory had eloquently urged New England's secession from the Union at the Hartford Convention of 1815, the family had taken a generally downward trend. By the time of Alexandra's arrival in Eastwick there was not a Lenox left in South County save one old widow, Abigail, in the stagnant quaint village of Old Wick; she went about the lanes muttering and cringing from the pebbles thrown at her by children who, called to account by the local constable, claimed they were defending themselves against her evil eye. The vast Lenox lands had long been broken up. The last of the effective male Lenoxes had caused to be built on an island the family still owned, in the tracts of salt marsh behind East Beach, a brick mansion in diminished but locally striking imitation of the palatial summer "cottages" being erected in Newport during this gilded age. Though a causeway had been constructed and repeatedly raised by fresh importation of gravel, the mansion always suffered the inconvenience of being cut off when the tide was high, and had been occupied fitfully by a succession of owners since 1920, and had been allowed by them to slide into disrepair. The great roof slates, some reddish and some a bluish gray, came crashing unobserved in the winter storms and lay like nameless tombstones in summer's lank tangle of uncut grass; the cunningly fashioned copper gutters and flashing turned green and rotten; the ornate octagonal cupola with a view to all points of the compass developed a list to the west; the massive end chimneys, articulated like bundles of organ pipes or thickly muscled throats, needed mortar and were dropping bricks. Yet the silhouette the mansion presented from afar was still rather chasteningly grand, Alexandra thought. She had parked on the shoulder of the beach road to gaze across the quarter-mile of marsh.

This was September, season of full tides; the marsh between here and the island this afternoon was a sheet of skyey water flecked by the tips of salt hay turning golden. It would be an hour or two before the causeway in and out became passable. The time now was after four; there was a stillness, and a clothy weight to the sky that hid the sun. Once the mansion would have been masked by an *allée* of elms continuing the causeway upward toward the front entrance, but the elms had died of Dutch elm disease and remained as tall stumps lopped of their wide-arching branches, standing like men in shrouds, leaning like that armless statue of Balzac by Rodin. The house had a forbidding, symmetrical face, with many windows that seemed slightly small—especially the third-story row, which went straight across beneath the roof without variation: the servants' floor. Alexandra had been in the building years ago, when, still trying to do the right wifely things, she had gone with Ozzie to a benefit concert held in its ballroom. She could remember little but room after room, scantly furnished and smelling of salt air and mildew and vanished pleasures. The slates of its neglected roof merged in tint with a darkness gathering in the north—no, more than clouds troubled the atmosphere. Thin white smoke was lifting from the left-hand chimney. Someone was inside.

That man with hairy backs to his hands.

Alexandra's future lover.

More likely, she decided, a workman or watchman he had hired. Her eyes smarted from trying to see so far, so intensely. Her insides like the sky had gathered to a certain darkness, a sense of herself as a pathetic onlooker. Female yearning was in all the papers and magazines now; the sexual equation had become reversed as girls of good family flung themselves toward brutish rock stars, callow unshaven guitarists from the slums of Liverpool or Memphis somehow granted indecent power, dark suns turning these children of sheltered upbringing into suicidal orgiasts. Alexandra thought of her tomatoes, the juice of violence beneath the plump complacent skin. She thought of her own older daughter, alone in her room with those Monkees and Beatles . . . one thing for Marcy, another for her mother to be mooning so, straining her eyes.

She shut her eyes tight, trying to snap out of it. She got back into the car with Coal and drove the half-mile of straight black road to the beach.

After season, if no one was about, you could walk with a dog unleashed. But the day was warm, and old cars and VW vans with curtained windows and psychedelic stripes filled the narrow parking lot; beyond the bathhouses and the pizza shack many young people wearing bathing suits lay supine on the sand with their radios as if summer and youth would never end. Alexandra kept a length of clothesline on the back-seat floor in deference to beach regulations. Coal shivered in distaste as she passed the loop through his studded collar. All muscle and eagerness, he pulled her along through the resisting sand. She halted to tug off her beige espadrilles and the dog gagged; she dropped the shoes behind a tuft of beach grass near the end of the boardwalk. The boardwalk had been scattered into its six-foot segments by a recent high tide, which had also left above the flat sand beside the sea a wrack of Clorox bottles and tampon sleeves and beer cans so long afloat their painted labels had been eaten away; these

unlabelled cans looked frightening—blank like the bombs
terrorists make and then leave in public places to bring the
system down and thus halt the war. Coal pulled her on, past a
heap of barnacled square-cut rocks that had been part of a
jetty built when this beach was the toy of rich men and not an
overused public playground. The rocks were a black-freckled
pale granite and one of the largest held a bolted bracket rusted
by the years to the fragility of a Giacometti. The emissions of
the young people's radios, rock of an airier sort, washed
around her as she walked along, conscious of her heaviness, of
the witchy figure she must cut with her bare feet and men's
baggy denims and worn-out green brocaded jacket, something from Algeria she and Ozzie had bought in Paris on their
honeymoon seventeen years ago. Though she turned a gyp-
syish olive in summer, Alexandra was of northern blood; her
maiden name had been Sorensen. Her mother had recited to
her the superstition about changing your initial when you
marry, but Alexandra had been a scoffer at magic then and on
fire to make babies. Marcy had been conceived in Paris, on an
iron bed.

Alexandra wore her hair in a single thick braid down her
back; sometimes she pinned the braid up like a kind of spine
to the back of her head. Her hair had never been a true clarion
Viking blond but of a muddy pallor now further dirtied by
gray. Most of the gray hair had sprouted in front; the nape
was still as finespun as those of the girls that lay here basking.
The smooth young legs she walked past were caramel in
color, with white fuzz, and aligned as if in solidarity. One
girl's bikini bottom gleamed, taut and simple as a drum in the
flat light.

Coal plunged on, snorting, imagining some scent, some
dissolving animal vein within the kelpy scent of the oceanside.
The beach population thinned. A young couple lay intertwined in a space they had hollowed in the pocked sand; the
boy murmured into the base of the girl's throat as if into a

microphone. An overmuscled male trio, their long hair flinging as they grunted and lunged, were playing Frisbee, and only when Alexandra purposefully let the powerful black Labrador pull her through this game's wide triangle did they halt their insolent tossing and yelping. She thought she heard the word "hag" or "bag" at her back after she had passed through, but it might have been an acoustic trick, a mistaken syllable of sea-slap. She was drawing near to where a wall of eroded concrete topped by a helix of rusted barbed wire marked the end of public beach; still there were knots of youth and seekers of youth and she did not feel free to set loose poor Coal, though he repeatedly gagged at the restraint of his collar. His desire to run burned the rope in her hand. The sea seemed unnaturally still—tranced, marked by milky streaks far out, where a single small launch buzzed on the sounding board of its level surface. On Alexandra's other side, nearer to hand, beach pea and woolly hudsonia crept down from the dunes; the beach narrowed here and became intimate, as you could see from the nests of cans and bottles and burnt driftwood and the bits of shattered Styrofoam cooler and the condoms like small dried jellyfish corpses. The cement wall had been spray-painted with linked names. Everywhere, desecration had set its hand and only footsteps were eased away by the ocean.

The dunes at one point were low enough to permit a glimpse of the Lenox mansion, from another angle and farther away; its two end chimneys stuck up like hunched buzzard's wings on either side of the cupola. Alexandra felt irritated and vengeful. Her insides felt bruised; she resented the overheard insult "hag" and the general vast insult of all this heedless youth prohibiting her from letting her dog, her friend and familiar, run free. She decided to clear the beach for herself and Coal by willing a thunderstorm. One's inner weather always bore a relation to the outer; it was simply a question of reversing the current, which occurred rather easily once power had been assigned to the primary pole, oneself as a woman. So many of Alexandra's remarkable powers had flowed from this mere reappropriation of her assigned self, achieved not until midlife. Not until midlife did she truly believe that she had a right to exist, that the forces of nature had created her not as an afterthought and companion—a bent rib, as the infamous *Malleus Maleficarum* had it—but as the mainstay of the continuing Creation, as the daughter of a daughter and a woman whose daughters in turn would bear daughters. Alexandra closed her eyes while Coal shivered and whimpered in fright and she willed this vast interior of herself—this continuum reaching back through the generations of humanity and the parenting primates and beyond them through the lizards and the fish to the algae that cooked up the raw planet's first DNA in their microscopic tepid innards, a continuum that in the other direction arched to the end of all life, through form after form, pulsing, bleeding, adapting to the cold, to the ultraviolet rays, to the bloating, weakening sun—she willed these so pregnant depths of herself to darken, to condense, to generate an interface of lightning between tall walls of air. And the sky in the north did rumble, so faintly only Coal could hear. His ears stiffened and swivelled, their roots in his scalp come alive. *Mertalia, Musalia, Dophalia*: in loud unspoken syllables she invoked the forbidden names. *Onemalia, Zitanseia, Goldaphaira, Dedulsaira*. Invisibly Alexandra grew huge, in a kind of maternal wrath gathering all the sheaves of this becalmed September world to herself, and the lids of her eyes flew open as if at a command. A blast of cold air hit from the north, the approach of a front that whipped the desultory pennants on the distant bathhouse straight out from their staffs. Down at that end, where the youthful naked crowd was thickest, a collective sigh of surprise arose, and then titters of excitement as the wind stiffened, and the sky toward Providence stood revealed as possessing the density of some translucent, empurpled rock. *Ghemynaea, Gegropheira, Cedani, Gilthar, Godieb.* At the base of this cliff of atmosphere cumulus clouds, moments ago as innocuous as flowers afloat in a pond, had begun to boil, their edges brilliant as marble against the blackening air. The very medium of seeing was altered, so that the seaside grasses and creeping glassworts near Alexandra's fat bare toes, corned and bent by years in shoes shaped by men's desires and cruel notions of beauty, seemed traced in negative upon the sand, whose tracked and pitted surface, suddenly tinted lavender, appeared to rise like the skin of a bladder being inflated under the stress of the atmospheric change. The offending youths had seen their Frisbee sail away from their hands like a kite and were hurrying to gather up their portable radios and their six-packs, their sneakers and jeans and tie-dyed tank tops. Of the couple who had made a hollow for themselves, the girl could not be comforted; she was sobbing while the boy with fumbling haste tried to relatch the hooks of her loosened bikini bra. Coal barked at nothing, in one direction and then the other, as the drop in barometric pressure maddened his ears.

Now the immense and impervious ocean, so recently tranquil all the way to Block Island, sensed the change. Its surface rippled and corrugated where sweeping cloud shadows touched it—these patches shrivelling, almost, like something burned. The motor of the launch buzzed more sharply. The sails at sea had melted and the air vibrated with the merged roar of auxiliary engines churning toward harbor. A hush caught in the throat of the wind, and then the rain began, great icy drops that hurt like hailstones. Footsteps pounded past Alexandra as honey-colored lovers raced toward cars parked at the far end, by the bathhouses. Thunder rumbled, at the top of the cliff of dark air, along whose face small scuds of paler gray, in the shape of geese, of gesticulating orators, of unravelling skeins of yarn, were travelling rapidly. The large hurtful drops broke up into a finer, thicker

rain, which whitened in streaks where the wind like a
harpist's fingers strummed it. Alexandra stood still while
cold water glazed her; she recited in her inner spaces,
Ezoill, Musil, Puri, Tamen. Coal at her feet whimpered;
he had wrapped her legs around with clothesline. His
body, its hair licked flat against the muscles, glistened
and trembled. Through veils of rain she saw that the
beach was empty. She undid the rope leash and set the dog
free.

But Coal stayed huddled by her ankles, alarmed as lightning flashed once, and then again, double. Alexandra counted
the seconds until thunder: five. By rough rule this made the
storm she had conjured up ten miles in diameter, if these
strokes were at the heart. Blunderingly thunder rumbled and
cursed. Tiny speckled sand crabs were emerging now from
their holes by the dozen and scurrying sideways toward the
frothing sea. The color of their shells was so sandy they
appeared transparent. Alexandra steeled herself and crunched
one beneath the sole of her bare foot. Sacrifice. There must
always be sacrifice. It was one of nature's rules. She danced
from crab to crab, crushing them. Her face from hairline to
chin streamed and all the colors of the rainbow were in this
liquid film, because of the agitation of her aura. Lightning
kept taking her photograph. She had a cleft in her chin and a
smaller, scarcely perceptible one in the tip of her nose; her
handsomeness derived from the candor of her broad brow
beneath the gray-edged wings of hair swept symmetrically
back to form her braid, and from the clairvoyance of her
slightly protuberant eyes, the gun-metal gray of whose irises
was pushed to the rims as if each utterly black pupil were an
anti-magnet. Her mouth had a grave plumpness and deep
corners that lent the appearance of a smile. She had attained
her height of five-eight by the age of fourteen and had
weighed one-twenty at the age of twenty; she was somewhere
around one hundred sixty pounds now. One of the libera-

tions of becoming a witch had been that she had ceased constantly weighing herself.

As the little sand crabs were transparent on the speckled sand, so Alexandra, wet through and through, felt transparent to the rain, one with it, its temperature and that of her blood brought into concord. The sky over the sea had now composed itself into horizontal fuzzy strips; the thunder was subsiding to a mutter and the rain to a warm drizzle. This downpour would never make the weather maps. The crab she had first crushed was still moving its claws, like tiny pale feathers touched by a breeze. Coal, his terror slipped at last, ran in circles, wider and wider, adding the quadruple gouges of his claws to the triangular designs of gull feet, the daintier scratches of the sandpipers, and the dotted lines of crab scrabble. These clues to other realms of being—to be a crab, moving sideways on tiptoe with eyes on stems! to be a barnacle, standing on your head in a little folding bucket kicking food toward your mouth!—had been cratered over by raindrops. The sand was soaked to the color of cement. Her clothes even to her underwear had been plastered against her skin so that she felt to herself like a statue by Segal, pure white, all the sinuous tubes and bones of her licked by a kind of mist. Alexandra strode to the end of the purged public beach, to the wire-topped wall, and back. She reached the parking lot and picked up her sodden espadrilles where she had left them, behind a tuft of *Ammophila breviligulata*. Its long arrowlike blades glistened, having relaxed their edges in the rain.

She opened the door of her Subaru and turned to call loudly for Coal, who had vanished into the dunes. "Come, doggie!" this stately plump woman sang out. "Come, baby! Come, angel!" To the eyes of the young people huddled with their sodden gritty towels and ignominious goosebumps inside the gray-shingled bathhouse and underneath the pizza shack's awning (striped the colors of tomato and cheese),

Alexandra appeared miraculously dry, not a hair of her massive braid out of place, not a patch of her brocaded green jacket damp. It was such unverifiable impressions that spread among us in Eastwick the rumor of witchcraft.

Alexandra was an artist. Using few tools other than tooth-picks and a stainless-steel butter knife, she pinched and pressed into shape little lying or sitting figurines, always of women in gaudy costumes painted over naked contours; they sold for fifteen or twenty dollars in two local boutiques called the Yapping Fox and the Hungry Sheep. Alexandra had no clear idea of who bought them, or why, or exactly why she made them, or who was directing her hand. The gift of sculpture had descended with her other powers, in the period when Ozzie turned into colored dust. The impulse had visited her one morning as she sat at the kitchen table, the children off at school, the dishes done. That first morning, she had used one of her children's Play-Doh, but she came to depend for clay upon an extraordinarily pure kaolin she dug herself from a little pit near Coventry, a slippery exposed bank of greasy white earth in an old widow's back yard, behind the mossy wreck of an outhouse and the chassis of a prewar Buick just like, by uncanny coincidence, one that Alexandra's father used to drive, to Salt Lake City and Denver and Albuquerque and the lonely towns between. He had sold work clothes, overalls and blue jeans before they became fashionable—before they became the world's garb, the cos-tume that sheds the past. You took your own burlap sacks to Coventry, and you paid the widow twelve dollars a bag. If the sacks were too heavy she helped you lift them; like Alexandra she was strong. Though at least sixty-five, she dyed her hair a glittering brass color and wore pants suits of turquoise or magenta so tight the flesh below her belt was bunched in sausagey rolls. This was nice. Alexandra read a message for herself here: Getting old could be jolly, if you stayed strong. The widow sported a high horselaugh and big gold loop earrings her brassy hair was always pulled back to display. A rooster or two performed its hesitant, preening walk in the tall grass of this unkempt yard; the back of the woman's lean clapboard house had peeled down to the bare gray wood, though the front was painted white. Alexandra, with the back of her Subaru sagging under the weight of the widow's clay, always returned from these trips heartened and exhilarated, full of the belief that a conspiracy of women upholds the world.

Her figurines were in a sense primitive. Sukie or was it Jane had dubbed them her "bubbies"—chunky female bodies four or five inches long, often faceless and without feet, coiled or bent in recumbent positions and heavier than expected when held in the hand. People seemed to find them comforting and took them away from the shops, in a steady, sneaking trickle that intensified in the summer but was there even in January. Alexandra sculpted their naked forms, stabbing with the toothpick for a navel and never failing to provide a nicked hint of the vulval cleft, in protest against the false smoothness there of the dolls she had played with as a girl; then she painted clothes on them, sometimes pastel bathing suits, sometimes impossibly clinging gowns patterned in polka dots or asterisks or wavy cartoon-ocean stripes. No two were quite alike, though all were sisters. Her procedure was dictated by the feeling that as clothes were put on each morning over our nakedness, so they should be painted upon rather than carved onto these primal bodies of rounded soft clay. She baked them two dozen at a time in a little electric Swedish kiln kept in a workroom off her kitchen, an unfinished room but with a wood floor, unlike the next room, a dirt-floored storage space where old flowerpots and lawn rakes, hoes and Wellington boots and pruning shears were kept. Self-taught, Alexandra had been at sculpture for five years—since before the divorce, to which it, like most manifestations of her blossoming selfhood, had contributed. Her children, especially Marcy, but Ben and little Eric too, hated the bubbies, thought them indecent, and once in their agony of embarrassment had shattered a batch that was cooling; but now they were reconciled, as if to defective siblings. Children are of a clay that to an extent remains soft, though irremediable twists show up in their mouths and a glaze of avoidance hardens in their eyes.

Jane Smart, too, was artistically inclined—a musician. She gave piano lessons to make ends meet, and substituted as choir director in local churches sometimes, but her love was the cello; its vibratory melancholy tones, pregnant with the sadness of wood grain and the shadowy largeness of trees, would at odd moonlit hours on warm nights come sweeping out of the screened windows of her low little ranch house where it huddled amid many like it on the curved roads of the Fifties development called Cove Homes. Her neighbors on their quarter-acre lots, husband and wife, child and dog, would move about, awakened, and discuss whether or not to call the police. They rarely did, abashed and, it may be, intimidated by the something naked, a splendor and grief, in Jane's playing. It seemed easier to fall back to sleep, lulled by the double-stopped scales, first in thirds, then in sixths, of Popper's études, or, over and over, the four measures of tied sixteenth-notes (where the cello speaks almost alone) of the second andante of Beethoven's Quartet No. 15, in A Minor. Jane was no gardener, and the neglected tangle of rhododendron, hydrangea, arborvitae, barberry, and box around her foundations helped muffle the outpour from her windows. This was an era of many proclaimed rights, and of blatant public music, when every supermarket played its Muzak version of "Satisfaction" and "I Got You, Babe" and wherever two or three teen-agers gathered together the spirit of Woodstock was proclaimed. Not the volume but the timbre of Jane's passion, the notes often fumbled at but resumed at the same somber and undivertible pitch, caught at the attention bothersomely. Alexandra associated the dark notes with Jane's dark eyebrows, and with that burning insistence in her voice that an answer be provided forthwith, that a formula be produced with which to wedge life into place, to nail its secret down, rather than drifting as Alexandra did in the faith that the secret was ubiquitous, an aromaless element in the air that the birds and blowing weeds fed upon.

Sukie had nothing of what she would call an artistic talent but she loved social existence and had been driven by the reduced circumstances that attend divorce to write for the local weekly, the Eastwick *Word*. As she marched with her bright lithe stride up and down Dock Street listening for gossip and speculating upon the fortunes of the shops, Alexandra's gaudy figurines in the window of the Yapping Fox, or a poster in the window of the Armenians' hardware store advertising a chamber-music concert to be held in the Unitarian Church and including *Jane Smart, cello* thrilled her like a glint of beach glass in the sand or a quarter found shining on the dirty sidewalk—a bit of code buried in the garble of daily experience, a stab of communication between the inner and outer world. She loved her two friends, and they her. Today, after typing up her account of last night's meetings at Town Hall of the Board of Assessors (dull: the same old land-poor widows begging for an abatement) and the Planning Board (no quorum: Herbie Prinz was in Bermuda), Sukie looked forward hungrily to Alexandra's and Jane's coming over to her house for a drink. They usually convened Thursdays, in one of their three houses. Sukie lived in the middle of town, which was convenient for her work, though the house, a virtually miniature 1760 saltbox on a kind of curved little alley off Oak called Hemlock Lane, was a great step down from the sprawling farmhouse—six bedrooms, thirty acres, a station wagon, a sports car, a Jeep, four dogs—that she and Monty had shared. But her girlfriends made it seem fun, a kind of pretense or interlude of enchantment; they usually affected some odd and colorful bit of costume for their gatherings. In a gold-threaded Parsi shawl Alexandra entered, stooping, at the side door to the kitchen; in her hands, like dumbbells or bloody evidence, were two jars of her peppery, basil-flavored tomato sauce.

The witches kissed, cheek to cheek. "Here sweetie, I know you like nutty dry things best *but*," Alexandra said, in that thrilling contralto that dipped deep into her throat like a Russian woman saying "*byelo*." Sukie took the twin gifts into her own, more slender hands, their papery backs stippled with fading freckles. "The tomatoes came on like a plague this year for some reason," Alexandra continued. "I put about a hundred jars of this up and then the other night I went out in the garden in the dark and shouted, 'Fuck you, the rest of you can all rot!' "

"I remember one year with the zucchini," Sukie responded, setting the jars dutifully on a cupboard shelf from which she would never take them down. As Alexandra said, Sukie loved dry nutty things—celery, cashews, pilaf, pretzel sticks, tiny little nibbles such as kept her monkey ancestors going in the trees. When alone, she never sat down to eat, just dipped into some yoghurt with a Wheat Thin while standing at the kitchen sink or carrying a 79 cent bag of onion-flavored crinkle chips into her TV den with a stiff bourbon. "I did *every*thing," she said to Alexandra, relishing exaggeration, her active hands flickering in the edges of her own vision. "Zucchini bread, zucchini soup, salad, frittata, zucchini stuffed with hamburger and baked, cut into slices and fried, cut into sticks to use with a dip, it was *wild*. I even threw a lot into the blender and told the children to put it on their bread instead of peanut butter. Monty was desperate; he said even his shit smelled of zucchini."

Though this reminiscence had referred, implicitly and

pleasurably, to her married days and their plenty, mention of an old husband was a slight breach of decorum and snatched away Alexandra's intention to laugh. Sukie was the most recently divorced and the youngest of the three. She was a slender redhead, her hair down her back in a sheaf trimmed straight across and her long arms laden with these freckles the cedar color of pencil shavings. She wore copper bracelets and a pentagram on a cheap thin chain around her throat. What Alexandra, with her heavily Hellenic, twice-cleft features, loved about Sukie's looks was the cheerful simian thrust: Sukie's big teeth pushed her profile below the brief nose out in a curve, a protrusion especially of her upper lip, which was longer and more complex in shape than her lower, with a plumpness on either side of the center that made even her silences seem puckish, as if she were tasting amusement all the time. Her eyes were hazel and round and rather close together. Sukie moved nimbly in her little comedown of a kitchen, everything crowded together and the sink stained and miniature, and beneath it a smell of poverty lingering from all the Eastwick generations who had lived here and had imposed their patchy renovations in the centuries when old hand-hewn houses like this were not considered charming. Sukie pulled a can of Planter's Beer Nuts, wickedly sugary, from a cupboard shelf with one hand and with the other took from the rubber-coated wire drainer on the sink a little paisley-patterned brass-rimmed dish to hold them. Boxes crackling, she strewed an array of crackers on a platter around a wedge of red-coated Gouda cheese and some supermarket pâté still in the flat tin showing a laughing goose. The platter was coarse tan earthenware gouged and glazed with the semblance of a crab. Cancer. Alexandra feared it, and saw its emblem everywhere in nature—in clusters of blueberries in the neglected places by rocks and bogs, in the grapes ripening on the sagging rotten arbor outside her kitchen windows, in the ants bringing up conical granular hills in the cracks in her asphalt driveway, in all blind and irresistible multiplications. "Your usual?" Sukie asked, a shade tenderly, for Alexandra, as if older than she was, had with a sigh dropped her body, without removing her shawl, into the kitchen's one welcoming concavity, an old blue easy chair too disgraceful to have elsewhere; it was losing stuffing at its seams and at the corners of its arms a polished gray stain had been left where many wrists had rubbed.

"I guess it's still tonic time," Alexandra decided, for the coolness that had come in with the thunderstorm some days ago had stayed. "How's your vodka supply?" Someone had once told her that not only was vodka less fattening but it irritated the lining of your stomach less than gin. Irritation, psychic as well as physical, was the source of cancer. Those get it who leave themselves open to the idea of it; all it takes is one single cell gone crazy. Nature is always waiting, watching for you to lose faith so she can insert her fatal stitch.

Sukie smiled, broader. "I knew you were coming." She displayed a brand-new Gordon's bottle, with its severed boar's head staring with a round orange eye and its red tongue caught between teeth and a curling tusk.

Alexandra smiled to see this friendly monster. "Plenty of tonic, puh-*leese*. The calories!"

The tonic bottle fizzed in Sukie's fingers as if scolding. Perhaps cancer cells were more like bubbles of carbonation, percolating through the bloodstream, Alexandra thought. She must stop thinking about it. "Where's Jane?" she asked.

"She said she'd be a little late. She's rehearsing for that concert at the Unitarians'."

"With that awful Neff," Alexandra said.

"With that awful Neff," Sukie echoed, licking quinine water from her fingers and looking in her bare refrigerator for a lime. Raymond Neff taught music at the high school, a pudgy effeminate man who yet had fathered five children upon his slovenly, sallow, steel-bespectacled, German-born wife. Like most good schoolteachers he was a tyrant, unctuous and insistent; in his dank way he wanted to sleep with everybody. Jane was sleeping with him these days. Alexandra had succumbed a few times in the past but the episode had moved her so little Sukie was perhaps unaware of its vibrations, its afterimage. Sukie herself appeared to be chaste vis-à-vis Neff, but then she had been available least long. Being a divorcee in a small town is a little like playing Monopoly; eventually you land on all the properties. The two friends wanted to rescue Jane, who in a kind of indignant hurry was always selling herself short. It was the hideous wife, with her strawy dull hair cut short as if with grass clippers and her carefully pronounced malapropisms and her goggle-eyed intent way of listening to every word, whom they disapproved of. When you sleep with a married man you in a sense sleep with the wife as well, so she should not be an utter embarrassment.

"Jane has such *beaut*iful possibilities," Sukie said a bit automatically, as she scrabbled with a furious monkey-motion in the refrigerator's icemaker to loosen some more cubes. A witch can freeze water at a glance but sometimes unfreezing it is the problem. Of the four dogs she and Monty had supported in their heyday, two had been loping silvery-brown Weimaraners, and she had kept one, called Hank; he was now leaning on her legs in the hope that she was struggling in the refrigerator on his behalf.

"But she *wastes* herself," Alexandra said, completing the sentence. "Wastes in the old-fashioned sense," she added, since this was during the Vietnam War and the war had given the word an awkward new meaning. "If she's serious about her music she should go somewhere serious with it, a city. It's a terrible waste, a conservatory graduate playing fiddle for a bunch of deaf old biddies in a dilapidated church."

"She feels safe here," Sukie said, as if they didn't.

"She doesn't even wash herself, have you ever noticed her

smell?" Alexandra asked, not about Jane but about Greta Neff, by a train of association Sukie had no trouble following, their hearts were so aligned on one wavelength.

"And those granny glasses!" Sukie agreed. "She looks like John Lennon." She made a kind of solemn sad-eyed thin-lipped John Lennon face. "I sink sen we can drink ouur— *sprechen Sie wass?*—bev-er-aitches neeoauu." There was an awful un-American diphthong that came out of Greta Neff's mouth, a kind of twisting of the vowel up against her palate.

Cackling, they took their drinks into the "den," a little room with peeling wallpaper in a splashy faded pattern of vines and fruit baskets and a bellied plaster ceiling at a strange sharp slant because the room was half tucked under the stairs that went up to the atticlike second floor. The room's one window, too high for a woman not standing on a stool to peer out of, had lozenge panes of leaded glass, thick glass bubbled and warped like bottle bottoms.

"A cabbagy smell," Alexandra amplified, lowering herself and her tall silvery drink onto a love seat covered in a crewelwork of flamboyant tattered swirls, stylized vines unravelling. "He carries it on his clothes," she said, thinking simultaneously that this was a little like Monty and the zucchini and that she was evidently inviting Sukie with this intimate detail to guess that she had slept with Neff. Why? It was nothing to brag about. And yet, it was. How he had sweated! For that matter she had slept with Monty, too; and had never smelled zucchini. One fascinating aspect of sleeping with husbands was the angle they gave you on their wives: they saw them as nobody else did. Neff saw poor dreadful Greta as a kind of quaint beribboned Heidi, a sweet bit of edelweiss he had fetched from a perilous romantic height (they had met in a Frankfurt beer hall while he was stationed in West Germany instead of fighting in Korea), and Monty . . . Alexandra squinted at Sukie, trying to remember what Monty had said of her. He had said little, being such a would-be gentleman. But once he had let slip, having come to Alexandra's bed from some awkward consultation at the bank, and being still preoccupied, the words "She's a lovely girl, but bad luck, somehow. Bad luck for others, I mean. I think she's fairly good luck for herself." And it was true, Monty had lost a great deal of his family's money while married to Sukie, which everyone had blamed simply on his own calm stupidity. *He* had never sweated. He had suffered from that hormonal deficiency of the wellborn, an inability to relate himself to the possibility of hard labor. His body had been almost hairless, with that feminine soft bottom.

"Greta must be great in the sack," Sukie was saying. "All those *Kinder*. *Fünf*, yet."

Neff had allowed to Alexandra that Greta was ardent but strenuous, very slow to come but determined to do so. She would make a grim witch: those murderous Germans. "We must be nice to her," Alexandra said, back to the subject of Jane. "Speaking to her on the phone yesterday, I was struck by how angry she sounded. That lady is burning up."

Sukie glanced over at her friend, since this seemed a slightly false note. Some intrigue had begun for Alexandra, some new man. In the split-second of Sukie's glance, Hank with his lolling gray Weimaraner tongue swept two Wheat Thins off the crab platter, which she had set down on a much-marred pine sea chest refinished by an antique dealer to be used as a coffee table. Sukie loved her shabby old things; there was a kind of blazonry in them, a costume of rags affected by the soprano in the second act of the opera. Hank's tongue was coming back for the cheese when Sukie caught the motion in the corner of her eye and slapped his muzzle; it was rubbery, in the hard way of automobile tires, so the slap hurt her own fingers. "Ow, you bastard," she said to the dog, and to her friend, "Angrier than anybody else?" meaning themselves. She took a rasping sip of neat bourbon. She drank whiskey summer and winter and the reason, which she had forgotten, was that a boyfriend at Cornell had once told her that it brought out the gold flecks in her green eyes. For the same vain reason she tended to dress in shades of brown and in suede with its animal shimmer.

"Oh yes. We're in lovely shape," the bigger, older woman answered, her mind drifting from this irony toward the subject of that conversation with Jane—the new man in town, in the Lenox mansion. But even as it drifted, her mind, like a passenger in an airplane who amidst the life-imperilling sensations of lifting off looks down to marvel at the enamelled precision and glory of the Earth (the houses with their roofs and chimneys so sharp, so finely made, and the lakes truly mirrors as in the Christmas yards our parents had arranged while we were sleeping; it was all true, and even maps are true!), took note of how lovely Sukie was, bad luck or not, with her vivid hair dishevelled and even her eyelashes looking a little mussed after her hard day of typing and looking for the right word under the harsh lights, her figure in its milky-green sweater and dark suede skirt so erect and trim, her stomach flat and her breasts perky and high and her bottom firm, and that big broad-lipped mouth on her monkeyish face so mischievous and giving and brave.

"Oh I *know* about him!" she exclaimed, having read Alexandra's mind. "I have such *tons* to tell, but I wanted to wait until Jane got here."

"I can wait," Alexandra said, suddenly resenting now, as if suddenly feeling a cool draft, this man and his place in her mind. "Is that a new skirt?" She wanted to touch it, to stroke it, its doelike texture, the firm lean thigh underneath.

"Resurrected for the fall," Sukie said. "It's really too long, the way skirts are going."

The kitchen doorbell rang: a tittering, ragged sound. "That connection's going to burn the house down some day," Sukie prophesied, darting from the den. Jane had let herself in already. She looked pale, her pinched hot-eyed face overburdened by a floppy furry tam-o'-shanter whose loud plaid fussily matched that of her scarf. Also she was wearing ribbed kneesocks. Jane was not physically radiant like Sukie and was afflicted all over her body with small patches of asymmetry, yet an appeal shone from her as light from a twisted filament. Her hair was dark and her mouth small, prim, and certain. She came from Boston originally and that gave her something there was no unknowing.

"That Neff is such a bitch," she began, clearing a frog from her throat. "He had us do the Haydn over and over. He said my intonation was prissy. *Prissy*. I burst into tears and told him he was a disgusting male chauv." She heard herself and couldn't resist a pun. "I should have told him to chauv it."

"They can't help it," Sukie said lightly. "It's just their way of asking for more love. Lexa's having her usual diet drink, a v-and-t. *Moi*, I'm ever deeper into the bourbon."

"I shouldn't be doing this, but I'm so fucking hurt I'm going to be a bad girl for once and ask for a martini."

"Oh, baby. I don't think I have any dry vermouth."

"No sweat, pet. Just put the gin on the rocks in a wine glass. You don't by any chance have a bit of lemon peel?"

Sukie's refrigerator, rich in ice, yoghurt, and celery, was barren of much else. She had her lunches at Nemo's Diner downtown, three doors away from the newspaper offices, past the framer's and the barber's and the Christian Science reading room, and had taken to having her evening meals there too, because of the gossip she heard in Nemo's, the mutter of Eastwick life all around her. The old-timers congregated there, the police and the highway crew, the out-of-season fishermen and the momentarily bankrupt businessmen. "Don't seem to have any oranges either," she said, tugging at the two produce drawers of sticky green metal. "I did buy some peaches at that roadside stand over on 4."

"Do I dare to eat a peach?" Jane quoted. "I shall wear white flannel trousers, and walk upon the beach." Sukie winced, watching the other woman's agitated hands—one tendony and long, from fingering the strings, and the other squarish and slack, from holding the bow—dig with a rusty dull carrot grater into the blushing cheek, the rosiest part, of the yellow pulpy peach. Jane dropped the rosy sliver in; a sacred hush, the spell of any recipe, amplified the tiny *plip*. "I can't start drinking utterly raw gin this early in life," Jane announced with puritanical satisfaction, looking nevertheless haggard and impatient. She moved toward the den with that rapid stiff walk of hers.

Alexandra guiltily reached over and snapped off the TV, where the President, a lugubrious gray-jawed man with pained dishonest eyes, had been making an announcement of great importance to the nation.

"Hi there, you gorgeous creature," Jane called, a bit loudly in this small slant space. "Don't get up, I can see you're all settled. Tell me, though—was that thunderstorm the other day yours?"

The peach skin in the inverted cone of her drink looked like a bit of brightly diseased flesh preserved in alcohol.

"I went to the beach," Alexandra confessed, "after talking to you. I wanted to see if this man was in the Lenox place yet."

"I *thought* I'd upset you, poor chicken," said Jane. "And was he?"

"There was smoke from the chimney. I didn't drive up."

"You should have driven up and said you were from the Wetlands Commission," Sukie told her. "The noise around town is that he wants to build a dock and fill in enough on the back of the island there to have a tennis court."

"That'll never get by," Alexandra told Sukie lazily. "That's where the snowy egrets nest."

"Don't be too sure," was the answer. "That property hasn't paid any taxes to the town for ten years. For somebody who'll put it back on the rolls the selectmen can evict a lot of egrets."

"Oh, isn't this *cozy!*" Jane exclaimed, rather desperately, feeling ignored. Their four eyes upon her then, she had to improvise. "Greta came into the church," she said, "right after he called my Haydn prissy, and laughed."

Sukie did a German laugh: "Hö hö hö."

"Do they still fuck, I wonder?" asked Alexandra idly, amid this ease with her friends letting her mind wander and gather images from nature. "How could he stand it? It must be like excited sauerkraut."

"No," Jane said firmly. "It's like—what's that pale white stuff they like so?—sauerbraten."

"They marinate it," Alexandra said. "In vinegar, with garlic, onions, and bay leaves. And I think peppercorns."

"Is that what he tells you?" Sukie asked Jane mischievously.

"We never talk about it, even at our most intimate," Jane prissily said. "All he ever confided on the subject was that she had to have it once a week or she began to throw things."

"A poltergeist," Sukie said, delighted. "A polterfrau."

'Really," Jane said, not seeing the humor of it, "you're right. She is an impossibly awful woman. So pedantic; so smug; such a *Na*zi. Ray's the only one who doesn't see it, poor soul."

"I wonder how much she guesses," Alexandra mused.

"She doesn't *want* to guess," Jane said, pressing home the assertion so the last word hissed. "If she guessed she might have to do something about it."

"Like turn him loose," Sukie supplied.

"Then we'd all have to cope with him," Alexandra said, envisioning this plump dank man as a tornado, a voracious natural reservoir, of desire. Desire did come in containers out of all proportion.

"Hang on, Greta!" Jane chimed in, seeing the humor at last.

All three cackled.

The side door solemnly slammed, and footsteps slowly marched upstairs. It was not a poltergeist but one of Sukie's children, home from school, where extracurricular activities had kept him or her late. The upstairs television came on with its comforting humanoid rumble.

Greedily Sukie had crammed too big a handful of salted nuts into her mouth; she flattened her palm against her chin to keep morsels from falling. Still laughing, she sputtered crumbs. "Doesn't *any*body want to hear about this new man?"

"Not especially," Alexandra said. "Men aren't the answer, isn't that what we've decided?"

She was different, a little difficult, when Jane was present, Sukie had often noticed. Alone with Sukie she had not tried to conceal her interest in this new man. The two women had in common a certain happiness in their bodies, which had often been called beautiful, and Alexandra was enough older (six years) to establish when just they were gathered, a certain maternal fit: Sukie frisky and chatty, Lexa lazy and sybilline. Alexandra tended to dominate, when the three were together, by being somewhat sullen and inert, making the other two come to her.

"They're not the answer," Jane Smart said. "But maybe they're the question." Her gin was two-thirds gone. The bit of peach skin was a baby waiting to be thrust out dry into the world. Beyond the graying lozenge panes blackbirds were noisily packing the day away, into its travelling bag of dusk.

Sukie stood to make her announcement. "He's rich," she said, "and forty-two. Never married, and from New York, one of the old Dutch families. He was evidently a child prodigy at the piano, and invents things besides. The whole big room in the east wing, where the billiard table still is, and the laundry area under it are to be his laboratory, with all these stainless-steel sinks and distilling tubes and everything, and on the west side, where the Lenoxes had this greenhousy whatchamacallum, a conservatory, he wants to install a big sunken tub, with the walls wired for stereo." Her round eyes, quite green in the late light, shone with the madness of it. "Joe Marino has the plumbing contract and was talking about it last night after they couldn't get a quorum because Herbie Prinz went to Bermuda without telling anybody. Joe was really freaked out: no estimate asked for, everything the best, price be damned. A *teak* tub eight feet in diameter, and the man doesn't like the feel of tile under his feet so the whole floor is going to be some special fine-grained slate you have to order from Tennessee."

"He sounds pompous," Jane told them.

"Does this big spender have a name?" Alexandra asked, thinking what a romantic Sukie was as well as a gossip columnist and wondering if a second vodka-and-tonic would give her a headache later, when she was home alone in her rambling former farmhouse with only the steady breathing of her sleeping children and Coal's restless scratching and the baleful staring of the moon to keep her stark-awake spirit company. In the West a coyote would howl in the lavender distance and even farther away a transcontinental train would pull its slithering miles of cars and these sounds would lead her spirit out of the window and dissolve its wakefulness in the delicate star-blanched night. Here, in the crabbed, water-logged East, everything was so close; night-sounds sur-rounded her house like a bristling thicket. Even these women, in Sukie's cozy little cubbyhole, loomed close, so that each dark hair of Jane's faint mustache and the upright amber down, sensitive to static, of Sukie's long forearms made Alexandra's eyes itch. She was jealous of this man, that the very shadow of him should so excite her two friends, who on other Thursdays were excited simply by her, her regally lazy powers stretching there like a cat's power to cease purring and kill. On those Thursdays the three friends would conjure up the spectres of Eastwick's little lives and set them buzzing and circling in the darkening air. In the right mood and into their third drinks they could erect a cone of power above them like a tent to the zenith, and know at the base of their bellies who was sick, who was sinking into debt, who was loved, who was frantic, who was burning, who was asleep in a remission of life's bad luck; but this wouldn't happen today. They were disturbed.

"Isn't that funny about his name?" Sukie was saying, staring up at the day's light ebbing from the leaded window. She could not see through the high wobbly lozenge panes, but in her mind's eye clearly stood her back yard's only tree, a slender young pear tree overburdened with pears, heavy yellow suspended shapes like costume jewels hung on a child. Each day now was redolent of hay and ripeness, the little pale late asters glowing by the side of the roads like litter. "They were all saying his name last night, and I heard it before from Marge Perley, it's on the tip of my tongue. . . "

"Mine too," Jane said. "*Damn*. It has one of those little words in it."

"De, da, du," Alexandra prompted hopelessly.

The three witches fell silent, realizing that, tongue-tied, they were themselves under a spell, of a greater.

Darryl Van Horne came to the chamber-music concert in the Unitarian Church on Sunday night, a bearish dark man with greasy curly hair half-hiding his ears and clumped at the back so that his head from the side looked like a beer mug with a monstrously thick handle. He wore gray flannels bagged at the backs of his knees somehow and an elbow-patched jacket of Harris Tweed in a curious busy pattern of green and black. A pink Oxford button-down shirt of the type fashionable in the Fifties and, on his feet, incongruously small and pointy black loafers completed the costume. He was out to make an impression.

"So you're our local sculptress," he told Alexandra at the reception afterwards, which was held in the church parlor, for the players and their friends, and centered about an unspiked punch the color of antifreeze. The church was a pretty enough little Greek Revival, with a shallow Doric-columned porch and a squat octagonal tower, on Cocumscussoc Way, off of Elm behind Oak, which the Congregationalists had put up in 1823 but which a generation later had gone under to the Unitarian tide of the 1840s. In this hazy late age of declining doctrine its interior was decorated here and there with crosses anyway, and the social parlor bore on one wall a large felt banner, concocted by the Sunday school, of the Egyptian tau cross, the hieroglyph for "life," surrounded by the four triangular alchemic signs for the elements. The category of "players and their friends" included everyone except Van Horne, who pushed into the parlor anyway. People knew who he was; it added to the excitement. When he spoke, his voice resounded in a way that did not quite go with the movements of his mouth and jaw, and this impression of an artificial element somewhere in his speech apparatus was reinforced by the strange slipping, patched-together impression his features made and by the excess of spittle he produced when he talked, so that he occasionally paused to wipe his coat sleeve roughly across the corners of his mouth. Yet he had the confidence of the cultured and well-to-do, stooping low to achieve intimacy with Alexandra.

"They're just little things," Alexandra said, feeling abruptly petite and demure, confronted by this brooding dark bulk. It was that time of the month when she was especially sensitive to auras. This thrilling stranger's was the shiny black-brown of a wet beaver pelt and stood up stiff behind his head. "My friends call them my bubbies," she said, and fought a blush. Fighting it made her feel slightly faint, in this crowd. Crowds and new men were not what she was used to.

"Little things," Van Horne echoed. "But so *potent*," he said, wiping his lips. "So full of psychic juice, you know, when you pick one up. They knocked me out. I bought all they had at, what's that place?—the Noisy Sheep—"

"The Yapping Fox," she said, "or the Hungry Sheep, two doors the other side of the little barbershop, if you ever get a haircut."

"Never if I can help it. Saps my strength. My mother used to call me Samson. But yeah, one of those. I bought all they had to show to a pal of mine, a really relaxed terrific guy who runs a gallery in New York, right there on Fifty-seventh Street. It's not for me to promise you anything, Alexandra—O.K. if I call you that?—but if you could bring yourself to create on a bigger scale, I bet we could get you a show. Maybe you'll never be Marisol but you could sure as hell be another Niki de Saint-Phalle. You know, those 'Nanas.' Now *those* have scale. I mean, she's *real*ly let go, she's not just futzin' around."

With some relief Alexandra decided she quite disliked this man. He was pushy, coarse, and a blabbermouth. His buying her out at the Hungry Sheep felt like a rape, and she would have to run another batch through the kiln now earlier than she had planned. The pressure his personality set up had intensified her cramps, which she had woken with that morning, days ahead of schedule; that was one of the signs of cancer, irregularities in your cycle. Also, she had brought with her from the West a regrettable trace of the regional prejudice against Indians and Chicanos, and to her eyes Darryl Van Horne didn't look *washed*. You could almost see little specks of black in his skin, as if he were a halftone reproduction. He wiped his lips with the hairy back of a hand, and his lips twitched with impatience while she searched her heart for an honest but polite response. Dealing with men was work, a chore she had become lazy at. "I don't *want* to be another Niki de Saint-Phalle," she said. "I want to be me. The potency, as you put it, comes from their being small enough to hold in the hand." Hastening blood made the capillaries in her face burn; she smiled at herself for being excited, when intellectually she had decided the man was a fraud, an apparition. Except for his money; that had to be real.

His eyes were small and watery, and looked rubbed. "Yeah, Alexandra, but what *is* you? Think small, you'll wind up small. You're not giving you a chance, with this old-giftie-shoppie mentality. I couldn't believe how little they were charging—a lousy twenty bucks, when you should be thinking five figures."

He was New York vulgar, she perceived, and felt sorry for him, landed in this subtle province. She remembered the wisp of smoke, how fragile and brave it had looked. She asked him forgivingly, "How do you like your new house? Are you pretty well settled in?"

With enthusiasm, he said, "It's hell. I work late, my ideas come to me at night, and every morning around seven-fifteen these fucking workmen show up! With their fucking radios! Pardon my Latin."

He seemed aware of his need for forgiveness; the need surrounded him, and rippled out from every clumsy, too-urgent gesture.

"You *gotta* come over and see the place," he said. "I need advice all over the lot. All my life I've lived in apartments where they decide everything for you, and the contractor I've got's an asshole."

"Joe?"

"You know him?"

"Everybody knows him," Alexandra said; this stranger should be told that insulting local people was not the way to win friends in Eastwick.

But his loose tongue and mouth tumbled on unabashed. "Little funny hat all the time?"

She had to nod, but perhaps not to smile. She sometimes hallucinated that Joe was still wearing his hat while making love to her.

"He's out to lunch every meal of the day," Van Horne said. "All he wants to talk about is how the Red Sox pitching collapsed again and how the Pats still don't have any pass defense. Not that the old guy doing the floor is any wizard either; this priceless slate, practically marble, up from Tennessee, and he lays it half with the rough side up, where you can see the marks of the quarry saw. These butchers you call workmen up here wouldn't last one day on a union job in Manhattan. No offense, I can see you're thinking, 'What a snob,' and I guess the hicks don't get much practice, putting up chicken coops; but no wonder it's such a weird-looking state. Hey, Alexandra, between us: I'm crazy about that huffy frozen look you get on your face when you get defensive and can't think what to say. And the tip of your nose is cute." Astonishingly, he reached out and touched it, the little cleft tip she was sensitive about, a touch so quick and improper she wouldn't have believed it happened but for the chilly tingle it left.

She didn't just dislike him, she hated him; yet still she stood there smiling, feeling trapped and faint and wondering what her irregular insides were trying to tell her.

Jane Smart came up to them. For the performance she had had to spread her legs and therefore was the only woman at the gathering in a full-length gown, a shimmering concoction of aqua silk and lace trim perhaps a touch too bridal. "Ah, *la artiste*," Van Horne exclaimed, and he seized her hand not in a handshake but like a manicurist inspecting, taking her hand upon his wide palm and then rejecting it, since it was the left he wanted, the tendony fingering hand with its glazed calluses where she pressed the strings. The man made a tender

sandwich of it between his own hairy two. "What intonation," he said. "What vibrato and stretch. Really. You think
I'm an obnoxious madman but I do know music. It's the one
thing makes me humble."

Jane's dark eyes lightened, indeed glowed. "Not prissy,
you think," she said. "Our leader keeps saying my intonation
is prissy."

"What an asshole," pronounced Van Horne, wiping spit
from the corners of his mouth. "You have precision but that's
not prissy necessarily; precision is where passion begins.
Without precision, *beaucoup de rien*, huh? Even your thumb,
on your thumb position: you really keep that pressure on,
where a lot of men crump out, it hurts too much." He pulled
her left hand closer to his face and caressed the side of her
thumb. "See that?" he said to Alexandra, brandishing Jane's
hand as if it were detached, a dead thing to be admired. "That
is one beautiful callus."

Jane tugged her hand back, feeling eyes gathering upon
them. The Unitarian minister, Ed Parsley, was taking notice
of the scene. Van Horne perhaps relished an audience, for he
dramatically let Jane's left hand drop and seized the un-
guarded right, as it hung at Jane's side, to shake it in her own
astonished face. "It's *this* hand," he almost shouted. "It's this
hand's the fly in the ointment. Your *bow*ing. God! Your
spiccato sounds like *marcato*, your *legato* like *détaché*
Honey, *string* those phrases together, you're not playing just
notes, one after the other, biddledy um-um-um, you're
playing *phras*es, you're playing human *out*cries!"

As if in silent outcry Jane's prim thin mouth dropped open
and Alexandra saw tears form second lenses upon her eyes,
whose brown was always a little lighter in color than you
remembered, a tortoiseshell color.

Reverend Parsley joined them. He was a youngish man
with a slippery air of doom about him; his face was like a
handsome face distorted in a slightly warped mirror—too

long from sideburn to nostril, as if perpetually being tugged forward, and the too full and expressive lips caught in the relentless smile of one who knows he is in the wrong place, on the wrong platform of the bus station in a country where no known language is spoken. Though just into his thirties, he was too old to be a window-trashing LSD-imbibing soldier in the Movement and this added to his sense of displacement and inadequacy, though he was always organizing peace marches and vigils and read-ins and proposing to his parish of dryasdust dutiful souls that they let their pretty old church become a sanctuary, with cots and hot plates and chemical toilet facilities, for the hordes of draft evaders. Instead, tasteful cultural events were sheltered here, where the acoustics were accidentally marvellous; those old builders perhaps did have secrets. But Alexandra, having been raised in the stark land mined for a thousand cowboy movies, was inclined to think that the past is often romanticized, that when it was the present it had that same curious hollowness we all feel now.

Ed looked up—he was not tall; this was another of his disappointments—at Darryl Van Horne quizzically. Then he addressed Jane Smart with a sharp shouldering-aside note in his voice: "Beautiful, Jane. Just a damn beautiful job all four of you did. As I was saying to Clyde Gabriel just now, I wish there had been a better way to advertise, to get more of the Newport crowd over here, though I know his paper did all it could, he took it that I was criticizing; he seems a lot on edge lately." Sukie was sleeping with Ed, Alexandra knew, and perhaps Jane had slept with him in the past. There was a quality men's voices had when you had slept with them, even years ago: the grain came up, like that of unpainted wood left out in the weather. Ed's aura—Alexandra couldn't stop seeing auras, it went with menstrual cramps—emanated in sickly chartreuse waves of anxiety and narcissism from his hair, which was combed away from an inflexible part and was somehow colorless without being gray. Jane was still fighting back tears and in the awkwardness Alexandra had become the introducer, this strange outsider's sponsor.

"Reverend Parsley—"

"Come on, Alexandra. We're better friends than that. The name's Ed, *please*." Sukie must talk about her a little while sleeping with him, so he felt this familiarity. Everywhere you turn people know you better than you know them; there is all this human spying. Alexandra could not make herself say "Ed," his aura of doom was so repulsive to her.

"—this is Mr. Van Horne, who's just moved into the Lenox place, you've probably heard."

"Indeed I have heard, and it's a delightful surprise to have you here, sir. Nobody had said you were a music-lover."

"In a half-ass way, you could say that. My pleasure, Reverend." They shook hands and the minister flinched.

"No 'Reverend,' please. Everybody, friend or foe, calls me Ed."

"Ed, this is a swell old building you have here. It must cost you a bundle in fire insurance."

"The Lord is our carrier," Ed Parsley joked, and his sickly aura widened in pleasure at this blasphemy. "To be serious, you can't rebuild this kind of plant, and the older members complain about all the steps. We've had people drop out of the choir because they can't make it up into the loft. Also, to my mind, an opulent building like this, with all its traditional associations, gets in the way of the message the modern-day Unitarian-Universalists are trying to bring. What I'd like to see is us open a storefront church right down there on Dock Street; that's where the young people gather, that's where business and commerce do their dirty work."

"What's dirty about it?"

"I'm sorry, I didn't catch your first name."

"Darryl."

"Darryl, I see you like to pull people's legs. You're a man

of sophistication and know as well as I do that the connection between the present atrocities in Southeast Asia and that new little drive-in branch Old Stone Bank has next to the Superette is direct and immediate; I don't need to belabor the point."

"You're right, fella, you don't," Van Horne said.

"When Mammon talks, Uncle Sam jumps."

"Amen," said Van Horne.

How nice it was, Alexandra thought, when men talked to one another. All that aggression: the clash of shirt fronts. Eavesdropping, she felt herself thrilled as when on a walk in the Cove woods she came upon traces in some sandy patch of a flurry of claws, and a feather or two, signifying a murderous encounter. Ed Parsley had sized Van Horne up as a banker type, an implementer of the System, and was fighting dismissal in the bigger man's eyes as a shrill and ineffectual liberal, the feckless agent of a nonexistent God. Ed wanted to be the agent of another System, equally fierce and far-flung. As if to torment himself he wore a clergyman's collar, in which his neck looked both babyish and scrawny; for his denomination such a collar was so unusual as to be, in its way, a protest.

"Did I hear," he said now, his voice gravelly in its insinuating sonority, "you offering a critique of Jane's cello-playing?"

"Just her bowing," Van Horne said, suddenly a bashful shambles, his jaw slipping and drooling. "I said the rest of it was great, her bowing just seemed a little choppy. Christ, you have to watch yourself around here, stepping on everybody's toes. I mentioned to sweet old Alexandra here about my plumbing contractor being none too swift and it turns out he's her best friend."

"Not best friend, just a friend," she felt obliged to intercede. The man, Alexandra saw even amid the confusions of this encounter, had the brute gift of bringing a woman out, of getting her to say more than she had intended. Here he had insulted Jane and she was gazing up at him with the moist mute fascination of a whipped dog.

"The Beethoven was especially splendid, don't you agree?" Parsley was still after Van Horne, to wring some concession out of him, the start of a pact, a basis they could meet on next time.

"Beethoven," the big man said with bored authority, "sold his soul to write those last quartets; he was stone deaf. All those nineteenth-century types sold their souls. Liszt. Paganini. What they did wasn't human."

Jane found her voice. "I practiced till my fingers bled," she said, gazing straight up at Van Horne's lips, which he had just rubbed with his sleeve. "All those terrible sixteenth-notes in the second andante."

"You keep practicing, little Jane. It's five-sixths muscle memory, as you know. When muscle memory takes over, the heart can start to sing its song. Until then, you're stymied. You're just going through the motions. Listen. Whyncha come over some time to my place and we'll fool around with a bit of old Ludwig's piano and cello stuff? That Sonata in A is an absolute honey, if you don't panic on the legato. Or that E Minor of Brahms: *fabuloso. Quel schmaltz!* I think it's still in the old fingers." He wiggled them, his fingers, at all of their faces. Van Horne's hands were eerily white-skinned beneath the hair, like tight surgical gloves.

Ed Parsley coped with his unease by turning to Alexandra and saying in sickly conspiracy, "Your friend appears to know whereof he speaks."

"Don't look at me, I just met the gentleman," Alexandra said.

"He was a child *pro*digy," Jane Smart told them, become somehow angry and defensive. Her aura, usually a rather dull mauve, had undergone a streaked orchid surge, betokening arousal, though by which man was not clear. The whole parlor to Alexandra's eyes was clouded by merged and pulsating auras, sickening as cigarette smoke. She felt dizzy, disenchanted; she longed to be home with Coal and her quietly ticking kiln and the expectant cold wet plasticity of clay in its burlap sacks hauled from Coventry. She closed her eyes and wished that this particular nexus around her—of arousal, dislike, radical insecurity, and a sinister will to dominate emanating not only from the dark stranger—would dissolve.

Several elderly parishioners were nudging forward for their share of Reverend Parsley's attention, and he turned to flatter them. The white hair of the women was touched in the caves of the curls of their perms with the tenderest golds and blues. Raymond Neff, profusely sweating and aglow with the triumph of the concert, came up to them all and, enduring in the deafness of celebrity their simultaneous compliments, jollily bore away Jane, his mistress and comrade in musical battle. She, too, had been glazed, shoulders and neck, by the exertions of the performance. Alexandra noticed this and was touched. What did Jane see in Raymond Neff? For that matter what did Sukie see in Ed Parsley? The smells of the two men when they had stood close had been, to Alexandra's nostrils, rank—whereas Joe Marino's skin had a certain sweet sourness, like the stale-milk aroma that arises from a baby's pate when you settle your cheek against its fuzzy bony warmth. Suddenly she was alone with Van Horne again, and feared she would have to bear again upon her breast the imploring inchoate weight of his conversation; but Sukie, who feared nothing, all russet and crisp and glimmering in her reportorial role, edged through the crowd and conducted an interview.

"What brings you to this concert, Mr. Van Horne?" she asked, after Alexandra had shyly performed introductions.

"My TV set's on the blink" was his sullen answer. Alexandra saw that he preferred to make the approaches himself; but there was no denying Sukie in her interrogating mood, her little pushy monkey-face bright as a new penny.

"And what has brought you to this part of the world?" was her next question.

"Seems time I got out of Gotham," he said. "Too much mugging, rent going sky-high. The price up here seemed right. This going into some paper?"

Sukie licked her lips and admitted, "I might put a mention in a column I write for the *Word* called 'Eastwick Eyes and Ears.'"

"Jesus, don't do that," the big man said, in his baggy tweed coat. "I came up here to cool the publicity."

"What kind of publicity were you receiving, may I ask?"

"If I told you, that'd be more publicity, wouldn't it?"

"Could be."

Alexandra marvelled at her friend, so cheerfully bold. Sukie's brazen ochre aura merged with the sheen of her hair. She asked, as Van Horne made as if to turn away, "People are saying you're an inventor. What sort of thing do you invent?"

"Toots, even if I took all night to explain it to ya, ya wouldn't understand. It mostly deals with chemicals."

"Try me," Sukie urged. "See if I understand."

"Put it in your 'Eyes and Ears' and I might as well write a circular letter to my competition."

"Nobody who doesn't live in Eastwick reads the *Word*, I promise. Even in Eastwick nobody reads it, they just look at the ads and for their own names."

"Listen, Miss—"

"Rougemont. Ms. I was married."

"What was he, a French Canuck?"

"Monty always said his ancestors were Swiss. He acted Swiss. Don't the Swiss have square heads, supposedly?"

"Beats me. I thought that was the Manchurians. They have skulls like cement blocks, that's how Genghis Khan could stack 'em up so neatly."

"Do you feel we've wandered rather far from the subject?"

"About the inventions, listen, I can't talk. I am *watched*."

"How exciting! For all of us," Sukie said, and she let her smile push her upper lip, creasing deliciously, up so far her nose wrinkled and a band of healthy gum showed. "How about for my eyes and ears only? And Lexa's here. Isn't she gorgeous?"

Van Horne turned his big head stiffly as if to check; Alexandra saw herself through his bloodshot blinking eyes as if at the end of a reversed telescope, a figure frighteningly small, cleft here and there and with wisps of gray hair. He decided to answer Sukie's earlier question: "I've been doing a fair amount lately with protective coatings—a floor finish you can't scratch with even a steak knife after it hardens, a coating you can spray on the red-hot steel as it's cooling so it bonds with the carbon molecules; your car body'll get metal fatigue before oxidization sets in. Synthetic polymers—that's the name of your brave new world, honeybunch, and it's just getting rolling. Bakelite was invented around 1907, synthetic rubber in 1910, nylon around 1930. Better check those dates if you use any of this. The point is, this century's just the infancy; synthetic polymers're going to be with us to the year one million or until we blow ourselves up, whichever comes sooner, and the beauty of it is, you can *grow* the raw materials, and when you run out of land you can grow 'em in the ocean. Move over, Mother Nature, we've got you beat. Also I'm working on the Big Interface."

"What interface is that?" Sukie was not ashamed to ask. Alexandra would just have nodded as if she knew; she had a lot still to learn about overcoming acculturated female recessiveness.

"The interface between solar energy and electrical energy," Van Horne told Sukie. "There *has* to be one, and once we find the combination you can run every appliance in your house right off the roof and have enough left over to recharge your electric car in the night. Clean, abundant, and *free*. It's coming, honeybunch, it's coming!"

"Those panels look so ugly," Sukie said. "There's a hippie in town who's done over an old garage so he can heat his water, I have no idea why, he never takes a bath."

"I'm not talking about collectors," Van Horne said. "That's Model T stuff." He looked about him; his head turned like a barrel being rolled on its edge. "I'm talking about a *paint*."

"A paint?" Alexandra said, feeling she should make a contribution. At least this man was giving her something new to think about, beyond tomato sauce.

"A paint," he solemnly assured her. "A simple paint you brush on with a brush and that turns the entire epidermis of your lovely home into an enormous low-voltaic cell."

"There's only one word for that," Sukie said.

"Yeah, what's that?"

"Electrifying."

Van Horne aped being offended. "Shit, if I'd known that's the kind of flirtatious featherheaded thing you like to say I wouldn't have wasted my time spilling my guts. You play tennis?"

Sukie stood up a little taller. Alexandra experienced a wish to stroke that long flat stretch from the other woman's breasts to below her waist, the way one longs to dart out a hand and stroke the belly a cat on its back elongates in stretching, the toes of its hind paws a-tremble in this moment of muscular ecstasy. Sukie was just so nicely *made*. "A bit," she said, her tongue peeking through her smile and adhering for a moment to her upper lip.

"You gotta come over in a couple weeks or so, I'm having a court put in."

Alexandra interrupted. "You can't fill wetlands," she said.

This big stranger wiped his lips and repulsively eyed her.

"Once they're filled," he said in his imperfectly synchronized, slightly slurring voice, "they're not wet."

"The snowy egrets like to nest there, in the dead elms out back."

"T, O, U, F, F," Van Horne said. "Tough."

From the sudden stariness of his eyes she wondered if he was wearing contact lenses. His conversation did seem distracted by a constant slipshod effort to keep himself together. "Oh," she said, and what Alexandra noticed now gave her, already slightly dizzy, the sensation of looking down a deep hole. His aura was gone. He had absolutely none, like a dead man or a wooden idol, above his head of greasy hair.

Sukie laughed, pealingly; her dainty round belly pumped under the waistband of her suede skirt in sympathy with her diaphragm. "I love that. May I quote you, Mr. Van Horne? Filled Wetlands No Longer Wet, Declares Intriguing New Citizen."

Disgusted by this mating dance, Alexandra turned away. The auras of all the others at the party were blinding now, like the peripheral lights along a highway as raindrops collect on the windshield. And very stupidly she felt within herself the obscuring moisture of an unwanted infatuation condensing. The big man was a bundle of needs; he was a chasm that sucked her heart out of her chest.

Old Mrs. Lovecraft, her aura the tawdry magenta of those who are well pleased with their lives and fully expect to go to Heaven, came up to Alexandra bleating, "Sandy dear, we *miss* you at the Garden Club. You *must*n't keep so to yourself."

"*Do* I keep to myself? I *feel* busy. I've been putting up tomatoes, it's just incredible the way they kept coming this fall "

"I *know* you've been gardening; Horace and I admire your house every time we drive down Orchard Road: that *cun*ning little bed you have by your doorway, chock-a-block full of button mums I've several times said to him, 'Let's *do* drop in,' but then I think, No, she might be making her little *things*, and we don't want to dis*turb* her inspiration."

Making her little things or love with Joe Marino, Alexandra thought: that was what Franny Lovecraft was implying. In a town like Eastwick there were no secrets, just areas of avoidance. When she and Oz were still together and new in town they had spent a number of evenings in the company of sweet old bores like the Lovecrafts; now Alexandra felt infinitely fallen from the world of decent and dreary amusements they represented.

"I'll come to some meetings this winter, when there's nothing else to do," Alexandra said, relenting. "When I'm homesick for nature," she added, though knowing she would never go, she was far beyond such tame delights. "I like the slide shows on English gardens; are you having any of them?"

"You *must* come next Thursday," Franny Lovecraft insisted, overplaying her hand as people of minor distinction—vice-presidents of savings banks, granddaughters of clipper-ship captains—will. "Daisy Robeson's son Warwick has *just* got back from three years in Iran, where he and his lovely little family had *such* a nice time, he was working as an adviser there, it somehow has all to do with oil, he says the Shah is performing *mir*acles, all this splendid modern architecture right in their capital city—oh, what *is* its name, I want to say New Delhi. . . ."

Alexandra offered no help though she knew the name Tehran; the devil was getting into her.

"At *any* rate, Wicky is going to give a slide show on Oriental rugs. You see, Sandy dear, in the Arab mind, the rug *is* a garden, it's an indoor garden in their tents and palaces in the middle of all that desert, and there's all manner of real flowers in the design, that to casual eyes looks so abstract. Now *does*n't that sound fascinating?"

"It does," Alexandra said. Mrs. Lovecraft had adorned her wrinkled throat, collapsed upon itself in folds and gulleys like

those of an eroded roadside embankment, with a strand of
artificial pearls of which the centrepiece was an antique
mother-of-pearl egg in which a tiny gold cross had been
tediously inlaid. With an irritated psychic effort, Alexandra
willed the frayed old string to break; fake pearls slipped down
the old lady's sunken front and cascaded in constellations to
the floor.

The floor of the church parlor was covered with industrial
carpeting the dull green of goose scat; it muffled the patter
of pearls. The crowd was slow to detect the disaster, and at
first only those in the immediate vicinity stooped to collect
them. Mrs. Lovecraft, her face blanched with shock beneath
the patches of rouge, was herself too arthritic and brittle to
stoop. Alexandra, while kneeling at the old lady's dropsical
feet, wickedly willed the narrow strained straps of her
once-fashionable lizardskin shoes to come undone. Wickedness was like food: once you got started it was hard to stop;
the gut expanded to take in more and more. Alexandra
straightened up and set a half-dozen retrieved pearls in her
victim's trembling, blue-knuckled, greedily cupped hand.
Then she backed away, through the widening circle of squatting searchers. These bodies squatting seemed grotesque
giant cabbages of muscle and avidity and cloth; their auras
were all confused like watercolors running together to make
gray. Her way to the door was blocked by Reverend Parsley,
his handsome waxy face with that Peer Gynt tweak of doom
to it. Like many a man who shaves in the morning, he sported
a visible stubble by nighttime.

"*Al*exandra," he began, his voice deliberately forced into its
most searching, low-pitched register. "I was *so* much hoping
to see you here tonight." He wanted her. He was tired of
fucking Sukie. In the nervousness of his overture he reached
up to scratch his quaintly combed head, and his intended
victim took the opportunity to snap the cheap expansion
band of his important-looking gold-plated watch, an Omega.

He felt it release and grabbed the expensive accessory where it was entangled in his shirt cuff before it had time to drop This gave Alexandra a second to slip past the smear of his startled face—a pathetic smear, as she was to remember it guiltily; as if by sleeping with him she could have saved him—into the open air, the grateful black air.

The night was moonless. The crickets stridulated their everlasting monotonous meaningful note. Car headlights swept by on Cocumscussoc Way, and the bushes by the church door, nearly stripped of leaves, sprang up sharp in the illumination like the complicated mandibles and jointed feelers and legs of insects magnified. The air smelled faintly of apples making cider by themselves, in their own skins where these apples fell uncollected and rotting in the neglected orchards that backed up onto the church property, empty land waiting for its developer. The sheltering humped shapes of cars waited in the gravel parking lot. Her own little Subaru figured in her mind as a pumpkin-colored tunnel at whose far end glowed the silence of her rustic kitchen, Coal's tail-thumping welcome, the breathing of her children as they lay asleep or feigning in their rooms, having turned off television the instant her headlights glared at the windows. She would check them, their bodies each in its room and bed, and then take twenty of her baked bubbies, cunningly stacked so that no two had touched and married, out of the Swedish kiln, which would still be ticking, cooling, talking to her as of the events in the house in the time in which she had been away—for time flowed everywhere, not just in the rivulet of the delta in which we have been drifting. Then, duty done to her bubbies, and to her bladder, and to her teeth, she would enter upon the spacious queendom of her bed, a kingdom without a king, all hers. Alexandra was reading an endless novel by a woman with three names and an airbrushed photograph of herself on the shiny jacket; a few pages of its interminable woolly adventures among cliffs and castles

served each night to smooth the border-crossing into uncon-
sciousness. In her dreams she ranged far and wide, above the
housetops, visiting rooms carved confusedly from the jumble
of her past but seemingly solid as her oneiric self stood in each
one, a ghost brimming with obscure mourning as she picked
up an apple-shaped pincushion from her mother's sewing
basket or waited while staring out at the snow-capped
mountains for a playmate long dead to telephone. In her
dreams omens cavorted around her as gaudily as papier-
mâché advertisements beckoning innocents this way and that
at an amusement park. Yet we never look forward to dreams,
any more than to the fabled adventures that follow death.

Gravel crackled at her back. A dark man touched the soft
flesh above her elbow; his touch was icy, or perhaps she was
feverish. She jumped, frightened. He was chuckling. "The
damnedest thing happened back in there just now. The old
dame whose pearls let loose a minute ago tripped over her
own shoes in her excitement and everybody's scared she
broke her hip."

"How sad," Alexandra said, sincerely but absent-
mindedly, her spirit drifting, her heart still thumping from the
scare he gave her.

Darryl Van Horne leaned close and thrust words into her
ear. "Don't forget, sweetheart. Think bigger. I'll check into
that gallery. We'll be in touch. Nitey-nite."

"You actually *went*?" Alexandra asked Jane with a dull
thrill of pleasure, over the phone.

"Why not?" Jane said firmly. "He really did have the
music for the Brahms Sonata in E Minor, and plays amazingly. Like Liberace, only without all that smiling. You wouldn't
think it; his hands don't look like they could do anything,
somehow."

"You were alone? I keep picturing that perfume ad." The

one which showed a young male violinist seducing his accompanist in her low-cut gown.

"Don't be vulgar, Alexandra. He feels quite asexual to me. And there are all these workmen around, including your friend Joe Marino, all dressed up in his little checked hat with a feather in it. And there's this constant rumbling from the backhoes moving boulders for the tennis court. Evidently they've had to do a lot of blasting."

"How can he get away with that, it's wetlands."

"I don't know, sweet, but he has the permit tacked up right on a tree."

"The poor egrets."

"Oh Lexa, they have all the rest of Rhode Island to nest in. What's nature for if it's not adaptable?"

"It's adaptable up to a point. Then it gets hurt feelings."

October's crinkled gold hung in her kitchen window; the big ragged leaves on her grape arbor were turning brown, from the edges in. Off to the left, toward her bog, a little stand of birches released in a shiver of wind a handful as of bright spear-points, twinkling as they fell to the lawn. "How long did you stay?"

"Oh," Jane drawled, lying. "About an hour. Maybe an hour and a half. He really *does* have some feeling for music and his manner when you're alone with him isn't as clownish as it may have seemed at the concert. He said being in a church, even a Unitarian one, gave him the creeps. I think behind all that bluffing he's really rather shy."

"Darling. You never give up, do you?"

Alexandra felt Jane Smart's lips move an inch back from the mouthpiece in indignation. Bakelite, the first of the synthetic polymers, that man had said. Jane was saying hissingly, "I don't see it's a question of giving up or not, it's a question of doing your thing. You do your thing moping around in your garden in men's pants and then cooking up your little figurines, but to make music you *must* have people. *Othe*r people."

"They're not figurines and I don't mope around."

Jane was going on, "You and Sukie are always poking fun of my being with Ray Neff and yet until this other man has shown up the only music I could make in town was with Ray."

Alexandra was going on, "They're *sculp*tures, just because they're not on a big scale like a Calder or Moore, you sound as vulgar as Whatsisname did, insinuating I should do something bigger so some expensive New York gallery can take fifty percent, even if they *were* to sell, which I very much doubt. Everything now is so trendy and violent."

"Is that what he said? So he had a proposition for you too."

"I wouldn't call it a proposition, just typical New York pushiness, sticking your nose in where it doesn't belong. They all have to be in on the action, any action."

"He's fascinated by us," Jane Smart asserted. "Why we all live up here wasting our sweetness on the desert air."

"Tell him Narragansett Bay has always taken oddballs in and what's he doing up here himself?"

"I wonder." In her flat Massachusetts Bay style Jane slighted the *r*. "He almost gives the impression that things got too hot for him where he was. And he does love all the space in the big house. He owns three pianos, honestly, though one of them is an upright that he keeps in his library; he has all these beautiful old books, with leather bindings and titles in Latin."

"Did he give you anything to drink?"

"Just tea. This manservant he has, that he talks Spanish to, brought it on a huge tray with a lot of liqueurs in funny old bottles that had that air, you know, of coming out of a cellar full of cobwebs."

"I thought you said you just had tea."

"Well really, Lexa, maybe I did have a sip of blackberry

cordial or something Fidel was very enthusiastic about called mescal; if I'd known I was going to have to make such a complete report I'd have written the name down. You're worse than the CIA."

"I'm sorry, Jane. I'm very jealous, I suppose. And my *peri*od. It's lasted five days now, ever since the concert, and the ovary on the left side *hurts*. Do you think it could be menopause?"

"At thirty-eight? Honey, really."

"Well then it must be cancer."

"It couldn't be cancer."

"Why couldn't it be?"

"Because you're you. You have too much magic to have cancer."

"Some days I don't feel like I have any magic. Anyway, other people have magic too." She was thinking of Gina, Joe's wife. Gina must hate her. The Italian word for witch was *strega*. All over Sicily, Joe had told her, they give each other the evil eye. "Some days my insides feel all tied in knots."

"See Doc Pat, if you're seriously worried," said Jane, not quite unsympathetically. Dr. Henry Paterson, a plump pink man their age, with wounded wide watery eyes and a beautiful gentle firm touch when he palpated. His wife had left him years ago. He had never grasped why or remarried.

"He makes me feel strange," Alexandra said. "The way he drapes you with a sheet and does everything under that."

"The poor man, what is he supposed to do?"

"Not be so sly. I have a body. He knows it. I know it. Why do we have to pretend with this sheet?"

"They all get sued," Jane said, "if there isn't any nurse in the room." Her voice had a double to it, like a television signal when a truck goes by. This wasn't what she had called to talk about. Something else was on her mind.

"What else did you learn at Van Horne's?" Alexandra asked.

"*Well*—promise you won't tell anybody."

"Not even Sukie?"

"E*spe*cially not Sukie. It's about her. Darryl is really rather remarkable, he picks everything up. He stayed at the reception later than we did, I went off to have a beer with the rest of the quartet at the Bronze Barrel—"

"Greta along?"

"Oh God yes. She told us all about Hitler, how her parents couldn't stand him because his German was so uncouth. Apparently on the radio he didn't always end his sentences with the verb."

"How awful for them."

"—and I guess you faded into the night after playing that dreadful trick with poor Franny Lovecraft's pearls—"

"What pearls?"

"Don't pretend, Lexa. You were naughty. I know your style. And then the shoes, she's been in bed ever since but I guess she didn't break anything; they were worried about her hip. Do you know a woman's bones shrink to about half by the time she gets old? That's why everything snaps. She was lucky: just contusions."

"I don't know, looking at her made me wonder if I was going to be so sweet and boring and bullying when I got to be that age, if I *do* get to be, which I doubt. It was like looking into a mirror at my own dreary future, and I'm sorry, it drove me *wild*."

"All *right*, sweetie; it's no skin off my nose. As I was trying to say, Darryl hung around to help clean up and noticed while Brenda Parsley was in the church kitchen putting the plastic cups and paper plates into the Trashmaster Ed and Sukie had both disappeared! Leaving poor Brenda to put the best face on it she could—but imagine, the humiliation!"

"They really should be more discreet."

Jane paused, waiting for Alexandra to say something more; there was a point here she was supposed to grasp and express, but her mind was off, entertaining images of cancer spreading within her like the clouds of galaxies whirling softly out into the blackness, setting a deadly star here, there. . . .

"He's such a wimp," Jane at last supplied, lamely, of Ed. "And why is she always implying to us that she's given him up?"

Now Alexandra's mind pursued the lovers into the night, Sukie's slim body like a twig stripped of bark, but with pliant and muscular bumps; she was one of those women just this side of boyishness, of maleness, but vibrant, so close to this edge, the femininity somehow steeped in the guiltless energy men have, their lives consecrated like arrows, flying in slender storms at the enemy, taught from their cruel boyhoods onward how to die. Why don't they teach women? Because it isn't true that if you have daughters you will never die. "Maybe a clinic," she said aloud, having rejected Doc Pat, "where they don't know me."

"Well I would think *some*thing," Jane said, "rather than going on tormenting yourself. And being rather boring, if I do say so."

"I think part of Ed's appeal to Sukie," Alexandra offered, trying to get back on Jane's wavelength, "may be her professional need to feel in the local swim. At any rate what's interesting is not so much her still seeing him as this Van Horne character's bothering to notice so avidly, when he's just come to town. It's flattering, I suppose we're meant to think."

"Darling Alexandra, in some ways you're still awfully unliberated. A man can be just a person too, you know."

"I know that's the theory, but I've never met one who thought he was. They all turn out to be men, even the faggots."

"Remember when we were wondering if he was one? Now he's after all of us!"

"I thought he wasn't after you, you were both after Brahms."

"We were. We are. Really, Alexandra. Relax. You *are* sounding *aw*fully crampy."

"I'm a mess. I'll be better tomorrow. It's my turn to have it, remember."

"Oh my God yes. I nearly forgot. That's the other thing I was calling about. I can't make it."

"Can't make a Thursday? What's happening?"

"Well, you'll sniff. But it's Darryl again. He has some lovely little Webern bagatelles he wants to try me on, and when I suggested Friday he said he has some roving Japanese investors coming by to look at his undercoating. I was thinking of swinging by Orchard Road this afternoon if you'd like, one of the boys wanted me to go watch him play soccer after school but I could just produce my face for a minute on the sidelines—"

"No thanks dear," Alexandra said. "I have a guest coming."

"Oh." Jane's voice was ice, dark ice with ash in it such as freezes in the winter driveway.

"Possibly," Alexandra softened it to. "He or she wasn't sure they could make it."

"Darling, I quite understand. No need to say any more."

It made Alexandra angry, to be put on the defensive, when she was the one being snubbed. She told her friend, "I thought Thursdays were sacred."

"They are, usually," Jane began.

"But I suppose in a world where nothing else is there's no reason for Thursdays to be." Why was she so hurt? Her weekly rhythm depended on the infrangible triangle, the cone of power. But she mustn't let her voice drag on, betraying her this way.

Jane was apologizing, "Just this one time—"

"It's *fine*, sweetie. All the more devilled eggs for me." Jane

Smart loved devilled eggs, chalky and sharp with paprika and a pinch of dry mustard, garnished with chopped chives or an anchovy laid across each stuffed white like the tongue of a toad.

"Were you really going to the trouble of devilled eggs?" she asked plaintively.

"Of course not, dear," Alexandra said. "Just the same old soggy Saltines and stale Velveeta. I must hang up."

An hour later, gazing abstracted past the furry bare shoulder (with its touching sour-sweet smell like a baby's pate) of Joe Marino as he with more rigor than inspiration pumped away at her while her bed groaned and swayed beneath the unaccustomed double weight, Alexandra had a vision. She saw the Lenox mansion in her mind's eye, clear as a piece of calendar art, with the one wisp of smoke that she had observed that day, its pathetic strand of vapor confused with the poignance of Jane's describing Van Horne as shy and hence clownish. Disoriented, had been more Alexandra's impression: like a man peering through a mask, or listening with wool in his ears. "Focus, for Chrissake," Joe snarled in her own ear, and came, helplessly, excited by his own anger, his bare furry body—the work-hardened muscles gone slightly punky with prosperity—heaving once, twice, and the third time, ending in a little shiver like a car with carbon build-up shuddering after the ignition has been turned off. She tried to catch up but the contact was gone.

"Sorry," he growled. "I thought we were doing great but you wandered off." He had been generous, too, in forgiving her the tag end of her period, though there was hardly any blood.

"My fault," Alexandra said. "Absolutely. You were lovely. I was lousy." *Plays amazingly*, Jane had said.

The ceiling in the wake of her vision wore a sudden clarity, as if seen for the first time: its impassive dead square stretch, certain small flaws in its surface scarcely distinguishable from the specks in the vitreous humor of her eyes, except that when she moved her focus these latter drifted like animalcules in a pond, like cancer cells in our lymph. Joe's rounded shoulder and the side of his neck were as indifferent and pale as the ceiling, and as smoothly traversed by these optical impurities, which were not usually part of her universe. but when they did intrude were hard to shake, hard not to see. A sign of old age. Like snowballs rolling downhill we accumulate grit.

She felt her front, breasts and belly, swimming in Joe's sweat and by this circuitous route her mind was returning to enjoyment of his body, its spongy texture and weight and confiding male aroma and rather miraculous, in a world of minor miracles, thereness. He was usually not there. Usually he was with Gina. He rolled off Alexandra with a wounded sigh. She had wounded his Mediterranean vanity. He was tan and bald on top, his shiny skull somewhat rippled, like the pages of a book we have left out in the dew, and it was part of his vanity to put back on, first thing, his hat. He said he felt cold without it. Hat in place, he showed a youngish profile, with the sharply hooked nose we see in Bellini portraits and with liverish deep dents beneath his eyes. She had been attracted to that sluggish debauched look, that hint of the leaden-eyed *barone* or doge or Mafioso who deals life and death with a contemptuous snick of his tongue and teeth. But Joe, whom she had seduced when he came to repair a toilet that murmured all night, proved to be toothless in this sense, a devout bourgeois honest down to the last brass washer, an infatuated father of five children under eleven, and an in-law to half the state. Gina's family had packed this coast from New Bedford to Bridgeport with kin. Joe was a glutton for loyalties; his heart belonged to more sports teams—Celtics, Bruins, Whalers, Red Sox, Pawtucket Sox, Pats, Teamen, Lobsters, Minutemen—than she had dreamed existed. Once a week he came and pumped away at her with much that same faithfulness. Adultery had been a step toward damnation for him, and he was honoring one more obligation, a satanic one. Also, it was something of a contraceptive measure; his fertility had begun to be frightening to him, and the more seed of his that Alexandra with her IUD absorbed, the less there was for Gina to work with. The affair was in its third summer and Alexandra should be ending it, but she liked Joe's taste—salty-sugary, like nougat—and the way the air shimmered about an inch above the gentle ridges of his skull. His aura had no malice or bad color to it; his thoughts, like his plumber's hands, were always seeking a certain fittingness. Fate had passed her from a maker of chrome fixtures to their installer.

To see the Lenox mansion as it had been in her vision, distinct in its bricks, its granite sills and quoins and Arguslike windows, so frontally, one would have to be hovering in midair above the marsh, flying. Rapidly the vision had diminished in size, as if receding in space, beckoning her. It became the size of a postage stamp and had she not closed her eyes it might have vanished like a pea down the drain. It was when her eyes were closed that he had come. Now she felt dazed, and splayed, as if the orgasm had been partly hers.

"Maybe I should cash it in with Gina and start up fresh somewhere with you," Joe was saying.

"Don't be silly. You don't want to do anything of the kind," Alexandra told him. High unseen in the windy day above her ceiling, geese in a V straggled south, honking to reassure one another: *I'm here, you're here.* "You're a good Roman Catholic with five *bambini* and a thriving business."

"Yeah, what am I doing here then?"

"You're bewitched. It's easy. I tore your picture out of the Eastwick *Word* when you'd been to a Planning Board meeting and smeared my menstrual fluid all over it."

"Jesus, you can be disgusting."

"You like that, don't you? Gina is never disgusting. Gina is as sweet as Our Lady. If you were any kind of a gentleman you'd finish me off with your tongue. There isn't much blood, it's the tag end."

Joe grimaced. "How's about I give you a rain check on that?" he said, and looked around for clothes to put on under his hat. Though growing pudgy, his body had a neatness; he had been a schoolboy athlete, deft with every ball, though too short to star. His buttocks were taut, even if his abdomen had developed a swag. A big butterfly of fine black hair rested on his back, the top edge of its wings along his shoulders and its feet feathering into the dimples flanking the low part of his spine. "I gotta check in at that Van Horne job," he said, tucking in a pink slice of testicle that had peeped through one leghole of his elasticized shorts. They were bikini-style and tinted purple, a new thing, to go with the new androgyny. Among Joe's loyalties was one to changes of male fashion. He had been one of the first men around Eastwick to wear a denim leisure suit, and to sense that hats were making a comeback.

"How's that going, by the way?" Alexandra asked lazily, not wanting him to go. A desolation had descended to her from the ceiling.

"We're still waiting on this silver-plated faucet unit that had to be ordered from West Germany, and I had to send up to Cranston for a copper sheet big enough to fit under the tub and not have a seam. I'll be glad when it's done. There's something not right about that set-up. The guy sleeps past noon usually, and sometimes you go and there's nobody there at all, just this long-haired cat rubbing around. I hate cats."

"They're disgusting," Alexandra said. "Like me."

"No, listen, Al. You're *mia vacca. Mia vacca bianca*. You're my big plate of ice cream. What else can a poor guy say? Every attempt I make to get serious you turn me off."

"Seriousness scares me," she said seriously. "Anyway in your case I know it's just a tease."

But it was she who teased him, by making the laces of his shoes, oxblood cordovans like college men wear, come loose as fast as he tied them in bows; finally Joe had to shuffle out, defeated in his vanity and tidiness, with the laces dragging. His steps diminished on the stairs, one within the other, smaller and smaller, and the slam of the door was like the solid little nub, a mere peg of painted wood, innermost in a set of nested Russian dolls. Starling song scraped at the windows toward the yard; wild blackberries drew them to the bog by the hundreds. Abandoned and unsatisfied in the middle of a bed suddenly huge again, Alexandra tried to recapture, by staring at the blank ceiling, that strangely sharp and architectural vision of the Lenox place; but she could only produce a ghostly afterimage, a rectangle of extra pallor as on an envelope so long stored in the attic that the stamp has flaked off without being touched.

Inventor, Musician, Art Fancier
Busy Renovating Old Lenox Manse
BY SUZANNE ROUGEMONT

Courtly, deep-voiced, handsome in a casual, bearish way, Mr. Darryl Van Horne, recently of Manhattan and now a contented Eastwick taxpayer, welcomed your reporter to his island.

Yes, his island, for the famous "Lenox Manse" that this newcomer has purchased sits surrounded by marsh and at high tide by sheer sheets of water!

Constructed circa 1895 in a brick English style, with a symmetrical façade and massive chimneys at either end, the new proprietor hopes to convert his acquisition to multiple usages—as laboratory for his fabulous experiments with chemistry and solar energy, as a concert hall containing no less than three pianos (which he plays expertly, believe me), and as a large gallery upon whose walls hang startling works by such contemporary masters as Robert Rauschenberg, Claus Oldenberg, Bob Indiana, and James Van Dine.

An elaborate solarium-cum-greenhouse, a Japanese bath that will be a luxurious vision of exposed copper piping and polished teakwood, and an AsPhlex composition tennis court are all under construction as the privately owned island rings with the sound of hammer and saw and the beautiful pale herons who customarily nest in the lee of the property seek temporary refuge elsewhere.

Progress has its price!

Van Horne, though a genial host, is modest about his many enterprises and hopes to enjoy seclusion and opportunity for meditation in his new residence.

"I was attracted," he told your inquiring reporter, "to Rhode Island by the kind of space and beauty it affords, rare along the Eastern Seaboard in these troubled and overpopulated times. I feel at home here already.

"This is one heck of a spot!" he added informally, standing with your reporter on the ruins of the old Lenox dock and gazing out upon the vista of marsh, drumlin, channel, low-lying shrubland, and distant ocean horizon visible from the second floor.

The house with its vast stretches of parqueted maple floor and high ceiling bearing chandelier rosettes of molded plaster plus dentil molding along the sides felt chilly on the day of our fall visit, with much of the new "master's" equipment and furniture still in its sturdy packing cases, but he assured your reporter that the coming winter held no terrors for our resourceful host.

Van Horne plans to install a number of solar panels over the slates of the great roof and furthermore feels close to the eventual perfection of a closely guarded process that will render consumption of fossil fuels needless in the near future. Speed the day!

The grounds now abandoned to sumac, ailanthus, chokecherry and other weed trees the new proprietor envisions as a semi-tropical paradise brimming with exotic vegetation sheltered for the winter in the Lenox mansion's elaborate solarium-cum-greenhouse. The period statuary adorning the once-Versailles-like mall, now unfortunately so eroded by years of weather that many figures lack noses and hands, the proud owner plans to restore indoors, substituting Fiberglas replicas along the stately mall (well remembered in its glory by elderly citizens of this area) in the manner of the celebrated caryatids at the Parthenon in Athens, Greece.

The causeway, Van Horne said with an expansive gesture so characteristic of the man, could be improved by the addition of anchored aluminum pontoon sections at the lowest portions.

"A dock would be a lot of fun," he volunteered in a possibly humorous vein. "You could run a Hovercraft over to Newport or up to Providence."

Van Horne shares his extensive residence with no more company than an assistant-cum-butler, Mr. Fidel Malaguer, and an adorable fluffy Angora kitten whimsically yclept Thumbkin, because the animal has extra thumbs on several paws.

A man of impressive vision and warmth, your reporter welcomed the newcomer to this fabled region of South County confident that she spoke on behalf of many neighbors.

The Lenox Manse has again become a place to keep an eye on!

"You went there!" Alexandra jealously accused Sukie, over the phone, having read the article in the *Word*.

"Sweetie, it was an assignment."

"And whose idea was the assignment?"

"Mine," Sukie admitted. "Clyde wasn't sure it was news. And sometimes in cases like this when you talk about what a lovely home et cetera the person gets robbed the next week and sues the newspaper." Clyde Gabriel, a stringy weary man with a disagreeable do-gooding wife, edited the *Word*. Apologetically Sukie asked, "What did you think of the piece?"

"Well, honey, it had color, but you *do* run on a bit and honestly—now don't be offended—you *must* watch your participles. They dangle all over the place."

"If it's less than five paragraphs you don't get a byline. And he got me drunk. First it was rum in the tea and then it was rum without the tea. That creepy spic kept bringing it on this enormous silver tray. I never saw such a big tray; it was like a tabletop, all engraved and chased or whatever."

"What about *him*? How did he act? Darryl Van Horne."

'Well he talked a blue streak I must say. Giving me a saliva bath half the time. It was hard to know how seriously to take some of the things—the pontoon bridge, for instance. He said the canisters if that's what they are could be painted green and would blend right in with the marsh grass. The tennis court is going to be green, even the fencing. It's almost done and he wants us all to come play while the weather isn't too bad yet."

"All of who?"

"All of *us*, you and me and Jane. He seemed very interested, and I told him a little bit, just the part everybody knows, about our divorces and finding ourselves and so on. And what a comfort especially you are. I don't find Jane all that comforting lately, I think she's looking for a husband behind our backs. And I don't mean awful Neff, either. Greta has him too socked in with those children. God, don't children get in the way? I keep having the most terrible fights with mine. They say I'm never home and I try to explain to the little shits that I'm *earn*ing a *liv*ing."

Alexandra would not be distracted from the encounter she wanted to envision, between Sukie and this Van Horne man. "You told him the dirt about us?"

"Is there dirt? I just don't let gossip get to me, Lexa, frankly. Hold your head up and keep thinking, *Fuck you*: that's how I get down Dock Street every day. No, of course I didn't. I was very discreet as always. But he did seem so curious. I think it might be you he loves."

"Well I don't love him. I hate complexions that dark. And I can't stand New York chutzpah. And his face doesn't fit his mouth, or his voice, or something."

"I found that rather appealing," Sukie said. "His clumsiness."

"What did he do clumsy, spill rum all over your lap?"

"And then lick it up, no. Just the way he lurched from one thing to another, showing me his crazy paintings—there must be a fortune on those walls—and then his lab and playing the piano a little, 'Mood Indigo,' I think it was, done to waltz time as sort of a joke. Then he went running around outdoors so one of the backhoes nearly knocked him into a pit, and wanted to know if I wanted to see the view from the cupola."

"You *did*n't go into the cupola with him! Not on your first date."

"Baby, you make me keep *say*ing. It wasn't a date, it was an as*sign*ment. No, I thought I had enough and I knew I was drunk and had this deadline." She paused. Last night there had been a high wind and this morning, Alexandra saw through her kitchen window, the birches and the grape arbor had been stripped of so many leaves that a new kind of light was in the air, that naked gray short-lived light of winter that shows us the lay of the land and how close the houses of our neighbors sit. "He *did* seem," Sukie was saying, "I don't know, almost too eager for publicity. I mean, it's just a little local paper. It's as if—"

"Go on," said Alexandra, touching the chill windowpane with her forehead as if to let her thirsty brain drink the fresh wide light.

"I just wonder if this business of his is really doing so well, or is it just whistling in the dark? If he's really making these things, shouldn't there be a factory?"

"Good questions. What sort of questions did he ask about us? Or, rather, what sort of things did you choose to tell him?"

"I don't know why you sound so huffy about it."

"I don't either. I mean, I really don't."

"I mean, I don't have to tell you any of this."

"You're right. I'm being awful. Please don't stop." Alexandra did not want her ill humor to close the window on the outside world that Sukie's gossip gave her.

"Oh," Sukie answered tantalizingly. "How cozy we are. How much we've discovered we prefer women to men, and so on."

"Did that offend him?"

"No, he said he preferred women to men too. They were much the superior mechanism."

"He said 'mechanism.' "

"Some word like that. Listen, angel, I must run, honest. I'm supposed to be interviewing the committee heads about the Harvest Festival."

"Which church?"

In the pause, Alexandra shut her eyes and saw an iridescent zigzag, as if a diamond on an unseen hand were etching darkness in electric parallel with Sukie's darting thoughts. "You know, the Unitarian. All the others think it's too pagan."

"May I ask, how are you feeling toward Ed Parsley these days?"

"Oh, the usual. Benign but distant. Brenda is *such* an impossible prig."

"What is she being impossibly priggish about, does he say?"

A certain reserve concerning sexual specifics obtained among the witches, but Sukie, by way of making up, moved against this constraint and broke into confession: "She doesn't do *any*thing for him, Lexa. And before he went to divinity school he knocked about quite a bit, so he knows what he's missing. He keeps wanting to run away and join the Movement."

"He's too old. He's over thirty. The Movement doesn't want him."

"He *knows* that. He de*spis*es himself. I *can't* be rejecting to him every time, he's too pathetic," Sukie cried out in protest.

Healing belonged to their natures, and if the world accused them of coming between men and wives, of tying the disruptive ligature, of knotting the *aiguillette* that places the kink of impotence or emotional coldness in the entrails of a marriage seemingly secure in its snugly roofed and darkened house, and if the world not merely accused but burned them alive in the tongues of indignant opinion, that was the price they must pay. It was fundamental and instinctive, it was womanly, to want to heal—to apply the poultice of acquiescent flesh to the wound of a man's desire, to give his closeted spirit the exaltation of seeing a witch slip out of her clothes and go skyclad in a room of tawdry motel furniture.

Alexandra released Sukie with no more implied rebuke of the younger woman's continuing to minister to Ed Parsley.

In the silence of her house, childless for two more hours, Alexandra battled depression, moving beneath its weight like a fish sluggish and misshapen at the bottom of the sea. She felt suffocated by her uselessness and the containing uselessness of this house, a mid-nineteenth-century farmhouse with musty small rooms and a smell of linoleum. She thought of eating, to cheer herself up. All things, even giant sea slugs, feed; feeding is their essence and teeth and hoofs and wings have all evolved from the millions of years of small bloody struggles. She made herself a sandwich of sliced turkey breast and lettuce on diet whole-wheat bread, all hauled from the Bay Superette this morning, with Comet and Calgonite and this week's issue of the *Word*. The many laborious steps lunch involved nearly overwhelmed her—taking the meat from the refrigerator and undoing its taped jacket of butcher paper, locating the mayonnaise on the shelf where it hid amid jars of jelly and salad oil, clawing loose from the head of lettuce its clinging crinkling skin of plastic wrap, arranging these ingredients on the counter with a plate, getting a knife from the drawer to spread the mayonnaise, finding a fork to fish a long spear of pickle from the squat jar where seeds clouded a thin green juice, and then making herself coffee to wash the taste of turkey and pickle away. Every time she returned to its place in the drawer the little plastic dip that measured the coffee grounds into the percolator, a few more grains of coffee accumulated there, in the cracks, out of reach: if she lived forever these grains would become a mountain, a range of dark brown Alps. All around her in this home was an inexorable silting of dirt: beneath the beds, behind the books, between the spines of the radiators. She put away all the ingredients and equipment her hunger had called forth. She went through some motions of housekeeping. Why was there nothing to sleep in but beds that had to be remade, nothing to eat from but dishes that had to be washed? Inca women had had it no worse. She was indeed as Van Horne had said a mechanism, a robot cruelly conscious of every chronic motion.

She had been a cherished daughter, in that high western town, with its main street like a wide and dusty football field, the drugstore and the tack shop and the Woolworth's and the barbershop scattered over the space like creosote bushes that poison the earth around them. She had been the life of her family, a marvel of amusing grace flanked by dull brothers, boys yoked to the clattering cart of maleness, their lives one team after another. Her father, returning from his trips selling Levi's, had looked upon the growing Alexandra as upon a plant that grew in little leaps, displaying new petals and shoots at each reunion. As she grew, little Sandy stole health and power from her fading mother, as she had once sucked milk from her breasts. She rode horses and broke her hymen. She learned to ride on the long saddle-shaped seats of motorcycles, clinging so tightly her cheek took the imprint of the studs on the back of the boy's jacket. Her mother died and her father sent her east to college; her high-school guidance counselor had fastened on something with the safe-sounding name of Connecticut College for Women. There in New London, as field-hockey captain and fine-arts major, she moved through the many brisk costumes of the East's four picture-postcard seasons and in the June of her junior year found herself one day all in white and the next with the many uniforms of wife lined up limp in her wardrobe. She had met Oz on a sailing day on Long Island that others had arranged; holding drink after drink steady in a fragile plastic glass, he had seemed neither sick nor alarmed, when she had been both, and this had impressed her. Ozzie had delighted in her too—her full figure and her western, mannish way of walking. The wind shifted, the sail flapped, the boat yawed, his grin flashed reassuringly in the sun-scorched gin-fed pink of his face; he had a one-sided sheepish smile a little like her father's. It was a fall into his arms, but by such fallings she dimly understood life to rise, from strength to strength. She shouldered motherhood, the garden club, car pools, and cocktail parties. She shared morning coffee with the cleaning lady and midnight cognac with her husband, mistaking drunken lust for reconciliation. Around her the world was growing—child after child leaped from between her legs, they built an addition onto the house, Oz's raises kept pace with inflation—and somehow she was feeding the world but no longer fed by it. Her depressions grew worse. Her doctor prescribed Tofranil, her psychotherapist analysis, her clergyman *Either/Or*. She and Oz lived at that time, in Norwich, within sound of church bells and as winter afternoons darkened and before school returned her children to her Alexandra would lie in her bed beaten flatter by every stroke, feeling as shapeless and ill-smelling as an old galosh or the pelt of a squirrel killed days before on the highway. As a girl she would lie on the bed in their innocent mountain town excited by her body, a visitor of sorts who had come out of nowhere to enclose her spirit; she had studied herself in the mirror, saw the cleft in her chin and the curious dent at the end of her nose, stood back to appraise the sloping wide shoulders and gourdlike breasts and the belly like a shallow inverted bowl glowing above the demure triangular bush and solid oval thighs, and decided to be friends with her body; she could have been dealt a worse. Lying on the bed, she would marvel at her own ankle, turning it in the window light—the taut glimmer of its bones and sinews, the veins of palest blue with their magical traffic of oxygen—or stroke her own forearms, downy and plump and tapered. Then in mid-marriage her own body disgusted her, and Ozzie's attempts to make love to it seemed an unkind gibe. It was the body outside, beyond the windows, that light-struck, water-riddled, foliate flesh of that other self the world to which beauty still clung; when divorce came it was as if she had flown through that window. The morning after the decree, she was up at four, pulling up dead pea plants and singing by moonlight, singing by the light of that hard white stone with the tilted sad unisex face—a celestial presence, and dawn in the east the gray of a cat. This other body too had a spirit.

Now the world poured through her, wasted, down the drain. A woman is a hole, Alexandra had once read in the memoirs of a prostitute. In truth it felt less like being a hole than being a sponge, a heavy squishy thing on this bed soaking out of the air all the futility and misery there is: wars nobody wins, diseases conquered so we can all die of cancer. Her children would be clamoring home, so awkward and needy, plucking, clinging, looking to her for nurture, and they would find not a mother but only a frightened fat child no longer cute, no longer amazing to a father whose ashes two years ago had been scattered from a crop-duster over his favorite mountain meadow, where the family used to go gathering wildflowers—alpine phlox and sky pilot with its skunky-smelling leaves, monkshood and shooting stars and avalanche lily that blooms in the moist places left as the snow line retreats. Her father had carried a flower guide; little Sandra would bring him fresh-plucked offerings to name, delicate blooms with shy pale petals and stems chilly, it seemed to the child, from being out all night in the mountainous cold.

The chintz curtains that Alexandra and Mavis Jessup, the decorator divorcee from the Yapping Fox, had hung at the bedroom windows bore a big splashy pattern of pink and white peonies. The folds of the draperies as they hung produced out of this pattern a distinct clown's face, an evil pink-and-white clown's face with a little slit of a mouth: the more Alexandra looked, the more such sinister clown's faces there were, a chorus of them amid the superimpositions of the peonies. They were devils. They encouraged her depression.

She thought of her little bubbies waiting to be conjured out of the clay and they were images of her—sodden, amorphous. A drink, a pill, might uplift and glaze her, but she knew the price: she would feel worse two hours later. Her wandering thoughts were drawn as if by the glamorous shuttle and syncopated clatter of machinery toward the old Lenox place and its resident, that dark prince who had taken her two sisters in as if in calculated insult to her. Even in his insult and vileness there was something to push against and give her spirit exercise. She yearned for rain, the relief of its stir beyond the blankness of the ceiling, but when she turned her eyes to the window, there was no change in the cruelly brilliant weather outside. The maple against her window coated the panes with gold, the last flare of outlived leaves. Alexandra lay on her bed helpless, weighed down by all the incessant uselessness there is in the world.

Good Coal came in to her, scenting her sorrow. His lustrous long body, glittering in its loose sack of dogskin, loped across the oval rug of braided rags and heaved without effort up onto her swaying bed. He licked her face in worry, and her hands, and nuzzled where for comfort she had loosened the waist of her dirt-hardened Levi's. She tugged up her blouse to expose more of her milk-white belly and he found the supernumerary pap there, a hand's-breadth from her navel, a small pink rubbery bud that had appeared a few years ago and that Doc Pat had assured her was benign and not cancerous. He had offered to remove it but she was frightened of the knife. The pap had no feeling, but the flesh around it tingled while Coal nuzzled and lapped as at a teat. The dog's body radiated warmth and a faint perfume of carrion. Earth has in her all these shades of decay and excrement and Alexandra found them not offensive but in their way handsome, decomposition's deep-woven plaid.

Abruptly Coal was exhausted by his suckling. He collapsed into the curve her grief-drugged body made on the bed. The big dog, sleeping, snored with a noise like moisture in a straw. Alexandra stared at the ceiling, waiting for something to happen. The watery skins of her eyes felt hot, and dry as cactus skins. Her pupils were two black thorns turned inwards.

Sukie turned in her story of the Harvest Festival ("Rummage Sale, Duck-the-Clown / Part of Unitarian Plans") to Clyde Gabriel in his narrow office and discovered him, disconcertingly, slumped at his desk with his head in his arms. He heard the sheets of her copy rustle in his wire basket and looked up. His eyes were red-rimmed but whether from crying or sleep or hangover or last night's sleeplessness she could not tell. She knew from rumor that he not only was a drinker but owned a telescope he would sometimes sit at for hours on his back porch, examining the stars. His oak-pale hair, thin on top, was mussed; he had puffy blue welts below his eyes and the rest of his face was faintly gray like newsprint. "Sorry," she said, "I thought you'd want to pop this in."

Without much raising his head off the desk he squinted at her pages. "Pop, schnop," he said, embarrassed by being found slumped over. "This item doesn't deserve a two-line head. How about 'Peacenik Parson Plans Poppycock'?"

"I didn't talk to Ed; it was his committee chairpersons."

"Oops, pardon me. I forgot you think Parsley's a great man."

"That isn't altogether what I think," Sukie said, standing extra erect. These unhappy or unlucky men it was her fate to be attracted to were not above pulling you down with them if you allowed it and didn't stand tall. His nasty sardonic side, which made some others of the staff cringe and which had soured his reputation around town, Sukie saw as a masked apology, a plea turned upside down. At a point earlier in his life he must have been beautiful with promise, but his handsomeness—high square forehead, broad could-be passionate mouth, and eyes a most delicate icy blue and framed by starry long lashes—was caving in; he was getting that dried-out starving look of the persistent drinker.

Clyde was a little over fifty. On the pegboard wall behind his desk, along with a sampler of headline sizes and some framed citations awarded to the *Word* under earlier managements, he had hung photographs of his daughter and son but none of his wife, though he was not divorced. The daughter, pretty in an innocent, moon-faced way, was an unmarried X-ray technician at Michael Reese Hospital in Chicago, on her way perhaps to becoming what Monty would have laughingly called a "lady doctor." The Gabriel son, a college dropout interested in theatre, had spent the summer on the fringes of summer stock in Connecticut, and had his father's pale eyes and the pouty good looks of an archaic Greek statue. Felicia Gabriel, the wife left off the wall, must have been a perky bright handful once but had developed into a sharp-featured little woman who could not stop talking. She was in this day and age outraged by everything: by the government and by the protesters, by the war, by the drugs, by dirty songs played on WPRO, by *Playboy*'s being sold openly at the local drugstores, by the lethargic town government and its crowd of downtown loafers, by the summer people scandalous in both costume and deed, by nothing's being quite as it would be if she were running everything. "Felicia was just on the phone," Clyde volunteered, in oblique apology for the sad posture in which Sukie had found him, "furious about this Van Horne man's violation of the wetlands regulations. Also she says your story about him was altogether too flattering; she says she's heard rumors about his past in New York that are pretty unsavory."

"Who'd she hear them from?"

"She won't say. She's protecting her sources. Maybe she

got the poop straight from J. Edgar Hoover." Such antiwifely irony added little animation to his face, he had been ironical at Felicia's expense so often before. Something had died behind those long-lashed eyes. The two adult children pictured on his wall had his ghostliness, Sukie had often thought: the daughter's round features like an empty outline in their perfection and the boy also eerily passive, with his fleshy lips and curly hair and silvery long face. This colorlessness in Clyde's instance was stained by the brown aromas of morning whiskey and cigarette tobacco and a strange caustic whiff the back of his neck gave off. Sukie had never slept with Clyde. But she had this mothering sense that she could give him health. He seemed to be sinking, clutching his steel desk like an overturned rowboat.

"You look exhausted," she was forward enough to tell him.

"I am. Suzanne, I really am. Felicia gets on the phone every night to one or another of her causes and leaves me to drink too much. I used to go use the telescope but I really need a stronger power, it barely brings the rings of Saturn in."

"Take her to the movies," Sukie suggested.

"I did, some perfectly harmless thing with Barbra Streisand—God, what a voice that woman has, it goes through you like a knife!—and she got so sore at the violence in one of the previews she went back and spent half the movie complaining to the manager. Then she came back for the last half and got sore because she thought they showed too much of Streisand's tits when she bent over, in one of these turn-of-the-century gowns. I mean, this wasn't even a PG movie, it was a G! It was all people singing on old trolley cars!" Clyde tried to laugh but his lips had lost the habit and the resultant crimped hole in his face was pathetic to look at. Sukie had an impulse to peel up her cocoa-brown wool sweater and unfasten her bra and give this dying man her perky breasts to suck; but she already had Ed Parsley in her life and one wry intelligent sufferer at a time was enough.

Every night she was shrinking Ed Parsley in her mind, so that when the call came she could travel sufficiently lightened across the flooded marsh to Darryl Van Horne's island. That's where the action was, not here in town, where oil-streaked harbor water lapped the pilings and placed a shudder of reflected light upon the haggard faces of the citizens of Eastwick as they plodded through their civic and Christian duties.

Still, Sukie's nipples had gone erect beneath her sweater in awareness of her healing powers, of being for any man a garden stocked with antidotes and palliatives. Her areolas tingled, as when once babies needed her milk or as when she and Jane and Lexa raised the cone of power and a chilly thrill, a kind of alarm going off, moved through her bones, even her finger and toe bones, as if they were slender pipes conveying streams of icy water. Clyde Gabriel bent his head to a piece of editing; touchingly, his colorless scalp showed between the long loose strands of oak-pale hair, an angle he never saw.

Sukie left the *Word* offices and stepped out onto Dock Street and walked to Nemo's for lunch; the perspective of sidewalks and glaring shopfronts pulled tight as a drawstring around her upright figure. The masts of sailboats moored beyond the pilings like a forest of slender varnished trees had thinned. At the south end of the street, at Landing Square, the huge old beeches around the little granite war memorial formed a fragile towering wall of yellow, losing leaves to every zephyr. The water as it turned toward winter cold became a steelier blue, against which the white clapboards of houses on the Bay side of the street looked dazzlingly chalky, every nail hole vivid. *Such beauty*! Sukie thought, and felt frightened that her own beauty and vitality would not always be part of it, that some day she would be gone like a lost odd-shaped piece from the center of a picture puzzle.

*   *   *

Jane Smart was practicing Bach's Second Suite for un-accompanied cello, in D Minor, the little black sixteenth-notes of the prelude going up and down and then up again with the sharps and flats like a man slightly raising his voice in conversation, old Bach setting his infallible tonal suspense engine in operation again, and abruptly Jane began to resent it, these notes, so black and certain and masculine, the fingering getting trickier with each sliding transposition of the theme and he not caring, this dead square-faced old Lutheran with his wig and his Lord and his genius and two wives and seventeen children, not caring how the tips of her fingers hurt, or how her obedient spirit was pushed back and forth, up and down, by these military notes just to give him a voice after death, a bully's immortality; abruptly she rebelled, put down the bow, poured herself a little dry vermouth, and went to the phone. Sukie would be back from work by now, throwing some peanut butter and jelly at her poor children before heading out to the evening's idiotic civic meeting.

"We *must* do something about getting Alexandra over to Darryl's place" was the burden of Jane's call. "I swung by late Wednesday even though she had told me not to because she seemed so hurt about our Thursday not working out, she has gotten much too dependent on Thursdays, and she looked just terribly down, *sick* with jealousy, first me and the Brahms and then your article, I must say your prose did somehow rub it in, and I couldn't get her to say a word about it and I didn't dare press the topic myself, why she hasn't been invited."

"But darling, she *has* been, as much as you and I were. When he was showing me his art works for the article he even pulled out an expensive-looking catalogue for a show this Niki Whatever had had in Paris and said he was saving it for Lexa to see."

"Well she won't go now until she's formally asked and I can tell it's eating the poor thing alive. I thought maybe you could say something."

"Sweetie, why me? You're the one who knows him better, you're over there all the time now with all this music."

"I've been there twice," Jane said, hissing the last word most positively. "You just have that way about you, you can get away with saying things to a man. I'm too definite somehow; it would come out as meaning too much."

"I'm not sure he even liked the article," Sukie fended. "He never called me about it."

"Why wouldn't he have liked it? It was lovely, and made him seem very romantic and dashing and impressive. Marge Perley has it up on her bulletin board and tells all her prospective clients that this was her sale."

At Sukie's end of the line a crying female child came up to her; her older brother, this child managed to explain between sobs while Jane's voice crackled on like static, wouldn't let her watch an education special about lions mating instead of a rerun of *Hogan's Heroes* on a UHF channel that *he* wanted to see. Peanut butter and jelly flecked this little girl's lips; her fine hair was an uncombed tangle. Sukie wanted to slap the repulsive child's dirty face and knock a little sense into those TV-glazed eyes. Greed, that was all TV taught, turning our minds to total pap. Darryl Van Horne had explained to her how TV was responsible for all the riots and war resistance; the commercial interruptions and the constant switching back and forth between channels had broken down in young people's brains the synapses that make logical connections, so that Make Love Not War seemed to them an actual idea.

"I'll think about it," she promised Jane hastily, and hung up. She had to go out to an emergency session of the Highway Department; last February's unexpected blizzards had used up all this year's snow-removal and road-salting budget and the chairman, Ike Arsenault, was threatening to resign. Sukie hoped to be able to leave early for a tryst with Ed Parsley at Point Judith. First she had to settle the squabble in the TV den. The children had their own set upstairs but to be perverse preferred to use hers; the noise filled the tiny house, and their glasses of milk and cocoa cups left rings on the sea chest refinished as a coffee table, and she would find bread crusts turning green between the love-seat cushions. She flounced in a fury and assigned the rudest brat to put the supper dishes into the dishwasher. "And be sure to rinse the peanut-butter knife, rinse and *wipe* it; if you just throw it in the heat bakes the peanut butter so you can *never* get it off." Before leaving the kitchen Sukie chopped up an Alpo can of blood-colored horsemeat and set it on the floor, in the plastic dog dish a child with a Magic Marker had letter HANK, for the ravenous Weimaraner to gobble. She crammed half a fistful of salted Spanish peanuts into her own mouth; bits of red skin stuck to her sumptuous lips.

She went upstairs. To get to Sukie's bedroom, you went up the narrow stair and turned left into a narrow slanted hall of unadorned boards and then right, through an authentic eighteenth-century door studded in a double X pattern of squarish cut nails. She shut this door and with a wrought-iron latch shaped like a claw locked herself in. The room was papered in an old pattern of vines growing straight up like bean plants on poles, and the cobwebbed ceilings sagged like the underside of a hammock. Large washers bolted at the worst cracks kept the plaster from falling down. A single geranium was dying on the sill of the room's one small window. Sukie slept in a sway-backed double bed that wore a threadbare coverlet of dotted Swiss. She had remembered there was a copy of last week's *Word* by her bedside; with a pair of curved nail scissors she carefully cut out her "Inventor, Musician, Art Fancier" article, breathing warmly upon it as her nearsighted eyes strained not to include a single adjacent letter of any item that did not concern Darryl Van Horne. This done, she wrapped the article face inwards around a heavy-hipped, tiny-footed naked bubby Alexandra had given Sukie for her thirtieth birthday two years ago but which for the purposes of magic would represent the creatrix herself. With a special string Sukie kept in a narrow cupboard beside the walled-in fireplace, a furry pale green jute such as gardeners used to tie up plants and whose properties included therefore that of encouraging growth, she tightly wound the package around until not a glint of the crackling print-filled paper showed. She tied it with a bow, then another, and a third, for magic. The fetish weighed pleasantly in the hand, a phallic oblong with the texture of a closely woven basket. Uncertain what the proper spell might be, she touched it lightly to her forehead, her two breasts, her navel that was a single link in the infinite chain of women, and, lifting her skirt but keeping her underpants on, her pudendum. For good measure she gave the thing a kiss. "Have fun, you two," she said, and, remembering a word of her schoolgirl Latin, chanted in a whisper, *"Copula, copula, copula."* Then she kneeled and put this hairy green charm underneath her bed, where she spotted about a dozen dust mice and a pair of lost pantyhose she was in too much of a hurry to retrieve. Already her nipples had stiffened, foreseeing Ed Parsley, his dark parked car, the sweeping accusatory beam of the Point Judith lighthouse, the crummy dank motel room he would have already paid eighteen dollars for, and the storms of his guilt she would have to endure once he was sexually satisfied.

On this afternoon of cold low silver sky Alexandra thought East Beach might be too windy and raw so she stopped the Subaru on a shoulder of the beach road not far from the Lenox causeway. Here was a wide stretch of marsh, the grass now bleached and pressed flat in patches by the action of the tides, where Coal could have a run. Between the speckled boulders that were the causeway's huge bones the sea deposited dead gulls and empty crab shells the dog loved to sniff and rummage among. Here also stood what was left of an entrance gate: two brick pillars capped by cement bowls of fruit and holding the rusting pivot pins for an iron gate that had vanished. While she stood gazing in the direction of the glowering symmetrical house, its owner pulled up behind her silently in his Mercedes. The car was an off-white that looked dirty; one front fender had been dented and the other repaired and repainted in an ivory that did not quite match. Alexandra was wearing a red bandanna against the wind, so when she turned she saw her face in the smiling dark man's eye as a startled oval, framed in red against the silver streaks over the sea, her hair covered like a nun's.

His car window had slid smoothly down on a motor. "You've come at last," he called, less with that prying clownish edge of the post-concert party than as a simple factual declaration by a busy man. His seamed face grinned. Beside him on the front seat sat a shadowy conical shape—a collie, but one in whose tricolor hair the black was unusually dominant. This creature yapped mercilessly when loyal Coal rallied from his far-ranging carrion-sniffing to his mistress's side.

She gripped her pet's collar to restrain him as he bristled and gagged, and lifted her voice to make it heard above the dogs' din. "I was just parking here, I wasn't . . ." Her voice came out frailer and younger than her own; she had been caught.

"I know, I know," Van Horne said impatiently. "Come on over anyway and have a drink. You haven't had your tour yet."

"I have to get back in a minute. The children will be coming home from school." But even as she said it Alexandra was dragging Coal, suspicious and resisting, toward her car. His run wasn't over, he wanted to say.

"Better hop in my jalopy with me," the man shouted. "The tide's coming in and you don't want to get stranded."

I don't? she wondered, obeying like an automaton, betraying her best friend by shutting Coal alone in the Subaru. He had expected her to join him and drive home. She cranked the driver's window down an inch, for air, and punched the locks on the doors. The dog's black face rumpled with incredulity. His ears were thrust out as far from his skull as their crimped inner folds would bear their floppy weight. These velvety pink folds she had often fondled by the fireside, examining them for ticks. She turned away. "Really just a minute," she stammered to Van Horne, torn, awkward, years fallen from her with their poise and powers.

The collie, whom Sukie's article had not mentioned, shed all ferocity and slunk gracefully into the back seat as she opened the Mercedes door. The car's interior was red leather; the front seats had been dressed in sheep hides, woolly side up. With an expensive punky sound the door closed at her side.

"Say howdy-do, Needlenose," Van Horne said, twisting his big head, like an ill-fitting helmet, toward the back seat. The dog did indeed have a very pointed nose, which he pushed into Alexandra's palm when she offered it. Pointed, moist, and shocking—the tip of an icicle. She pulled her hand back quickly.

"The tide won't be in for hours," she said, trying to return her voice to its womanly register. The causeway was dry and full of potholes. His renovations had not extended this far.

"The bastard can fool you," he said. "How the hell've you been, anyway? You look depressed."

"I do? How can you tell?"

"I can tell. Some people find fall depressing, others hate spring. I've always been a spring person myself. All that growth, you can feel Nature groaning, the old bitch; she doesn't want to do it, not again, no, anything but *that*, but she *has* to. It's a fucking torture rack, all that budding and pushing, the sap up the tree trunks, the weeds and the insects getting set to fight it out once again, the seeds trying to remember how the hell the DNA is supposed to go, all that competition for a little bit of nitrogen; Christ, it's cruel. Maybe I'm too sensitive. I bet you revel in it. Women aren't that sensitive to things like that."

She nodded, hypnotized by the bumpy road diminishing under her, growing at her back. Brick pillars twin to those at the far end stood at the entrance to the island, and these still had their gate, its iron wings flung wide for years and the rusted scrolls become a lattice for wild grapevines and poison ivy and even interpenetrated by young trees, swamp maples, their little leaves turning the tenderest red, almost a rose. One of the pillars had lost its crown of mock fruit.

"Women take pain in their stride pretty much," Van Horne was going on. "Me, I can't stand it. I can't even bring myself to swat a housefly. The poor thing'll be dead in a couple days anyway."

Alexandra shuddered, remembering houseflies landing on her lips as she slept, their feathery tiny feet, the electric touch of their energy, like touching a frayed cord while ironing. "I like May," she admitted lamely. "Except every year it does feel, as you say, more of an effort. For gardeners, anyway."

Joe Marino's green truck, to her relief, was not parked anywhere out front of the mansion. The heavy work on the tennis court seemed to have been done; instead of the golden earthmovers Sukie had described, a few shirtless young men were with dainty pinging noises fastening wide swatches of green plastic-coated fencing to upright metal posts all around what at the distance, as she looked down from a curve of the driveway to where the snowy egrets used to nest in the dead elms, seemed a big playing card in two flat colors imitating grass and earth; the grid of white lines looked sharp with signification, as compulsively precise as a Wiccan diagram. Van Horne had stopped the car so she could admire. "I looked into that HarTrue and even if you see your way past the initial expense the maintenance of any kind of clay is one

hell of a headache. With this AsPhlex composition all you
need do is sweep the leaves off it now and then and with any
luck you can play right into December. Couple of days more
it'll be ready to baptize; my thought was with you and your
two buddies we might have a foursome."

"My goodness, are we up to such an honor? I'm really in
no shape—"she began, meaning her game. Ozzie and she for a
time had played a lot of doubles with other couples, but in the
years since, though Sukie once or twice a summer got her out
for some Saturday singles on the battered public courts
toward Southwick, she had really played hardly at all.

"Then *get* in shape," Van Horne said, misunderstanding,
spitting in his enthusiasm. "Move around, get rid of that flub.
Hell, thirty-eight is *young*."

He knows my age, Alexandra thought, more relieved than
offended. It was nice to have yourself known by a man; it was
getting to be known that was embarrassing: all that self-
conscious verbalization over too many drinks, and then the
bodies revealed with the hidden marks and sags like disappointing presents at Christmastime. But how much of love,
when you thought about it, was not of the other but of
yourself naked in his eyes: of that rush, that little flight, of
shedding your clothes, and being you at last. With this
overbearing strange man she felt known, essentially, already.
His being awful rather helped.

He put the car into motion and coasted around the
crackling driveway circle and halted at the front door. Two
steps led up to a paved, pillared porch holding in tesserae of
green marble the inlaid initial *L*. The door itself, freshly
painted black, was so massive Alexandra feared it would pull
its hinges loose when the owner swung it open. Inside the
foyer, a sulphurous chemical smell greeted her; Van Horne
seemed oblivious of it, it was his element. He ushered her in,
past a stuffed hollow elephant foot full of knobbed and
curved canes and one umbrella. He was not wearing baggy

tweed today but a dark three-piece suit as if he had been somewhere on business. He gestured right and left with excited stiff arms that returned to his sides like collapsed levers. "Lab's over there, past the pianos, used to be the ballroom, nothing in there but a ton of equipment half of it still in crates, we've hardly begun to roll yet, but when we do, boy, we're going to make dynamite look like firecrackers. Here on the other side, let's call it the study, half my books still in cartons in the basement, some of the old sets I don't want to put out in the light till I can get an air-control unit set up, these old bindings, you know, and even the threads hold 'em together turn into dust like mummies when you lift the lid . . . cute room, though, isn't it? The antlers were here, and the heads. I'm no hunter myself, get up at four in the morning go out and blast some big-eyed doe never did anybody any harm in the world in the face with a shotgun, crazy. People are crazy. People are really wicked, you have to believe it. Here's the dining room. The table's mahogany, six leaves if I want to give a banquet, myself I prefer dinners on the intimate side, four, six people, give everybody a chance to shine, strut their stuff. You invite a mob and mob psychology takes over, a few leaders and a lot of sheep. I have some super candelabra still packed, eighteenth-century, expert I know says positively from the workshop of Robert Joseph Auguste though it doesn't have the hallmark, the French were never into hallmarks like the English, the de*tail* on it you wouldn't believe, imitation grapevines down to the tiniest little curlicue tendril, you can even see a little bug or two on 'em, you can even see where insects chewed the leaves, everything done two-thirds scale; I hate to get it up here in plain view until I have a foolproof burglar alarm installed, though burglars generally don't like to tackle a place like this, only one way in and out, they like to have an escape hatch. Not that that's any insurance policy, they're getting bolder, the drugs make the bastards desperate, the drugs and the general breakdown in respect for any damn thing at all; I've heard of people gone for only half an hour and cleaned out, they keep track of your routines, your every move, you're watched, that's one thing you can be sure of in this society, baby: you are *watched*."

Of Alexandra's responses to this outpouring she had no consciousness: polite noises, no doubt, as she held herself a distance behind him in fear of being accidentally struck as the big man wheeled and gestured. She was aware of, beyond his excited dark shape as he lavishly bragged, a certain penetrating bareness: a shabbiness of empty corners and rugless scratched floors, of ceilings whose cracks and buckled patches had gone untouched for decades, of woodwork whose once-white paint had yellowed and chipped and of elegant hand-printed panoramic wallpapers drooping loose in the corners and along the dried-out seams; vanished paintings and mirrors were remembered by rectangular and oval ghosts of lesser discoloration. For all his talk of glories still to be unpacked, the rooms were badly underfurnished; Van Horne had the robust instincts of a creator but with only, it seemed, half the needed raw materials. Alexandra found this touching and saw in him something of herself, her monumental statues that could be held in the hand.

"*Now*," he announced, booming as if to drown out these thoughts in her head, "here's the room I wanted you to see. *La chambre de résistance*." It was a long living room, with a portentous fireplace pillared like the façade of a temple—leafy Ionic pillars carved to support a mantel above which a great bevelled mirror gave back the room a speckled version of its lordly space. She looked at her own image and removed the bandanna, shaking down her hair, not fixed in a braid today but with a sticky twistiness still in it. As her voice had come out of her startled mouth younger than she was, so she looked younger in this antique, forgiving mirror. It was slightly tipped; she looked up into it, pleased that the flesh beneath her chin did not show. In the bathroom mirror at home she looked terrible, a hag with cracked lips and a dented nose and with broken veins in her septum, and when, driving in the Subaru, she stole a peek at herself in the rearview mirror, she looked worse yet, corpselike in color, the eyes quite wild and a single stray lash laid like a beetle leg across one lower lid. As a tiny girl Alexandra had imagined that behind every mirror a different person waited to peek back out, a different soul. Like so much of what we fear as a child, it turned out to be in a sense true.

Van Horne had put around the fireplace some boxy modern stuffed chairs and a curved four-cushioned sofa, refugees from a New York apartment obviously, and well worn; but the room was mostly furnished with works of art, including several that took up floor space. A giant hamburger of violently colored, semi-inflated vinyl. A white plaster woman at a real ironing board, with an actual dead cat from a taxidermist's rubbing at her ankles. A vertical stack of Brillo cartons that close inspection revealed to be not airy stamped cardboard but meticulously silk-screened sheets mounted on great cubes of something substantial and immovable. A neon rainbow, unplugged and needing a dusting.

The man slapped an especially ugly assemblage, a naked woman on her back with legs spread; she had been concocted of chicken wire, flattened beer cans, an old porcelain chamber pot for her belly, pieces of chrome car bumper, items of underwear stiffened with lacquer and glue. Her face, staring straight up at the sky or ceiling, was that of a plaster doll such as Alexandra used to play with, with china-blue eyes and cherubic pink cheeks, cut off and fixed to a block of wood that had been crayoned to represent hair. "Here's the genius of the bunch for my money," Van Horne said, wiping the corners of his mouth dry with a two-finger pinching motion. "Kienholz. A Marisol with guts. You know, the tac*til*ity; there's nothing monotonous or pre-ordained about it. That's the kind of thing *you* should be setting your sights toward.

The richness, the *Vielfältigkeit*, the, you know, the ambiguity. No offense, friend Lexa, but you're a Johnny-one-note with those little poppets of yours."

"They're not poppets, and this statue is rude, a joke against women," she said languidly, feeling splayed and out of focus, in tune with the moment—a gliding sensation, the world passing through her or she moving the world, a cosmic confusion such as when the train silently tugs away from the station and it seems the platform is sliding backwards. "My little bubbies aren't jokes, they're meant affectionately." Yet her hand wandered on the assemblage and found there the glossy yet resistant texture of life. On the walls of this long room, once perhaps hung with Lenox family portraits from eighteenth-century Newport, there now hung or protruded or dangled gaudy travesties of the ordinary—giant pay telephones in limp canvas, American flags duplicated in impasto, oversize dollar bills rendered with deadpan fidelity, plaster eyeglasses with not eyes but parted lips behind the lenses, relentless enlargements of our comic strips and advertising insignia, our movie stars and bottle caps, our candies and newspapers and traffic signs. All that we wish to use and discard with scarcely a glance was here held up bloated and bright: permanized garbage. Van Horne gloated, snorted, and repeatedly wiped his lips as he led Alexandra through his collection, down one wall and back the other; and in truth she saw that he had acquired of this mocking art specimens of good quality. He had money and needed a woman to help him spend it. Across his dark vest curved the gold chain of an antique watch fob; he was an inheritor, though ill at ease with his inheritance. A wife could put him at ease.

The tea with rum came, but formed a more sedate ceremony than she had imagined from Sukie's description. Fidel materialized with that ideal silence of servants, a tidy scar placed so flatteringly beneath one cheekbone it seemed appliquéd to his mocha skin, a deliberate fillip to his small slanting features. The long-haired cat called Thumbkin, with the deformed paws mentioned in the *Word*, leaped onto Alexandra's lap just as she lifted her cup to sip; its liquid content scarcely swayed. The horizon of sea visible through the Palladian windows from where she sat stayed level also: the world was in part a gently shuffled deck of horizontal liquids, it occurred to her, thinking of the cold dense stratum of the sea where only giant eyeless slugs moved beneath the pressure, and then of mist licking the autumnal surface of a woodland pond, and of the spheres of ever-thinner gas that our astronauts pierce without puncturing, so the sky's blue does not leak away. She felt at peace here, which she had not expected, here in these rooms virtually empty but for their overload of sardonic art, rooms eloquent of a bachelor's lacks. Her host seemed pleasanter too. The manner of a man who wants to sleep with you is slicing and aggressive, testing, foreshadowing his eventual anger if he succeeds, and there seemed little of that in Van Horne's manner today. He looked tired, slumped in his tatty boxy armchair covered in a mushroom-colored corduroy. She fantasized that the business appointment for which he had put on his solemn three-piece suit had been a disappointment, perhaps a petition for a bank loan that had been refused. With plain need he poured extra rum into his tea from the bottle of Mount Gay his butler had set at his elbow, on a Queen Anne piecrust table. "How did you come to acquire such a large and wonderful collection?" Alexandra asked him.

"My investment adviser" was his disappointing answer. "Smartest thing financially you can ever do except strike oil in your back yard is buy a name artist before he has the name. Think of those two Russkis who picked up all that Picasso and Matisse cheap in Paris just before the war and now it sits over there in Leningrad where nobody can lay their eyes on it. Think of the lucky fools who took an early Pollock off his hands for the price of a bottle of Scotch. Even hit or miss you'll average out better than the stock market. One Jasper Johns makes up for an awful lot of junk. Anyway, I love the junk."

"I see you do," Alexandra said, trying to help him. How could she ever rouse this heavy rambling man to fall in love with her? He was like a house with too many rooms, and the rooms with too many doors.

He did lurch forward in his chair, spilling tea. He had done it so often, evidently, that by reflex he spread his legs and the tan liquid flipped between them to the carpet. "Greatest thing about Orientals," he said. "They don't show your sins." With the sole of one little pointy black shoe—his feet were almost monstrously small for his bulk—he rubbed the tea stain in. "I *hated*," he volunteered, "that abstract stuff they were trying to sell us in the Fifties; Christ, it all reminded me of Eisenhower, a big blah. I want art to *show* me something, to tell me where I'm at, even if it's Hell, right?"

"I guess so. I'm really very dilettantish," Alexandra said, less comfortable now that he did seem to be rousing. What underwear had she put on? When had she last had a bath?

"So when this Pop came along, I thought, Jesus, this is the stuff for me. So fucking cheerful, you know—going down but going down with a smile. Like the late Romans in a way. 'Djou ever read Petronius? *Fun*ny. Funny, God, you can look at that goat Rauschenberg put in the rubber tire and laugh until sundown. I was in this gallery years ago on Fifty-seventh Street—that's where I'd like to see you, as I guess I've been saying to the point where it's boring—and the dealer, this faggot called Mischa, they used to call him Mischa the Muff, hell of a knowledgeable guy though, showed me these two beer cans by Johns—Ballantine ale, actually—in bronze, but painted up so sweet, with that ever-so-exact but slightly free way Johns has, and one with a triangle in the top where a beer opener had been and the other virgin, unopened. Mischa says to me, 'Pick that one up.' 'Which one?' I say. 'Any one,' he says. I pick up the virgin one. It's heavy. 'Pick up the other one,' he says. 'Really?' I ask. 'Go ahead,' he says. I do. It's lighter! The beer had been drunk!! In terms of the art, that is. I nearly came in my pants, that was such a turn-on when I saw the light."

He had sensed that Alexandra did not mind his talking dirty. She in fact rather liked it; it had a secret sweetness, like the scent of carrion on Coal's coat. She must go. Her dog's big heart would break in that little locked car.

"I asked him what the price was for these beer cans and Mischa told me and I said, 'No way.' There are limits. How much cash can you tie up in two fake beer cans? Alexandra, no kidding, if I'd taken the plunge I would have quintupled my money by now, and that wasn't so many years ago. Those cans are worth more than their weight in pure gold. I honestly believe, when future ages look back on us, when you and I are just a pair of skeletons lying in those idiotic expensive boxes they make you buy, our hair and bones and fingernails pillowed on all this ridiculous satin these fat-cat funeral directors rip you off for, Jesus I'm getting carried away, they can just take my *corpus* and dump it on the dump would suit me fine, when you and I are dead is all I mean to say, those beer cans, ale cans I should be saying, are going to be our Mona Lisa. We were talking about Kienholz; you know there's this entire sawed-off Dodge car he did, with a couple inside fucking. The car sits on a mat of artificial turf and a little ways away from it he put a little other patch of Astroturf or whatever he used, about the size of a checkerboard, with a single empty beer bottle on it! To show they'd been drinking and chucked it out. To give the lovers' lane ambience. That's genius. The little extra piece of mat, the apartness. Somebody else would have just put the beer bottle on the main mat. But having it separate is what makes it art. Maybe *that's* our Mona Lisa, that empty of Kienholz's. I mean, I was out there in L.A. looking at this crazy sawed-off Dodge and tears came to my eyes. I'm not shitting you, Sandy. Tears." And he held his unnaturally white, waxy-looking hands in front of his eyes as if to pluck these watery reddish orbs from his skull.

"You travel," she said.

"Less than I used to. I'm just as glad. You go everywhere but it's always you unpacks the bag. Same bag, same you. You girls up here have the right idea. Find a Nowheresville and make your own space. All the junk comes after you anyway, with the TV and the global village and all." He slumped in his mushroom chair, empty at last of phrases. Needlenose trotted into the room and curled at his master's feet, tucking his long nose under his tail.

"Speaking of travel," Alexandra said. "I must run. I locked my poor doggie in the car, and my children will be home from school by now." She set down her teacup—monogrammed with *N*, strangely, instead of any of Van Horne's initials—on his scratched and chipped Mies van der Rohe glass table and stood to her height. She was wearing her brocaded Algerian jacket over a silver-gray cotton turtleneck, with her slacks of forest-green serge. A pang of relief at her waist as she stood reminded her of how uncomfortably tight these slacks had become. She had vowed to lose weight; but winter was the worst time for it, one nibbled to keep warm, to keep the early dark at bay, and anyway in this bulky man's eyes, turned upwards appraising the jut of her breasts, she read no demand to change her shape. Joe called her in their privacy his cow, his woman-and-a-half. Ozzie used to say she was better at night than two more blankets. Sukie and Jane called her gorgeous. She brushed from the serge tightly covering her pelvis several long white hairs Thumbkin had deposited there. She retrieved her bandanna with a scarlet flick from the arm of the curved sofa.

"But you haven't seen the lab!" Van Horne protested. "Or the hot-tub room, we *fin*ally got the mother finished, all but some accessory wiring. Or the upstairs. My big Rauschenberg lithographs are all upstairs."

"Perhaps there will be another time," Alexandra said, her voice quite settled now into her womanly contralto. She was enjoying leaving. Seeing him frantic, she was confident again of her powers.

"You ought at least to see my bedroom," Van Horne pleaded, leaping up and barking his shin on a corner of the glass table so that pain slipped his features awry. "It's all in black, even the sheets," he told her; "it's damn hard to buy good black sheets, what they call black is really navy blue. And in the hall I've just got some very subtly raunchy oils by a newish painter called John Wesley, no relation to the crazy Methodist, he does what look like illustrations to children's animal books until you realize what they're showing. Squirrels fucking and stuff like that."

"Sounds fun," Alexandra said, and moved briskly in a wide arc, an old hockey-player's move, so the chair blocked him for a moment and he could only loudly follow as she sailed out of the room with its ugly art, on through the library, past the music room, into the hall with the elephant's foot, where the rotten-egg smell was strongest but the breath of the out-of-doors could be scented too. The black door had been left its natural two-toned oak on this side.

Fidel had appeared from nowhere to position himself with a hand on the great brass latch. To Alexandra he seemed to be looking past her face toward his master; they were going to trap her here. In her fantasy she would count to five and start to scream; but there must have been a nod, for the latch clicked on the count of three.

Van Horne said behind her, "I'd offer to give you a ride back to the road but the tide may be up too far." He sounded out of breath: emphysema from too many cigarettes or inhaling those Manhattan bus fumes. He did need a wife's care.

"But you promised it wouldn't be!"

"Listen, what the hell do I know? I'm more of a stranger here than you are. Let's walk down and have a gander."

Whereas the driveway curved around, the grass mall, lined with limestone statues the weather and vandals had robbed of hands and noses, led directly down to where the causeway met the edge of the island. An untidy shore of weeds—seaside goldenrod, beach clotbur with its huge loose leaves—and gravel and a rubble of old asphalt paving spread behind the vine-entangled gate. The weeds trembled in a chill wind off the flooded marsh. The sky had lowered its bacon stripes of gray; the most luminous thing in sight was a great egret, not a snowy, loitering in the direction of the beach road, its yellow bill close to the color of her abandoned Subaru. Between here and there a tarnished glare of water had overswept the causeway. The scratch of tears arose in Alexandra's throat. "How *could* this have happened, we haven't been an hour!"

"When you're having fun . . ." he murmured.

"It wasn't *that* much fun! I can't get back!"

"Listen," Van Horne said close to her ear, and lightly closed his fingers on her upper arm, so she just felt his touch through the cloth. "Come on back and phone your kids and we'll have Fidel whip up a light supper. He does a terrific chili."

"It's not the *kids*, it's the *dog*," she cried. "Coal will be frantic. How deep is it?"

"I don't know. A foot, maybe two toward the middle. I could try to splash through with the car but get stuck out there it's bye-bye to a lot of fine old German machinery. Get saltwater in your brakes and differential, a car never drives the same. Like having your cherry popped."

"I'll wade," Alexandra said, and shook her arm free of his fingers, but not before, as if he had read her mind, he gave her a sharp quick pinch.

"Your pants'll get soaked," he said. "That water's brutal this time of year."

"I'll take my slacks off," she said, leaning on him to pull off her sneakers and socks. The spot where he had pinched her burned but she refused to acknowledge this presumptuous injury. After he had seemed so boyish and befuddled, spilling his tea and confiding his love of art. He was in truth a monster. Gravel prodded her bare feet. If she was going to do this she mustn't hesitate. "Here goes," she said. "Don't look."

She undid the side zipper of her slacks and pushed down at the waistband and her thighs joined the egret for brightness in this scene of rust and gray. Afraid she might topple on the unsteady stones, she bent over and pushed the shiny green serge past her pink ankles and blue-veined feet, and stepped out. Startled air lapped her naked legs. She made a bundle of sneakers and slacks and walked away from Van Horne down the causeway. Not looking back, she felt his eyes on her, her heavy thighs, their vulnerable ripple and jiggle. No doubt he had been watching with his hot tired eyes when she bent over. Alexandra had forgotten what underpants she had put on this morning and was relieved, glancing down, to discover them a plain beige, not ridiculously flowered or indecently cut like most you had to buy in the stores these days, designed for slim young hippies or groupies, half your ass hanging out behind and the crotch narrow as a rope. The air, endlessly tall, was cool on her skin. She enjoyed her own nakedness usually, especially in the open, taking a sunbath after lunch in her back yard on a blanket those first warm days of April and May before the bugs come. And under the full moon, gathering herbs skyclad.

So little used these years since the Lenoxes left, the causeway had grown grassy; barefoot she trod the center mane like the top of a soft broad wall. Color had drained from its wands of *Spartina patens* and the stretches of marsh on either side had turned sere. Where water first overcrept the surface of the road the matted grass gently swung in the transparent inches. The tide, infiltrating, made chuckling, hissing noises. Behind her, Darryl Van Horne was shouting something, encouragement or warning or apology, but Alexandra was too intent on the shock of her toes' first immersion to hear. How serious, how stark, the cold of this water was! Another element, where her blood was an alien. Brown pebbles stared up at her refracted and meaninglessly vivid, like the letters of an alphabet one doesn't know. The marsh grass had become seaweed, indolent and adrift, streaming leftwards with the rising water. Her own feet looked small, refracted like the pebbles. She must wade through quickly, while still numb. The tide covered her ankles now, and the distance to dry road was great, farther than she could have thrown a pebble. A dozen more shocking strides, and the water was up to her knees, and she could feel the sideways suck of its mindless flow. The coldest thing about this pull was that it would be here whether she was or not. It had been here before she was born and would be here when she was dead. She did not think it could knock her down, but she felt herself leaning against its force. And her ankles had begun to cry out, the numbness eaten through, the ache unendurable except that it must be endured.

Alexandra could no longer see her own feet, and the nodding tips of marsh grass no longer kept her company. She began to try to run, splashing; the splashing drowned out the sound of her host still shouting gibberish at her back. The intensity of her gaze enlarged the Subaru. She could see Coal's hopeful silhouette in the driver's seat, his ears lifted as high as they would go as he sensed rescue approaching. The icy pull came high on her thighs and her underpants were getting splashed. Foolish, so foolish, so vain and falsely girlish, she deserved this for leaving her only friend, her true and uncomplicated friend. Dogs perch on the edge of understanding, their bright eyes polished by the yearning to comprehend; an hour no worse than a minute to them, they live in a world without time, without accusation, without acceptance because there was no foresight. The water with its deathgrip rose to her crotch; a noise was forced from her throat. She was close enough to alarm the egret, who with a halt uncertain motion, like that of an old man tentatively reaching to brace himself on the arms of his chair, beat the air with the inverted W of his wings and rose, dragging his black stick feet behind him. Him? Her? Turning her own head with its bedraggled hair, Alexandra did see in the opposite direction, toward the ashen sand-hills of the beach, another white hole in the day's gray, another great egret, this one's mate though acres separated them under this dirty striped sky.

At the first bird's lift-off, the murderous clamps of the ocean had loosened a little on her thighs, sliding down as she waded on upwards, breathless, weeping with the shock and comedy of it, to the dry stretch of causeway that led to her car. Where the tide had been deepest there had been a kind of exultation, and now this ebbed. Alexandra shivered like a dog and laughed at her own folly, in seeking love, in getting stranded. The spirit needs folly as the body needs food; she felt healthier for this. Visions of herself as drowned, tinted greenish and locked stiff in the twist of last agony like those two embracing women in that amazing painting *Undertow* by Winslow Homer, had not come true. Drying, her feet hurt as if stung by a hundred wasps.

Manners demanded that she turn and wave in derisive flirtatious triumph toward Van Horne. He, a little black Y between the brick uprights of his crumbling gate, waved back with both arms held straight out. He applauded, beating his hands together to make a noise that arrived across the intervening plane of water a fraction of a second delayed. He shouted something of which she only heard the words "You *can* fly!" She dried her beaded, goose-bumped legs with the red bandanna and pulled herself into her slacks while Coal woofed and pounded his tail on the vinyl within the Subaru. His happiness was infectious. She smiled to herself, wondering whom she should call first to tell about this, Sukie or Jane. At last she too had been initiated. Where he had pinched, her upper arm still burned.

The little trees, the sapling sugar maples and the baby red oaks squatting close to the ground, were the first to turn, as if green were a feat of strength, and the smallest weaken first. Early in October the Virginia creeper had suddenly drenched in alizarin crimson the tumbled boulder wall at the back of her property, where the bog began; the drooping parallel daggers of the sumac then showed a red suffused with orange. Like the slow sound of a great gong, yellow overspread the woods, from the tan of beech and ash to the hickory's spotty gold and the flat butter color of the mitten-shaped leaves of the sassafras, mittens that can have a thumb or two or none. Alexandra had often noticed how adjacent trees of the same species, sprung from two seeds spinning down together the same windy day, yet have leaves notched in different rhythms, and one turns as if bleached, from dull to duller, while the other looks as if each leaf were hand-painted by a Fauvist in clashing patches of red and green. The ferns underfoot in fading declared an extravagant variety of forms. Each cried out, *I am, I was*. There was thus in fall a rebirth of identity out of summer's mob of verdure. The breadth of the event, from the beach plums and bayberries along Block Island Sound to the sycamores and horse-chestnut trees lining the venerable streets (Benefit, Benevolent) on Providence's College Hill, answered to something diffuse and gentle within Alexandra, her sense of merge, her passive ability to contemplate a tree and feel herself a rigid trunk with many arms running to their tips with sap, to become the oblong cloud oddly alone in the sky or the toad hopping from the mower's path into deeper damper grass—a wobbly bubble on leathery long legs, a spark of fear behind a warty broad forehead. She was that toad, and as well the cruel battered black blades attached to the motor's poisonous explosions. The panoramic ebb of chlorophyll from the swamps and hills of the Ocean State lifted Alexandra up like smoke, like the eye above a map. Even the exotic imports of the Newport rich—the English walnut, the Chinese smoke tree, the *Acer japonicum*—were swept into this mass movement of surrender. A natural principle was being demonstrated, that of divestment. We must lighten ourselves to survive. We must not cling. Safety lies in lessening, in becoming random and thin enough for the new to enter. Only folly dares those leaps that give life. This dark man on his island was possibility. He was the new, the magnetic, and she relived their stilted teatime together moment by moment, as a geologist lovingly pulverizes a rock.

Some shapely young maples with the sun behind them became blazing torches, a skeleton of shadow within an incandescent halo. The gray of naked branches more and more tinged the woods beside the roads. The sullen conical evergreens lorded where other substance had dissolved. October did its work of undoing day by day and came to its last day still fair, fair enough for outdoor tennis.

Jane Smart in her pristine whites tossed up the tennis ball. It became in midair a bat, its wings circled in small circumference at first and, next instant, snapped open like an umbrella as the creature flicked away with its pink blind face. Jane shrieked, dropped her racket, and called across the net, "That was not funny." The other witches laughed, and Van Horne, who was their fourth, belatedly, halfheartedly enjoyed the joke. He had powerful, educated strokes but did seem to have trouble seeing the ball, in the slant late-afternoon sun that beamed in rays through the sheltering stand of larches here at the back end of his island; the larches were dropping their needles and these had to be swept from the court. Jane's own eyes were excellent, preternaturally sharp. Bats' faces looked to her like flattened miniature versions of children pressing their noses against a candy-store window, and Van Horne, who played incongruously dressed in basketball sneakers and a Malcolm X T-shirt and the trousers of an old dark suit, had something of this same childish greed on his bewildered, glassy-eyed face. He coveted their wombs, was Jane's belief. She prepared to toss and serve again, but even as she weighed the ball in her hand it took on a liquid heft and a squirming wartiness. Another transformation had been wrought. With a theatrical sigh of patience, she set the toad down on the blood-red composition surface over by the bright green fence and watched it wriggle through. Van Horne's feeble-minded and wrynecked collie, Needlenose, raced around the outside of the fence to inspect; but he lost the toad in the tumble of earth and blasted rocks the bulldozers had left here.

"Once more and I quit," Jane called across the net. She and Alexandra had been pitted against Sukie and their host. "The three of you can play Canadian doubles," she threatened. With the bespectacled gesturing face on Van Horne's T-shirt it seemed there were five of them present anyway. The next tennis ball in her hand went through some rapid textural changes, first slimy like a gizzard then prickly like a sea urchin, but she resolutely refused to look at it, to cede it that reality, and when it appeared against the blue sky above her head it was a fuzzy yellow Wilson, which, following instruction books she had read, she imagined as a clockface to be struck at two o'clock. She brought the strings smartly through this phantom and felt from the surge of follow-through that the serve would be good. The ball kicked toward Sukie's throat and she awkwardly defended her breasts with the racket held in the backhand position. As if the strings had become noodles, the ball plopped at her feet and rolled to the sideline.

"Super," Alexandra muttered to Jane. Jane knew her partner loved, in different erotic keys, both their opponents, and their partnering, which Sukie had arranged at the outset of the match with a suspect twirl of her racket, must give Alexandra some jealous pain. The other two were a mesmerizing team, Sukie with her coppery hair tied in a bouncing ponytail and her slender freckled limbs swinging from a little peach tennis dress, and Van Horne with his machinelike swiftness, animated as when playing the piano by a kind of demon. His effectiveness was only limited by moments of dim-sighted uncoordination in which he missed the ball entirely. Also, his demon tended to play at a constant *forte* that sent some of his shots, when a subtle chop into a vacant space would have won the point, skimming out just past the base line.

As Jane prepared to serve to him, Sukie called gaily, "Foot fault!" Jane looked down to see not her sneaker toe across the line but the line itself, though a painted one, across the front of her sneaker and holding it fast like a bear trap. She shook off the illusion and served to Darryl Van Horne, who returned the ball with a sharp forehand that Alexandra alertly poached, directing the ball at Sukie's feet; Sukie managed to scoop it on the short hop into a lob that Jane, having come to the net at her partner's adroit and aggressive poach, just reached in time to turn it into another lob, which Van Horne, eyes flashing fire, set himself to smash with a grunting overhead and which he would have smashed, had not a magical small sparkling storm, what they call in many parts of the world a dust devil, arisen and caused him to snap a sheltering right hand to his brow with a curse. He was left-handed and wore contact lenses. The ball remained suspended at the level of his waist while he blinked away the pain; then he stroked it with a forehand so firm the orb changed color from optical yellow to a chameleon green that Jane could hardly see against the background of green court and green fence. She swung where she sensed the ball to be and the contact felt sweet; Sukie had to scramble to make a weak return, which Alexandra volleyed down into the opponents' forecourt so vehemently it bounced impossibly high, higher than the setting sun. But Van Horne skittered back quicker than a crab underwater and tossed his metal racket toward the stratosphere, slowly twirling, silvery. The disembodied racket returned the ball without power but within the base lines, and the point continued, the players interlacing, round and round, now clockwise, now widdershins, the music of it all enthralling, Jane Smart felt: the counterpoint of their four bodies, eight eyes, and sixteen extended limbs scored upon the now nearly horizontal bars of sunset red filtered through the larches, whose falling needles pattered like distant applause. When the rally and with it the match was at last over, Sukie complained, "My racket kept feeling dead."

"You should use catgut instead of nylon," Alexandra suggested benignly, her side having won.

"It felt absolutely leaden; I kept having shooting pains in my forearm trying to lift it. Which one of you hussies was doing that? Absolutely not fair."

Van Horne also pleaded in defeat. "Damn contact lenses," he said. "Get even a speck of dust behind them it's like a fucking razor blade."

"It was lovely tennis," Jane pronounced with finality. Often she was cast, it seemed to her, in this role of peacemaking parent, of maiden aunt devoid of passion, when in fact she was seething.

The end of Daylight Saving Time had been declared and darkness came swiftly as they filed up the path to the many lit windows of the house. Inside, the three women sat in a row on the curved sofa in Van Horne's long, art-filled, yet somehow barren living room, drinking the potions he brought them. Their host was a master of exotic drinks,

drinks alchemically concocted of tequila and grenadine and crème de cassis and Triple Sec and Seltzer water and cranberry juice and apple brandy and additives even more arcane, all kept in a tall seventeenth-century Dutch cabinet topped by two startled angel's heads, their faces split, right through the blank eyeballs, by the aging of the wood. The sea seen through his Palladian windows was turning the color of wine, of dogwood leaves before they fall. Between the Ionic pillars of his fireplace, beneath the ponderous mantel, stretched a ceramic frieze of fauns and nymphs, naked figures white on blue. Fidel brought hors d'oeuvres, pastes and dips of crushed sea creatures, *empanadillas, calamares en su tinta* that were consumed with squeals of disgust, with fingers that turned the same muddy sepia as the blood of these succulent baby squids. Now and then one of the witches would exclaim that she *must* do something about the children, either go home to make their suppers or at least phone the house to put the oldest daughter officially in charge. Tonight was already deranged: it was the night of trick-or-treat, and some of the children would be at parties and others out begging on the shadowy crooked streets of downtown Eastwick. Toddling in rustling groups along the fences and hedges would be little pirates and Cinderellas wearing masks with fixed grimaces and live moist eyes darting in papery eyeholes; there would be ghosts in pillow cases carrying shopping bags rattling with M & M's an Hershey Kisses. Doorbells would be constantly ringing. A few days ago Alexandra had gone shopping with her baby, little Linda, in the Woolworth's at the mall, the lights of this trashy place brave against the darkness outside, the elderly overweight clerks weary amid their child-tempting gimcracks at the end of the day, and for a moment Alexandra had felt the old magic, seeing through this nine-year-old child's wide gaze the symbolic majesty of the cut-rate spectres, the authenticity of the packaged goblin—mask, costume, and plastic trick-or-treat sack all for $3.98. America teaches its children that every passion can be transmuted into an occasion to buy. Alexandra in a moment of empathy became her own child wandering aisles whose purchasable wonders were at eye level and scented each with its own potent essence of ink or rubber or sugary dough. But such motherly moments came to her ever more rarely as she took possession of her own self, a demigoddess greater and sterner than any of the uses others might have for her. Sukie next to her on the sofa arched her back inward, stretching in her scant peach dress so that her white frilled panties showed, and said with a yawn, "I really should go home. The poor darlings. That house right in the middle of town, it must be besieged."

Van Horne was sitting opposite her in his corduroy armchair; he had been perspiring glowingly and had put on an Irish knit sweater, of natural wool still smelling oilily of sheep, over the stencilled image of gesticulating, buck-toothed Malcolm X. "Don't go, my friend," he said. "Stay and have a bath. That's what I'm going to do. I stink."

"Bath?" Sukie said. "I can take one at home."

"Not in an eight-foot teak hot tub you can't," the man said, twisting his big head with such violent roguishness that bushy Thumbkin, alarmed, jumped off his lap. "While we're all having a good long soak Fidel can cook up some paella or tamales or something."

"Tamale and tamale and tamale," Jane Smart said compulsively. She was sitting on the end of the sofa, beyond Sukie, and her profile had an angry precision, Alexandra thought. The smallest of them physically, she got the most drunk, trying to keep up. Jane sensed she was being thought about; her hot eyes locked onto Alexandra's. "What about you, Lexa? What's your thought?"

"Well," was the drifting answer, "I *do* feel dirty, and I ache. Three sets is too much for this old lady."

"You'll feel like a million after this experience," Van Horne assured her. "Tell you what," he said to Suki. "Run on home, check on your brats, and come back here soon as you can."

"Swing by my house and check on mine too, could you sweetie?" in chimed Jane Smart.

"Well I'll see," Sukie said, stretching again. Her long freckled legs displayed at their tips dainty sneakerless feet in little tasselled Peds like lucky rabbit's-feet. "I may not be back at all. Clyde was hoping I could do a little Halloween color piece—just go downtown, interview a couple trick-or-treaters on Oak Street, ask at the police station if there's been any destruction of property, maybe get some of the old-timers hanging around Nemo's to talking about the bad old days when they used to soap windows and put buggies on the roof and things."

Van Horne exploded. "Why're you always mothering that sad-ass Clyde Gabriel? He scares me. The guy is sick."

"That's why," Sukie said, very quickly.

Alexandra perceived that Sukie and Ed Parsley were at last breaking up.

Van Horne picked up on it too. "Maybe I should invite him over here some time."

Sukie stood and pushed her hair back from her face haughtily. She said, "Don't do it on my account, I see him all day at work." There was no telling, from the way she snatched up her racket and flung her fawn sweater around her neck, whether she would return or not. They all heard her car, a pale gray Corvair convertible with front-wheel drive and her ex-husband's vanity plate ROUGE still on the back, start up and spin out and crackle away down the drive. The tide was low tonight, low under a new moon, so low ancient anchors and rotten dory ribs jutted into starlight where saltwater covered them for all but a few hours of each month.

Sukie's departure left the three remaining more comfortable with themselves, at ease in their relatively imperfect skins. Still in their sweaty tennis clothes, their fingers dyed by squid ink, their throats and stomachs invigorated by the peppery sauces of Fidel's tamales and enchiladas, they walked with fresh drinks into the music room, where the two musicians showed Alexandra how far they had proceeded with the Brahms E Minor. How the man's ten fingers did thunder on the helpless keys! As if he were playing with hands more than human, stronger, and wide as hay rakes, and never fumbling, folding trills and arpeggios into the rhythm, gobbling them up. Only his softer passages lacked something of expressiveness, as if there were no notch in his system low enough for the tender touch necessary. Dear stubby Jane, brows knitted, struggled to keep up, her face turning paler and paler as concentration drained it, the pain in her bowing arm evident, her other hand scuttling up and down, pressing the strings as if they were too hot to pause upon. It was Alexandra's motherly duty to applaud when the tense and tumultuous performance was over.

"It's not my cello, of course," Jane explained, unsticking black hair from her brow.

"Just an old Strad I had lying around," Van Horne joked and then, seeing that Alexandra would believe him—for there was coming to be in her lovelorn state nothing she did not believe within his powers and possessions—amended this to: "Actually, it's a Ceruti. He was Cremona too, but later. Still, an O.K. old fiddlemaker. Ask the man who owns one." Suddenly he shouted as loudly as he had made the harp of the piano resound, so that the thin black windowpanes in their seats of cracked putty vibrated in sympathy. "Fidel!" he called into the emptiness of the vast house. "Margaritas! ¡Tres! Bring them into the bath! ¡Tráigalas al baño! ¡Rápidamente!!"

So the moment of divestment was at hand. To embolden Jane, Alexandra rose and followed Van Horne at once; but perhaps Jane needed no emboldening after her private musical sessions in this house. It was the ambiguous essence of Alexandra's relation with Jane and Sukie that she was the leader, the profoundest witch of the three, and yet also the slowest, a bit in the dark, a bit—yes—innocent. The other two were younger and therefore slightly more modern and less beholden to nature with its massive patience, its infinite care and imperious cruelty, its ancient implication of a slow-grinding, anthropocentric order.

The procession of three passed through the long room of dusty modern art and then a small chamber hastily crammed with stacked lawn furniture and unopened cardboard boxes. New double doors, the inner side padded with black vinyl quilting, sealed off the heat and damp of the rooms Van Horne had added where the old copper-roofed conservatory used to be. The bathing space was floored in Tennessee slate and lit by overhead lights sunk in the ceiling, itself a dark pegboardy substance. "Rheostatted," Van Horne explained in his hollow, rasping voice. He twisted a luminous knob inside the double doors so these upside-down ribbed cups brimmed into a brightness photographs could have been taken by and then ebbed back to the dimness of a developing room. These lights were sunk above not in rows but scattered at random like stars. He left them at dim, in deference perhaps to their puckers and blemishes and the telltale false teats that mark a witch. Beyond this darkness, behind a wall of plate glass, vegetation was underlit green by buried bulbs and lit from above by violet growing lamps that fed spiky, exotic shapes—plants from afar, selected and harbored for their poisons. A row of dressing cubicles and two shower stalls, all black like the boxes in a Nevelson sculpture, occupied another wall of the space, which was dominated as by a massive musky sleeping animal by the pool itself, a circle of water with burnished teak rim, an element opposite from that icy tide Alexandra had braved some weeks ago: this water was so warm the very air in here started sweat on her face. A small squat console with burning red eyes at the tub's near edge contained, she supposed, the controls.

"Take a shower first if you feel so dirty," Van Horne told her, but himself made no move in that direction. Instead he went to a cabinet on another wall, a wall like a Mondrian but devoid of color, cut up in doors and panels that must all conceal a secret, and took out a white box, not a box but a long white skull, perhaps a goat's or a deer's, with a hinged silver lid. Out of this he produced some shredded something and a packet of old-fashioned cigarette papers at which he began clumsily fiddling like a bear worrying a fragment of beehive.

Alexandra's eyes were adjusting to the gloom. She went into a cubicle and slipped out of her gritty clothes and, wrapping herself in a purple towel she found folded there, ducked into the shower. Tennis sweat, guilt about the children, a misplaced bridal timidity—all sluiced from her. She held her face up into the spray as if to wash it away, that face given to you at birth like a fingerprint or Social Security number. Her head felt luxuriously heavier as her hair got wet. Her heart felt light like a small motor skimming on an aluminum track toward its inevitable connection with her rough strange host. Drying herself, she noticed that the monogram stitched into the nap of the towel seemed to be an *M*, but perhaps it was *V* and *H* merged. She stepped back into the shadowy room with the towel wrapped around her. The slate presented a fine reptilian roughness to the soles of her feet. The caustic pungence of marijuana scraped her nose like a friendly fur. Van Horne and Jane Smart, shoulders gleaming, were already in the tub, sharing the joint. Alexandra walked to the tub edge, saw the water was about four feet deep, let her towel drop, and slipped in. Hot. Scalding. In the old days, before burning her completely at the stake they would pull pieces of flesh from a witch's flesh with red-hot tongs; this was a window into that, that furnace of suffering.

"Too hot?" Van Horne asked, his voice even hollower

more mock-manly, amid these sequestered, steamy acoustics.

"I'll get used," she said grimly, seeing that Jane had. Jane looked furious that Alexandra was here at all, making waves, gently though she had tried to lower herself into the agonizing water. Alexandra felt her breasts tug upwards, buoyant. She had slipped in up to her neck and so had no dry hand to accept the joint; Van Horne placed it between her lips. She drew deep and held in the smoke. Her submerged trachea burned. The water's temperature was becoming one with her skin and, looking down, she saw how they had all been dwindled, Jane's body distorted with wedge-shaped wavering legs and Van Horne's penis floating like a pale torpedo, uncircumcised and curiously smooth, like one of those vanilla plastic vibrators that have appeared in city drugstore display windows now that the revolution is on and the sky is the limit.

Alexandra reached up and behind her to the towel she had dropped and dried her hands and wrists enough to accept in her turn the little reefer, fragile as a chrysalis, as it was passed among the three of them. She had had pot before; her older boy, Ben, in fact grew it in their back yard, in a patch past the tomato plants, which it superficially resembled. But it had never been part of their Thursdays: alcohol, calorie-rich goodies, and gossip had been transporting enough. After several deep tokes amid this steam Alexandra imagined she felt herself changing, growing weightless in the water and in the tub of her skull. As when a sock comes through the wash turned inside out and needs to be briskly reached into and pulled, so the universe; she had been looking at it as at the back side of a tapestry. This dark room with its just barely discernible seams and wires was the other side of the tapestry, the consoling reverse to nature's sunny fierce weave. She felt clean of worry. Jane's face still expressed worry, but her mannish brows and that smudge of insistence in her voice no longer intimidated Alexandra, seeing their source in the thick black pubic bush which beneath the water seemed to sway back and forth almost like a penis.

"God," Darryl Van Horne announced aloud, "I'd love to be a woman."

"For heaven's sake, why?" Jane sensibly asked.

"Think what a female body can do—make a baby and then make milk to feed it."

"Well think of your own body," Jane said, "the way it can turn food into shit."

"*Jane*," Alexandra scolded, shocked by the analogy, which seemed despairing, though shit too was a kind of miracle if you thought about it. To Van Horne she confirmed, "It *is* wonderful. At the moment of birth there's nothing left of your ego, you're just a channel for this effort that comes from beyond."

"Must be," he said, dragging, "a fantastic high."

"You're so drugged you don't notice," the other woman said, sourly.

"Jane, that isn't true. It wasn't true for me. Ozzie and I did the whole natural-childbirth thing, with him in the room giving me ice chips to suck, I got so dehydrated, and helping me breathe. With the last two babies we didn't even have a doctor, we had a monitrice."

"Do you know," Van Horne stated, going into that pedantic, ponderous squint that Lexa instinctively loved, as a glimpse of the shy clumsy boy he must have been, "the whole witchcraft scare was an attempt—successful, as it turned out—on the part of the newly arising male-dominated medical profession, beginning in the fourteenth century, to get the childbirth business out of the hands of midwives. That's what a lot of the women burned were—midwives. They had the ergot, and atropine, and probably a lot of right instincts even without germ theory. When the male doctors took over they worked blind, with a sheet around their necks, and brought all the diseases from the rest of their practice with them. The poor cunts died in droves."

"Typical," said Jane abrasively. She had evidently decided that being nasty would keep her in the forefront of Van Horne's attention. "If there's one thing that infuriates me more than male chauvs," she told him now, "it's creeps who take up feminism just to work their way into women's underpants."

But her voice, it seemed to Alexandra, was slowing, softening, as the water worked upon them from without and the cannabis from within. "But baby you're not even wearing underpants," Alexandra pointed out. It seemed an illumination of some merit. The room was growing brighter, with nobody touching a dial.

"I'm not kidding," Van Horne pursued, that myopic little boy-scholar still in him, worming to understand. His face was set on the water's surface as on a platter; his hair was long as John the Baptist's and merged with the curls licked flat on his shoulders. "It comes from the heart, can't you girls tell? I love women. My mother was a brick, smart and pretty, Christ. I used to watch her slave around the house all day and around six-thirty in wanders this little guy in a business suit and I think to myself, 'What's this wimp butting in for?' My old dad, the hard-working wimp. Tell me honest, how does it feel when the milk flows?"

"How does it feel," Jane asked irritably, "when you come?"

"Hey come on, let's not get ugly."

Alexandra perceived genuine alarm on the man's heavy, seamed face; for some reason coming was a tender area in his mind.

"I don't see what's ugly," Jane was saying. "You want to talk physiology, I'm just offering a physiological sensation that women can't have. I mean, we don't come that way. Quite. Don't you love that word they have for the clitoris, 'homologous'?"

Alexandra offered, apropos of giving milk, "It feels like when you have to go pee and can't and then suddenly you can."

"That's what I love about women," Van Horne said. "Their homely similes. There's no such word as 'ugly' in your vocabulary. Men, Christ, they're so squeamish about everything—blood, spiders, blow jobs. You know, in a lot of species the bitch or sow or whatever eats the afterbirth?"

"I don't think you realize," Jane said, striving for a dry tone, "what a chauvinistic thing that is to say." But her dryness took a strange turn as she stood on tiptoe in the tub, so her breasts lifted silvery from the water; one was a little higher and smaller than the other. She held them in her two hands and explained to a point in space between the man and the other woman, as if to the invisible witness of her life, a witness we all carry with us and seldom address aloud, "I always wanted my breasts to be bigger. Like Lexa's. She has lovely big boobs. Show him, sweet."

"Jane, *please*. You're making me blush. I don't think it's the size that matters so much to men, it's the, it's the *tilt*, and the way they go with the whole body. And what you yourself think of them. If you're pleased, others will be. Am I right or wrong?" she asked Van Horne.

But he would not be held to the role of male spokesman. He too stood up out of the water and cupped his hairy-backed palms over his vestigial male nipples, tiny warts surrounded by wet black snakes. "Think of *evolv*ing all that," he beseeched. "The machinery, all that plumbing, of the body of one sex to make food, food more exactly suited to the baby than any formula you can cook up in a lab. Think of evolving sexual pleasure. Do squids have it? What about plankton? With them, they don't have to think, but we, we think. To keep us in the game, what a bait they had to rig up! There's more built into it than one of these crazy reconnaissance planes that costs the taxpayers a zillion before it gets shot down. Suppose they left it out, nobody would fuck anybody and the species would stop dead with everybody admiring sunsets and the Pythagorean theorem."

Alexandra liked the way his mind worked; she had no trouble following it. "I adore this room," she announced dreamily. "At first I didn't think I would. All the black, except for the nice copper tubing Joe put in. Joe can be sweet, when he takes off his hat."

"Who's Joe?" Van Horne asked.

"This conversation," Jane said, so the *s*'s in her words slightly burned, "seems to have descended to a rather primitive level."

"I could put on some music," Van Horne said, touchingly anxious that they not be bored. "We're all wired up for four-track stereo."

"*Shh*," Jane said. "I heard a car on the driveway."

"Trick-or-treaters," Van Horne suggested. "Fidel'll give 'em some razor-blade apples we've been cooking up."

"Maybe Sukie's come back," Alexandra said. "I love you, Jane; you have such good ears."

"Aren't they nice?" the other woman agreed. "I *do* have pretty ears, even my father always said. Look." She held her hair back from one and then, turning her head, the other. "The only trouble is, one's a little higher than the other, so any glasses I wear sit cockeyed on my nose."

"They're rather square," Alexandra said.

Taking it as a compliment, Jane added, "And nice and flat to the skull. Sukie's are cupped out like a monkey's, have you ever noticed?"

"Often."

"Her eyes are too close together, too, and her overbite should have been corrected when she was young. And her nose, just a little blob really. I honestly don't know how she makes it all work as well as she does."

"I don't think Sukie will be coming back," Van Horne said. "She's too tied up with these neurotic creeps that run this town."

"She is and she isn't," someone said; Alexandra thought it had to be Jane but it sounded like her own voice.

"Isn't this cozy and nice?" she said, to test her own voice. It sounded deep, a man's voice.

"Our home away from home," Jane said, sarcastically, Alexandra supposed. It was really by no means easy to attain etheric harmony with Jane.

The sound Jane had heard was not Sukie, it was Fidel, bringing margaritas, on the enormous engraved silver tray Sukie had once mentioned to Alexandra admiringly, each broad wineglass on its thin stem rimmed with chunky sea-salt. It looked odd to Alexandra, so at home in her nudity had she already become, that Fidel was not naked too, but wearing a pajamalike uniform the color of army chinos.

"Dig this, ladies," Van Horne called, boyish in his boasting and also in the look of his white behind, for he had gotten out of the water and was fiddling with some dials at the far black wall. There was a greased rumble and, overhead, the ceiling, not perforated here but of dull corrugated metal as in a tool shed, rolled back to disclose the inky sky and its thin splash of stars. Alexandra recognized the sticky web of the Pleiades and giant red Aldebaran. These preposterously far bodies and the unseasonably warm but still sharp autumn air and the Nevelson intricacies of the black walls and the surreal Arp shapes of her own bulbous body all fitted around her sensory self exactly, as tangible as the steaming bath and the chilled glass stem pinched between her fingertips, so that she was as it were interlocked with a multitude of ethereal bodies. These stars condensed as tears and cupped her warm eyes. Idly she turned the stem in her hand to the stem of a fat yellow rose and inhaled its aroma. It smelled of lime juice. Her lips came away loaded with salt crystals fat as dewdrops. A thorn in the stem had pricked one finger and she watched a single drop of blood well up at the center of the whorl of a fingerprint. Darryl Van Horne was bending over to fuss at some more of his controls and his white bottom glowingly seemed the one part of him that was not hairy or repellently sheathed by a kind of exoskeleton but authentically his self, as we take in most people the head to be their true self. She wanted to kiss it, his glossy innocent unseeing ass. Jane passed her something burning which she obediently put to her lips. The burning inside Alexandra's trachea mingled with the hot angry look of Jane's stare as under the water her friend's hand fishlike nibbled and slid across her belly, around those buoyant breasts she had said she coveted.

"Hey don't leave me out," Van Horne begged, and splashed back into the water, shattering the moment, for Jane's little hand, with its callused fingertips like fish teeth, floated away. They resumed their conversing, but the words drifted free of meaning, the talk was like touching, and time fell in lazy loops through the holes in Alexandra's caressed consciousness until Sukie did come back, bringing time back with her.

In she hurried with autumn caught in the suede skirt with its frontal ties of rawhide and her tweed jacket nipped at the waist and double-pleated at the back like a huntswoman's, her peach tennis dress left at home in a hamper. "Your kids are fine," she informed Jane Smart, and did not seem nonplussed to find them all in the tub, as if she knew this room already, with its slates, its bright serpents of copper, the jagged piece of illumined green jungle beyond, and the ceiling with its cold rectangle of sky and stars. With her wonderful matter-of-fact quickness, first setting down a leather pocketbook big as a saddlebag on a chair Alexandra had not noticed before—there was furniture in the room, chairs and mattresses, black so they blended in—Sukie undressed, first slipping off her low-heeled square-toed shoes, and then removing the hunting jacket, and then pushing the untied suede skirt down over her hips, and then unbuttoning the silk blouse of palest beige, the tint of an engraved invitation, and pushing down her half-slip, the pink-brown of a tea rose, and her white panties with it, and lastly uncoupling her bra and leaning forward with extended arms so the two emptied cups fell down her arms and into her hands, lightly; her exposed breasts swayed outward with this motion. Sukie's breasts were small enough to keep firm in air, rounded cones whose tips had been dipped in a deeper pink without there being any aggressive jut of buttonlike nipple. Her body seemed a flame, a flame of soft white fire to Alexandra, who watched as Sukie calmly stooped to pick her underthings up from the floor and drop them onto the chair that was like a shadow materialized and then matter-of-factly rummaged in her big loose-flapped pocketbook for some pins to put up her hair of that pale yet plangent color called red but that lies between apricot and the blush at the heart of yew wood. Her hair was this color wherever it was, and her pinning gesture bared the two tufts, double in shape like two moths alighted sideways, in her armpits. This was progressive of her; Alexandra and Jane had not yet broken with the patriarchal command to shave laid upon them when they were young and learning to be women. In the Biblical desert women had been made to scrape their armpits with flint; female hair challenged men, and Sukie as the youngest of the witches felt least obliged to trim and temper her natural flourishing. Her slim body, freckled the length of her forearms and shins, was yet ample enough for her outline to undulate as she walked toward them, into the sallow floor lights that guarded the rim of the tub, out of the black background of this place, its artificial dark monotone like that of a recording studio; the edge of the apparition of her naked beauty undulated as when in a movie a series of stills are successively imposed upon the viewer to give an effect of fluttering motion, disturbing and spectral, in silence. Then Sukie was close to them and restored to three dimensions, her so lovely long bare side marred endearingly by a pink wart and a livid bruise (Ed Parsley in a fit of radical guilt?) and not only her limbs freckled but her forehead too, and a band across her nose, and even, a distinct constellation, on the flat of her chin, a little triangular chin crinkled in determination as she sat on the tub edge and, taking a breath, with arched back and tensed buttocks eased herself into the smoking, healing water. "Holy Mo," Sukie said.

"You'll get used," Alexandra reassured her. "It's heavenly once you make your mind up."

"You kids think this is hot?" Darryl Van Horne bragged anxiously. "I set the thermostat twenty degrees higher when it's just me. For a hangover it's great. All those poisons, they bake right out."

"What were they doing?" Jane Smart asked. Her head and throat looked shrivelled, Alexandra's eyes having dwelt so long and fondly on Sukie.

"Oh," Sukie answered her, "the usual. Watching old movies on Channel Fifty-six and getting themselves sick on the candy they'd begged."

"You didn't by any chance swing by my house?" Alexandra asked, feeling shy, Sukie was so lovely and now beside her in the water; waves she made laved Alexandra's skin.

"Baby, Marcy is seventeen," Sukie said. "She's a big girl. She can cope. Wake up." And she touched Alexandra on the shoulder, a playful push. Reaching the little distance to give the push lifted one of Sukie's rose-tipped breasts out of the water; Alexandra wanted to suck it, even more than she had wanted to kiss Van Horne's bottom. She suffered a prevision of the experience, her face laid sideways in the water, her hair streaming loose and drifting into her lips as they shaped their receptive O. Her left cheek felt hot, and Sukie's green glance showed she was reading Alexandra's mind. The auras of the three witches merged beneath the skylight, pink and violet and tawny, with Van Horne's stiff brown collapsible thing over his head like a clumsy wooden halo on a saint in an impoverished Mexican church.

The girl Sukie had spoken of, Marcy, had been born when Alexandra was only twenty-one, having dropped out of college at Oz's entreaties to be his wife, and she was reminded now of her four babies, how as they came one by one it was the female infants suckling that tugged at her insides more poignantly, the boys already a bit like men, that aggressive vacuum, the hurt of the sudden suction, the oblong blue skulls bulging and bullying above the clusters of frowning muscles where their masculine eyebrows would some day sprout. The girls were daintier, even those first days, such hopeful thirsty sweet clinging sugar-sacks destined to become beauties and slaves. Babies: their dear rubbery bowlegs as if they were riding tiny horses in their sleep, the lovable swaddled crotch the diaper makes, their flexible violet feet, their skin everywhere fine as the skin of a penis, their grave indigo stares and their curly mouths so forthrightly drooling. The way they ride your left hip, clinging lightly as vines to a wall to your side, the side where your heart is. The ammonia of their diapers. Alexandra began to cry, thinking of her lost babies, babies swallowed by the children they had become, babies sliced into bits and fed to the days, the years. Tears slid warm and then by contrast to her hot face cool down the sides of her nose, finding the wrinkles hinged at her nostril wings, salting the corners of her mouth and dribbling down her chin, making a runnel of the little cleft there. Amid all these thoughts Jane's hands had never left her; Jane intensified her caresses, massaging now the back of Alexandra's neck, then the *musculus trapezius* and on to the deltoids and the pectorals, oh, that did ease sorrow, Jane's strong hand, that pressure now above, now below the water, below even the waist, the little red eyes of the thermal controls keeping poolside watch, the margarita and marijuana mixing their absolving poisons in the sensitive hungry black realm beneath her skin, her poor neglected children sacrificed so she could have her powers, her silly powers, and only Jane understanding, Jane and Sukie, Sukie lithe and young next to her, touching her, being touched, her body woven not of aching muscle but of a kind of osier, supple and gently speckled, the nape beneath her pinned-up hair of a whiteness that never sees the sun, a piece of pliant alabaster beneath the amber wisps. As Jane was doing to Alexandra Alexandra did to Sukie, caressed her. Sukie's body in her hands seemed silk, seemed heavy slick fruit, Alexandra so dissolved in melancholy triumphant affectionate feelings there was no telling the difference between caresses given and caresses received; shoulders and arms and breasts emergent, the three women drew closer to form, like graces in a print, a knot, while their hairy swarthy host, out of the water, scrabbled through his black cabinets. Sukie in a strange practical voice that Alexandra heard as if relayed from a great distance into this recording studio was discussing with this Van Horne man what music to put on his expensive and steam-resistant stereo system. He was naked and his swinging gabbling pallid genitals had the sweetness of a dog's tail curled tight above the harmless button of its anus.

Our town of Eastwick was to gossip that winter—for here as in Washington and Saigon there were leaks; Fidel made friends with a woman in town, a waitress at Nemo's, a sly black woman from Antigua called Rebecca—about the evil doings at the old Lenox place, but what struck Alexandra this first night and ever after was the amiable human awkwardness of it all, controlled as it was by the awkwardness of their eager and subtly ill-made host, who not only fed them and gave them shelter and music and darkly suitable furniture but provided the blessing without which courage of our contemporary sort fails and trickles away into ditches others have dug, those old ministers and naysayers and proponents of heroic constipation who sent lovely Anne Hutchinson, a woman ministering to women, off into the wilderness to be scalped by redmen in their way as fanatic and unforgiving as Puritan divines. Like all men Van Horne demanded the women call him king, but his system of taxation at least dealt in assets—bodies, personal liveliness—they did have and not in spiritual goods laid up in some nonexistent Heaven. It was Van Horne's kindness to subsume their love for one another into a kind of love for himself. There was something a little abstract about his love for them and something therefore formal and merely courteous in the obeisances and favors they granted him—wearing the oddments of costume he provided, the catskin gloves and green leather garters, or binding him with the *cingulum*, the nine-foot cord of plaited red wool. He stood, often, as at that first night, above and beyond them, adjusting his elaborate and (his proud claims notwithstanding) moisture-sensitive equipment.

He pressed a button and the corrugated roof rumbled back across the section of night sky. He put on records—first Joplin, yelling and squawking herself hoarse on "Piece of My Heart" and "Get It While You Can" and "Summertime" and "Down on Me," the very voice of joyful defiant female despair, and then Tiny Tim, tiptoeing through the tulips with a thrilling androgynous warbling that Van Horne couldn't get enough of, returning the needle to the beginning grooves over and over, until the witches clamorously demanded Joplin again. On his acoustical system the music surrounded them, arising in all four corners of the room; they danced, the four clad in only their auras and hair, with shy and minimal motions, keeping within the music, often turning their backs, letting the titanic ghostly presences of the singers soak them through and through. When Joplin croaked "Summertime" at that broken tempo, remembering the words in impassioned spasms as if repeatedly getting up off the canvas in some internal drug-hazed prizefight, Sukie and Alexandra swayed in each other's arms without their feet moving, their fallen hair stringy and tangled with tears, their breasts touching, nuzzling, fumbling in pale pillow fight lubricated by drops of sweat worn on their chests like the broad bead necklaces of ancient Egypt. And when Joplin with that deceptively light-voiced opening drifted into the whirlpool of "Me and Bobby McGee," Van Horne, his empurpled penis rendered hideously erect by a service Jane had performed for him on her knees, pantomimed with his uncanny hands—encased it seemed in white rubber gloves with wigs of hair and wide at the tips like the digits of a tree toad or lemur—in the dark above her bobbing head the tumultuous solo provided by the inspired pianist of the Full Tilt Boogie band.

On the black velour mattresses Van Horne had provided, the three women played with him together, using the parts of his body as a vocabulary with which to speak to one another; he showed supernatural control, and when he did come his semen, all agreed later, was marvellously cold. Dressing after midnight, in the first hour of November, Alexandra felt as if she were filling her clothes—she played tennis in slacks, to hide somewhat her heavy legs—with a weightless gas, her flesh had been so rarefied by its long immersion and assimilated poisons. Driving home in her Subaru, whose interior smelled of dog, she saw the full moon with its blotchy mournful face in the top of her tinted windshield and irrationally thought for a second that astronauts had landed and in an act of imperial atrocity had spray-painted that vast sere surface green.

ii *Malefica*

"I will not be other than I am; I find too much content in
my condition; I am always caressed."
—*a young French witch, c. 1660*

"HE HAS?" Alexandra asked over the phone. At her
kitchen windows the Puritan hues of November
prevailed, the arbor a tangle of peeling vines, the birdfeeder
hung up and filled now that the first frosts had shrivelled the
berries of the woods and bog.

"That's what Sukie says," said Jane, her *s*'s burning. "She
says she saw it long coming but didn't want to say anything
to betray him. Not that telling just us would be betraying
anybody, if you ask me."

"But how long has Ed known the girl?" A row of
Alexandra's teacups, hung on brass hooks beneath a pantry
shelf, swayed as if an invisible hand had caressed them in the
manner of a harpist.

"Some months. Sukie thought he seemed different with
her. He just wanted mostly to talk, to use her as a sounding
board. She's glad: think of the venereal diseases she might
have gotten. All these flower children have crabs at the least,
you know."

The Reverend Ed Parsley had run off with a local teen-ager,

was the long and short of it. "Have I ever seen this girl?"
Alexandra asked.

"Oh certainly," Jane said. "She was always in that gang in
front of the Superette after about eight at night, waiting for a
drug pusher I suppose. A pale smudgy face wider than it was
high, somehow, with dirty flaxen hair just hanging down any
old how, and dressed like a little female lumberjack."

"No love beads?"

Jane answered seriously. "Well, no doubt she owned some,
to wear when she wanted to go to a debutante party. Can't
you picture her? She was one of those picketing the town
meeting last March and threw sheep's blood they got at the
slaughterhouse all over the war memorial."

"I can't, honey, maybe because I don't want to. These kids
in front of the Superette always frighten me, I just hustle out
between them without looking to the right or the left."

"You shouldn't be frightened, they're not even seeing you.
To them you're just part of the landscape, like a tree."

"Poor Ed. He did look so harassed lately. When I saw him
at the concert, he even seemed to want to cling to *me*. I
thought that was being disloyal to Sukie, so I shook him off."

"The girl isn't even from Eastwick, she was always hanging
around here but she lived up in Coddington Junction, some
perfectly awful broken home in a trailer there, living with her
common-law stepfather because her mother was always on
the road doing something in a carnival, they call it acrobatics."

Jane sounded so prim, you would think she was a virgin
spinster if you hadn't seen her functioning with Darryl Van
Horne. "Her name is Dawn Polanski," Jane was going on. "I
don't know if her parents called her Dawn or she called
herself that, people like that do give themselves names now,
like Lotus Blossom and Heavenly Avatar or whatever."

Her toughened little hands had been incredibly busy, and
when the cold semen had spurted out, it was Jane who had

appropriated most of it. Other women's sexual styles are something you are left mostly to guess at and perhaps wisely, for it can be *too* fascinating. Alexandra tried to blink the pictures out of her mind and asked, "But what are they going to *do?*"

"I daresay they have no idea, after they go to some motel and screw till they're sick of it. Really, it *is* pathetic." It was Jane who had stroked her first, not Sukie. Picturing Sukie, the soft white flame her body had been, posing on the slates, opened a little hollow space in Alexandra's abdomen, near her left ovary. Her poor insides: she was sure one day she'd have an operation, and they'd open it all too late, just crawling with black cancer cells. Except they probably weren't black but a brighter red, and shiny, like cauliflower of a bloody sort. "Then I suppose," Jane was saying, "they'll head for some big city and try to join the Movement. I think Ed thinks it's like joining the army: you find a recruitment center and they give you a physical and if you pass they take you in."

"It seems so deluded, doesn't it? He's too old. As long as he stayed around here he seemed rather young and dashing, or at least *in*teresting, and he had his church, it gave him a forum of sorts. . . ."

"He hated being respectable," Jane broke in sharply. "He thought it was a sellout."

"Oh my, what a world," Alexandra sighed, watching a gray squirrel make his stop-and-start wary way across the tumbled stone wall at the edge of her yard. A batch of her bubbies was baking in the ticking kiln in the room off the kitchen; she had tried to make them bigger, but as she did so the crudities of her self-taught technique, her ignorance of anatomy, seemed to matter more. "What about Brenda, how is she taking it?"

"About as you'd expect. Hysterically. She was virtually openly condoning Ed's carrying on on the side but she never thought he'd leave her. It's going to be a problem for the church, too. All she and the kids have is the parsonage and it's not theirs, of course. They'll have to be kicked out eventually." The calm crackle of malice in Jane's voice took Alexandra a bit aback. "She'll have to get a job. She'll find out what it's like, being on your own."

"Maybe we . . . " *Should befriend her*, was the unfinished thought.

"*Never*," telepathic Jane responded. "She was just too fucking smug, if you ask me, being Mrs. Minister, sitting there like Greer Garson behind the coffee urn, snuggling up to all the old ladies, you should have seen her breeze in and out of that church during our rehearsals. I know," she said, "I shouldn't take such satisfaction in another woman's comeuppance, but I do. You think I'm wrong. You think I'm wicked."

"Oh no," Alexandra said, insincerely. But who is to say what wicked is? Poor Franny Lovecraft could have broken her hip that night and be on a walker till she stepped into her grave. Alexandra had come to the phone holding a wooden stirring spoon and idly, as she waited for Jane to be milked of all her malice, she bent the thing with her mind waves so that its handle curled back like a dog's tail and rested in the carved bowl of the spoon. Then she bade the snakelike circle coil slowly up her arm. The abrasive caress of the wood set her teeth on edge. "And how about Sukie?" Alexandra asked, "Isn't she sort of left too?"

"She's delighted. She enco*u*raged him, she told me, to find what he could with this Dawn creature. I think she'd had her little ride with Ed."

"But does that mean she's going to go after Darryl now?" The spoon had draped itself around her neck and was touching its bowl end to her lips. It tasted of salad oil. She flickered her tongue against its wood and her tongue felt feathery, forked. Coal was nuzzling against her legs, worriedly, smelling magic, which had a tiny burnt odor like a gas jet when first turned on.

"I daresay," Jane was saying, "she has other plans. She's not as attracted to Darryl as you are. Or as I am, for that matter. Sukie likes men to be *down*. Keep your eye on Clyde Gabriel, is my advice."

"Oh that awful wife," Alexandra exclaimed. "She should be put out of her misery." She was scarcely minding what she was saying, for to tease Coal she had put the writhing spoon on the floor and the hair on his withers had bristled; the spoon lifted its head, and Coal's lips tugged up from his teeth, and his eyes kindled to attack.

"Let's do it," Jane Smart briskly replied.

Distracted by this sharp new wickedness in Jane, and a bit frightened by it, Alexandra let the spoon unbend; it dropped its head and clattered flat on the linoleum. "Oh I don't think it's for us to do," she protested, mildly.

"I always did despise him and am not in the least surprised," Felicia Gabriel announced in her flat self-satisfied manner, as if addressing a small crowd of friends who unanimously thought she was wonderful, though in fact she was speaking to her husband, Clyde. He had been trying to comprehend through his drunken post-supper fog a *Scientific American* article on the newer anomalies of astronomy. She stood with a nagging expectant tension in the doorway of the shelf-lined room he tried to use as a study now that Jenny and Chris were no longer around to pollute it with electronic noises, with Joan Baez and the Beach Boys.

Felicia had never outgrown the presumingness of a pretty and vivacious high-school girl. She and Clyde had gone through the public schools of Warwick together, and what a fetching live-wire she had been, in on every extracurricular activity from student council to girls' volleyball and a straight

A average to boot, not to mention being the first female captain ever of the debating team. A thrilling voice that would lift out above all the others in the impossibly high part of "The Star-Spangled Banner": it cut right through him like a knife. She had had dozens of boyfriends; she had been a real catch. He kept reminding himself of this. At night, when she fell asleep beside him with that depressing promptitude of the virtuous and hyperactive, leaving him to wrestle for hours alone with the demons of insomnia an evening's worth of liquor had planted in his system, he would examine her still features by moonlight, and the shadowed fit of her shut lids in their sockets and of her lips buttoned over some unspoken utterance of dream debate would disclose to his inspection an old perfection of nicely whittled bones. Felicia seemed frail when unconscious. He would lie propped up on one elbow and gaze at her, and the form of the peppy teen-ager he had loved would be restored to him, in her fuzzy pastel sweaters and her long plaid skirts swinging down the halls lined with tall green metal lockers, along with a sensation of being again his gangling "brainy" teen-aged self; a giant insubstantial column of lost and wasted time would arise from the bedroom walls so that they seemed to be lying like two crumpled bodies at the base of an airshaft. But now she stood erect before him, unignorable, dressed in the black skirt and white sweater in which she had chaired the evening's meeting of the Wetlands Watchdog Committee, where she had heard the news about Ed Parsley, from Mavis Jessup.

"He was *weak*," she stated, "a weak man somebody had once told he was handsome. He never looked handsome to me, with that pseudo-aristocratic nose and those slidy eyes. He never should have entered the ministry, he had no call, he thought he could charm God just as he charmed the old ladies into overlooking that he was a hollow man. To me—Clyde, *look* at me when I'm talking—he utterly failed to project the qualities of a man of God."

"I'm not sure the Unitarians care that much about God," he mildly answered, still hoping to read. Quasars, pulsars, stars emitting every millisecond jets of more matter than is contained in all the planets: perhaps in such cosmic madness he himself was looking for the old-fashioned heavenly God. Back in those innocent days when he had been "brainy" he had written for special credit in biology a long paper called "The Supposed Conflict Between Science and Religion," concluding that there was none. Though the paper had been given an A+, thirty-five years ago, by pie-faced, effeminate Mr. Thurmann, Clude saw now that he had lied. The conflict was open and implacable and science was winning.

"Whatever they care about it's more than staying young forever, which is what drove Ed Parsley into the arms of that pathetic little tramp," Felicia announced. "He must have taken a good look one day at that perfectly deplorable Sukie Rougemont you're so fond of and realized that she was over thirty and he better find a younger mistress or he'd be dragged into growing up himself. That saint Brenda Parsley, why she put up with it I have no idea."

"Why? Why not? What options did she have?" Clyde hated to hear her rant yet he could not resist replying now and then.

"Well, she'll kill him. This new one will absolutely kill him. He'll be dead inside of a year in some hovel where she's led him, his arms full of needle marks, and Ed Parsley will get none of my sympathy. I'll spit on his grave. Clyde, you must stop reading that magazine. What did I just say?"

"You'll thspit on his grave."

Semiconsciously he had imitated a slight strangeness in her diction. He looked up in time to see her remove a piece of tinted fuzz from between her lips. She rolled the fuzz into a tight pellet with rapid nervous fingers at her side while she talked on. "Brenda Parsley was telling Marge Perley it might have been that your friend Sukie gave him a push so she could give this Van Horne creature her undivided attention, though from what I hear around town his attention is divided ... three ways every ... Thursday night."

The uncharacteristic hesitation in her phrasing led him to look up from the jagged graphs of pulsar flashes; she had removed something else from her mouth and was making another pellet, staring him down as if daring him to notice. When she had been a high-school girl she had had shining round eyes, but now her face, without growing fat, with every year was pressing in upon these lamps of her soul; her eyes had become piggy, with a vengeful piggy glitter.

"Sukie's not a friend," he said mildly, determined not to fight. *Just this once, not a fight*, he Godlessly prayed. "She's an employee. We have no friends."

"You better *tell* her she's an employee because from the way she acts down there she's the veritable queen of the place. Walks up and down Dock Street as if she owns it, swinging her hips and in all that junk jewelry, everybody laughing at her behind her back. Leaving her was the smartest thing Monty ever did, about the *only* smart thing he ever did. I don't know why those women bother to go on living, whores to half the town and not even getting paid. And those poor neglected children of theirs, it's a positive crime."

At a certain point, which she invariably pressed through to reach, he couldn't bear it any more: the mellowing anaesthetic effect of the Scotch was abruptly catalyzed into rage. "And the reason we have no friends," he growled, letting the magazine with its monstrous celestial news drop to the carpet, "is you talk too Goddamn much."

"Whores and neurotics and a disgrace to the community. And *you*, when the *Word* is supposed to give some voice to the community and its legitimate concerns, instead give employment to this, this *per*son who can't even write a decent English sentence, and allow her space to drip her ridiculous poison into everybody's ears and let her have that much of a hold over the people of the town, the few good people that are left, frightened as they are into the corners by all this vice and shamelessness everywhere."

"Divorced women have to work," Clyde said, sighing, slowing his breathing, fighting to keep reasonable, though there was no reasoning with Felicia when her indignation started to flow, it was like a chemical, a kind of chemical reaction. Her eyes shrank to diamond points, her face became frozen, paler and paler, and her invisible audience grew larger, so she had to raise her voice. "Married women," he explained to her, "don't have to do anything and can fart around with liberal causes."

She didn't seem to hear him. "That dreadful man," she called to the multitudes, "building a tennis court right into the wetlandth, they thay"—she swallowed—"they say he uses the island to smuggle drugs, they row it in in dorieth when the tide ith high—"

This time there was no hiding it; she pulled a small feather, striped blue as from a blue jay, out of her mouth, and quickly made a fist around it at her side.

Clyde stood up, his feelings quite changed. Anger and the sense of entrapment fell from him; her old pet name emerged from his mouth. "Lishy, what on earth . . . ?" He doubted his eyes; saturated with galactic strangeness, they might be playing tricks. He pried open her unresisting fist. A bent wet feather lay upon her palm.

Felicia's tense pallor relaxed into a blush. She was embarrassed. "It's been happening lately," she told him. "I have no idea why. This scummy taste, and then these *things*. Some mornings I feel as if I'm choking, and pieces like straw, dirty straw, come out when I'm brushing my teeth. But I know I've not eaten anything. My breath is terrible. Clyde! I don't know what's *hap*pening to me!"

As this cry escaped her, Felicia's body was given an anxious twist, a look of being about to fly off somewhere, that reminded Clyde of Sukie: both women had fair dry skin and an ectomorphic frame. In high school Felicia had been drenched in freckles and her "pep" had been something like his favorite reporter's nimble, impudent carriage Yet one woman was heaven and the other hell. He took his wife into his arms. She sobbed. It was true; her breath smelled like the bottom of a chicken coop. "Maybe we should get you to a doctor," he suggested. This flash of husbandly emotion, in which he enfolded her frightened soul in a cape of concern, burned away much of the alcohol clouding his mind.

But after her moment of wifely surrender Felicia stiffened and struggled. "*No.* They'll make out I'm crazy and tell you to put me away. Don't think I don't know your thoughts. You wish I was dead. You bastard, you *do*. You're just like Ed Parsley. You're all bastards. Pitiful, corrupt . . . all you care about ith awful women. . . . " She writhed out of his arms; in the corner of his eye her hand snatched at her mouth. She tried to hide this hand behind her but, furious above all at the way that truth, for which men die, was mixed in with her frantic irrelevant self-satisfaction, he gripped her wrist and forced her clenched fingers open. Her skin felt cold, clammy. In her unclenched palm lay curled a wet pinfeather, as from a chick, but an Easter chick, for the little soft feather had been dyed lavender.

"He sends me letters," Sukie told Darryl Van Horne, "with no return address, saying he's gone underground. They've let him and Dawn into a group that's learning how to make bombs out of alarm clocks and cordite. The System doesn't stand a chance." She grinned monkeyishly.

"How does that make you feel?" the big man smoothly asked, in a hollow psychiatric voice. They were having lunch at a restaurant in Newport, where no one else from Eastwick was likely to be. Elderly waitresses in starchy brown miniskirts, with taffeta aprons tied behind in big bows evocative of Playboy bunny tails, brought them large menus, printed brown on beige, full of low-cal things on toast. Her weight was not among Sukie's worries: all that nervous energy, it burned everything up.

She squinted into space, trying to be honest, for she sensed that this man offered her a chance to be herself. Nothing would shock or hurt him. "It makes me feel relieved," she said. "That he's off my hands. I mean, what he wanted wasn't something a woman could give him. He wanted power. A woman can give a man power over herself in a way, but she can't put him in the Pentagon. That's what excited Ed about the Movement as he imagined it, that it was going to replace the Pentagon with an army of its own and have the same, you know, kind of thing—uniforms and speeches and board rooms with big maps and all. That really turned me off, when he started raving about that. I like *gentle* men. My father was gentle, a veterinarian in this little town in the Finger Lakes region, and he loved to read. He had all first editions of Thornton Wilder and Carl Van Vechten, with these plastic covers to protect the jackets. Monty used to be pretty gentle too, except when he'd get this shotgun down and go out with the boys and blast all these poor birds and furry things. He'd bring home these rabbits he had blasted up the ass, because of course they were trying to run away. Who wouldn't? But that only happened once a year—around now, as a matter of fact, is what must have made me think of it. That hunting smell is in the air. Small game season." Her smile was marred by the paste of cracker and bean spread that clung in dark spots between her teeth; the waitress had brought this free hors d'oeuvre to the table and Sukie had stuffed her face.

"How about old Clyde Gabriel? He gentle enough for you?" Van Horne lowered his big woolly barrel of a head when he was burrowing into a woman's secret life. His eyes had the hot swarming half-hidden look of children's when they put on Halloween masks.

"He might have been once, but he's pretty far gone. Felicia has done bad things to him. Sometimes at the paper, when some little layout girl just beginning the job has, I don't know, put a favored advertiser in a lower-left corner, he goes, really, wild. The girl has nothing to do but burst into tears. A lot of them have quit."

"But not you."

"He's easy on me for some reason." Sukie lowered her eyes—a lovely sight, with her reddish arched brows and her lids just touched with lavender make up and her sleek shimmering apricot hair demurely backswept and held in place on both sides by barrettes whose copper backs were echoed by a necklace close to her throat of linked copper crescents.

Her eyes lifted and flashed their green. "But then I'm a good reporter. I really am. Those baggy old men in Town Hall who make all the decisions—Herbie Prinz, Ike Arsenault—they really like me, and tell me what's up."

While Sukie consumed the crackers and bean spread, Van Horne puffed on a cigarette, doing it awkwardly, in the Continental manner, the burning tip cupped near the palm. "What's with you and these married types?"

"Well, the advantage of a wife is she saves you from making any decisions. That's what was beginning to frighten me about Brenda Parsley: she really had ceased to be any check on Ed, they were so far gone as a couple. We used to spend whole nights in these awful fleabags together. And it wasn't as if we were making love, after the first half-hour; he was going on about the wickedness of the corporate power structure's sending our boys to Vietnam for the benefit of their stockholders, not that I ever understood how it was benefiting them exactly, or got much impression that Ed really cared about those boys, the actual soldiers were just white and black trash as far as he was concerned. . . . " Her eyes had dropped and lifted again; Van Horne felt a surge of possessive pride in her beauty, her vital spirit. His. His toy. It was lovely how in a pensive pause her upper lip dominated her lower. "Then *I*," she said, "had to get up and go home and make breakfast for the kids, who were terrified because I'd been gone all night, and stagger right off to the paper—*he* could sleep all day. Nobody knows what a minister is supposed to be doing, just give his silly sermon on Sundays, it's really such a ripoff."

"People don't terrifically mind," Darryl said sagely, "being ripped off, is something I've discovered over the years." The waitress with her varicose legs exposed to mid-thigh brought Van Horne skinned shrimp tails on decrusted triangles of bread, and Sukie chicken à la king, cubed white meat and sliced mushrooms oozing in their cream over a scalloped flaky patty shell, and also brought him a Bloody Mary and her a Chablis spritzer paler than lemonade, because Sukie had to go back and write up the latest wrinkle in the Eastwick Highway Departments budget embarrassments as winter with its blizzards drew ever closer. Dock Street had been battered this summer by an unusually heavy influx of tourists and eight-axle trucks, so the slabs of mesh-reinforced concrete over the culverts there by the Superette were disintegrating; you could look right down into the tidal creek through the potholes. "So you think Felicia's an evil woman," Van Horne pursued, apropos of wives.

"I wouldn't say evil, exactly . . . yes I would. She really is. She's like Ed in a way, all causes and no respect for actual people around her. Poor Clyde sinking right in front of her eyes, and she's on the phone with this petition to restore a dress code at the high school. Coat and ties for the boys and nothing but skirts for the girls, no jeans or hotpants. They talk about fascists a lot now but she really is one. She got the news store to put *Playboy* behind the counter and then had a fit because some photography annual had a little tit and pussy in it, the models on some Caribbean beach, you know, with the sun sparkling all over them through a Polaroid filter. She actually wants poor Gus Stevens put in jail for having this magazine on his rack that his suppliers just brought him, they didn't ask. She wants *you* put in jail, for that matter, for unauthorized landfill. She wants everybody put in jail and the person she really *has* put in jail is her own husband."

"Well." Van Horne smiled, his red lips redder from the tomato juice in his Bloody Mary. "And you want to give him a parole."

"It's not just that; I'm at*trac*ted," Sukie confessed, suddenly close to tears, this whole matter of attraction so senseless, and silly. "He's so grateful for just the . . . the minimum."

"Coming from you, minimum is pretty max," Van Horne said gallantly. "You're a winner, tiger."

"But I'm not," Sukie protested. "People have these fantasies about redheads, we're supposed to be hot I suppose, like those little cinnamony candy hearts, but really we're just people, and though I bustle around a lot and try, you know, to look smart, at least by Eastwick standards, I don't think of myself as having the *real* whatever it is—power, mystery, womanliness—that Alexandra has, or even Jane in her kind of lumpy way, you know what I mean?" With other men also Sukie had noticed this urge of hers to talk about the two other witches, to seek coziness conversationally in evoking the three of them, this triune body under its cone of power being the closest approach to a mother she had ever had; Sukie's own mother—a busy little birdy woman physically like, come to think of it, Felicia Gabriel, and like her fascinated by doing good—was always out of the house or on the phone to one of her church groups or committees or boards; she was always taking orphans or refugees in, little lost Koreans were the things in those years, and then abandoning them along with Sukie and her brothers in the big brick house with its back yard sloping down to the lake. Other men, Sukie felt, minded when her thoughts and tongue gravitated to the coven and its coziness and mischief, but not Van Horne; it was his meat somehow, he was like a woman in his steady kindness, though of course terribly masculine in form: when he fucked you it hurt.

"They're dogs," he said now, simply. "They don't have your nifty knockers."

"Am I wrong?" she asked, feeling she could say anything to Van Horne, throw any morsel of herself into that dark cauldron of a simmering, smiling man. "With Clyde. I mean, I know all the books say you should *never*, with an employer, you lose your job then afterwards, and Clyde's so desperately unhappy there's something dangerous about it in any case. The whites of his eyeballs are yellow; what's that a sign of?"

"Those whites of his eyeballs were marinating," Van Horne assured her, "when you were still playing with Barbie dolls. You go to it, girl. Easy on the guilt trip. We didn't deal the deck down here, we just play the cards."

Thinking that if they talked about it any more, her affair with Clyde would be as much Darryl's as hers, Sukie steered the conversation away from herself; for the rest of the luncheon Van Horne talked about himself, his hopes of finding a loophole in the second law of thermodynamics. "There *has* to be one," he said, beginning to sweat and wipe his lips in excitement, "and it's the same fucking loophole whereby everything crossed over from nonbeing. It's the singularity at the bottom of the Big Bang. Yeah, and what *about* gravity? These smug scientists everybody thinks are so sacred talk as if we've all understood it ever since Newton rigged those formulas but the fact is it's a *hell*uva mystery; Einstein says it's like a screwy graph paper that's getting bent all the time but, Sukie baby, don't drift off, it's a *force*. It lifts the tides; step out of an airplane it'll suck you right down, and what kind of a force is it that operates across space instantly and has nothing to do with the electromagnetic field?" He was forgetting to eat; flecks of spit were appearing on the lacquered tabletop. "There's a formula out there, there's gotta be, and it's going to be as elegant as good old $E = mc^2$. The sword from the stone, you know what I mean?" His big hands, disturbing like the leaves of those tropical house plants that look plastic though we know they're natural, made a decisive sword-pulling motion. Then, with salt and pepper and a ceramic ashtray bearing a prim pink image of Newport's historical Old Colony House, Van Horne tried to illustrate sub-atomic particles and his faith that a combination could be found to generate electricity without further energy input. "It's like ju-jitsu: you toss the guy over your shoulder with more force than he came at you with. Levering. You gotta *swing* those electrons." His repulsive hands showed how. "You think just mechanically or chemically on this, you're licked; the old second law's got you every time. You know what Cooper pairs are? No? You're kidding. You a journalist or not? The news isn't all who's screwing who, you know. They're pairs of loosely bound electrons that make up the heart of superconductors. Know anything about superconductors? No? O.K., their resistance is zero. I don't mean it's very small, I mean it's *zero*. Well, suppose we found some Cooper *trip*lets. You'd have resistance of *less* than zero. There's gotta be an element, like selenium was for the Xerox process. Those assholes up in Rochester didn't have a thing until they hit upon selenium, out of the blue, they just fell into it. Well, once we get our equivalent of selenium, there's no stopping us, Sukie babes. You get down there under the chemical skin, every roof in the world can become a generator with just a coat of paint. This photovoltaic cell they use in the satellites is just a sandwich, really. What you need isn't ham, cheese, and lettuce—translate that silicon, arsenic, and boron—what you need is ham salad, where the macro arrangement isn't an issue. All *I* have to do is figure out the fucking mayonnaise."

Sukie laughed and, still hungry, took a breadstick from a miniature beanpot on the table and unwrapped it and began to nibble. To her it all sounded like fantastical presumption. There were all these men in Rochester and Schenectady, she had grown up with the type, science majors with little straight mouths and receding hairlines and those plastic liners in their shirt pockets in case their pens leaked, working away systematically at these problems, with government funds and nice little wives and children to go home to at night. But then she recognized this thought as sheer prejudice left over from her old life, before sheer womanhood had exploded within her and she realized that the world men had systematically made was all dreary poison, good for nothing really but battlefields and waste sites. Why couldn't a wild man like Darryl blunder into one of the universe's secrets? Think of Thomas Edison, deaf because as a boy he had been lifted into a cart by his ears. Think of that Scotsman, what was his name, watching the steam lift the lid of the kettle and then cooking up railroads. It was on the tip of her tongue to tell Van Horne how for fun she and Jane Smart had been casting spells on Clyde's awful wife; using a Book of Common Prayer Jane had stolen from the Episcopalian church where she sometimes pinch-hit as choir director, they had solemnly baptized a cookie jar Felicia and would toss things into it—feathers, pins, sweepings from Sukie's incredibly ancient little house on Hemlock Lane.

There, not ten hours after her lunch with Darryl Van Horne, she entertained Clyde Gabriel. The children were asleep. Felicia had gone off in a caravan of buses from Boston, Worcester, Hartford, and Providence to protest something in Washington: they were going to chain themselves to pillars in the Capitol and clog everything, human grit in the wheels of government. Clyde could stay the night, if he arose before the first child awoke. He made a touching mock-husband, with his bifocals and flannel pajamas and a little partial denture that he discreetly wrapped in a Kleenex and tucked into a pocket of his suit coat when he thought Sukie wasn't watching.

But she was, for the bathroom door didn't altogether close, due to the old frame of the house settling over the centuries, and she had to sit on the toilet some minutes waiting for the pee to come. Men, they were able to conjure it up immediately, that was one of their powers, that thunderous splashing as they stood lordly above the bowl. Everything about them was more direct, their insides weren't the maze women's were, for the pee to find its way through. Sukie, waiting, peeked out; Clyde, with an elderly tilt to his head and that bump on the back of his skull studious men have, crossed the vertical slit that she could see of her bedroom. From the angle of his arms she saw he was taking a thing out of his mouth. There was a brief pink glint of false gum and then he was slipping his little packet of folded Kleenex into the side pocket of his coat where he would not forget it when he groped out of her room at dawn. Sukie sat with her lovely oval knees together and her breath held: since girlhood she had liked to spy on men, this other race interwoven with hers, so full of bravado and dirty tough talk but such babies really, as they proved whenever you gave them your breasts to suck or opened your crotch for them to go down on, the way they burrowed there and wanted to crawl back in. She liked to sit just as she was only on a chair and spread her legs so her bush felt all big and the curls of it glittery and let them just lap and kiss and eat. Hair pie, a boy she used to know in New York State called it.

The pee at last came. She turned off the bathroom light and went into the bedroom, where the only illumination arose from the street lamp up at the corner of Hemlock Lane and Oak Street. She and Clyde had never spent a night together before, though lately they had taken to driving into the Cove woods at lunchtime (she walking along Dock Street as far as the war monument and he picking her up in his Volvo there); the other day she had grown bored with kissing his sad dry face with its long nostril hairs and tobaccoey breath and, to amuse herself and him, had unzipped his fly and swiftly, sweetly (she herself felt) jerked him off, coolly watching. These comic jets of semen, like the cries of a baby animal in the claws of a hawk. He had been flabbergasted by her witch's trick; when he laughed his lips pulled back strangely, exposing back rows of jagged teeth with pockets of blackened silver. That had been a little frightening, corrosion and pain and time all bared. She felt timid again, stepping unseeing into her own room with this man in it, her eyes not yet adjusted from the bathroom. Where Clyde sat in the corner his pajamas glowed like a fluorescent bulb that has just been switched off. A red cigarette tip glowed near his head. She could see herself, her white flanks and nervous ribbed sides, more clearly than she saw him, for several mirrors—gilt-framed, ancient, inherited from an Ithaca aunt—hung on her walls. These mirrors were mottled with age; the damp plaster walls of old stone houses had eaten the mercury off their backs. Sukie preferred such mirrors to perfect ones; they gave her back her beauty with less cavil. Clyde's voice growled, "Not sure I'm up to this."

"If not you, who?" Sukie asked the shadows.

"Oh, I can think of a number," he said, nevertheless standing and beginning to unbutton his pajama top. The glowing cigarette had been transferred to his mouth and its red tip bounced as he spoke.

Sukie felt a chill. She had expected to be folded instantly into his arms, with long, starved, bad-breath kisses such as they had shared in the car. Her prompt nakedness put her at a disadvantage; she had devalued herself. These frightful fluctuations a woman must endure on the stock exchange of male minds, up and down from minute to minute, as their ids and superegos haggle. She had half a mind to turn and closet herself again in the bright bathroom, and damn him. He had not moved. His dehydrated once-handsome face, taut at the cheekbones, was scrunched wiseguy-style around the cigarette, one eye held shut against the smoke. That was how he would sit editing copy, his soft pencil scurrying and slashing, his jaundiced eyes sheltered under a green eyeshade, his cigarette smoke loosing drifting galactic shapes in the cone of his desk light, his own cone of power. Clyde loved to cut, to find an entire superfluous paragraph that could be disposed of without a seam; though lately he had grown tender with her own prose, correcting only the misspellings. "How big a number?" she asked. He thought she was a whore. Felicia must keep telling him that. The chill Sukie had felt: was it the cold of the room, or the thrilling sight of her own white flesh simultaneously haunting the three mirrors?

Clyde killed his cigarette and finished undoing his pajamas. Now he was naked too. The amount of pallor in the mirrors doubled. His penis was impressive, lank like him, dangling in that helpless heavy-headed way penises have, this most precarious piece of flesh. His skin slithered anxiously against hers as he at last attempted an embrace; he was bony but surprisingly warm.

"Not too big," he answered. "Just enough to make me jealous. God, you're lovely. I could cry."

She led him into bed, trying to suppress any movements that might wake the children. Under the covers his head with its sharp angles and scratchy whiskers rested heavily on her breast; his cheekbone grated on her clavicle. "This shouldn't make you cry," she said soothingly, easing bone off bone. "It's supposed to be a happy thing." As Sukie said this, Alexandra's broad face swam into her mind: broad, a bit sun-browned even in winter from her walks outdoors, the gentle clefts at her chin and the tip of her nose giving her an impassive goddesslike strangeness, the blankness of one who holds to a creed: Alexandra believed that nature, the physical world, was a happy thing. This huddling man, this dogskin of warm bones, did not believe that. The world for him had been rendered tasteless as paper, composed as it was of inconsequent messy events that flickered across his desk on their way to the moldering back files. Everything for him had become secondary and sour. Sukie wondered about her own strength, how long she could hold these grieving, doubting men on her own chest and not be contaminated.

"If I could have you every night, it might be a happy thing," Clyde Gabriel conceded.

"Well, then," Sukie said, in a mother's tone, staring frightened at the ceiling, trying to launch herself into the agreed-upon surrender, that flight into sex her body promised others. This man's body out of its half-century released a complex masculine odor that included the rotted scent of whiskey—a taint she had often noticed, bending over him at the desk as his pencil jabbed at her typewritten copy. It was part of him, something woven in. She stroked the hair on his skull with its long bump of intelligence. His hair was thinning: how fine it was! As if every hair truly had been numbered. His tongue began to flick at her nipple, rosy and erect. She caressed the other, rolling it between thumb and forefinger, to arouse herself. His sadness had been cast into her, and she could not quite shake it. His climax, though he was slow to come in that delicious way of older men, left her own demon unsatisfied. She needed more of him, though now he wanted to sleep. Sukie asked, "Do you feel guilty toward Felicia, being with me this way?" It was an unworthy, flirtatious thing to say, but sometimes after being fucked she felt a desperate sliding, a devaluation too steep.

The room's single window held stony moonlight. Bald November reigned outside. Lawn chairs had been taken in, the lawns were dead and flat as floors, the outdoors was bare as a house after the movers had come. The little pear tree bejewelled with fruit had become a set of sticks. A dead geranium stood in a pot on the windowsill. The narrow cupboard beside the cold fireplace held green string. A charm slept beneath the bed. Clyde fetched his answer up from a depth near dreams. "No guilt," he said. "Just rage. That bitch has gabbled and prattled my life away. I'm usually numb. Your being so lovely wakes me up a little, and that's not good. It shows me what I've missed, what that self-righteous boring bitch has made me miss."

"I think," Sukie said, still flirtatious, "I'm supposed to be a little extra, I'm not supposed to make you *an*gry." Meaning, too, that she was not the one to take him on and get him out from under, he was too sad and poisoned; though she did feel wifely stirrings, still, viewing such men in their dailiness— that stoop their shoulders have when they got up from a chair, the shamefaced awkward way they step in and out of their trousers, how docilely they scrape their whiskers off their faces every day and go out in the world looking for money.

"It makes me dizzy, what you show me," Clyde said, lightly stroking her firm breasts, her flat long abdomen. "You're like a cliff. I want to jump."

"Please don't jump," Sukie said. She heard a child, her youngest, turning in her bed. The house was so small, they were all in one another's arms at night, through the papered odd-shaped walls.

Clyde fell asleep with his hand on her belly, so she had to lift his heavy arm—the soft rasp of his snoring stopped, then resumed—to slide herself from the sway-backed bed. She tried to pee again and failed, took her nightie and bathrobe from the back of the bathroom door, and checked on the restless child, whose covers had all been kicked in the agitation of some nightmare to the floor. Back in bed Sukie lulled herself by flying in her mind to the old Lenox place—the tennis games they could play all winter now that Darryl extravagantly had installed a great canvas bubble-top held up by warm air, and the drinks Fidel would serve them afterwards with their added color-spots of lime and cherry and mint and pimiento, and the way their eyes and giggles and gossip would interlace like the wet circles their glasses left on the glass table in Darryl's huge room where Pop Art was gathering dust. Here, the women were free, on holiday from the stale-smelling life that snored at their sides. When Sukie slept, she dreamed of yet another woman, Felicia Gabriel, her tense triangular face, talking, talking, angrier and angrier, her face coming closer, the tip of her tongue the color of a bit of pimiento, wagging in relentless level indignation behind her teeth, now flickering between her teeth, touching Sukie here, there, maybe we shouldn't, but it does feel, who's to say what's natural, whatever exists has to be natural, and nobody's watching anyway, nobody, oh, such a hard rapid little red tip, so considerate really, so good. Sukie briefly awoke to realize that the climax Clyde had failed to give her the apparition of Felicia had sought to. Sukie finished the effort with her own left hand, out of rhythm with Clyde's snores. The tiny staggering shadow of a bat passed in front of the moon and this too Sukie found consoling, the thought of something awake besides her mind, as when a late-night trolley car screeched around a distant unseen corner in the night when she was a girl in New York State, in that little brick city like a fingernail at the end of a long icy lake.

Being in love with Sukie made Clyde drink more; drunk, he could sink more relaxedly into the muck of longing. There was now an animal inside him whose gnawing was companionable, a kind of conversation. That he had once longed for Felicia this way made his situation seem all the more satisfactorily hopeless. It was his misfortune to see through everything. He had not believed in God since he was seven, in patriotism since he was ten, in art since the age of fourteen, when he realized he would never be a Beethoven, a Picasso, or a Shakespeare. His favorite authors were the great seers-through—Nietzsche, Hume, Gibbon, the ruthless jubilant lucid minds. More and more he blacked out somewhere between the third and fourth Scotches, unable to remember next morning what book he had been holding in his lap, what meetings Felicia had returned from, when he had gone to bed, how he had moved through the rooms of the house that felt like a vast and fragile husk now that Jennifer and Christopher were gone. Traffic shuddered on Lodowick Street outside like the senseless pumping of Clyde's heart and blood. In his solitary daze of booze and longing he had pulled down from a high dusty shelf his college Lucretius, scribbled throughout with the interlinear translations of his studious, hopeful college self. *Nil igitur mors est ad nos neque pertinet hilum, quandoquidem natura animi mortalis habetur.* He leafed through the delicate little book, its Oxford-blue spine worn white where his youthful moist hands had held it over and over. He looked in vain for that passage where the swerve of atoms is described, that accidental undetermined swerve whereby matter complicates, and all things are thus, through accumulating collisions, including men in their miraculous freedom, brought into being; for without this swerve all atoms would fall ever downwards through the *inane profundum* like drops of rain.

It had been his habit for years to step out into the relative quiet of the back yard before going up to bed and to gaze for a minute at the implausible spatter of stars; it was a knife edge of possibility, he knew, that allowed these fiery bodies to be in the sky, for had the primeval fireball been a shade more homogeneous no galaxies could have formed and had it been a shade less the galaxies would have billions of years ago consumed themselves in a heterogeneity too rash. He would stand by the corroding portable barbecue grill, never used now that the kids were gone, and remind himself to wheel it into the garage now that winter was in the air, and never manage to do it, night after night, lifting his face thirstily to that enigmatic miracle arching overhead. Light sank into his eyes that had started on its way when cave men prowled the vast world in little bands like ants on a pool table. Cygnus, its unfinished cross, and Andromeda, its flying V with, clinging near the second star, the bit of fuzz that—his neglected telescope had often made clear—is a spiral galaxy beyond the Milky Way. Night after night the heavens were the same; Clyde was like a photographic plate exposed again and again; the stars had bored themselves into him like bullet holes in a tin roof.

Tonight his old college *De Rerum Natura* folded its youthfully annotated pages and slipped between his knees. He was thinking of going out for his ritual stargaze when Felicia barged into his study. Though of course it was not his study but theirs, as every room in the house was theirs, and every flaking clapboard and bit of crumbling insulation on the old single-strand copper wiring was theirs, and the rusting barbecue and above the front doorway the wooden eagle plaque with its red, white, and blue weathered in the rain of atoms to rose, yellow, and black.

Felicia unwound striped wool scarves from around her head and throat and stamped her booted feet in indignation. "There are *such* stupid people running this town; they actually voted to change the name of Landing Square to Kazmierczak Square, in honor of that idiotic boy who went off and got himself killed in Vietnam." She pulled off her boots.

"Well," Clyde said, determined to be tactful. Since Sukie's flesh and fur and musk had flooded those cells of his brain set aside for a mate, Felicia seemed diaphanous, an image of a woman painted on tissue paper that might blow away. "That area hasn't really been a boat landing for eighty years. It got all silted in the blizzard of '88." He was innocently proud to be specific; along with astronomy, Clyde, in the days when his head was clear, used to be interested in terrestrial disasters: Krakatoa blowing its top and shrouding the Earth in dust, the Chinese flood of 1931 that killed nearly four million, the Lisbon earthquake of 1755 that struck when all the faithful were in church.

"But it was so *pleas*ant," Felicia said, giving that irrelevant quick smile which showed she thought her words inarguable, "up there at the end of Dock Street, with the benches for the old people, and that old granite obelisk that didn't look like a war memorial at all."

"It might still be pleasant," he offered, wondering if one more inch of Scotch would mercifully knock him out.

"No it won't," Felicia said definitely. She stripped off her coat. She was wearing a broad copper bracelet that Clyde had never seen before. It reminded him of Sukie, who sometimes left her jewelry on but nothing else and walked in nakedness glinting, in the shadowy rooms where they made love. "Next thing they'll want to be naming Dock Street and then Oak Street and then Eastwick itself after some lower-class dropout who couldn't think of anything better to do than go over there and napalm villages."

"Kazmierczak was a pretty good kid, actually. Remember, a few years back, he was their quarterback, and on the honor roll at the same time? That's why people took it so hard when he got killed last summer."

"Well *I* didn't take it hard," Felicia said, smiling as if her point had been clinched. She came near the fire he had built in the grating, to warm her hands now that her mittens were off. She half-turned her back and fiddled with her mouth, as if disentangling a hair from her lips. Clyde didn't know why this by now familiar gesture angered him, since of all the unattractive traits that had come upon her with age this one affliction could not be construed as her fault. In the morning he would see feathers, straw, pennies still slick with saliva stuck to her pillow and want to shake her awake, his own head thundering. "It's not ath if," she insisted, "he was even born and bred in Eastwick. His family moved here about five

years ago, and his father refuthes to get a job, just works on
the highway crew long enough to get another six months of
unemployment. He was at the meeting tonight, wearing a
black tie with egg stains all over it. Poor Mrs. K., she tried to
dress up so as not to look like a tart but I'm afraid she failed."

Felicia had a considerable love for the underprivileged in
the abstract but when actual cases got close to her she tended
to hold her nose. There was a fascinating spin to Felicia and
Clyde couldn't always resist giving a poke to keep her going.
"I don't think Kazmierczak Square has such a bad ring to it,"
he said.

Felicia's beady furious eyes flashed. "No you wouldn't.
You wouldn't think Shithouse Square had such a bad ring to
it either. You don't give a damn about the world we pass on
to our children or the wars we inflict on the innocent or
whether or not we poison ourselves to death, you're poisoning yourself to death right now though what do you care,
drag the whole globe down with you ith the way you look at
it." The diction of her tirade had become thick and she carefully lifted from her tongue a small straight pin and what
looked like part of an art-gum eraser.

"Our children," he sneered. "I don't see them around to
receive the world in whatever shape we pass it on." He
drained the glass of Scotch—a taste of smoke and heather
amid the cubes of fluoridated water. Ice rattled against his
upper lip; he thought of Sukie's lips, their cushiony expression of pleasure even when she was trying to be solemn and
sad. He made her sad, was one of his sorrows. Her lipstick
tasted ever so faintly of cherry and sometimes left a line across
her two front teeth. He stood to replenish his glass, and
staggered. Bits of Sukie—her plump parallel toes tipped with
scarlet, her copper necklace of crescents, the pale orange tufts
in her armpits—fluttered about him unsteadily. The bottle
lived on a lower shelf, beneath a long uniform set of Balzac
like so many miniature brown coffins.

"Yes, that's another thing you can't stand, the way Jenny and Chris have gone off, as if you can keep children home forever, as if the world doesn't have to *change* and *grow*. Wake up, Clyde. You thought life was going to be just like those children's books Mommy and Daddy kept piling on your bed every time you were sick, all those Wee Astronomers and Children's Classics and coloring books with safe little outlines and nice pointy crayons in their snug little boxes, when the fact is it's an *or*ganism, Clyde—the world is an organism, it's vital, it's sensitive, it's moving *on*, Clyde, while you sit over there playing with that silly little paper of yours as if you were still Mommy's pet sick in bed. Your so-called reporter Sukie Rougemont was there tonight at the meeting, her piggy little nose in the air, giving me that I-know-something-you-don't-know-look."

Language, he was thinking, perhaps *is* the curse, that took us out of Eden. And here we are trying to teach it to these poor good-natured chimpanzees and grinning dolphins. The Johnnie Walker bottle chortled obligingly in its tilted throat.

"Don't you think, *ooh*," Felicia was going on, exclaiming as the vortex of fury gripped her, "don't you think I don't know about you and that minx, I can read you like a book and don't you forget it, how you'd like to fuck her if you had the guts but you don't, you don't."

The picture of Sukie as she was, blurred and gentle and with a sort of distended amazement in her expression beneath him, when she was being fucked, came into his mind and the strong honey of it paralyzed his tongue, which had wanted to protest, *But I do*.

"You sit here," Felicia was going on, with a chemical viciousness that had become independent of her body, a possession controlling her mouth, her eyes, "you sit here mooning about Jenny and Chris who've at least had the guts and the sense to kiss this Godforsaken town good-bye forever and try to make careers for themselves where things are *hap*pening, you sit here mooning but you know what they used to say to me about you? You really want to know, Clyde? They would say, 'Hey, Mom, wouldn't it be great if Dad would leave us? But, you know,' they would have to add, 'he just doesn't have the guts.' " Scornfully, as if still in the voice of others: " 'He just doesn't—have—the guts.' "

The polish, Clyde thought, the polish of her rhetoric was what made it truly insufferable: the artful pauses and repetitions, the way she had picked up the word "guts" and turned it into a musical theme, the way she was making her orotund points before a huge mental audience rapt to the uttermost tier of the bleachers. A crowd of thumbtacks had come up from her gullet during the climax of her peroration, but not even this had stopped her. Felicia spat them swiftly into her hand and tossed them into the log fire he had built. They faintly sizzled; their colored heads blackened. "No gutth at all," she said, extracting one last tack and flicking it through the gap between the bricks and the fire screen, "but he wants to turn the entire town into a memorial for this horrible war. It must all fit, it must be, what do they call it, a syndrome. A drunken weakling wants the entire world to go down with him. Hitler, that's who you remind me of, Clyde. Another weak man the world didn't stand up to. Well, it's not going to happen this time." Now the imaginary crowd had gotten behind her—troops she was leading. "*We're standing up to evil,*" she called, her eyes focused above and beyond his head.

And she stood with legs braced as if he might try to knock her down. But he had taken a step her way because the fire, under its mouthful of wet tacks, seemed to be dying. He pulled back the screen and gave the spread logs a poke with the brass-handled poker. The logs snuggled closer, with sparks. He was reminded of himself and Sukie: a curious benison attendant upon sex with Sukie was how sleepy her proximity made him; at the slithering touch of her skin a blissful languor would steal upon him, after a life of insomnia.

Before and after sex her naked body rode so lightly at his side he seemed to have found his spot in space at last. Just thinking of this peace the red-haired divorcee bestowed drew a merciful blankness across his brain.

Perhaps minutes passed. Felicia was vehemently talking. His children's vigorous contempt for him had become involved with his criminal willingness to sit in a chair while unjust wars, fascist governments, and profit-greedy exploiters ravaged the world. The poker's smooth heft was still in his hand. In its chemical indignation her face had gone white as a skull; her eyes burned like the tiny flames of votive candles deep in the waxy pockets they have hollowed. Her hair seemed to be standing up in a ragged, skimpy halo. Most horribly, things kept coming out of her mouth—parrot feathers, dead wasps, bits of eggshell all mixed in an unstoppable thin gruel she kept wiping from her chin in a rhythmic gesture like cocking a gun. He saw these extrusions as a sign; this woman was possessed, she bore no relation to the woman he in good faith had married. "Hey come on, Lishy," Clyde begged, "let's cool it. Let's call it a day." The chemical and mechanical action that had replaced her soul surged on; in her trance of indignation she had ceased to see and hear. Her voice would wake the neighbors. Her voice was growing louder, fed inexhaustibly from within. His drink was in his left hand; he lifted the poker in his right and slashed it down across her head, just to interrupt the flow of energy for a moment, to plug the hole through which too much was pouring. The bone of her skull gave off a surprising high-pitched noise, as if two blocks of wood had been playfully knocked together. Her eyeballs rolled upward, displaying their whites, and her lips parted involuntarily, showing on her tongue an impossibly blue small feather. He knew he was making a mistake but the silence felt heaven-sent. His own chemicals took over; he hit her head with the poker again and again, pursuing it in its slow fall to the floor, until the sound the blows made was more liquid than that of wood knocking wood. He had plugged this hole in cosmic peace forever.

An immense sheath of relief slid upward from Clyde Gabriel, a film slipping from his sweat-coated body like a polyethylene protecting bag being pulled from a clean suit. He sipped on the Scotch and avoided looking at the floor. He thought of the stars outside and of the impervious pattern they would be making on this night of his life as on every other in the aeons since the galaxy condensed. Though he still had a lot to do, and some of it very difficult, a miraculously refreshed perspective gave each of his actions a squared-off clarity, as if indeed he had been returned to those illustrated children's books Felicia had scornfully conjured up. How curious of her to do so: she had been right, he had loved those days of staying home from school sick. She knew him too well. Marriage is like two people locked up with one lesson to read, over and over, until the words become madness. He thought she whimpered from the floor but decided it was only the fire digesting a tiny vein of sap.

As a conscientious, neatness-loving child Clyde had relished architectural drawings—ones that showed every molding and lintel and ledge and made manifest the triangular diminishments of perspective. With ruler and blue pencil he used to extend the diminishing lines of drawings in magazines and comic books to the vanishing point, even when the point lay well off the page. That such a point existed was a pleasing concept to him, and perhaps his first glimpse into adult fraudulence was the discovery that in many flashy-looking drawings the artists had cheated: there was no exact vanishing point. Now Clyde in person had arrived at this place of final perspective, and everything was ideally lucid and crisp around him. Vast problematical areas—next Wednesday's issue of the *Word*, the arrangement of his next tryst with Sukie, that perpetual struggle of lovers to find privacy and a bed that did not feel tawdry, the recurrent pain of putting back on his underclothes and leaving her, the necessity to consult with Joe Marino about the no-longer-overlookable decrepitude of this house's old furnace and deteriorating pipes and radiators, the not dissimilar condition of his liver and stomach lining, the periodic blood tests and consultations with Doc Pat and all the insincere resolutions his deplorable condition warranted, and now no end of complication with the police and the law courts—were swept away, leaving only the outlines of this room, the lines of its carpentry clean as laser beams.

He tossed down the last of his drink. It scraped his guts. Felicia had been wrong to say he didn't have any. In setting the tumbler on the fireplace mantel he could not avoid the peripheral vision of her stocking feet, fallen awkwardly apart as if in mid-step of an intricate dance. She had in truth been a nimble jitterbugger at Warwick High. That wonderful pumping, wah-wahing big-band sound even little local bands could fabricate in those days. The tip of her girlish tongue would show between her teeth as she set herself to be twirled. He stooped and picked up the Lucretius from the floor and returned it to its place on the shelf. He went down into the cellar to look for a rope. The disgraceful old furnace was chewing its fuel with a strained whine; its brittle rusty carapace leaked so much heat the basement was the coziest part of the house. There was an old laundry room where the previous owners had left an antique Bendix with wringers and an old-fashioned smell of naphtha and even a basket of clothespins on the round tin lid of its tub. The games he used to play with clothespins, crayoning them into little long-legged men wearing round hats somewhat like sailor hats. Clothesline, nobody uses clothesline any more. But here was a coil, neatly looped and tucked behind the old washer in a world of cobwebs. The transparent hand of Providence, Clyde suddenly realized, was guiding him. With his own, opaque hands—veiny, gnarled, an old man's claws, hideous— he gave the rope a sharp yank and inspected six or eight feet of it for frayed spots that might give way. A rusty pair of metal shears lay handy and he cut off the needed length.

As when climbing a mountain, take one step at a time and don't look too far ahead up the path: this resolve carried him smoothly back up the stairs, holding the dusty rope. He turned left into the kitchen and looked up. The ceiling here had been lowered in renovation and presented a flimsy surface of textured cellulose tiles held in a grid of aluminum strapping. The house had nine-foot plaster ceilings in the other downstairs rooms; the ornate chandelier canopies, none of which still held a chandelier, might not take his weight even if he climbed a stepladder and found a protuberance to knot the clothesline around.

He went back into his library to pour one more drink. The fire was burning a bit less merrily and could do with another log; but such an attention lay on that vast sheet of concerns no longer relevant, no longer his. It took some getting used to, how hugely much no longer mattered. He sipped the drink and felt the smoky amber swallow descend toward a digestion that was also off the board, in the dark, not to occur. He thought of the cozy basement and wondered whether, if he promised just to live there in one of the old coal bins and never go outdoors, all might be forgiven and smoothed over. But this cringing thought polluted the purity he had created in his mind minutes ago. Think again.

Perhaps the rope was the problem. He had been a newspaperman for thirty years and knew of the rich variety of methods whereby people take their own lives. Suicide by automobile was actually one of the commonest; automotive suicides were buried every day by satisfied priests and unaffronted loved ones. But the method was uncertain and messily public and at this vanishing point all the aesthetic prejudices Clyde had suppressed in living seemed to be welling up along with images from his childhood Some people, given the blaze in the fireplace, the awful evidence on the floor, and the thoroughly wooden house, might have made a pyre for themselves. But this would leave Jenny and Chris with no inheritance and Clyde was *not* one of those like Hitler who wanted to take the world with him; Felicia had been crazy in this comparison. Further, how could he trust himself not to save his scorched skin and flee to the lawn? He was no Buddhist monk, trained in discipline of that craven beast the body and able to sit in calm protest until the charred flesh toppled. Gas was held to be painless but then he was no mechanic either, to find the masking tape and string putty to seal off the many windows of the kitchen whose roominess and sunniness had been one of the factors in Felicia's and his decision to buy the house thirteen years ago this December. All of this year's December, it occurred to him with a guilty joy, December with its short dark tinselly days and ghastly herd buying and wooden homage to a dead religion (the dime-store carols, the pathetic crêche at Landing— Kazmierczak—Square, the Christmas tree erected at the other end of Dock Street in that great round marble urn called the Horse Trough), all of December was among the many things now off Clyde's sublimely simplified calendar. Nor would he have to pay next month's oil bill. Or gas bill. But he disdained the awkward wait gas would require, and he did not want his last view of reality to be the inside of a gas oven as he held his head in it on all fours in the servile position of a dog about to be fed. He rejected the messiness with knives and razor blades and bathtubs. Pills were painless and tidy but one of Felicia's causes had been a faddish militance against the pharmaceutical companies and what she said was their attempt to create a stoned America, a nation of drug-dependent zombies. Clyde smiled, the deep crease in his cheek leaping up. Some of what the old girl said had made sense. She hadn't been entirely babble. But he did not think she was right about Jennifer and Chris; he had never expected or desired them to stay home forever, he was offended only by Chris's going into such a flaky profession as the stage and Jenny's moving so far away, to Chicago no less, and letting herself be bombarded by X-rays, her ovaries exposed so she might never bear him any grandchildren. They too were off the map, grandchildren. Having children is something we think we ought to do because our parents did it, but when it is over the children are just other members of the human race, rather disappointingly. Jenny and Chris had been good quiet children and there had been something a bit disappointing in that too; by being good they had been evading Felicia, who when younger and not so plugged into altruism had had a terrible temper (sexual frustration no doubt at the root of it, but how can any husband keep a woman protected and excited at the same time?), and in the process the children had evaded him also. Jenny when about nine used to worry about death and once asked him why he didn't say prayers with her like the other daddies and though he didn't have much of an answer that was the closest together they had ever drawn. He had always been trying to read and her coming to him had been an interruption. With a better pair of parents Jenny could have grown to be a saint, such light pale clear eyes, a face as smooth as a photographed face after the retoucher is done with it. Until he had had a girl baby Clyde had never really seen female genitals, so sweet and puffy like twin little pale buns off a pastry tray.

The town had grown very silent around them, around him: not a car was stirring on Lodowick Street, His stomach hurt. It usually did, this time of night: an incipient ulcer. Doc Pat had told him, If you *must* keep drinking, at least eat. One of the unfortunate side effects of his affair with Sukie was skipping lunch in order to fuck. She sometimes brought a jar of cashews but with his bad teeth he wasn't that fond of nuts any more; the crumbs got under the appliance and cut his gums.

Amazing, women, the way loving never fills them up. If you do a good job they want more the next minute, as bad as getting out a newspaper. Even Felicia, for all she said she hated him. This time of night he would be having one more nip by the dying fire, giving her time to get herself into bed and fall asleep waiting for him. Having talked herself out, she toppled in a minute into the oblivion of the just. He wondered now if she had been hypoglycemic; in the mornings she had been clearheaded and the ghostly audience she gave her speeches to had dispersed. She had never seemed to grasp how much she infuriated him. Some mornings, on a Saturday or Sunday, she would keep her nightie on as provocation, by way of making up. You would think a man and woman living together so many hours of their lives would find a moment to make up in. Missed opportunities. If tonight he had just ridden it out and let her get safely upstairs . . . But that possibility, too, along with his grandchildren and the healing of his liquor-pitted stomach and his troubles with his little denture, was off the map.

Clyde had the sensation of there being several of him, like ghost images on TV. This time of night he, in a parade of such ghost images, would mount the stairs. The stairs. The limp dry old rope still dangled in his hand. Its cobwebs had come off on his corduroy trousers. Lord give me strength.

The staircase was a rather grand Victorian construction that doubled back after a midway landing with a view of the back yard and its garden, once elaborate but rather let go in recent years. A rope tied to the base of one of the upstairs balusters should provide enough swing room over the stairs below, which could serve as a kind of gallows platform. He carried the rope upstairs to the second-floor landing. He worked rapidly, fearing the alcohol might overtake him with a blackout. A square knot was right over left, then left over right. Or was it? His first attempt produced a granny. It was hard to move his hands through the narrow spaces between the squared baluster bases; his knuckles got skinned. His hands seemed to be a great distance from his eyes, and to have become luminous, as though plunged into an ethereal water. It took prodigies of calculation to figure where the loop in the rope should come (not more than six or eight inches under the narrow facing board with its touchingly fine Victorian molding, or his feet might touch the stairs and that blind animal his body would struggle to keep alive) and how big the loop for his head should be. Too big, he would fall through; too snug, he might merely strangle. The hangman's art: the neck should break, he had read more than once in his life, thanks to a sudden sharp pressure on the cervical vertebrae. Prisoners in jail used their belts with blue-faced results. Chris had been in Boy Scouts but that had been years ago and there had been a scandal with the scoutmaster that had broken up the den. Clyde finally produced a messy kind of compound slip knot and let the noose hang over the side. Viewed from above, by leaning over the banister, the perspective was sickening; the rope lightly swayed and kept swaying, turned into a pendulum by some waft of air that moved uninvited through this drafty house.

Clyde's heart was no longer in it but with the methodical determination that had put ten thousand papers to bed he went into the warm cellar (the old furnace chewing, chewing fuel) and fetched the aluminum stepladder. It felt feather-light; the might of angels was descending upon him. He also carried up some lumber scraps and with these set the ladder on the carpeted stairs so that, one pair of plastic feet resting three risers lower than the other on pieces of wood, the stepless crossbraced rails were vertical and the entire tilted A-shape would topple over at a nudge. The last thing he would see, he estimated, would be the front doorway and the leaded fanlight of stained glass, its vaguely sunriselike symmetrical pattern lit up by the sodium glow of a distant street lamp. By light nearer to hand, scratches on the aluminum seemed traces left by the swerving flight of atoms in a bubble chamber. Everything was touched with transparency; the many tapering, interlocked lines of the staircase were as the architect had dreamed them; it came to Clyde Gabriel, rapturously, that there was nothing to fear, of course our spirits passed through matter like the sparks of divinity they were, of course there would be an afterlife of infinite opportunities, in which he could patch things up with Felicia, and have Sukie too, not once but an infinity of times, just as Nietzsche had conjectured. A lifelong fog was lifting; it was all as clear as rectified type, the meaning that the stars had been singing out to him, *candida sidera*, tingeing with light sluggish spirit sunk in its proud muck.

The aluminum ladder shivered slightly, like a highstrung youthful steed, as he trusted his weight to it. One step, two, then the third. The rope nestled dryly around his neck; the ladder trembled as he reached up and behind to slip the knot tighter, snug against what seemed the correct spot. Now the ladder was swinging violently from side to side; the agitated blood of its jockey was flailing it toward the hurdle, where it lifted, as he had foreseen, at the most delicate urging, and fell away. Clyde heard the clatter and thump. What he had not expected was the burning, as though a hot rasp were being pulled up through his esophagus, and the way the angles of wood and carpet and wallpaper whirled, whirled so widely it seemed for a second he had sprouted eyes in the back of his head. Then a redness in his overstuffed skull was followed by blackness, giving way, with the change of a single letter, to blankness.

"Oh baby, how horrible for you," Jane Smart said to Sukie, over the phone.

"Well it's not as if I'd had to see any of it myself. But the guys down at the police station were plenty vivid. Apparently she didn't have any face *left*." Sukie was not crying but her voice had that wrinkled quality of paper that has been damp and though dry will never lie flat again.

"Well she was a *vile* woman," Jane said firmly, comforting, though her head with its eyes and ears was still back in the suite of Bach unaccompanieds—the exhilarating, somehow malevolently onrushing Fourth, in E-flat Major. "So boring, so self-righteous," she hissed. Her eyes rested on the bare floor of her living room, splintered by repeated heedless socketing of her cello's pointed steel foot.

Sukie's voice faded in and out, as though she were letting the telephone drop away from her chin. "I've never known a man," she said, a bit huskily, "gentler than Clyde."

"Men are violent," Jane said, her patience wearing thin. "Even the mildest of them. It's biological. They're full of rage because they're just accessories to reproduction."

"He hated even to correct anybody at work," Sukie went on, as the sublime music—its diabolical rhythms, its wonderfully cruel demands upon her dexterity—slowly faded from Jane's mind, and the sting from the side of her left thumb, where she had been ardently pressing the strings. "Though once in a while he would blow up at some proofreader who had let just *oo*dles of things slip through."

"Well darling, it's obvious. That's why. He was keeping it all inside. When he blew up at Felicia he had thirty years' worth of rage, no wonder he took off her head."

"It's not fair to say he took off her head," Sukie said. "He just kind of—what's that phrase everybody's using these days?—*was*ted it."

"And then wasted himself," prompted Jane, hoping by such efficient summary to hasten this conversation along so she could return to her music; she liked to practice two hours in the mornings, from ten to noon, and then give herself a tidy lunch of cottage cheese or tuna salad spooned into a single large curved lettuce leaf. This afternoon she had set up a matinee with Darryl Van Horne at one-thirty. They would work for an hour on one of the two Brahmses or an amusing little Kodály Darryl had unearthed in a music shop tucked in the basement of a granite building on Weybosset Street just beyond the Arcade, and then have, their custom was, Asti Spumante or some tequila milk Fidel would do in the blender, and a bath. Jane still ached, at both ends of her perineum, from their last time together. But most of the good things that come to a woman come through pain and she had been flattered that he should want her without an audience, unless you counted Fidel and Rebecca padding in and out with trays and towels; there was something precarious about Darryl's lust that was flattered and soothed by the three of them being there together and that needed the most extravagant encouragements when Jane was with him by herself. She added to Sukie irritably, "That he was clear-minded enough to carry it through is what I find surprising."

Sukie defended Clyde. "Liquor never made him confused unusually, he really drank as a kind of medicine. I think a lot of his depression must have been metabolic; he once told me his blood pressure was one-ten over seventy, which in a man his age was really wonderful."

Jane snapped, "I'm sure a lot of things about him were wonderful for a man of his age. I certainly preferred him to that deplorable Ed Parsley."

"Oh, Jane, I know you're dying to get me off the phone, but speaking of Ed . . ."

"Yess?"

"Have you been noticing how close Brenda has grown to the Neffs?"

"I've rather lost track of the Neffs, frankly."

"I know you have, and good for you," Sukie said. "Lexa and I always thought he abused you and you were much too gifted for his little group; it really was just jealousy, his saying your bowing or whatever he said was prissy."

"Thank you, sweet."

"Anyway, the two of them and Brenda are apparently thick as thieves now, they eat out at the Bronze Barrel or that new French place over toward Pettaquamscutt all the time and evidently Ray and Greta have encouraged her to put in for Ed's position at the church and become the new Unitarian minister. Apparently the Lovecrafts are all for it too and Horace you know is on the church board."

"But she's not ordained. Don't you have to be ordained? The Episcopalians where I fill in are very strict about things like that; you can't even join as a member unless a bishop has put his hands somewhere, I think on your head."

"No, but she *is* in the parsonage with those brats of theirs—absolutely undisciplined, neither Ed or Brenda believed in ever saying No—and making her the new minister might be more graceful than getting her to leave. Maybe there's a course or something you can take take by mail."

"But can she preach? You *do* have to preach."

"Oh I don't think that would be any real problem. Brenda has wonderful posture. She was studying to be a modern dancer when she met Ed at an Adlai Stevenson rally; she was in one of the warm-up acts and he was to ask the blessing. He told me about it more than once, I used to wonder if he wasn't still in love with her after all."

"She is a ridiculous vapid woman," Jane said.

"Oh Jane, don't."

"Don't what?"

"Don't sound like that. That's the way we used to talk about Felicia, and look what happened."

Sukie had become very small and curled over at her end of the line, like a lettuce leaf wilting. "Are you blaming *us*?" Jane asked her briskly. "Her sad sot of a husband I would think instead should be blamed."

"On the surface, sure, but we *did* cast that spell, and put those things in the cookie jar when we got tiddly, and things did keep coming out of her mouth, Clyde mentioned it to me so innocently, he tried to get her to go to a doctor but she said medicine ought to be entirely nationalized in this country the way it is in England and Sweden. She hated the drug companies, too."

"She was full of hate, darling. It was the hate coming out of her mouth that did her in, not a few harmless feathers and pins. She had lost touch with her womanhood. She needed pain to remind her she was a woman. She needed to get down on her knees and drink some horrible man's nice cold come. She needed to be beaten, Clyde was right about that, he just went at it too hard."

"Please, Jane. You frighten me when you talk like that, the things you say."

"Why *not* say them? Really, Sukie, you sound infantile." Sukie was a weak sister, Jane thought. They put up with her for the gossip she gathered and that kid-sister shine she used to bring to their Thursdays but she really was just a conceited immature girl, she couldn't please Van Horne the way that Jane did, that burning stretching; even Greta Neff, washed-out old bag as she was with her granny glasses and pathetic pedantic accent, was more of a woman in this sense, a woman who could hold whole kingdoms of night within her, burning. "Words are just words," she added.

"They're not: they make things *hap*pen!" Sukie wailed, her voice shrivelled to a pathetic wheedle. "Now two people are dead and two children are orphans because of us!"

"I don't think you can be an orphan after a certain age," Jane said. "Stop talking nonsense." Her *s*'s hissed like spit on a stove top. "People stew in their own juice."

"If I hadn't slept with Clyde he wouldn't have gone so crazy, I'm sure of it. He loved me so, Jane. He used to just hold my foot in his hands and kiss between each pair of toes."

"Of course he did. That's the kind of thing men are supposed to do. They're supposed to adore us. They're shits, try to keep that in mind. Men are absolutely shits, but we get them in the end because we can suffer better. A woman can outsuffer a man every time." Jane felt huge in her impatience; the black notes she had swallowed that morning bristled within her, alive. Who would have thought the old Lutheran had so much jism? "There will always be men for you, sweetie," she told Sukie. "Don't bother your head about Clyde any more. You gave him what he asked for, it's not your fault he couldn't handle it. Listen, truly. I must run." Jane Smart lied, "I have a lesson coming in at eleven."

In fact her lesson was not until four. She would rush back from the old Lenox place aching and steamy-clean and the sight of those grubby little hands on her pure ivory keys mangling some priceless simplified melody of Mozart's or Mendelssohn's would make her want to take the metronome and with its heavy base mash those chubby fingers as if she were grinding beans in a pestle. Since Van Horne had come into her life Jane was more passionate than she had ever been about music, that golden high-arched exit from this pit of pain and ignominy.

"She sounded so harsh and strange," Sukie said to Alexandra over the phone a few days later. "It's as if she thinks she has the inside track with Darryl and is fighting to protect it."

"That's one of his diabolical arts, to give each of us that impression. I'm really quite sure it's me he loves," said Alexandra, laughing with cheerful hopelessness. "He has me doing these bigger pieces of sculpture now, varnished papier-mâché is what this Saint-Phalle woman uses, I don't know how she does it, the glue gets all over your fingers, into your hair, *yukk*. I get one side of a figure looking right and then the other side has no shape at all, just a bunch of loose ends and lumps."

"Yes he was saying to me when I lose my job at the *Word* I

should try a novel. I can't imagine sitting down day after day to the same story. And the people's names—people just don't *exist* without their real names."

"Well," Alexandra sighed, "he's challenging us. He's stretching us."

Over the phone she did sound stretched—more diffuse and distant every second, sinking into a translucent quicksand of estrangement. Sukie had come back to her house after the Gabriels' funeral, and no child was home from school yet, yet the little old house was sighing and muttering to itself, full of memories and mice. There were no nuts or munchies in the kitchen and as the next best consolation she had reached for the phone. "I miss our Thursdays," she abruptly confessed, childlike.

"I know, baby, but we have our tennis parties instead. Our baths."

"They frighten me sometimes. They're not as cozy as we used to be by ourselves."

"*Are* you going to lose your job? What's happening with that?"

"Oh I don't know, there are so many rumors. They say the owner rather than find a new editor is going to sell out to a chain of small-town weeklies the gangsters operate out of Providence. Everything is printed in Pawtucket and the only local news is what a correspondent phones in from her home and the rest is statewide feature articles and things they buy from a syndicate and they give them away to everybody like supermarket fliers."

"Nothing is as cozy as it used to be, is it?"

"*No*," Sukie blurted, but could not quite, like a child, cry.

A pause occurred, where in the old days they could hardly stop talking. Now each woman had her share, her third, of Van Horne to be secretive about, their solitary undiscussed visits to the island which in stark soft gray December had become more beautiful than ever; the ocean's silver-tinged horizon was visible now from those upstairs Arguslike windows behind which Van Horne had his black-walled bedroom, visible through the leafless beeches and oaks and swaying larches surrounding the elephantine canvas bubble that held the tennis court, where the snowy egrets used to nest. "How was the funeral?" Alexandra at last asked.

"Well, you know how they are. Sad and gauche at the same time. They were cremated, and it seemed so strange, burying these little rounded boxes like Styrofoam coolers, only brown, and smaller. Brenda Parsley said the prayer at the undertaker's, because they haven't found a replacement for Ed yet, and the Gabriels weren't anything really, though Felicia was always going on about everybody else's Godlessness. But the daughter wanted I guess some kind of religious touch. Very few people came, actually, considering all the publicity. Mostly *Word* employees putting in an appearance hoping to keep their jobs, and a few people who had been on committees with Felicia, but she had quarrelled you know with almost everybody. The people at Town Hall are delighted to have her off their backs, they all called her a witch."

"Did you speak to Brenda?"

"Just a bit, out at the cemetery. There were so few of us."

"How did she act toward you?"

"Oh, very polished and cool. She owes me one and she knows it. She wore a navy-blue suit with a ruffled silk blouse that did look wonderfully ministerial. And her hair done in a different way, swept back quite severely and without those bangs like the woman in Peter, Paul, and Mary that used to make her look, you know, puppyish. An improvement, really. It was Ed used to make her wear those miniskirts, so he'd feel more like a hippie, which was really rather humiliating, if you have Brenda's piano legs. She spoke quite well, especially at the graveside. This lovely fluting voice floating out over the headstones. She talked about how much into community service both the deceased were and tried to make some connection between their deaths and Vietnam, the moral confusion of our times, I couldn't quite follow it."

"Did you ask her if she hears from Ed?"

"Oh I wouldn't dare. Anyway I doubt it, since *I* never do any more. But she did bring him up. Afterwards, when the men were tugging the plastic grass around, she looked me very levelly in the eye and said his leaving was the best thing ever happened to her."

"Well, what else can she say? What else can any of us say?"

"Lexa sweet, whatever do you mean? You sound as though you're weakening."

"Well, one does get weary. Carrying everything alone. The bed is so cold this time of year."

"You should get an electric blanket."

"I have one. But I don't like the feeling of electricity on top of me. Suppose Felicia's ghost comes in and pours a bucket of cold water all over the bed, I'd be electrocuted."

"Alexandra, don't. Don't scare me by sounding so depress- ed. We all look to you for whatever it is. Mother-strength."

"Yes, and that's depressing too."

"Don't you believe in any of it any more?"

In freedom, in witchcraft. Their powers, their ecstasy.

"Of course I do, poops. Were the children there? What do they look like?"

"Well," Sukie said, her voice regaining animation, giving the news, "rather remarkable. They both look like Greek statues in a way, very stately and pale and perfect. And they stick together like twins even though the girl is a good bit older. Jennifer, her name is, is in her late twenties and the boy is college-age, though he's not in college; he wants to be something in show business and spends all his time getting rides back and forth between Los Angeles and New York. He was a stagehand at a summer-theatre place in Connecticut and the girl flew in from Chicago where she's taken a leave from her job as an X-ray technician. Marge Perley says they're going to stay here in the house a while to get the estate settled; I was thinking maybe we should do something with them. They seem such babes in the woods, I hate to think of their falling into Brenda's clutches."

"Baby, they've surely heard all about you and Clyde and blame you for everything."

"Really? How could they? I was being nothing but kind."

"You upset his internal balances. His ecology."

Sukie confessed, "I don't like feeling guilty."

"Who does? How do you think I feel, poor dear quite unsuitable Joe keeps offering to leave Gina and that swarm of fat children for me."

"But he never will. He's too Mediterranean. Catholics never get conflicted like us poor lapsed Protestants do."

"Lapsed," Alexandra said. "Is that how you think of yourself? I'm not sure I ever had anything to lapse from."

There entered into Sukie's mind, broadcast from Alexandra's, a picture of a western wooden church with a squat weather-beaten steeple, high in the mountains and unvisited. "Monty was very religious," Sukie said. "He was always talking about his ancestors." And on the same wavelength the image of Monty's drooping milk-smooth buttocks came to her and she knew at last for certain that he and Alexandra had had an affair. She yawned, and said, "I think I'll go over to Darryl's and unwind. Fidel is developing some wonderful new concoction he calls a Rum Mystique."

"Are you sure it isn't Jane's day?"

"I think she was having her day the day I talked to her. Her talk was really excited."

"It burns."

"Exactly. Oh, Lexa, you really should see Jennifer Gabriel, she's delicious. She makes me look like a tired old hag. This pale round face and these pale blue eyes like Clyde had and a pointy chin like Felicia had and the most delicate little nose, with a fine straight edge like something you would sculpture with a butter knife but slightly dented into her face, like a cat's if you can picture it. And such skin!"

"Delicious," Alexandra echoed, driftingly. Alexandra used to love her, Sukie knew. That first night at Darryl's, dancing to Joplin, they had clung together and wept at the curse of heterosexuality that held them apart as if each were a rose in a plastic tube. Now there was a detachment in Alexandra's voice. Sukie remembered that charm she made, with its magical triple bow, and reminded herself to take it out from under her bed. Spells go bad, lose efficacy, within about a month, if no human blood is involved.

And a few more days later Sukie met the female Gabriel orphan walking without her brother along Dock Street: on that wintry, slightly crooked sidewalk, half the shops shuttered for the winter and the others devoted to scented tinted candles and Austrian-style Christmas ornaments imported from Korea, these two stars shone to each other from afar and tensely let gravitational attraction bring them together, while the windows of the travel agency and the Superette, of the Yapping Fox with its cable-knit sweaters and sensible plaid skirts and of the Hungry Sheep with its slightly slinkier wear, of Perley Realty with its faded snapshots of Cape-and-a-halfs and great dilapidating Victorian gems along Oak Street waiting for an enterprising young couple to take them over and make the third floor into apartments, of the bakery and the barbershop and the Christian Science reading room all stared. The Eastwick branch of the Old Stone Bank had installed against much civic objection a drive-in window, and Sukie and Jennifer had to wait as if on opposite banks of a stream while several cars nosed in and out of the slanted accesses carved into the sidewalk. The downtown was much too cramped and historic, the objectors, led by the late Felicia

Gabriel, had pointed out in vain, for such a further complication of traffic.

Sukie at last made it to the younger woman's side, around the giant fins of a crimson Cadillac being guardedly steered by fussy, dim-sighted Horace Lovecraft. Jennifer wore a dirty old buff parka wherein the down had flattened and one of Felicia's scarves, a loose-knit purple one, wrapped several times around her throat and chin. Several inches shorter than Sukie, she seemed an undernurtured waif, her eyes watery and nostrils pink. The thermometer that day stood near zero.

"How's it going?" Sukie asked, with forced cheer.

In size and age this girl was to Sukie as Sukie was to Alexandra; though Jennifer was wary she had to yield to superior powers. "Not so bad," she responded, in a small voice whittled smaller by the cold. She had acquired in Chicago a touch of Midwestern nasality in her pronunciation. She studied Sukie's face and took a little plunge, adding confidingly, "There's so much stuff; Chris and I are overwhelmed. We've both been living like gypsies, and Mommy and Daddy kept *every*thing—drawings we both did in kindergarten, our grade-school report cards, boxes and boxes of old photographs. . . ."

"It must be sad."

"Well, that, and *frus*trating. They should have made some of these decisions themselves. And you can see how things were let slide these last years; Mrs. Perley said we'd be cheating ourselves if we didn't wait to sell it until after we can get it painted in the spring. It would cost maybe two thousand and add ten to the value of the place."

"Look. You look frozen." Sukie herself was snug and imperial-looking in a long sheepskin coat, and a hat of red fox fur that picked up the copper glint of her own. "Let's go over to Nemo's and I'll buy you a cup of coffee."

"Well . . ." The girl wavered, looking for a way out, but tempted by the idea of warmth.

Sukie pressed her offensive. "Maybe you hate me, from things you've heard. If so, it might do you good to talk it out."

"Mrs. Rougemont, why would I hate you? It's just Chris is at the garage with the car, the Volvo—even the car they left us was way overdue for its checkup."

"Whatever's wrong with it will take longer to fix than they said," Sukie said authoritatively, "and I'm sure Chris is happy. Men love garages. All that banging. We can sit at a table in the front so you can see him go by if he does. Please. I want to say how sorry I am about your parents. He was a kind boss and I'm in trouble too, now that he's gone."

A badly rusted '59 Chevrolet, its trunk shaped like gull wings, nearly brushed them with its chrome protuberances as it lumbered up over the curb toward the browny-green drive-in window; Sukie touched the girl's arm to safeguard her. Then, not letting go, she urged her across the street to Nemo's. Dock Street had been widened more than once as motor traffic increased in this century; its crooked sidewalks had been pared in places to the width of a single pedestrian and some of the older buildings jutted out at odd angles. Nemo's Diner was a long aluminum box with rounded corners and a broad red stripe along its sides. In mid-morning it held only the counter crowd—underemployed or retired men several of whom with casual handlift or nod greeted Sukie, but less gladly, it seemed to her, than before Clyde Gabriel had let horror into the town.

The little tables at the front were empty, and the picture window that overlooked the street here sweated and trickled with condensation. As Jennifer squinted against the light, small creases leaped up at the corners of her ice-pale eyes and Sukie saw that she was not quite so young as she had seemed on the street, swaddled in rags. Her dirty parka, patched with iron-on rectangles of tan vinyl, she laid a bit ceremoniously across the chair beside her, and coiled the long purple skein of scarf upon it. Underneath, she wore a simple gray skirt and white lamb's-wool sweater. She had a tidy plump figure; and there was a roundness to her that seemed too simple—her arms and breasts and cheeks and throat all defined with the same neat circular strokes.

Rebecca, the slatternly Antiguan Fidel was known to keep company with, came with crooked hips and her heavy gray lips twisted wryly shut on all she knew. "Now what you ladies be liking?"

"Two coffees," Sukie asked her, and on impulse also ordered johnnycakes. She had a weakness for them; they were so crumby and buttery and today would warm her insides.

"Why did you say I might hate you?" the other woman asked, with surprising directness, yet in a mild slight voice.

"Because." Sukie decided to get it over with. "I was your father's—whatever. You know. Lover. But not for long, only since summer. I didn't mean to mess anybody up, I just wanted to give him something, and I'm all I have. And he *was* lovable, as you know."

The girl showed no surprise but became more thoughtful, lowering her eyes. "I know he was," she said. "But not much recently, I think. Even when we were little, he seemed distracted and sad. And then smelled funny at night. Once I knocked some big book out of his lap trying to cuddle and he started to spank me and couldn't seem to stop." Her eyes lifted as her mouth shut on further confession; there was a curious vanity, the vanity of the meek, in the way her nicely formed, unpainted lips sealed so neatly one against the other. Her upper lip lifted a bit in faint distaste. "*You* tell me about him. My father."

"What about him?"

"What he was like."

Sukie shrugged. "Tender. Grateful. Shy. He drank too much but when he knew he was going to see me he would try not to, so he wouldn't be—stupid. You know. Sluggish."

"Did he have a lot of girlfriends?"

"Oh no. I don't think so." Sukie was offended. "Just me, was my conceited impression. He loved your mother, you know. At least until she became so—obsessed."

"Obsessed with what?"

"I'm sure you know better than I. With making the world a perfect place."

"That's rather nice, isn't it, that she wanted it to be?"

"I suppose." Sukie had never thought of it as nice, Felicia's public nagging: a spiteful ego trip, rather, with more than an added pinch of hysteria. Sukie did not appreciate being put on the defensive by this bland little ice maiden, who from the sound of her voice might be getting a cold. Sukie volunteered, "You know, if you're single in a town like this you pretty much have to take what you can find."

"No I don't know," said Jennifer, but softly. "But then I guess I don't know much about that sort of thing altogether."

Meaning what? That she was a virgin? It was hard to know if the girl was empty or if her strange stillness manifested an exceptionally complete inner poise. "Tell me about you," Sukie said. "You're going to become a doctor? Clyde was so proud of that."

"Oh, but it's a fraud. I keep running out of money and flunking anatomy. It was the chemistry I liked. The technician job is really as far as I'm ever going to go. I'm stuck."

Sukie told her, "You should meet Darryl Van Horne. He's trying to get us all *un*stuck."

Jennifer unexpectedly smiled, her little flat nose whitening with the tension. Her front teeth were round as a child's. "What a grand name," she said. "It sounds made up. Who is he?"

But she must, Sukie thought, have heard about our sabbats. The girl was difficult to see through; patches of an unnatural innocence, as though she had been skipped by life, blocked telepathy as lead blocks X-rays. "Oh, a sort of eccentric youngish middle-aged man who's bought the old Lenox place. You know, the big brick mansion toward the beach."

"The haunted plantation, we used to call that. I was fifteen when my parents moved here and really never got to know the area terribly well. There's an enormous amount to it, though it looks like nothing on the map."

Insolent tropical Rebecca brought their coffee in Nemo's heavy white mugs, and the golden johnnycakes; along with the pronounced warm fragrances of these there carried across the glazed table a spicy sour smell that Sukie linked to the waitress herself, her broad pelvis and heavy coffee-colored breasts, as she leaned over to set the mugs and plates in place. "Is there anything wanting now of you ladies' happi-ness?" the waitress asked, looking down upon them from the great slopes of herself. Her head looked rather small and sinewy— her black hair done in corn rows of tight braids—upon the mass of her flesh.

"Is there any cream, Becca?" Sukie asked.

"I get you de one." Putting down the little aluminum pitcher, she told them, "You can say 'cream' if you likes, milk is what de boss puts in every mornin'."

"Thank you, darling, I *meant* milk." But for a little joke Sukie quickly said to herself the white spell *Sator arepo tenet opera rotas*, and the milk poured thick and yellow, cream. Curdled flecks rotated on the circular surface of her coffee. Johnnycake turned to buttery fragments in her mouth. Indian ghosts of cornmeal slipped through the forest of her taste-buds. She swallowed and said, of Van Horne, "He's nice. You'd like him, once you got over his manner."

"What's wrong with his manner?"

Sukie wiped crumbs from her smiling lips. "He comes on rough, but it's a put-on really. He's really no threat, anybody can manage Darryl. A couple of my girlfriends and I play tennis with him in this fantastic big canvas bubble he's put up. Do you play?"

Jennifer's round shoulders shrugged. "A little. Mostly at summer camp. And a bunch of us used to go use the U. of C. courts occasionally."

"How long are you going to be around, before you go back to Chicago?"

Jennifer was watching the curds swirl in her own coffee. "A while. It may take until summer to sell the house, and Chris has nothing much to do as it turns out and we get along easily; we always have. Maybe I won't go back. As I said, it wasn't working out that great at Michael Reese."

"Were you having man trouble?"

"Oh *no*." Her eyes lifted, displaying below her pale irises arcs of pure youthful white. "Men don't seem all that interested in me."

"But why not? If I may say so, you're lovely."

The girl lowered her eyes. "Isn't this funny milk? So thick and sweet. I wonder if it's gone bad."

"No, I think you'll find it very fresh. You haven't eaten your johnnycake."

"I nibbled at it. I never was that crazy about them, they're just fried dough."

"That's why we Rhode Islanders like them. They come as they are. I'll finish yours if you don't want it."

"I must do something wrong that men sense. I used to talk about it with my friends sometimes. *My* girlfriends."

"A woman needs woman friends," Sukie said complacently.

"I didn't have that many of those either. Chicago is a tough town. These birdlike little ethnic women studying all night and full of all the answers. If you ask them anything personal, though, like what you're doing wrong with these men you have to meet, they clam right up."

"It's hard to be right with men, actually," Sukie told her. "They're very angry with us because we can have babies and they can't. They're terribly jealous, poor dears: Darryl tells us

: 177 :

that. I don't really know whether or not to believe him; as I say, a lot of him is pure put-on. At lunch the other day he was trying to describe his theories to me, they all have to do with some chemical whose name begins with 'silly.' "

"Selenium. It's a magical element. It's the secret of those doors in airports that open automatically in front of you. Also it takes the green color out of glass that iron gives it. Selenic acid can dissolve gold."

"Well, my goodness, you do know a thing or two. If you're that into chemistry, maybe you could be Darryl's assistant."

"Chris keeps saying I should just hang out in our house with him a while, at least until we sell it. He's fed up with New York, *it's* too tough. He says the gays control all the fields he's interested in—window dressing, stage design."

"I think you should."

"Should what?"

"Hang around. Eastwick's amusing." Rather impatiently— the morning was wasting—Sukie brushed all the johnnycake crumbs from the front of her sweater. "This is *not* a tough town. This is a *sweet*ie-pie town." She washed down the crumbs in her mouth with a last sip of coffee and stood.

"I feel that," the other woman said, getting the signal and beginning to gather up her scarf, her pathetic patched parka. Dressed and on her feet, Jenny performed a surprising, thrilling mannish action: she took Sukie's hand in a firm grip. "Thank you," she said, "for talking to me. The only other person who has taken any interest in us, except for the lawyers of course, is that nice lady minister, Brenda Parsley."

"She's a minister's wife, not a minister, and I'm not sure she's so nice either."

"Her husband behaved horribly to her, everybody tells me."

"Or she to him."

"I *knew* you'd say something like that," Jennifer said, and smiled, not unpleasantly; but it made Sukie feel naked, she could be seen right through, with no lead vest of innocence to protect her. Her life was lived in full view of the town; even this little stranger knew a thing or two.

Before Jennifer flicked the scarf into place Sukie noticed that around her neck hung a thin gold chain of the type that for some people supports a cross. But at the base of the girl's slender soft white throat hung the Egyptian tau cross, its loop at the top like the head of a tiny man—an ankh, symbol of life and death both, an ancient sign of mysteries come newly into vogue.

Seeing Sukie's eyes linger there, Jennifer looked oppositely at the other's necklace of copper moons and said, "My mother was wearing copper. A broad plain bracelet I'd never seen before. As if—"

"As if what, dear?"

"As if she were trying to ward something off."

"Aren't we all?" said Sukie cheerily. "I'll be in touch about tennis."

The space inside Van Horne's great bubble was acoustically and atmospherically weird: the sounds of shouts and of balls being hit seemed smothered even as they rang out, and a faint prickly sensation of pressure weighed on Sukie's freckled brow and forearms. The amber hair of these forearms stood up as if electrified. Beneath the overarching firmament of dun canvas everything seemed in slightly slow motion; the players moved through an aura of compression, though in fact the limp dome stayed inflated because the air within it, pumped by a tireless fan through a boxy plastic mouth sealed by duct tape low in one corner, was warmer than the winter air outside. Today was the shortest day of the year. An earth hard as iron lay locked beneath a sky whose mottled clouds spit snow like ashes sucked up a chimney and then dispersed with the smoke. Thin powdery lines appeared next to brick edges and exposed tree roots but melted in the wan noon sun; there was no accumulation, though every shop and bank with its seasonal pealing and cotton mimicry was inviting Christmas to be white. Dock Street, as early darkness overtook the muffled shoppers, looked harried, its gala lights a forestallment of sleep, a desperate hollow-eyed attempt to live up to some promise in the bitter black air. Playing tennis in their tights and leg warmers and ski sweaters and double pairs of socks stuffed into their sneakers, the young divorced mothers of Eastwick were taking a holiday from the holiday.

Sukie feared guiltily that she might have spoiled it for the others by bringing Jennifer Gabriel along. Not that Darryl Van Horne had objected to her suggestion over the phone; it was his nature to welcome new recruits and perhaps their little circle of four was becoming narrow for him. Like most men, especially wealthy men, especially wealthy men from New York City, he was easily bored. But Jennifer had taken the liberty of bringing her brother along, and Darryl would surely be appalled by the entry into his home of this boy, who was in the newest fashion of youth inarticulate and sullen, with glazed eyes, a slack fuzzy jaw, and tangled curly hair so dirty as to be scarcely blond. Instead of tennis sneakers he had worn beat-up rubber-cleated running shoes that even in the chill vastness of the bubble gave off a stale foul smell of male sweat. Sukie wondered how pristine Jennifer could stand a housemate so slovenly. Monty for all his faults had been fastidious, always taking showers and rinsing out coffee cups she had abandoned on an end table after a phone conversation. The boy had borrowed a racket and shown no ability to hit the ball over the net, and no embarrassment at his inability, only a sluggish petulance. Ever the courteous host and seeming gentleman, Darryl, though all suited up to play, in an outfit of maroon jogging pants and purple down vest that made him look like a macaw, had suggested that the four females enjoy a set of ladies' doubles while he took Christopher away for a tour of the library, the lab, the little conservatory of poisonous tropical plants. The boy followed with languid ingratitude as Darryl gestured and spouted words; through the walls of the bubble they could hear him exclaiming all the way up the path to the house. Sukie did feel guilty.

She took Jenny as her partner in case the girl proved inept, though in warming up she had shown a firm stroke from both sides; in play she showed herself to be a spunky sound-enough player, though without much range—which may have been partly deference to Sukie's leggy, reaching style. At about the age of eleven, Sukie, learning the game on an old rhododendron-screened macadam court a friend of her family's had on his lake-side estate, had been complimented by her father for a spectacular, lunging "get"; and ever after she had been a "fetching" style of player, even lagging in one corner and then the other to make her returns seem spectacular. It was the ball right in on her fists Sukie sometimes couldn't handle. She and Jenny quickly went up four games to one on Alexandra and Jane, and then the tricks began. Though the object coming into Sukie's forehand was an optic-yellow Wilson, what she got her racket on—knees bent, head down, power flowing forward and up for a topspin return—was a gob of putty; the weight of it took a chip out of her elbow, it felt like. What dribbled up to the net between Jennifer's feet was inarguably, again, a tennis ball. On the next point the serve came to her backhand and, braced against another lump of putty, she felt something lighter than a sparrow fly from her strings; it disappeared into the shadowy vault of the dome, beyond the ring of clear plastic portholes that admitted light, and fell far out of bounds in the form of an optic-yellow Wilson.

"Play fair, you two fiends," Sukie shouted across the net.

Jane Smart called back flutingly, "Keep your eye on the ball, sugar, and bad things won't happen."

"The hell you say, Jane Pain. I put perfect swings into both those shots." Sukie was angry because it wasn't *fair*, when her partner was an innocent. Jennifer, who had been poised on the half-court line, had seen only the outcome of these shots and turned now to show Sukie a forgiving, encouraging face, heart-shaped and flushed a bright pink. On the next exchange, the girl darted to the net after a weak return from Jane, and Sukie willed Alexandra to freeze; Jenny's sharp volley thudded against the big woman's immobilized flesh. Released from the spell in a twinkling, Alexandra rubbed the stung spot on her thigh.

Reproachfully she told Sukie, "That would have really hurt if I weren't wearing woolies under my tights."

A welt would arise there, though, and Sukie apologetically pleaded, "Come on, let's just play real tennis." But both opponents were sore now. A grinding pain seized Sukie's joints as she stretched to volley an easy shot coming over the center of the net; pulled up short, she helplessly watched the blurred ball bounce on the center stripe. But she heard Jenny's feet drum behind her and saw the ball, miraculously returned, drop between Jane and Alexandra, who had thought they had the point won. This brought the game back to deuce, and Sukie, still staggered by that sudden ache injected into her joints but determined to protect her partner from all this *malefica*, said the blasphemous backwards words *Retson Retap* three times rapidly to herself and created an air pocket, a fault in the crystal of space, above their opponents' forecourt, so that Jane double-faulted twice, the ball diving in mid-trajectory as from a table edge.

That made the game score five to one and brought the serve to Jenny. When she tossed the ball up, it became an egg and spattered all over her upturned face, through the gut strings. Sukie threw down her racket in disgust and it became a snake, that then had nowhere to slither to, the great bubble being sealed all along the edge; frantically the creature, damned at the dawn of creation, whipped its S's and zetas of motion back and forth across the blood-colored AsPhlex that framed the green court, its diagrammed baselines and boundaries. "All right," Sukie announced. "That does it. The game's over." Little Jenny with an inadequate feminine handkerchief was trying to wipe away from around her eyes the webby watery albumen and the yolk with its fleck of blood. The egg had been fertilized. Sukie took the hanky from her and dabbed. "I'm sorry, so sorry," she said. "They just can't stand to lose, they are terrible women."

"At least," Alexandra called across the net apologetically, "it wasn't a *rot*ten egg."

"It's all right," Jennifer said, a little breathless but her voice still level. "I knew you all have these powers. Brenda Parsley told me."

"That idiotic blabbermouth," Jane Smart said. The other two witches had come around the net to help wipe Jennifer's face. "We don't have any powers she doesn't, now that she's been left."

"Is that what does it, being left?" Jenny asked.

"Or doing the leaving," Alexandra said. "The strange thing is it doesn't make any difference. You'd think it would. Anyway, I'm sorry about the egg. But my thigh's going to be black and blue tomorrow because Sukie wouldn't let me move; it wasn't really playing the game."

Sukie said, "It was as much playing the game as what you were doing to me."

"You mis-hit those shots plain and simple," Jane Smart called over; she had gone to the edge of the court to look for something.

"I thought too," said Jennifer softly, courting the others, "your head came up, at least on the backhand."

"You weren't watching."

"I was. And you have a tendency to straighten your knees at impact."

"I *don't*. You're supposed to be my *part*ner. You're supposed to en*cour*age me."

"You were wonderful," the girl said obediently.

Jane returned holding in her cupped palm a little heap of black sand she had scraped up with her fingernails at the side of the court. "Close your eyes," she ordered Jennifer, and threw the sand directly into her face. Magically, the glutinous remains of egg evaporated, leaving, however, the grit, which gave the smooth upturned features a startled barbaric look, as if wearing a speckled mask.

"Maybe it's time for our bath," Alexandra remarked, gazing maternally at Jennifer's gritty face.

Sukie wondered how they could have their usual bath with these strangers among them and blamed herself, for having been too forthcoming in inviting them. It was her mother's fault; back home in New York State there had always been extra people at the dinner table, people in off the street, possible angels in disguise to her mother's way of thinking. Aloud Sukie protested, "But Darryl hasn't played yet! Or Christopher," she added, though the boy had been lackadaisical and arrogantly inept.

"They don't seem to be coming back," Jane Smart observed.

"Well we better go do something or we'll all catch cold," Alexandra said. She had borrowed Jenny's damp handkerchief (monogrammed *J*) and with an intricately folded corner of it was removing, grain by grain, the sand from the girl's docile round face, tilted up toward this attention like a pink flower to the sun.

Sukie felt a pang of jealousy. She swung her arms and said, "Let's go up to the house," though her muscles still had lots of tennis in them. "Unless somebody wants to play singles."

Jane said, "Maybe Darryl."

"Oh he's too marvellous, he'd slaughter me."

"I don't think so," Jenny said softly, having observed their host warm up and as yet unable to see, fully, the wonder of him. "You have much better form. He's quite wild, isn't he?"

Jane Smart said coldly, "Darryl Van Horne is quite the most civilized person I know. And the most tolerant." Irritably she went on, "Lexa dear, do stop fussing with that. It'll all come off in the bath."

"I didn't bring a bathing suit," said Jennifer, her eyes wide and questing from face to face.

"It's quite dark in there, nobody can see anything," Sukie told her. "Or if you'd rather you can go home."

"Oh, no. It's too depressing. I keep imagining Daddy's body hanging in midair and that makes me too scared to go up and start sorting the things in the attic."

And it occurred to Sukie that whereas the three of them all had children they should be tending to, Jennifer and Christopher *were* children, tending to themselves. She suffered a sad vision of Clyde's prick, a father's, which could have been her own father's and in truth *had* seemed a relic of sorts, with a jaundiced tinge on its underside when erect and enormously long gray hairs, like hairs from an old woman's head, snaking down from the testicles. No wonder he had overreacted when she spread her legs. Sukie led the other women out of the tennis bubble, whose oval door unzipped from either side and had to be used quickly, to keep the warm air from escaping. The dying December day nipped at their faces, their sneakered feet. Coal, that loathsome Labrador of Alexandra's, and Darryl's blotchy nervous collie, Needlenose, who had together trapped and torn apart some furry creature in the island's little woods, came and romped around them, their black muzzles bloody. The earth of the once gently bellied lawn leading up to the house had been torn by bulldozers to build the court this fall and the clumps of sod and clay, frozen hard, made a moonscape treacherous to tread. Tears of cold in Sukie's eyes gave her companions a rainbow aura and it hurt her cheeks to talk. On the firmness of the driveway she broke into a sprint; at her back the others followed like a single clumsy beast on the gravel. The great oak door yielded to her push as if sensate, and in the marble-floored foyer, with its hollow elephant's foot, a sulphurous pillow of heat hit her in the face. Fidel was nowhere in sight. Following a mutter of voices, the women found Darryl and Christopher sitting on opposite sides of the round leather-topped table in the library. Old comic books and a tea tray were arranged on the table between them. Above them hung the melancholy stuffed moose and deer heads that had been left by the sporting Lenoxes: mournful glass eyes that did not blink though burdened with dust. "Who won?' Van Horne asked. "The good or the wicked?"

"Which witch is which?" Jane Smart asked, flinging herself down on a crimson beanbag chair under a cliff of bound arcana, pale-spined giant volumes identified in spidery Latin. "The fresh blood won," she said, "as it usually does." Fluffy, malformed Thumbkin had been standing still as a statuette on the hearth tiles, so close to the fire the tips of her whiskers seemed to spark; now with great dignity she stalked over to Jane's ankles and, as if Jane's white athletic socks were scratching posts, sunk the arcs of her claws deeply in, her tail at the same time shivering bolt upright as though she were blissfully urinating. Jane yowled and with the toe of one sneakered foot hoisted the animal high into space. Thumbkin spun like a great snowflake before noiselessly landing on her double paws over near where the brass-handled poker, tongs, and ash shovel glittered in their stand. The offended cat's eyes blinked and then joined their brass glitter; the vertical pupils narrowed in their yellow irises, contemplating the gathering.

"They began to use dirty tricks," Sukie tattled. "I feel gypped."

"That's how you tell a real woman," joked Darryl Van

Horne in his throaty, faraway voice. "She always feels gypped."

"Darryl, don't be dreary and epigrammatical," Alexandra said. "Chris, does that tea taste as good as it looks?"

" 'TsO.K.," the boy managed to get out, sneering and not meeting anyone's eye.

Fidel had materialized. His khaki jacket looked more mussed than usual. Had he been with Rebecca in the kitchen?

"Té para las señoras y la señorita, por favor," Darryl told him. Fidel's English was excellent and increasingly idiomatic, but it was part of their master-servant relationship that they spoke Spanish as long as Van Horne knew the words.

"Sí, señor."

"Rápidamente," Van Horne pronounced.

"Sí, sí." Away he went.

"Oh isn't this cozy!" Jane Smart exclaimed, but in truth something about it dissatisfied Sukie and made her sad: the whole house was like a stage set, stunning from one angle but from others full of gaps and unresolved shabbiness. It was an imitation of a real house somewhere else.

Sukie pouted, "I didn't get the tennis out of my system. Darryl: come down and play singles with me. Just until the light goes. You're all suited up for it and everything."

He said gravely, "What about young Chris here? He hasn't played either."

"He doesn't want to I'm sure," Jennifer interjected in a sisterly voice.

"I stink," the boy agreed. He really was blah, Sukie thought. A girl his age would be so amusing, so alert and socially sensitive, gathering in impressions, turning them into flirtation and sympathy, making the room her web, her nest, her theatre. Sukie felt herself quite frantic, standing and tossing her hair, verging on rudeness and exhibitionism, and she didn't quite know what to blame, except that she was embarrassed at having brought the Gabriels here—never again!—and hadn't had sex with a man since Clyde committed suicide two weeks ago. She had found herself lately at night thinking of Ed, wondering what he was doing off in the underground with that little low-class smudge Dawn Polanski.

Darryl, intuitive and kind for all his coarse manner, rose in his red jogging pants and put his purple down vest back on, plus a Day-Glo orange hunting cap with a bill and earflaps that he sometimes wore for a joke, and took up his racket, an aluminum Head. "One quick set," he warned, "with a seven-point tie breaker, if it goes to six-six. First ball turns into a toad, you forfeit. Anybody want to come watch?" Nobody did, they were waiting for their *té*. Lonely as a married couple then, the two of them went out into the dimming gray afternoon—the silent woods and bushes lavender and the sky an enamelled green in the east—down to the dome with its graveyard closeness and quiet.

The tennis was grand; not only did Darryl play like a robot, clumsy-looking but infallible, but he drew forth from Sukie amazing shots, impossible gets turned into singing winners, the segmented breadths and widths of the court miniaturized by her unnatural speed and adroitness. The ball hung like a moon as she raced for it; her body became an instrument of thought, present wherever she willed it. She even brought off a few backhand overheads. She felt herself stretch at the top of her serves like a bow releasing an arrow. She was Diana, Isis, Astarte. She was female grace and strength shed, for this silver moment, of its rough garb of servitude. Gloom gathered in the corners of the dun bubble; the portholes of sky hovered overhead like a mammoth crown of aquamarines; her eyes could no longer see the dark opponent scrambling and thumping and heaving on the far side of the net. The ball kept coming back, and with pace, springing up at her face like a predator repeatedly reborn from the painted asphalt. Hit, hit, she kept hitting, and the ball got smaller and smaller—the size of a golf ball, the size of a golden pea, and at last there was no bounce on the inky far side of the net, just a leathery swallowing sound, and the game was over. "That was bliss," Sukie announced, to whoever was there.

Van Horne's voice scraped and rumbled forward, saying, "I was a pal to you, how's about being a pal to me?"

"O.K.," Sukie said. "What do I do?"

"Kiss my ass," he said huskily. He offered it to her over the net. It was hairy, or downy, depending on how you felt about men. Left, right . . .

"And in the middle," he demanded.

The smell seemed to be a message he must deliver, a word brought from afar, not entirely unsweet, a whiff of camel essence coming through the flaps of the silken tents of the Dragon Throne's encampment in the Gobi Desert.

"Thanks," Van Horne said, pulling up his pants. In the dark he sounded like a New York taxi driver, raspy. "Seems silly to you, I know, but it gives me a helluva boost."

They walked together up the hill, Sukie's sweat caking on her skin. She wondered how they would manage the hot tub with Jennifer Gabriel there and showing no disposition to leave. Back in the house, the loutish brother was alone in the library, reading a big blue volume that Sukie in a glance over his shoulder saw to be bound comic books. A caped man in a blue hood with pointed ears: Batman. "The complete fucking set," Van Horne boasted. "It cost me a bundle, some of those old ones, going back to the war, that if I'd had the sense to save as a kid I could have made a fortune on. Christ I wasted my childhood waiting for next month's issue. Loved The Joker. Loved The Penguin. Loved the Batmobile in its underground garage. You're both too young to have gotten the bug."

The boy uttered a simplete sentence. "They used to be on TV."

"Yeah, but they camped it up. They didn't have to do that. They made it all a joke, that was damn poor taste. The old comic books, there's real evil there. That white face used to haunt my dreams, I'm not kidding. How do you feel about Captain Marvel?" Van Horne pulled from the shelves a volume from another set, bound in red rather than blue, and with a comic fervor boomed, "Sha-ZAM!" To Sukie's surprise he settled himself in a wing chair and began to leaf through, his big face skidding with pleasure.

Sukie followed the faint sound of female voices through the long room of moldering Pop Art, the small room of unpacked boxes, and the double doors leading to the slate-lined bath. The lights in their round ribbed wells had been rheostatted to low. The stereo's red eye was watching over the gentle successions of a Schubert sonata. Three heads of pinned-up hair were disposed upon the surface of steaming water. The voices murmured on, and no head turned to watch Sukie undress. She slid from her many stiff layers of tennis clothes and walked through the humid air naked, sat on the stone edge, and arched her back to give herself to the water, at first too fiery to bear but then not, not. Oh. Slowly she became a new self. Water like sleep sucks our natural heaviness away. Alexandra's and Jane's familiar bodies bobbed about her; their waves and hers merged in one healing agitation. Jennifer Gabriel's round head and round shoulders rested in the center of her vision; the girl's round breasts floated just beneath the surface of the transparent black water and in it her hips and feet were foreshortened like a misbegotten fetus's. "Isn't this lovely?" Sukie asked her.

"It is."

"He has all these controls," Sukie explained.

"Is he going to come in with us?" Jennifer asked, afraid.

"I think not," Jane Smart said, "this time."

"Out of deference to you, dear," Alexandra added.

"I feel so safe. Should I?"

"Why not?" one of the witches asked.

"Feel safe while you can," another advised.

"The lights are like stars, aren't they? Random, I mean."

"Watch this." They all knew the controls now. At the push of a finger the roof rumbled back. The first pale piercings—planets, red giants—showed early evening's mothering turquoise dome to be an illusion, a nothing. There were spheres beyond spheres, each transparent or opaque as the day and year turned.

"My goodness. The outdoors."

"Yess."

"Yet I don't feel cold."

"Heat rises."

"How much money do you think he put into all this?"

"Thousands."

"But why? For what purpose?"

"For us."

"He loves us."

"Only us?"

"We don't really know."

"It's not a useful question."

"Aren't you content?"

"Yes."

"Yess."

"But I'm thinking Chris and I should be getting back. The pets should be fed."

"What pets?"

"Felicia Gabriel used to say we shouldn't waste protein on pets when everybody in Asia was starving."

"I didn't know Clyde and Felicia had pets."

"They didn't. But shortly after we got here somebody put a puppy in the Volvo one night. And a cat came to the door a little later."

"Think of us. We have children."

"Poor neglected little scruffy things," Jane Smart said in a mocking tone that indicated she was imitating another voice, a voice "out there" raised in hostile gossip against them.

"Well I was raised very protectively," Sukie offered, "and it got to be oppressive. Looking back on it I don't think my parents were doing me any favors, they were working out some problems of their own."

"You can't live others' lives for them," said Alexandra driftingly.

"Women must stop serving everybody and then getting even psychologically. That's been our politics up to now."

"Oh. That does feel good," Jenny said.

"It's therapy."

"Close the roof again. I want to feel *cozy*."

"And shut off the fucking Schubert."

"Suppose Darryl comes in."

"With that hideous kid."

"Christopher."

"Let them."

"Mm. You're strong."

"My art, it giffs me muskles efen ünter me fingernails, like."

"Lexa. How much tequila was in your tea?"

"How late does the supermarket toward Old Wick stay open?"

"I have no idea, I absolutely have stopped going there. If the Superette downtown doesn't have it, we don't eat it."

"But they have hardly any fresh vegetables and no fresh meat."

"Nobody notices. All they want are those frozen dinners so they don't have to come to the table and interrupt TV, and hero sandwiches. The onions they slop in! I think it's what made me stop kissing the brats good night."

"My oldest, it's incredible, nothing but crinkle chips and Pecan Sandies since he was twelve and still he's six foot two, and not a cavity. The dentist says he's never seen such a beautiful mouth."

"It's the fluoride."

"I *like* Schubert. He isn't always *after* you like Beethoven is."

"Or Mahler."

"Oh my God, Mahler."

"He really is monstrously too much."

"My turn."

"*My* turn."

"Ooh, lovely. You've found the spot."

"What does it mean when your neck always hurts, and up near your armpits?"

"That's lymph. Cancer."

"Please, don't even joke."

"Try menopause."

"I wouldn't care about that."

"I look forward to it."

"You do wonder, sometimes, if being fertile isn't over-rated."

"You hear terrible things about IUDs now."

"The best subs, funnily enough, are from that supertacky-looking pizza shack at East Beach. But they close October to August. I hear the man and his wife go to Florida and live with the millionaires in Fort Lauderdale, that's how well they do."

"That one-eyed man who cooks in a tie-dyed undershirt?"

"I've never been sure if it's really one eye or is he always winking?"

"It's his wife does the pizzas. I wish I knew how she keeps the crusts from getting soggy."

"I have all this tomato sauce and my children have gone on strike against spaghetti."

"Give it to Joe to take home."

"He takes enough home."

"Well, he leaves you something, too."

"Don't be coarse."

"*What* does he take home?"

"Smells."

"Memories."

"Oh. My goodness."

"Just let yourself float."

"We're all here."

"We're right with you."

"I feel that," Jenny said in a voice even smaller and softer than her usual one.

"How very lovely you are."

"Wouldn't it be funny to be that young again?"

"I can't believe I ever was. It must have been somebody else."

"Close your eyes. One last nasty piece of grit right here in the corner. There."

"Wet hair is really the problem, this time of year."

"The other day my breath froze my scarf right to my face."

"I'm thinking of getting mine layered. They say the new barber on the other side of Landing Square, in that little long building where they used to sharpen saws, does a wonderful job."

"On women?"

"They have to, men have stopped getting them. They've upped the price, though. Seven fifty, that's without any wave or wash or anything."

"The last thing I did for my father was wheel him into the barber for a haircut. He knew it was his last, too. He announced it to everybody, all these men sitting around. 'This is my daughter, who's bringing me in for the last haircut I'll have in my life.'"

"Kazmierczak Square. Have you seen the new sign?"

"Horrible. I can't believe it'll last."

"People forget. The schoolchildren now, World War Two to them is just a myth."

"Don't you wish you still had skin like this? Not a scar, not a mole."

"Actually, there is a little pink thing I noticed the other day, up high. Higher."

"Oh yess. That hurt?"

"No."

"Good."

"Did you ever notice, once you start investigating yourself for lumps like they say you should, they seem to be everywhere? The body is just *ter*ribly complicated."

"Please don't even make me think about it."

"In the new dictionary they got at the paper there are these transparencies bound in with regular pages at the entry 'Man,' only a woman's body is there too. Veins, muscles, bones, each on a sheet of their own, it's incredible. How it all fits."

"I don't think it's really complicated, it's just our thinking about it makes it complicated. Like a lot of things."

"How wonderfully round they are. Perfect semicircles.'

"Hemispheres."

"That sounds so political."

"Hemispheres of influence."

"That *is* one of the unjoys. Erogenous-zone sag. I looked at my bottom in the mirror the other day and here were these definite undeniable puckers. Maybe that's why I have a stiff neck."

"Nemo's makes a pretty good sausage sub."

"Too many hot red peppers. Fidel is getting to Rebecca. He's flavoring her."

"What color do you think their babies would be?"

"Beige."

"Mocha."

"Does that feel too intrusive?"

"Not exactly."

"How well she speaks!"

"Oh God: the trouble with being young and beautiful is nobody helps you really appreciate it. When I was twenty-two and at my peak I guess all I did was worry about pleasing my mother-in-law and if I was as good in bed as these whores Monty knew in college."

"It's like being rich. You know you have something and you get uptight about being taken advantage of."

"Darryl doesn't seem to let it worry him."

"How rich *is* he, really?"

"He still hasn't paid Joe's bill, I know."

"That's how the rich are. They hold their money and collect the interest."

"Pay attention, love."

"How can I not?"

"My fingertips are all shrivelled."

"Maybe it's time we see if amphibians can lay their eggs on land."

"Okey-dokey."

"Here we go."

Splashing, they emerged cumbersomely: silver born in a chemical tumult from lead. They groped for towels.

"Where *is* he?"

"Asleep? I gave him a pretty strenuous game, if I do say so."

"They say, unless you use oil afterwards, water isn't good for your skin past a certain age."

"We have ointments."

"We have buckets of ointments."

"Just stretch out. Are you still relaxed?"

"Oh yes. I really am."

"Here's another, just under your pretty little boob. Like a tiny pink snout." Dark as the room was, it did not seem strange that this could be seen, for the pupils of the four of them had expanded as if to overflow their gray, hazel, brown, and blue irises. One witch pinched Jennifer's false teat and asked, "Feel anything?"

"No."

"Good."

"Feel any shame?" another asked.

"No."

"Good," pronounced the third.

"*Is*n't she good?"

"She is."

"Just think, 'Float.' "

"I feel I'm flying."

"So do we."

"All the time."

"We're right with you."

"It's killing."

"I love being a woman, really," Sukie said.

"You might as well," Jane Smart said dryly.

"I mean, it's not just propaganda," Sukie insisted.

"My baby," Alexandra was saying.

"Oh" escaped Jenny's lips.

"Gently. Gentler."

"This is paradise."

"Well, *I* thought," Jane Smart said over the phone emphatically, as if certain of being contradicted, "she was a bit *too* ingratiating. Too demure and Alice-in-Wonderlandish. I think she's up to something."

"But what would that be? We're all poor as church mice and a town scandal besides." Alexandra's mind was still in her work-room, with the half-fleshed-out armatures of two floating, lightly interlocked women wondering, as she patted handfuls of paste-impregnated shredded paper here and there, why she couldn't muster the confidence she used to bring to her little clay figurines, her little hefty bubbies meant to rest so securely on end tables and rumpus-room mantels.

"Think of the situation," Jane directed. "Suddenly she's an orphan. Obviously she was making a mess of things out in Chicago. The house is too big to heat and pay taxes on. But she has nowhere else to go."

Lately Jane seemed intent on poisoning every pot. Outside the window, the sparrow-brown twigs of an as yet snowless winter moved in a cold breeze, and the swaying birdfeeder needed refilling. The Spofford children were home for Christmas vacation but had gone ice-skating, giving Alexandra an hour to work in; it shouldn't be wasted. "I thought Jennifer was a nice addition," she said to Jane. "We mustn't get ingrown."

"We mustn't ever leave Eastwick either," Jane surprisingly said. "Isn't it horrible about Ed Parsley?"

"What about him? Has he come back to Brenda?"

"In pieces he'll come back" was the cruel reply. "He and Dawn Polanski blew themselves up in a row house in New Jersey trying to make bombs." Alexandra remembered his ghostly face the night of the concert, her last glimpse of Ed, his aura tinged with sickly green and the tip of his long vain nose seeming to be pulled so that his face was slipping sideways like a rubber mask. She could have said then that he was doomed. Jane's harsh image of coming back in pieces sliced Alexandra, her crooked arm and hand floating away with the telephone and Jane's voice in it, while her eyes and body let the window mullions pass through them like the parallel wires of an egg slicer. "He was identified by the fingertips of a hand they found in the rubble," Jane was saying. "Just this hand by itself. It was all over television this morning, I'm surprised Sukie hasn't called you."

"Sukie's been a little huffy with me, maybe she felt upstaged by Jennifer the other night. Poor Ed," Alexandra said, feeling herself drift away as in a slow explosion. "She must be devastated."

"Not so it showed when I talked to her a half-hour ago.

She sounded mostly worried about how much of a story the new management at the *Word* would want; there's this boy in Clyde's office now younger than we are, he's been sent by the owners, who everybody thinks are front men for the Mafia that hangs out, you know, on Federal Hill. He's just out of Brown and knows nothing about editing."

"Does she blame herself?"

"No, why would she? She never urged Ed to leave Brenda and run off with that ridiculous little slut, she was doing what she could to hold the marriage together. Sukie told me she told him to stick with Brenda and the ministry at least until he had looked into public relations. That's what these ministers and priests who leave the church go into, public relations."

"I don't know, general involvement," Alexander weakly said. "Did they find Dawn's hands too?"

"I don't know what they found of Dawn's but I don't see how she could have escaped unless . . ." *Unless she were a witch* was the unspoken thought.

"Even that wouldn't do much against cordite, or whatever they call it. Darryl would know."

"Darryl thinks I'm ready for some Hindemith."

"Sweetie, that's wonderful. I wish he'd tell me I'm ready to go back to my bubbies. I miss the money, for one thing."

"Alexandra S. Spofford," Jane Smart chastised. "Darryl's trying to do something wonderful for you. Those New York dealers get ten thousand dollars for just a doodle."

"Not my doodles," she said, and hung up depressed. She didn't want to be a mere ingredient in Jane's poison pot, part of the daily local stew, she wanted to look out of her window and see miles and miles of empty golden land, dotted with sage, and the tips of the distant mountains a white as vaporous as that of clouds, only coming to a point.

Sukie must have forgiven Alexandra for being too taken

with Jenny, for she called after Ed's memorial service to give an account. Snow had fallen in the meantime: one does forget that annual marvel, the width of it all, the air given presence, the diagonal strokes of the streaming flakes laid across everything like an etcher's hatching, the tilted big beret the birdbath wears next morning, the deepening in color of the dry brown oak leaves that have hung on and the hemlocks with their drooping deep green boughs and the clear blue of the sky like a bowl that has been decisively emptied, the excitement that vibrates off the walls within the house, the suddenly supercharged life of the wallpaper, the mysteriously urgent intimacy the potted amaryllis on the window enjoys with its pale phallic shadow. "Brenda spoke," Sukie said. "And some sinister fat man from the Revolution, in a beard and ponytail. Said Ed and Dawn were martyrs to pig tyranny, or something. He became quite excited, and there was a gang with him in Castro outfits that I was afraid would start beating us up if anybody muttered or got out of line somehow. But Brenda was quite brave, really. She's gotten rather wonderful."

"She has?" A sheen, was how Alexandra remembered Brenda: a sleekly blond head of hair done up in a tight twist, turning away at the concert party amid the peacock confusion of auras. From other encounters her mind's eye could supply a long, rather chalky face, with complacent lips more brightly painted than one quite expected, with that vehement gloss of a rose about to drop its petals.

"She has her outfit down to a T now—dark suits with padded shoulders, and a silk necktie in front so broad it looks like a napkin she forgot to take out after eating lobster. She spoke for about ten minutes, about what a caring minister Ed had been, *so* interested in Eastwick and its delicate ecology and its conflicted young people and all that, until his conscience—and here, on the word 'conscience,' Brenda got her voice to break, you would have loved it, she dabbed with her hanky at her eyes, just one tear from each eye, ex*act*ly enough—until his conscience, she said, demanded he take his energies away from the confines of this town, where they were so much appreciated"—Sukie's powers of mimicry were in full gear now; Alexandra could see her upper lip crinkling and protruding drolly—"and devote them, these wonderful energies, to trying to correct the *dread*ful, my dear, malaise that is poisoning the heartblood of our nation. She said our nation is laboring under a malignant spell and looked me right in the eye."

"What did you do?"

"Smiled. It wasn't *me* who got him down there in New Jersey with the bomb squad, it was Dawn. Very little mention of her, by the way, when the fat man got done. Like none. Apparently they never found any pieces of her, just bits of clothing that could have come out of a closet. She was such a scruffy little thing maybe she sailed out through the roof. The Polanskis or whatever their name is, the stepfather and the mother, showed up, though, dressed like something out of a Thirties movie. I guess they don't get out of their trailer that often. I kept looking at the mother wondering about these acrobatics she does for the circus, I must say she's kept her figure; but her *face*. Frightening. So tough it was growing things all over it like you have on your heel from bad shoes. Nobody knew what to say to them, since the girl was just Ed's floozie and not even officially dead at that. Even Brenda didn't quite know how to handle it at the door, since the family was at the root of her troubles in a way, but I must say, she was magnificent—very courteous and *grande dame*, gave them her sympathy with a glistening eye. Brenda's not our sort, I know, but I really do admire the way she's picked herself up and made something of her situation. Speaking of situations . . ."

"Yes?" Alexandra asked on cue. The pause had been a probe to see if she was still paying attention. Alexandra had been idly making dots with her fingertips on the fogged patches in the lower panes of her kitchen window— semiconscious conjurings of snow, or Sukie's freckles, or the holes in the telephone mouthpiece, or the paint dabs with which Niki de Saint-Phalle decorated her internationally successful "Nanas." Alexandra was glad Sukie was talking to her again; she sometimes feared that if it were not for Sukie she would lose all contact with the world of daily events and go off sailing into the stratosphere just like little Dawn blown out of that house in New Jersey.

"I've been fired," Sukie said.

"Baby! You haven't! How could they, you're the only undreary thing about that paper now."

"Well, maybe you could say I quit. The boy who's taken Clyde's place, with some Jewish name I can't remember, Bernstein, Birnbaum, I don't even *want* to remember it, cut my obituary of Ed from a column and a half to two little dumb paragraphs; he said they had a space problem this week because another poor local has been killed in Vietnam but I know it's because everybody's told him Ed had been my lover and he's afraid of my going overboard in print and people tittering. A long time ago Ed had given me these poems he wrote in the style of Bob Dylan and I *had* put a couple of them in but wouldn't have complained if they'd come and asked me to cut those; but they even took out how he founded the Fair Housing Group and was in the top third of his class at Harvard Divinity School. I said to the boy, 'You've just come to Eastwick and I don't think you realize what a beloved figure Reverend Parsley was,' and this brat from Brown smiled and said, 'I've heard about his being beloved,' and I said, 'I quit. I work hard on my copy and Mr. Gabriel almost never cut a word.' That made this insufferable child smile all the more and there was nothing to do but walk out. Actually, before I walked out I took the pencil out of his hand and broke it right in front of his eyes."

Alexandra laughed, grateful to have such a spirited friend, a friend in three dimensions unlike those evil clown faces in her bedroom. "Oh Sukie, you honestly did?"

"Yes, and I even said, 'Go break a leg,' and threw the two pieces on his desk. The smug little kike. But now what do I do? All I have is about seven hundred dollars in the bank."

"Maybe Darryl. . ." Alexandra's thoughts did fly to Darryl Van Horne at all hours: his overeager face with its flecks of spit, and certain dusty corners of his home awaiting a woman's touch, and such moments as the frozen one after he had laughed his harsh brittle bark, when his jaw snapped shut and the world as it were had to come unstuck from a momentary spell. These images did not visit Alexandra's brain by invitation or with a purpose but as one radio station overlaps another as we travel a winding road. Whereas Sukie and Jane seemed to have gathered fresh strength and vehemence from their rites on the island, Alexandra found her independent existence had gone from clay to paper in substance and her sustaining ties with nature had slackened. She had let her roses head into winter unmulched; she had not composted the leaves as in other Novembers; she kept forgetting to fill the birdfeeder and no longer bothered to rap on the window to drive the greedy gray squirrels away. She dragged herself about with a lassitude that even Joe Marino noticed, and that discouraged him. Boredom in a wife is part of the social contract, but boredom in a mistress undermines a man. All Alexandra wanted was to soak her bones in the teak hot tub and lean her head on Van Horne's hairy matted torso while Tiny Tim warbled over the stereo, "Livin' in the sunlight, lovin' in the moonlight, havin' a wonderful time!"

"Darryl has his hands full," Sukie told her. "The town is about to shut off his water for nonpayment of his bill and he's, at my suggestion I guess, hired Jenny Gabriel to be his lab assistant."

"At your suggestion?"

"Well, she *was* this technician out in Chicago, and now here she is pretty much all alone. . . ."

"Sukie, your darling guilt. Aren't you sly?"

"I thought I owed her a *lit*tle something, and she does look awfully cute and serious in this little white coat over there. A bunch of us were over there yesterday."

"There was a party over there yesterday and nobody told me?"

"Not a real party. Nobody got undressed."

She must get hold of herself, Alexandra told herself. She must find a new center to her life.

"It was for less than an hour, baby, honest. It just happened. The man from town water was there too, with a court order or whatever they have to have. Then he couldn't find the turn-off and accepted a drink and we all tried on his hardhat. You know Darryl loves you best."

"He doesn't. I'm not as pretty as you are and I don't do all the things for him that Jane does."

"But you're his body type," Sukie reassured her. "You look good together. Sweetie, I really ought to run. I heard that Perley Realty might take on a new trainee in anticipation of the spring rush."

"You're going to sell real estate?"

"I might have to. I have to do something, I'm spending millions on orthodontia, and I can't imagine why; Monty had beautiful teeth, and mine aren't bad, just that slight overbite."

"But is Marge—what did you say about Brenda?—our sort?"

"If she gives me a job she is."

"I thought Darryl wanted you to write a novel."

"Darryl wants, Darryl wants," Sukie said. "If Darryl'll pay my bills he can have what he wants."

Cracks were appearing, it seemed to Alexandra after Sukie hung up, in what had for a time appeared perfect. She was behind the times, she realized. She wanted things never to change, or, rather, to repeat always in the same way, as nature does. The same tangle of poison ivy and Virginia creeper on the tumbled wall at the edge of the marsh, the same glinting mineral mix in the pebbles of the road. How magnificent and abysmal pebbles are! They lie all around us billions of years old, not only rounded smooth by centuries of the sea's tumbling but their very matter churned and remixed by the rising of mountains and their chronic eroding, not once but often in the vast receding cone of aeons, snow-capped mountains arisen where Rhode Island and New Jersey now have their marshes, while oceans spawned diatoms where now the Rockies rise, fossils of trilobites embedded in their cliffs. Museums had dazed Alexandra as a girl with their mineral exhibits, interlocked crystalline prisms in colors vulgar save that they came straight from nature, lepidolite and chrysoberyl and tourmaline with their regal names all struck off like giant frozen sparks in the churning of the earth, the very granite outcrops around us fluid, the continents bobbing in basalt. At times she felt dizzy, tied to all this massive incremental shifting, her consciousness a fleck of mica. The sensation persisted that she was not merely riding the universe but a partner to it, herself enormous within, capable of extracting medicine from the seethe of weeds and projecting rainstorms out of her thought. She and the seethe were one.

In winter, when the leaves fell, forgotten ponds moved closer, iced-over and brilliant, through the woods, and the summer-cloaked lights of the town loomed neighborly, and placed a whole new population of shadows and luminous rectangles upon the wallpaper of the rooms her merciless insomnia set her to wandering through. Her powers afflicted her most at night. The clown faces created by the overlapping peonies of her chintz curtains thronged the shadows and chased her from the bedroom. The sound of the children's breathing pumped through the house, as did the groans of the furnace. By moonlight, with a curt confident gesture of plump hands just beginning to show on their backs the mottling of liver spots, she would bid the curly-maple sideboard (which had been Oz's grandmother's) move five inches to the left; or she would direct a lamp with a base like a Chinese vase—its cord waggling and waving behind it in midair like the preposterous tail plumage of a lyrebird—to change places with a brass-candlestick lamp on the other side of the living room. One night a dog's barking in the yard of one of the neighbors beyond the line of willows at the edge of her yard irritated her exceptionally; without sufficient reflection she willed it dead. It had been a puppy, unused to being tied, and she thought too late that she might as easily have untied the unseen leash, for witches are above all adepts of the knot, the *aiguillette*, with which they promote enamorments and alliances, barrenness in women or cattle, impotence in men, and discontent within marriages. With knots they torment the innocent and entangle the future. The puppy had been known to her children and next morning the youngest of them, baby Linda, came home in tears. The owners were sufficiently incensed to have the vet perform an autopsy. He found no poison or sign of disease. It was a mystery.

The winter passed. In the darkroom of overnight blizzards, New England picture postcards were developed; the morning's sunshine displayed them in color. The not-quite-straight sidewalks of Dock Street, shovelled in patches, manifested patterns of compressed bootprints, like dirty white cookies with treads. A jagged wilderness of greenish ice cakes swung in and out with the tides, pressing on the bearded, barnacled pilings that underlay the Bay Superette. The new young editor of the *Word*, Toby Bergman, slipped on a frozen slick outside the barber shop and broke his leg. Ice backup during the owners' winter vacation on Sea Island, Georgia, forced gallons of water to seep by capillary action between the shingles of the Yapping Fox gift shop and to pour down the front inside wall, ruining a fortune in Raggedy Ann dolls and découpage by the handicapped.

The town in winter, deprived of tourists, settled more compactly upon itself, like a log fire burning late into the evening. A dwindled band of teen-agers hung out in front of the Superette, waiting for the psychedelic-painted VW van the drug dealer from south Providence drove. On the coldest days they stood inside and, until chased by the choleric manager (a moonlighting tax accountant who got by on four hours sleep a night), clustered in the warmth to one side of the electric eye, beside the Kiwanis gumball machine and the other that for a nickel released a handful of stale pistachios in shells dyed a psychedelic pink. Martyrs of a sort they were, these children, along with the town drunk, in his basketball sneakers and buttonless overcoat, draining blackberry brandy from a paper bag as he sat on his bench in Kazmierczak Square, risking nightly death by exposure; martyrs too of a sort were the men and women hastening to adulterous trysts, risking disgrace and divorce for their fix of motel love—all sacrificing the outer world to the inner, proclaiming with this priority that everything solid-seeming and substantial is in fact a dream, of less account than a merciful rush of feeling.

The crowd inside Nemo's—the cop on duty, the postman taking a breather, the three or four burly types collecting unemployment against the spring rebirth of construction and fishing—became as winter wore on so well known to one another and the waitresses that even ritual remarks about the weather and the war dried up, and Rebecca filled their orders without asking, knowing what they wanted. Sukie Rougemont, no longer needing gossip to fuel her column "Eastwick Eyes and Ears" in the *Word*, preferred to take her clients and prospective buyers into the more refined and feminine atmosphere of the Bakery Coffee Nook a few doors away, between the framer's shop run by two fags originally from Stonington

and the hardware store run by a seemingly endless family of
Armenians; different Armenians, in different sizes but all
with intelligent liquid eyes and kinky hair glistening low on
their foreheads, waited on you each time. Alma Sifton, the
proprietress of the Bakery Coffee Nook, had begun in what
had been an old clam shack, with simply a coffee urn and two
tables where shoppers who didn't want to run the gauntlet of
stares in Nemo's might have a pastry and rest their feet; then
more tables were added, and a line of sandwiches, mostly
salad spreads (egg, ham, chicken), easily dished up. By her
second summer Alma had to build an addition to the Nook
twice the size of the original and put in a griddle and
microwave oven; the Nemo's kind of greasy spoon was
becoming a thing of the past.

Sukie loved her new job: getting into other people's houses,
even the attics and cellars and laundry rooms and back halls,
was like sleeping with men, a succession of subtly different
flavours. No two homes had quite the same style or smell.
The energetic bustling in and out of doors and up and down
stairs and saying hello and good-bye constantly to people
who were themselves on the move, and the gamble of it all
appealed to the adventuress in her, and challenged her charm.
Her sitting hunched over at a typewriter inhaling other
people's cigarette smoke all day had not been healthy. She
took a night course in Westerly and passed her exam and got
her real-estate license by March.

Jane Smart continued to give lessons and fill in on the organ
at South County churches and to practice her cello. There
were certain of the Bach unaccompanied suites—the Third,
with its lovely bourrée, and the Fourth, with that opening
page of octaves and descending thirds which becomes a
whirling, inconsolable outcry, and even the almost impossible
Sixth, composed for an instrument with five strings—where
she felt for measures at a time utterly *with* Bach, his mind
exactly coterminous with hers, his vanished passion, lesser

even than dust dispersed, stretching her fingers and flooding her cerebral lobes with triumph, his insistent questioning of the harmonics an operation of her own perilous soul. So this was the immortality men had built their pyramids and rendered their blood sacrifices for, this rebirth of a drudging old wife-fucking Lutheran *Kapellmeister* in the nervous system of a late-twentieth-century bachelor girl past her prime. Small comfort it must bring to his bones. But the music did talk, in its syntax of variation and reprise, reprise and variation; the mechanical procedures accumulated to form a spirit, a breath that rippled the rapid mathematics of it all like those footsteps wind makes on still, black water. It was communion. Jane did not see much of the Neffs, now that they were involved in the circle Brenda Parsley had gathered around her, and would have been endlessly solitary but for the crowd at Darryl Van Horne's.

Where once there had been three and then four, now there were six, and sometimes eight, when Fidel and Rebecca were enlisted in the fun—in the game of touch football, for instance, that they played with a beanbag in the echoing length of the big living room, the giant vinyl hamburger and silkscreened Brillo boxes and neon rainbow all pushed to one side, jumbled beneath the paintings like junk in an attic. A certain contempt for the physical world, a voracious appetite for immaterial souls, prevented Van Horne from being an adequate caretaker of his possessions. The parqueted floor of the music room, which he had had sanded and polyurethaned at significant expense, already held a number of pits gouged by the endpin of Jane Smart's cello. The stereo equipment in the hot-tub room had been soaked so often there were pops and crackles in every record played. Most spectacularly, a puncture had mysteriously deflated the tennis-court dome one icy night, and the gray canvas lay sprawled there in the cold and snow like the hide of a butchered brontosaurus, waiting for spring to come, since Darryl saw no point in bothering with it until the court could be used as an outdoor court again. In the touch-football games, he was always one of the quarterbacks, his nearsighted bloodshot eyes rolling as he faded back to pass, the corners of his mouth flecked with a foam of concentration. He kept crying out, "The pocket, the pocket!"—begging for protection, wanting Sukie and Alexandra, say, to block out Rebecca and Jenny moving in for the tag, while Fidel circled out for the bomb and Jane Smart cut back for the escape-hatch buttonhook. The women laughed and bumbled at the game, unable to take it seriously. Chris Gabriel languidly went through the motions, like a disbelieving angel, misplaced in all this adult foolishness. Yet he usually came along, having made no friends of his own age; the small towns of America are generally empty of people of his age, at college as they are, or in the armed forces, or beginning their careers amid the temptations and hardships of a city. Jennifer worked many afternoons with Van Horne in his lab, measuring out grams and deciliters of colored powders and liquids, deploying large copper sheets coated with this or that doped compound under batteries of overhead sunlamps while tiny wires led to meters monitoring electrical current. One sharp jump of the needle, Alexandra was led to understand, and more than the riches of the Orient would pour in upon Van Horne; in the meantime, there was an acrid and desolate chemical stink dragged up from the dungeons of the universe, and a mess of unscrubbed aluminum sinks and spilled and scattered elements, and plastic siphons clouded and melted as if by sulphurous combustion, and glass beakers and alembics with hardened black sediments crusted to the bottoms and sides. Jenny Gabriel, in a stained white smock and the clunky big sunglasses she and Van Horne wore in the perpetual blue glare, moved through this hopeful chaos with curious authority, sure-fingered and quietly decisive. Here, as in their orgies, the girl—more than a girl, of course; indeed, only ten years younger than Alexandra—moved uncontaminable and in a sense untouched and yet among them, seeing, submitting, amused, unjudging, as if nothing were quite new to her, though her previous life seemed to have been one of exceptional innocence, the very barbarity of the times serving, in Chicago, to keep her within her citadel. Sukie had told the others how the girl had all but confided, in Nemo's, that she was still a virgin. Yet the girl disclosed her body to them with a certain shameless simplicity during the baths and the dances and submitted to their caresses not insensitively, and not without reciprocating. The touch of her hands, neither brusquely powerful like that of Jane's callused tips nor rapid and insinuating as with Sukie, had a penetration of its own, a gentle lingering as if in farewell, a forgiving slithering inquisitive something, ever less tentative, that pushed through to the bone. Alexandra loved being oiled by Jennifer, oiled while lying stretched on the black cushions or on several thicknesses of towels spread on the slates, the dampness of the bath enfolded and lifted up amid essences of aloe and coconut and almond, of sodium lactate and valerian extract, of aconite and cannabis indica. In the misted mirrors that Van Horne had installed on the outside of the shower doors, folds and waves of flesh glistened, and the younger woman, pale and perfect as a china figurine, could be seen kneeling in those angled deep distances mirrors create. The women developed a game called Serve Me, a sort of charade, though nothing like the charades Van Horne tried to organize in his living room when they were drunk but which collapsed beneath their detonations of mental telepathy and the clumsy fervor of his own mimicry, which disdained word-by-word enactments but sought to concentrate in one ferocious facial expression such full titles as *The History of the Decline and Fall of the Roman Empire* and *The Sorrows of Young Werther* and *The Origin of Species*. *Serve me*, the thirsty skins and spirits clamored, and patiently Jennifer oiled each witch, easing the transforming oils into the frowning creases, across the spots, around the bulges, rubbing against the grain of time, dropping small birdlike coos of sympathy and extollation.

"You have a lovely neck."

"I've always thought it was too short. Stubby. I've always hated my neck."

"Oh, you shouldn't have. Long necks are grotesque, except on black people."

"Brenda Parsley has an Adam's apple."

"Let's not be unkind. Let's think serene-making thoughts."

"Do me. Do me next, Jenny," Sukie nagged in a piping child's voice; she reverted quite dramatically, and while stoned was not above sucking her thumb.

Alexandra groaned. "What indecent bliss. I feel like a big sow rolling around."

"Thank God you don't smell that way," Jane Smart said. "Or does she, Jenny?"

"She smells very sweet and clean," Jenny primly said. From within that transparent bell of innocence or unknowing her slightly nasal voice came from as if far away, though distinctly; in the mirrors she was, kneeling, the shape and size and luster of one of those hollow porcelain birds, with holes at either end, from which children produce a few whistled notes.

"Jenny, the backs of my thighs," Sukie begged. "Just slowly along the backs, incredibly slowly. And use your fingernails. Don't be afraid of the insides of the thighs. The backs of the knees are wonderful. *Won*derful. Oh my God." Her thumb slid into her mouth.

"We're going to wear Jenny out," Alexandra warned in a considerate, drifting, indifferent voice.

"No, I like it," the girl said. "You're all so appreciative."

"We'll do you," Alexandra promised. "As soon as we get over this drugged feeling."

"I don't really care about being rubbed that much," Jenny

confessed. "I'd rather do it than have it done to me, isn't that perverse?"

"It works out very well for us," Jane said, hissing the last word.

"Yes it does," Jenny agreed politely.

Van Horne, out of respect perhaps for the delicate initiate, seldom bathed with them now, or if he did he left the room swiftly, his hairy body wrapped from waist to knees in a towel, to keep Chris entertained with a game of chess or backgammon in the library. He made himself available afterwards, however, wearing clothes of increasing foppishness—a silk paisley strawberry-colored bathrobe, for instance, with bellbottom slacks of a fine green vertical stripe protruding below, and a mauve foulard stuffed about his throat—and affecting an ever-more-preening manner of magisterial benevolence, to preside over tea or drinks or a quick supper of Dominican *sancocho* or Cuban *mondongo*, of Mexican *pollo picado con tocino* or Colombian *soufflé de sesos*. Van Horne watched his female guests gobble these spicy delicacies rather ruefully, puffing tinted cigarettes through a curious twisted horn holder he lately brandished; he had himself lost weight and seemed feverish with hopes for his selenium-based solution to the problem of energy. Away from this topic, he often fell apathetically silent, and sometimes left the room abruptly. In retrospect, Alexandra and Sukie and Jane Smart might have concluded that he was bored with them; but they were themselves so far from bored with him that boredom did not enter their imaginations. His vast home, which they had nicknamed Toad Hall, expanded their meagre domiciles; in Van Horne's realm they left their children behind and became children themselves.

Jane came faithfully for her sessions of Hindemith and Brahms and, most recently attempted, Dvořák's swirling, dizzying Concerto for cello in B Minor. Sukie as that winter slowly melted away began to trip back and forth with notes and diagrams for her novel, which she and her mentor believed could be preplanned and engineered, a simple verbal machine for the arousal and then the relief of tension. And Alexandra timidly invited Van Horne to come view the large, weightless, enamelled statues of floating women she had patted together with gluey hands and putty knives and wooden salad spoons. She felt shy, having him to her house, which needed fresh paint in all the downstairs rooms and new linoleum on the kitchen floor; and between her walls he did seem diminished and aged, his jaw blue and the collar of his button-down Oxford frayed, as if shabbiness were infectious. He was wearing that baggy green-and-black tweed jacket with leather elbow-patches in which she had first met him, and he seemed so much an unemployed professor, or one of those sad men who as eternal graduate students haunt every university town, that she wondered how she had ever read into him so much magic and power. But he praised her work: "Baby, I think you've found your *shtik*! That sort of corny carny quality Lindner has, but with you there's not that metallic hardness, more of a Miró feeling, and sexy—sex-*ee*, hoo boy!" With an alarming speed and clumsiness, he loaded three of her papier-mâché figures into the back seat of his Mercedes, where they looked to Alexandra like gaudy little hitch-hikers, corky bright limbs tangled and the wires that would suspend them from a ceiling snarled. "I'm driving to New York day after tomorrow more or less, and I'll show these to my guy on Fifty-seventh Street. He'll nibble, I'll bet my bottom buck; you've really caught something in the cultural works now, a sort of end-of-the-party feel. That unreality. Even the clips of the war on TV look unreal, we've all seen too many war movies."

Out in the open air, next to her car, dressed in a sheepskin coat with grimy cuffs and elbows, the matching sheepskin hat too small for his bushy head, he looked to Alexandra beyond capture, a lost cause; but, with an unpredictable lurch, he yielded to the bend of her mind and came back into the house with her and, breathing wheezily, up to her bedroom, to the bed she had lately denied to Joe Marino. Gina was pregnant again and that made it just too heavy. Darryl's potency had something infallible and unfeeling about it, and his cold penis hurt, as if it were covered with tiny little scales; but today, his taking her poor creations so readily with him to sell, and his stitched-together, slightly withered appearance, and the grotesque peaked sheepskin hat on his head, all had melted her heart and turned her vulva super-receptive. She could have mated with an elephant, thinking of becoming the next Niki de Saint-Phalle.

The three women, meeting downtown on Dock Street, checking in with one another by telephone, silently shared the sorority of pain that went with being the dark man's lover. Whether Jenny too carried this pain her aura did not reveal. When discovered by an afternoon visitor in the house, she always was wearing her lab coat and a frontal, formal attitude of efficiency. Van Horne used her, in part, because she was opaque, with her slightly brittle, deferential manner, her trait of letting certain vibrations and insinuations pass right through her, the somehow schematic roundness to her body. Within a group each member falls into a slot of special usefulness, and Jenny's was to be condescended to, to be "brought along," to be treasured as a version of each mature, divorced, disillusioned, empowered woman's younger self, though none had been quite like Jenny, or had lived alone with her younger brother in a house where her parents had met violent deaths. They loved her on their own terms, and, in fairness, she never indicated what terms she would have preferred. The most painful aspect of the afterimage the girl left, at least in Alexandra's mind, was the impression that she had trusted them, had confided herself to them as a woman usually first confides herself to a man, risking destruction in the determination to *know*. She had knelt among them like a docile slave and let her white round body shed the glow of its perfection upon their darkened imperfect forms sprawled wet on black cushions, under a roof that never slid back after, one icebound night, Van Horne had pushed the button and a flash made a glove of blue fire around his hairy hand.

Insofar as they were witches, they were phantoms in the communal mind. One smiled, as a citizen, to greet Sukie's cheerful pert face as it breezed along the crooked sidewalk; one saluted a certain grandeur in Alexandra as in her sandy riding boots and old green brocaded jacket she stood chatting with the proprietress of the Yapping Fox—Mavis Jessup, herself divorced, and hectic in complexion, and her dyed red hair hanging loose in Medusa ringlets. One credited to Jane Smart's angry dark brow, as she slammed herself into her old moss-green Plymouth Valiant, with its worn door latch, a certain distinction, an inner boiling such as had in other cloistral towns produced Emily Dickinson's verses and Emily Brontë's inspired novel. The women returned hellos, paid bills, and in the Armenians' hardware store tried, like everybody else, to describe with finger sketches in the air the peculiar thingamajiggy needed to repair a decaying home, to combat entropy; but we all knew there was something else about them, something as monstrous and obscene as what went on in the bedroom of even the assistant high-school principal and his wife, who both looked so blinky and tame as they sat in the bleachers chaperoning a record hop with its bloodcurdling throbbing.

We all dream, and we all stand aghast at the mouth of the caves of our deaths; and this is our way in. Into the nether world. Before plumbing, in the old outhouses, in winter, the accreted shit of the family would mount up in a spiky frozen stalagmite, and such phenomena help us to believe that there is more to life than the airbrushed ads at the front of magazines, the Platonic forms of perfume bottles and nylon nightgowns and Rolls-Royce fenders. Perhaps in the passage ways of our dreams we meet, more than we know: one white lamplit face astonished by another. Certainly the fact of witchcraft hung in the consciousness of Eastwick; a lump, a cloudy density generated by a thousand translucent overlays, a sort of heavenly body, it was rarely breathed of and, though dreadful, offered the consolation of completeness, of rounding out the picture, like the gas mains underneath Oak Street and the television aerials scraping *Kojak* and Pepsi commercials out of the sky. It had the uncertain outlines of something seen through a shower door and was viscid, slow to evaporate: for years after the events gropingly and even reluctantly related here, the rumor of witchcraft stained this corner of Rhode Island, so that a prickliness of embarrassment and unease entered the atmosphere with the most innocent mention of Eastwick.

iii *Guilt*

Recall the famous witch trials: the most acute and humane
judges were in no doubt as to the guilt of the accused; the
"witches" *themselves did not doubt it*—and yet there was
no guilt.

—*Friedrich Nietzsche, 1887*

"Y ou HAVE?" Alexandra asked Sukie, over the phone.
It was April; spring made Alexandra feel dopey and
damp, slow to grasp even the simplest thing through the
omnipresent daze of sap running again, of organic filaments
warming themselves once again to crack mineral earth and
make it yield yet more life. She had turned thirty-nine in
March and there was a weight to this too. But Sukie sounded
more energetic than ever, breathless with her triumph. She
had sold the Gabriel place.

"Yes, a lovely serious rather elderly couple called Hallybread. He teaches physics over at the University in Kingston
and she I think counsels people, at least she kept asking me
what *I* thought, which I guess is part of the technique they
learn. They had a house in Kingston for twenty years but he
wants to be nearer the sea now that he's retired and have a
sailboat. They don't mind the house's not being painted yet,
they'd rather pick the color themselves, and they have
grandchildren and step-grandchildren that come and visit so
they can use those rather dreary rooms on the third floor

where Clyde kept all his old magazines, it's a wonder the weight didn't break the beams."

"What about the emanations, will that bother them?" For some of the other prospects who had looked at the house this winter had read of the murder and suicide and were scared off. People are still superstitious, even with all of modern science.

"Oh yes, they had read about it when it happened. It made a big splash in every paper in the state except the *Word*. They were amazed when somebody, not me, told them this had been the house. Professor Hallybread looked at the staircase and said Clyde must have been a clever man to make the rope just long enough so his feet didn't hit the stairs. I said, Yes, Mr. Gabriel had been very clever, always reading Latin and these abstruse astrological things, and I guess I began to look teary, thinking of Clyde, because Mrs. Hallybread put her arm around me and began to act, you know, like a counsellor. I think it may have helped sell the house actually, it put us on this footing where they could hardly say no."

"What are their names?" Alexandra asked, wondering if the can of clam chowder she was warming on the stove would boil over. Sukie's voice through the telephone was seeking painfully to infuse her with vernal vitality. Alexandra tried to respond and take an interest in these people she had never met, but her brain cells were already so littered with people she had met and grown to know and got excited by and even loved and then had forgotten. That cruise on the *Coronia* to Europe twenty years ago with Oz had by itself generated enough acquaintances to populate a lifetime—their mates at the table with the edge that came up in rough weather, the people in blankets beside them on the deck having bouillon at elevenses, the couples they met in the bar at midnight, the stewards, the captain with his square-cut ginger beard, everyone so friendly and interesting because they were young, young; youth is a kind of money, it makes people fawn. Plus the people she had gone to high school and Conn. College with. The boys with motorcycles, the pseudo-cowboys. Plus a million faces on city streets, mustached men carrying umbrellas, curvaceous women pausing to straighten a stocking in the doorway of a shoe store, cars like cartons of faces like eggs driving constantly by—all real, all with names, all with souls they used to say, now compacted in her mind like dead gray coral.

"Kind of cute names," Sukie was saying. "Arthur and Rose. I don't know if you'd like them or not, they seemed practical more than artistic."

One of the reasons for Alexandra's depression was that Darryl had some weeks ago returned from New York with the word that the manager of the gallery on Fifty-seventh Street had thought her sculptures were too much like those of Niki de Saint-Phalle. Furthermore, two of the three had returned damaged; Van Horne had taken Chris Gabriel along to help with the driving (Darryl became hysterical on the Connecticut Turnpike: the trucks tailgating him, hissing and knocking on all sides of him, these repulsive obese drivers glaring down at his Mercedes from their high dirty cabs) and on the way home they had picked up a hitch-hiker in the Bronx, so the pseudo-Nanas riding in the back were shoved over to make room. When Alexandra had pointed out to Van Horne the bent limbs, the creases in the fragile papier-mâché, and the one totally torn-off thumb, his face had gone into its patchy look, his eyes and mouth too disparate to focus, the glassy left eye drifting outward toward his ear and saliva escaping the corners of his lips. "Well Christ," he had said, "the poor kid was standing out there on the Deegan a couple blocks from the worst slum in the fucking country, he coulda got mugged and killed if we hadn't picked him up." He thought like a taxi driver, Alexandra realized. Later he asked her, "Why don'tcha try working in wood at least? You think Michelangelo ever wasted his time with gluey old newspapers?"

"But where will Chris and Jenny go?" she mustered the wit to ask. Also on her mind uncomfortably was Joe Marino, who even while admitting that Gina was in a family way again was increasingly tender and husbandly toward his former mistress, coming by at odd hours and tossing sticks at her windows and talking in all seriousness down in her kitchen (she wouldn't let him into the bedroom any more) about his leaving Gina and their setting themselves up with Alexandra's four children in a house somewhere in the vicinity but out of Eastwick, perhaps in Coddington Junction. He was a shy decent man with no thought of finding another mistress; that would have been disloyal to the team he had assembled. Alexandra kept biting back the truth that she would rather be single than a plumber's wife; it had been bad enough with Oz and his chrome. But just thinking a thought so snobbish and unkind made her feel guilty enough to relent and take Joe upstairs to her bed. She had put on seven pounds during the winter and that little extra layer of fat may have been making it harder for her to have an orgasm; Joe's naked body felt like an incubus and when she opened her eyes it seemed his hat was still on his head, that absurd checked wool hat with the tiny brim and little iridescent brown feather.

Or it may have been that somewhere someone had tied an *aiguillette* attached to Alexandra's sexuality.

"Who knows?" Sukie asked in turn. "I don't think they know. They don't want to go back to where they came from, I know that. Jenny is so sure Darryl's close to making a breakthrough in the lab she wants to put all her share of the house money into his project."

This did shock Alexandra, and drew her full attention, either because any talk of money is magical, or because it had not occurred to her that Darryl Van Horne needed money. That *they* all needed money—the child-support checks ever later and later, and dividends down because of the war and the overheated economy, and the parents resisting even a dollar raise in the price of a half-hour's piano lesson by Jane Smart, and Alexandra's new sculptures worth less than the newspapers shredded to make them, and Sukie having to stretch her smile over the weeks between commissions—was assumed, and gave a threadbare gallantry to their little festivities, the extravagance of a fresh bottle of Wild Turkey or a jar of whole cashews or a tin of anchovies. And in these times of national riot, with an entire generation given over to the marketing and consumption of drugs, ever more rarely came the furtive wife knocking on the back door for a gram of dried orchis to stir into an aphrodisiac broth for her flagging husband, or the bird-loving widow wanting henbane with which to poison her neighbor's cat, or the timid teen-ager hoping to deal for an ounce of distilled moonwort or woadwaxen so as to work his will upon a world still huge in possibilities and packed like a honeycomb with untasted treasure. Nightclad and giggling, in the innocent days when they were freshly liberated from the wraps of housewifery, the witches used to sally out beneath the crescent moon to gather such herbs where they nestled at the rare and delicate starlit junction of suitable soil and moisture and shade. The market for all their magic was drying up, so common and multiform had sorcery become; but if they were poor, Van Horne was rich, and his wealth theirs to enjoy for their dark hours of holiday from their shabby sunlit days. That Jenny Gabriel might offer him money of her own, and he accept, was a transaction Alexandra had never envisioned. "Did you talk to *her* about this?"

"I told her I thought it would be crazy. Arthur Hallybread teaches physics and he says there is absolutely no foundation in electromagnetic reality for what Darryl is trying to do."

"Isn't that the sort of thing professors always say, to anybody with an idea?"

"Don't be so defensive, darling. I didn't know you cared."

"I don't care, really," Alexandra said, "what Jenny does

with her money. Except she *is* another woman. How did she react when you said this to her?"

"Oh, you know. Her eyes got bigger and stared and her chin turned a little more pointy and it was as if she hadn't heard me. She has this stubborn streak underneath all the docility. She's too good for this world."

"Yes, that is the message she gives off, I suppose," Alexandra said slowly, sorry to feel that they were turning on her, their own fair creature, their *ingénue*.

Jane Smart called a week or so later, furious. "Couldn't you have *guessed*? Alexandra, you *do* seem abstracted these days." Her *s*'s hurt, stinging like match tips. "She's moving in! He's invited her and that foul little brother to move in!"

"Into Toad Hall?"

"Into the old *Len*ox place," Jane said, discarding the pet name they had once given it as if Alexandra were stupidly babbling. "It's what she's been angling for all along, if we'd just opened our foolish eyes. We were so *nice* to that vapid girl, taking her in, doing our thing, though she always *did* hold back as if really she were above it all and time would tell, like some smug little Cinderella squatting in the ashes knowing there was this glass slipper in her future—oh, the *prissi*ness of her now is what gets me, swishing about in her cute little white lab coat and getting *paid* for it, when he owes everybody in town and the bank is thinking of foreclosing but it doesn't want to get stuck with the property, the upkeep is a *night*mare. Do you know what a new slate roof for that pile would run to?"

"Baby," Alexandra said, "you sound so financial. Where did you learn all this?"

The fat yellow lilac buds had released their first small bursts of heart-shaped leaves and the arched wands of forsythia, past bloom, had turned chartreuse like miniature willows. The gray squirrels had stopped coming to the feeder, too busy mating to eat, and the grapevines, which look so dead all winter, were beginning to shade the arbor again. Alexandra felt less sodden this week, as spring muddiness dried to green; she had returned to making her little clay bubbies, getting ready for the summer trade, and they were slightly bigger, with subtler anatomies and a deliberately Pop intensity to their coloring: she had learned something over the winter, by her artistic misadventure. So in this mood of rejuvenation she had trouble quickly sharing Jane's outrage; the pain of the Gabriel children's moving into a house that had felt fractionally hers sank in slowly. She had always held to the conceited fantasy that in spite of Sukie's superior beauty and liveliness and Jane's greater intensity and commitment to witchiness, she, Alexandra, was Darryl's favorite—in size and in a certain psychic breadth most nearly his match, and destined, somehow, to *reign* with him. It had been a lazy assumption.

Jane was saying, "Bob Osgood told me." He was the president of the Old Stone Bank downtown: stocky, the same physical type as Raymond Neff, but without a teacher's softness and that perspiring bullying manner teachers get; solid and confident, rather, from association with money Bob Osgood was, and utterly, beautifully bald, with a freshly minted shine to his skull and a skinned pinkness catching at his ears and his eyelids and nostrils, even his tapering quick fingers, as if he had stepped fresh from a steam room.

"You *see* Bob Osgood?"

Jane paused, registering distaste at the direct question as much as uncertainty how to answer. "His daughter Deborah is the last lesson on Tuesdays, and picking her up he's stayed once or twice for a beer. You know what an impossible bore Harriet Osgood is; poor Bob can't get it up to go home to her."

"Get it up" was one of those phrases the young had made

current; it sounded a bit false and harsh in Jane's mouth. But then Jane *was* harsh, as people from Massachusetts tend to be. Puritanism had landed smack on that rock and after regaining its strength at the expense of the soft-hearted Indians had thrown its steeples and stone walls all across Connecticut, leaving Rhode Island to the Quakers and Jews and antinomians and women.

"Whatever happened to you and those nice Neffs?" Alexandra asked maliciously.

Harshly Jane laughed, as it were hawked into the mouthpiece of the telephone. "*He* can't get it up at all these days; Greta has reached the point where she tells anybody in town who'll listen, and she practically asked the boy doing checkout at the Superette to come back to the house and fuck her."

The *aiguillette* had been tied; but who had tied it? Witchcraft, once engendered in a community, has a way of running wild, out of control of those who have called it into being, running so freely as to confound victim and victimizer.

"Poor Greta," Alexandra heard herself mumble. Little devils were gnawing at her stomach; she felt uneasy, she wanted to get back to her bubbies and then, once they were snug in the Swedish kiln, to raking the winter-fallen twigs out of her lawn, and attacking the thatch with a pitchfork.

But Jane was on her own attack. "Don't give me that pitying earth-mother crap," she said, shockingly. "What are we going to *do* about Jennifer's moving in?"

"But sweetest, what can we do? Except show how hurt we are and have everybody laughing at us. Don't you think the town won't be amused enough anyway? Joe tells me some of the things people whisper. Gina calls us the *streghe* and is afraid we're going to turn the baby in her tummy into a little pig or a thalidomide case or something."

"Now you're talking," Jane Smart said.

Alexandra read her mind. "Some sort of spell. But what

difference would it make? Jenny's there, you say. She has *his* protection."

"Oh it will make a difference believe you me," Jane Smart pronounced in one long shaking utterance of warning like a tremulous phrase drawn from a single swoop of her bow.

"What does Sukie think?"

"Sukie thinks just as I do. That it's an outrage. That we've been betrayed. We've nursed a viper, my dear, in our bos*ooms*. And I don't mean the vindow viper."

This allusion did make Alexandra nostalgic for the nights, which in truth had become rarer as winter wore on, when they would all listen, nude and soaking and languid with pot and California Chablis, to Tiny Tim's many voices surrounding them in the stereophonic darkness, warbling and booming and massaging their interiors; the stereophonic vibrations brought into relief their hearts and lungs and livers, slippery fatty presences within that purple inner space for which the dim-lit tub room with its asymmetrical cushions was a kind of amplification. "I would think things will go on much as before," she reassured Jane. "He loves *us*, after all. And it's not as if Jenny does half the things we do for him; it was us she liked to cater to. The way that upstairs rambles, it's not as if they'll all be sharing quarters or anything."

"Oh Lexa," Jane sighed, fond in despair. "It's really *you* who're the innocent."

Having hung up, Alexandra found herself less than reassured. The hope that the dark stranger would eventually claim her cowered in its corner of her imagining; could it be that her queenly patience would earn itself no more reward than being used and discarded? The October day when he had driven her up to the front door as to something they mutually possessed, and when she had to wade away through the tide as if the very elements were begging her to stay: could such treasured auguries be empty? How short life is, how quickly its signs exhaust their meaning. She caressed the underside of her left breast and seemed to detect a small lump there. Vexed, frightened, she met the bright beady gaze of a gray squirrel that had stolen into the feeder to rummage amid the sunflower-seed husks. He was a plump little gentleman in a gray suit with white shirtfront, come bright-eyed to dine. The effrontery, the greed. His tiny gray hands, mindless and dry as bird feet, were arrested halfway to his chest by sudden awareness of her gaze, her psyche's impingement; his eyes were set sideways in the oval skull so as to seem in their convexity opaque turrets, slanted and gleaming. The spark of life inside the tiny skull wanted to flee, to twitch away to safety, but Alexandra's sudden focus froze the spark even through glass. A dim little spirit, programmed for feeding and evasion and seasonal copulation, was meeting a greater. *Morte, morte, morte,* Alexandra said firmly in her mind, and the squirrel dropped like an instantly emptied sack. One last spasm of his limbs flipped a few husks over the edge of the plastic feeder tray, and the luxuriant frosty plume of a tail flickered back and forth a few more seconds; then the animal was still, the dead weight making the feeder with its conical green plastic roof swing on the wire strung between two posts of an arbor. The program was cancelled.

Alexandra felt no remorse; it was a delicious power she had. But now she would have to put on her Wellingtons and go outside and with her own hand lift the verminous body by its tail and walk to the edge of her yard and throw it into the bushes over the stone wall, where the bog began. There was so much dirt in life, so many eraser crumbs and stray coffee grounds and dead wasps trapped inside the storm windows, that it seemed all of a person's time—all of a woman's time, at any rate—was spent in reallocation, taking things from one place to another, dirt being as her mother had said simply matter in the wrong place.

* * *

Comfortingly, that very night, while the children were lurking around Alexandra demanding, depending upon their ages, the car, help with their homework, or to be put to bed, Van Horne called her, which was unusual, since his sabbats usually arose as if spontaneously, without the deigning of his personal invitation, but through a telepathic, or telephonic, merge of the desires of his devotees. They would find themselves there without quite knowing how they came to be there. Their cars—Alexandra's pumpkin-colored Subaru, Sukie's gray Corvair, Jane's moss-green Valiant—would take them, pulled by a tide of psychic forces. "Come on over Sunday night," Darryl growled, in that New York taxi-driver rasp of his. "It's a helluva depressing day, and I got some stuff I want to try out on the gang."

"It's not easy," Alexandra said, "to get a sitter on a Sunday night. They've got to get up for school in the morning and want to stay home and watch Archie Bunker." In her unprecedented resistance she heard resentment, an anger that Jane Smart had planted but whose growth was being fed now with her own veins.

"Ah come on. Those kids of yours are ancient, how come they still need sitters?"

"I can't saddle Marcy with the three younger, they don't accept her discipline. Also she may want to drive over to a friend's house and I don't want her not to be able to; it's not fair to burden a child with your own responsibilities."

"What gender friend the kid seeing?"

"It's none of your business. A girlfriend, as it happens."

"Christ, don't snap at *me*, it wasn't me conned you into having those little twerps."

"They're *not* twerps, Darryl. And I do neglect them."

Interestingly, he did not seem to mind being talked back to, which she had not done before: perhaps it was the way to his heart. "Who's to say," he responded mildly, "what's neglect?

If my mother had neglected me a little more I might be a better all-round guy."

"You're an O.K. guy." It felt forced from her, but she liked it that he had bothered to seek reassurance.

"Thanks a fuck of a lot," he answered with a jolting coarseness. "We'll see you when you get here."

"Don't be huffy."

"Who's huffy? Take it or leave it. Sunday around seven. Dress informal."

She wondered why next Sunday should be depressing to him. She looked at the kitchen calendar. The numerals were interlaced with lilies.

Easter evening turned out to be a warm spring night with a south wind pulling the moon backwards through wild, blanched clouds. The tide had left silver puddles on the causeway. New green marsh grass was starting up in the spaces between the rocks; Alexandra's headlights swung shadows among the boulders and across the tree-intertwined entrance gate. The driveway curved past where the egrets used to nest and now the collapsed tennis-court bubble lay creased and hardened like a lava flow; then her car climbed, circling the mall lined by noseless statues. As the stately silhouette of the house loomed, the grid of its windows all alight, her heart lifted into its holiday flutter; always, coming here, night or day, she expected to meet the momentous someone who was, she realized, herself, herself unadorned and untrammelled, forgiven and nude, erect and perfect in weight and open to any courteous offer: the beautiful stranger, her secret self. Not all the next day's weariness could cure her of the exalted expectation that the Lenox place aroused. Your cares evaporated in the entry hall, where the sulphurous scents greeted you, and an apparent elephant's-foot umbrella stand holding a cluster of old-fashioned knobs and handles on second glance turned out to be a single painted casting, even to the little strap and snap button holding the umbrella furled—one more mocking work of art.

Fidel took her jacket, a man's zippered windbreaker. More and more Alexandra found men's clothes comfortable; first she began to buy their shoes and gloves, then corduroy and chino trousers that weren't so nipped at the waist as women's slacks were, and lately the nice, roomy, efficient jackets men hunt and work in. Why should they have all the comfort while we martyr ourselves with spike heels and all the rest of the slave-fashions sadistic fags wish upon us?

"*Buenas noches, señora,*" Fidel said. "*Es muy agradable tenerla nuevamente en esta casa.*"

"The mister have all sort of gay party planned," Rebecca said behind him. "Oh there big changes afoot."

Jane and Sukie were already in the music room, where some oval-backed chairs with a flaking silvery finish had been set out; Chris Gabriel slouched in a corner near a lamp, reading *Rolling Stone*. The rest of the room was candlelit; candles in all the colors of jellybeans had been found for the cobwebbed sconces along the wall, each draft-tormented little flame doubled by a tin mirror. The aura of the flames was an acrid complementary color: green eating into the orange glow yet constantly repelled, like the viscid contention amid unmixing chemicals. Darryl, wearing a tuxedo of an old-fashioned double-breasted cut, its black dull as soot but for the broad lapels, came up and gave her his cold kiss. Even his spit on her cheek was cold. Jane's aura was slightly muddy with anger and Sukie's rosy and amused, as usual. They had all, in their sweaters and dungarees, evidently underdressed for the occasion.

The tuxedo did give Darryl a less patchy and shambling air than usual. He cleared his froggy throat and announced, "Howzabout a little concert? I've been working up some ideas here and I want to get you girls' feedback. The first number is entitled"—he froze in mid-gesture, his sharp little greenish teeth gleaming, his spectacles for the night so small

that the pale-plastic frames seemed to have his eyes trapped—
"The 'A Nightingale Sang in Berkeley Square Boogie.' "

Masses of notes were struck off as if more than two hands
were playing, the left hand setting up a deep cloudy stride
rhythm, airy but dark like a thunderhead growing closer
above the treetops, and then the right hand picking out, in
halting broken phrases so that the tune only gradually
emerged, the rainbow of the melody. You could see it, the
misty English park, the pearly London sky, the dancing
cheek-to-cheek, and at the same time feel the American
rumble, the good gritty whorehouse tinkling only this conti-
nent could have cooked up, in the tasselled brothels of a
southern river town. The melody drew closer to the bass, the
bass moved up and swallowed the nightingale, a wonderfully
complicated flurry ensued while Van Horne's pasty seamed
face dripped sweat onto the keyboard and his grunts of effort
smudged the music; Alexandra pictured his hands as white
waxy machines, the phalanges and flexor tendons tugging and
flattening and directly connected to the rods and felts and
strings of the piano, this immense plangent voice one hyper-
developed fingernail. The themes drew apart, the rainbow
reappeared, the thunderhead faded into harmless air, the
melody was restated in an odd high minor key reached
through an askew series of six descending, fading chords
struck across the collapsing syncopation.

Silence, but for the hum of the piano's pounded harp.

"Fantastic," Jane Smart said dryly.

"Really, baby," Sukie urged upon their host, exposed and
blinking now that his exertion was over. "I've never heard
anything like it."

"I could cry," Alexandra said sincerely, he had stirred such
memories within her, and such inklings of her future; music
lights up with its pulsing lamp the cave of our being.

Darryl seemed disconcerted by their praise, as if he might
be dissolved in it. He shook his shaggy head like a dog drying

itself, and then seemed to press his jaw back into place with the same two fingers that wiped the corners of his mouth. "That one mixed pretty well," he admitted. "O.K., let's try this one now. It's called 'The How High the Moon March.'" This mix went less well, though the same wizardry was in operation. A wizardry, Alexandra thought, of theft and transformation, with nothing of guileless creative engendering about it, only a boldness of monstrous combination. The third offering was the Beatles' tender "Yesterday," broken into the stutter-rhythms of a samba; it made them all laugh, which hadn't been the effect of the first and which wasn't perhaps the intention. "So," Van Horne said, rising from the bench. "That's the idea. If I could work up a dozen or so of these a friend of mine in New York says he has an in with a recording executive and maybe we can raise a modicum of moolah to keep this establishment afloat. So what's your input?"

"It may be a bit . . . special," Sukie offered, her plump upper lip closing upon her lower in a solemn way that looked nevertheless amused.

"What's special?" Van Horne asked, pain showing, his face about to fly apart. "Tiny Tim was special. Liberace was special. Lee Harvey Oswald was special. To get any attention at all in this day and age you got to be way out."

"This establishment needs moolah?" Jane Smart asked sharply.

"So I'm told, toots."

"Honey, by whom?" Sukie asked.

"Oh," he said, embarrassed, squinting out through the candlelight as if he could see nothing but reflections, "a bunch of people. Banker types. Prospective partners." Abruptly, in tune perhaps with the old tuxedo, he ducked into horror-movie clowning, bobbing in his black outfit as if crippled, his legs hinged the wrong way. "That's enough business," he said. "Let's go into the living room. Let's get *smashed*."

Something was up. Alexandra felt a sliding start within her; an immense slick slope of depression was revealed as if by the sliding upwards of an automatic garage door, the door activated by a kind of electric eye of her own internal sensing and giving on a wide underground ramp whose downward trend there was no reversing, not by pills or sunshine or a good night's sleep. Her life had been built on sand and she knew that everything she saw tonight was going to strike her as sad.

The dusty ugly works of Pop Art in the living room were sad, and the way several fluorescent tubes in the track lighting overhead were out or flickered, buzzing. The great long room needed more people to fill it with the revelry it had been designed for; it seemed to Alexandra suddenly an ill-attended church, like those that Colorado pioneers had built along the mountain roads and where no one came any more, an ebbing more than a renunciation, everybody too busy changing the plugs in their pickup truck or recovering from Saturday night, the parking places outside gone over to grass, the pews with their racks still stocked with hymnals visible inside. "Where's Jenny?' she asked aloud.

"The lady still cleaning up in de labora*tory*," Rebecca said. "She works so hard, I worry sickness take her."

"How's it all going?" Sukie asked Darryl. "When can I paint my roof with kilowatts? People still stop me on the street and ask about that because of the story I wrote on you."

"Yeah," he snarled, ventriloquistically, so the voice emerged from well beside his head, "and those old fogies you sold the Gabriel dump to bad-mouthing the whole idea, I hear. Fuck 'em. They laughed at Leonardo. They laughed at Leibniz. They laughed at the guy who invented the zipper, what the hell was his name? One of invention's unsung greats. Actually, I've been wondering if microörganisms aren't the way to go—use a mechanism that's already set in place and self-replicates. Biogas technology: you know who's way ahead in that department? The Chinese, can you believe it?"

"Couldn't we just use less electricity?" Sukie asked, interviewing out of habit. "And use our bodies more? Nobody needs an electric carving knife."

"You need one if your neighbor has one," Van Horne said. "And then you need another to replace the one you get. And another. And another. Fidel! *Deseo beber!*"

The servant in his khaki pajamas, abjectly shapeless and yet also with a whisper of military menace, brought drinks, and a tray of *huevos picantes* and palm hearts. Without Jenny here, surprisingly, conversation lagged; they had grown used to her, as someone to display themselves to, to amuse and shock and instruct. Her wide-eyed silence was missed. Alexandra, hoping that art, any art, might staunch the internal bleeding of her melancholy, moved among the giant hamburgers and ceramic dartboards as if she had never seen them before; and indeed some of them she hadn't. On a four-foot plinth of plywood painted black, beneath a plastic pastry bell, rested an ironically realistic replica—a three-dimensional Wayne Thiebaud—of a white-frosted wedding cake. Instead of the conventional bride and groom, however, two nude figures stood on the topmost tier, the female pink and blonde and rounded and the black-haired man a darker pink, but for the dead-white centimeter of his semi-erect penis. Alexandra wondered what the material of this fabrication was: the cake lacked the scoring of cast bronze and also the glaze of enamelled ceramic. Acrylicked plaster was her guess. Seeing that no one but Rebecca, passing a tray of tiny crabs stuffed with *xu-xu* paste, was observing her, Alexandra lifted the bell and touched the frostinglike rim of the object. A tender dab of it came away on her finger. She put the finger in her mouth. Sugar. It was real frosting, a real cake, and fresh.

Darryl, with wide splaying gestures, was outlining another energy approach to Sukie and Jane. "With geothermal, once you get the shaft dug—and why the hell not? they make tunnels twenty miles long over in the Alps every day of the week—your only problem is keeping the energy from burning up the converter. Metal will melt like lead soldiers on Venus. You know what the answer is? Unbelievably simple. Stone. You got to make all your machinery, all the gearing and turbines, out of stone. They can do it! They can chisel granite now as fine as they can mill steel. They can make springs out of poured cement, would you believe?—particle size is what it all boils down to. Metal has had it, just like flint when the Bronze Age came in."

Another work of art Alexandra hadn't noticed before was a glossy female nude, a mannequin without the usual matte skin and the hinged limbs, a Kienholz in its assaultiveness but smooth and minimally defined in the manner of Tom Wesselmann, crouching as if to be fucked from behind, her face blank and bland, her back flat enough to be a tabletop. The indentation of her spine was straight as the groove for blood in a butcher's block. The buttocks suggested two white motorcycle helmets welded together. The statue stirred Alexandra with its blasphemous simplification of her own, female form. She took another margarita from Fidel's tray, savored the salt (it is a myth and absurd slander that witches abhor salt; saltpeter and cod liver oil, both associated with Christian virtue, are what they cannot abide), and sauntered up to their host. "I feel sexy and sad," she said. "I want to take my bath and smoke my joint and get home. I swore to the babysitter I'd be home by ten-thirty; she was the fifth girl I tried and I could hear her mother shouting at her in the background. These parents don't want them to come near us."

"You're breaking my heart," Van Horne said, looking sweaty and confused after his gaze into the geothermal furnace. "Don't rush things. I don't feel smashed yet. There's a schedule here. Jenny's about to come down."

Alexandra saw a new light in Van Horne's glassy bloodshot

eyes; he looked scared. But what could scare *him*?

Jenny's tread was silent on the carpeted curved front staircase; she came into the long room with her hair pulled back like Eva Perón's and wearing a powder-blue bathrobe that swept the floor. Above each of her breasts the robe bore as decoration three embroidered cuts like large buttonholes, which reminded Alexandra of military chevrons. Jenny's face, with its wide round brow and firm triangular chin, was shiny-clean and devoid of make-up; nor did a smile adorn it. "Darryl, don't get drunk," she said. "You make even less sense when you're drunk than when you're sober."

"But he gets in*spi*red," Sukie said with her practiced sauciness, feeling her way with this new woman, in residence and somehow in charge.

Jenny ignored her, looking around, past their heads. "Where's dear Chris?"

From the corner Rebecca said, "Young man in de liberry reading his magazines."

Jenny took two steps forward and said, "Alexandra. Look." She untied her cloth belt and spread the robe's wings wide, revealing her white body with its roundnesses, its rings of baby fat, its cloud of soft hair smaller than a man's hand. She asked Alexandra to look at that translucent wart under her breast. "Do you think it's getting bigger or am I imagining it? And up here," she said, guiding the other woman's fingers into her armpit. "Do you feel a little lump?"

"It's hard to say," Alexandra said, flustered, for such touching occurred in the steamy dark of the tub room but not in the bald fluorescent light here. "We're all so full of little lumps just naturally. I don't feel anything."

"You aren't con*cen*trating," Jenny said, and with a gesture that in another context would have seemed loving took Alexandra's wrist in her fingers and led her right hand to the other armpit. "There's sort of the same thing there too. Please, Lexa. Concentrate."

A faint bristle of shaven hair. A silkiness of applied powder. Underneath, lumps, veins, glands, nodules. Nothing in nature is quite homogeneous; the universe was tossed off freehand. "Hurt?" she asked.

"I'm not sure. I feel *some*thing."

"I don't think it's anything," Alexandra pronounced.

'Could it be connected with this somehow?" Jenny lifted her firm conical breast to further expose her transparent wart, a tiny cauliflower or pug face of pink flesh gone awry.

"I don't think so. We all get those."

Suddenly impatient, Jenny closed her bathrobe and pulled the belt tight. She turned to Van Horne. "Have you told them?"

"My dear, my dear," he said, wiping the corners of his smiling mouth with a trembling thumb and finger. "We must make a ceremony of it."

"The fumes today have given me a headache and I think we've all had enough ceremonies. Fidel, just bring me a glass of soda water, *aqua gaseosa, o horchata, por favor. Pronto, gracias.*"

"The wedding cake," exclaimed Alexandra, with an icy thrill of clairvoyance.

"Now you're cooking, little Sandy," Van Horne said. "You've got it. I saw you poke and lick that finger," he teased.

"It wasn't that so much as Jenny's manner. Still, I can't believe it. I know it but I can't believe it."

"You better believe it, ladies. The kid here and I were married as of yesterday afternoon at three-thirty p.m. The craziest little justice of the peace up in Apponaug. He stuttered. I never thought you could have a stutter and still get the license. D-d-d-do you, D-D-D-D-D—"

"Oh Darryl, you didn't!" Sukie cried, her lips pulled so far back in a mirthless grin that the hollows at the top of her upper gums showed.

Jane Smart hissed at Alexandra's side.

"How could you two do that to us?" Sukie asked.

The word "us" surprised Alexandra, who felt this announcement as a sudden sore place in her abdomen alone.

"So sneakily," Sukie went on, her cheerful party manner slightly stiff on her face. "We would at least have given her a shower."

"Or some casserole dishes," Alexandra said bravely.

"She did it," Jane was saying seemingly to herself but of course for Alexandra and the others to overhear. "She actually managed to pull it off."

Jenny defended herself; the color in her cheeks was high. "It wasn't so much managing, it just came to seem natural, me here all the time anyway, and naturally . . ."

"Naturally nature took its nasty natural course," Jane spit out.

"Darryl, what's in it for you?" Sukie asked him, in her frank and manly reporter's voice.

"Oh, you know," he said sheepishly. "The standard stuff. Settle down. Security. Look at her. She's beautiful."

"Bullshit," Jane Smart said slowly, the word simmering.

"With all respect, Darryl, and I *am* fond of our little Jenny," Sukie said, "she *is* a bit of a blah."

"Come on, cut it out, what sort of reception is this?" the big man said helplessly, while his robed bride beside him didn't flinch, taking shelter as she always had behind the brittle shield of innocence, the snobbery of ignorance. It was not that her brain was less efficient than theirs, within its limits it was more so; but it was like the keyboard of an adding machine as opposed to that of typewriters. Van Horne was trying to collect his dignity. "Listen, you bitches," he said. "What's this attitude that I owe you anything? I took you in, I gave you eats and a little relief from your lousy lives—"

"Who made them lousy?" Jane Smart swiftly asked.

"Not me. I'm new in town."

Fidel brought in a tray of long-stemmed glasses of champagne. Alexandra took one and tossed its contents at Van Horne's face; the rarefied liquid fell short, wetting only the area of his fly and one pants leg. All she had achieved was to make him seem the victim and not herself. She threw the glass vehemently at the sculpture of intertwined automobile bumpers; here her aim was better, but the glass in mid-flight turned into a barn swallow, and flicked itself away. Thumbkin, who had been licking herself on the satin love seat, worrying with avid tongue the tiny pink gap in her raiment of long white fur, perked up and gave chase; with that comical deadly solemnity of cats, green eyes flattened across the top, she stalked along the back of the curved four-cushion sofa and batted in frustration at the air when she reached the edge. The bird took shelter by perching upon a hanging Styrofoam cloud by Marjorie Strider.

"Hey, this isn't at all the way I pictured it," Van Horne complained.

"How *did* you picture it, Darryl?" Sukie asked.

"As a blast. We thought you'd be pleased as hell. You brought us together. You're like Cupids. You're like the maids of honor."

"I *never* thought they'd be pleased," Jenny corrected. 'I just didn't think they'd be quite so ill-mannered."

"Why *would*n't they be pleased?" Van Horne held his rubbery strange hands open in a supplicatory fashion, arguing with Jenny, and they did look the very tableau of a married couple. "We'd be pleased for *them*," he said, "if some schnook came along and took 'em off the market. I mean, what's this jealousy bag, with the whole damn world going up in napalm? How fucking bourgeois can you get?"

Sukie was the first to soften. Perhaps she just wanted to nibble something. "All right," she said. "Let's eat the cake. It better have hash in it."

"The best. Orinoco beige."

Alexandra had to laugh, Darryl was so funny and hopeful and discombobulated. "There is no such thing."

"Sure there is, if you know the right people. Rebecca knows the guys who drive that crazy-painted van down from south Providence. *La crème de la crooks*, honest. You'll fly out of here. Wonder what the tide's doing?"

So he did remember: her braving the ice-cold tide that day, and him standing on the far shore shouting "You *can* fly!"

The cake was set on the tablelike back of the crouching nude. The marzipan figures were removed and broken and passed around for them to eat in a circle. Alexandra got the prick—tribute of a sort. Darryl mumbled *"Hoc est enim corpus meum"* as he did the distribution; over the champagne he intoned, *"Hic est enim calix sanguinis mei."* Across from Alexandra, Jenny's face had turned a radiant pink; she was allowing her joy to show, she was dyed clear through by the blood of triumph. Alexandra's heart went out to her, as if to a younger self. They all fed cake to one another with their fingers; soon its tiered cylinders looked eviscerated by jackals. Then they linked dirty hands and, their backs to the crouching statue, upon whose left buttock Sukie with lipstick and frosting had painted a grinning snaggle-toothed face, they danced in a ring, chanting in the ancient fashion, *"Emen hatan, Emen hetan"* and *"Har, har, diable, diable, saute ici, saute là, joue ici, joue là!"*

Jane, by now the drunkest of them, tried to sing all the stanzas to that unspeakable Jacobean song of songs, "Tinkletum Tankletum," until laughter and alcohol broke her memory down. Van Horne juggled first three, then four, then five tangerines, his hands a frantic blur. Christopher Gabriel stuck his head out of the library to see what all the hilarity was about. Fidel had been holding back some marinated capybara balls, which now he served forth. The night was becoming a success; but when Sukie proposed that they all go have a bath now, Jenny announced with a certain firmness, "The tub's been drained. It had gotten all scummy, and we're waiting for a man from Narragansett Pool Hygiene to come and give the teak a course of fungicide."

So Alexandra got home earlier than expected and surprised the babysitter intertwined with her boyfriend on the sofa downstairs. She backed out of the room and reëntered ten minutes later and paid the embarrassed sitter. The girl was an Arsenault and lived downtown; her friend would drive her home, she said. Alexandra's next action was to go upstairs and tiptoe into Marcy's room and verify that her daughter, seventeen and a woman's size, was virginally asleep. But for hours into the night the vision of the pallid undersides of the Arsenault girl's thighs clamped around the nameless boy's furry buttocks, his jeans pulled down just enough to give his genitals freedom while she had been stripped of all her clothes, burned in Alexandra's brow like the moon sailing backwards through tattered, troubled clouds.

They met, the three of them, somewhat like old times, in Jane Smart's house, the ranch house in the Cove development that had been such a comedown, really, for Jane after the lovely thirteen-room Victorian, with its servants' passageways and ornamental ball-and-stick work and Tiffany-glass chandeliers, that she and Sam in their glory days had owned on Vane Street, one block back from Oak, away from the water. Her present house was a split-level ranch standing on the standard quarter-acre, its shingled parts painted an acid blue. The previous owner, an underemployed mechanical engineer who had finally gone to Texas in pursuit of work, had spent his abundant spare time "antiquing" the little house, putting up pine cabinets and false boxed beams, and knotty wainscoting with induced chisel scars, and even installing light switches in the form of wooden pump handles and a toilet bowl sheathed in oaken barrel staves. Some walls were hung with old carpentry tools, plow planes and frame saws and drawknives; and a small spinning wheel had been cunningly incorporated into the banister at the landing where the split in levels occurred. Jane had inherited this fussy overlay of Puritania without overt protest; but her contempt and that of her children had slowly eroded the precious effect. Whittled light switches were snapped in rough haste. Once one stave had been broken by a kick, the whole set of them collapsed around the toilet bowl. The cute boxy toilet-paper holder had come apart too. Jane gave her piano lessons at the far end of the long open living room, up six steps from the kitchen-dinette-den level, and the uncarpeted living-room floor showed the ravages of an apparently malign fury; the pin of her cello had gouged a hole wherever she had decided to set her stand and chair. And she had roamed the area fairly widely, rather than play in one settled place. Nor did the damage end there; everywhere in the newish little house, built of green pine and cheap material in a set pattern like a series of dances enacted by the construction crews, were marks of its fragility, scars in the paint and holes in the plasterboard and missing tiles on the kitchen floor. Jane's awful Doberman pinscher, Randolph, had chewed chair rungs and had clawed at doors until troughs were worn in the wood. Jane really did live, Alexandra told herself in extenuation, in some unsolid world part music, part spite.

"So what shall we do about it?" Jane asked now, drinks distributed and the first flurry of gossip dispersed—for there could be only one topic today, Darryl Van Horne's astounding, insulting marriage.

"How smug and 'at home' she was in that big blue bathrobe," Sukie said. "I hate her. To think it was me that brought her to tennis that time. I hate myself." She crammed her mouth with a handful of salted pepita seeds.

"And she was quite competitive, remember?" Alexandra

said. "That bruise on my thigh didn't go away for weeks."

"That should have told us something," Sukie said, picking a green husk from her lower lip. "That she wasn't the helpless little doll she appeared. It's just I felt so guilty about Clyde and Felicia."

"Oh *stop* it," Jane insisted. "You *did*n't feel guilty, how *could* you feel guilty? It wasn't your screwing Clyde rotted his brain, it wasn't you who made Felicia such a horror."

"They had a symbiosis," Alexandra said consideringly. "Sukie's being so lovely for Clyde upset it. I have the same problem with Joe except I'm pulling out. Gently. To defuse the situation. People," she mused. "People *are* explosive."

"Don't you just *hate* her?" Sukie asked Alexandra. "I mean, we all understood he was to be yours if he was to be anybody's, among the three of us, once the novelty and everything wore off. Isn't that so, Jane?"

"It is not so" was the definite response. "Darryl and I are both musical. And we're dirty."

"Who say's Lexa and I aren't dirty?" Sukie protested.

"You work at it," Jane said. "But you have other tendencies too. You both have goody-goody sides. You haven't committed yourselves the way I have. For me, there is nobody except Darryl."

"I thought you said you were seeing Bob Osgood," Alexandra said.

"I said I was giving his daughter Deborah piano lessons," Jane responded.

Sukie laughed. "You should see how uppity you look, saying that. Like Jenny when she called us all ill-mannered."

"And didn't she boss him around, in her chilly little way," Alexandra said. "I knew they were married just from the way she stepped into the room, making a late entrance. And he was different. Less outrageous, more tentative. It was sad."

"We *are* committed, sweetie," Sukie said to Jane. "But what can we do, except snub them and go back to being our old cozy selves? I think it may be nicer now. I feel closer to the two of you than for months. And all those hot hors d'oeuvres Fidel made us eat were getting to my stomach."

"What can we *do*?" Jane asked rhetorically. Her black hair, brushed from a central part in two severe wings, fell forward, eclipsing her face, and was swiftly brushed back. "It's obvious. We can *hex* her."

The word, like a shooting star suddenly making its scratch on the sky, commanded silence.

"You can hex her yourself if you feel that vehement," Alexandra said. "You don't need us."

"I do. It needs the three of us. This mustn't be a little hex, so she'll just get hives and a headache for a week."

Sukie asked after a pause, "What *will* she get?"

Jane's thin lips clamped shut upon a bad-luck word, the Latin for "crab." "I think it's obvious, from the other night, where her anxieties lie. When a person has a fear like that it takes just the teeniest-weeniest psychokinetic push to make it come true."

"Oh, the poor child," Alexandra involuntarily exclaimed, having the same terror herself.

"Poor child nothing," said Jane. "She is"—and her thin face put on additional hauteur—"Mrs Darryl Van Horne."

After another pause Sukie asked, "How would it work?"

"Perfectly straightforwardly. Alexandra makes a wax figure of her and we stick pins in it under our cone of power."

"Why must *I* make it?" Alexandra asked.

"Simple, my darling. You're the sculptress, we're not. And you're still in touch with the larger forces. My spells lately tend to go off at about a forty-five degree angle. I tried to kill Greta Neff's pet cat about six months ago when I was still seeing Ray, and from what he let drop I gather I killed all the rodents in the house instead. The walls stank for weeks but the cat stayed disgustingly healthy."

Alexandra asked, "Jane, don't you ever get scared?"

"Not since I accepted myself for what I am. A fair cellist, a dreadful mother, and a boring lay."

Both the other women protested this last, gallantly, but Jane was firm: "I give good enough head, but when the man is on top and in me something resentful takes over."

"Just try imagining it's your own hand," Sukie suggested. "That's what I do sometimes."

"Or think of it that *you're* fucking *him*," Alexandra said. "That he's just something you're toying with."

"It's too late for all that. I like what I am by now. If I were happier I'd be less effective. Here's what I've done for a start. When Darryl was passing the marzipan figures around I bit off the head of the one representing Jenny but didn't swallow it, and spit it out when I could in my handkerchief. Here." She went to her piano bench, lifted the lid, and brought out a crumpled handkerchief; gloatingly she unfolded the handkerchief for their eyes.

The little smooth candy head, further smoothed by those solvent seconds in Jane's mouth, did have a relation to Jenny's round face—the washed-out blue eyes with their steady gaze, the blond hair so fine it lay flat on her head like paint, a certain blankness of expression that had something faintly challenging and defiant and, yes, galling about it.

"That's good," Alexandra said, "but you also need something more intimate. Blood is best. The old recipes used to call for *sang de menstruës*. And hair, of course. Fingernail clippings."

"Belly-button lint," chimed in Sukie, silly on two bourbons.

"Excrement," Alexandra solemnly continued, "though if you're not in Africa or China that's hard to come by."

"Hold on. Don't go away," Jane said, and left the room.

Sukie laughed. "I should write a story for the Providence *Journal-Bulletin*, 'The Flush Toilet and the Demise of Witchcraft.' They said I could submit features as a free-lancer to

them if I wanted to get back into writing." She had kicked off
her shoes and curled her legs under her as she leaned on one
arm of Jane's acid-green sofa. In this era even women well
into middle age wore miniskirts, and Sukie's kittenish posture
exposed almost all the thigh she had, plus her freckled,
gleaming knees, perfect as eggs. She was in a wool pullover
dress scarcely longer than a sweater, sharp orange in color;
this color made with the sofa's vile green the arresting clash
one finds everywhere in Cézanne's landscapes and that would
be ugly were it not so oddly, boldly beautiful. Sukie's face
wore that tipsy slurred look—eyes too moist and sparkling,
lipstick rubbed away but for the rims by too much smiling
and chattering—that Alexandra found sexy. She even found
sexy Sukie's least successful feature, her short, fat, and rather
unchiselled nose. There was no doubt, Alexandra thought to
herself dispassionately, that since Van Horne's marriage her
heart had slipped its moorings, and that away from the shared
unhappiness of these two friends there was little but desolation. She could pay no attention to her children; she could see
their mouths move but the sounds that came out were jabber
in a foreign language.

"Aren't you still doing real estate?" she asked Sukie.

"Oh I am, honey. But it's *such* thin pickings. There are
these hundreds of other divorcees running around in the mud
showing houses."

"You made that sale to the Hallybreads."

"I know I did, but that just about brought me even with
my debts. Now I'm slipping back into the red again and I'm
getting desperate." Sukie smiled broadly, her lips spreading
like cushions sat on. She patted the empty place beside her.
"Gorgeous, come over and sit by me. I feel I'm shouting. The
acoustics in this hideous little house, I don't know how she
can stand hearing herself."

Jane had gone up the little half-flight of stairs to where the
bedrooms were in this split-level, and now returned with a

linen hand towel folded to hold some delicate treasure. Her aura was the incandescent purple of Siberian iris, and pulsed in excitement. "Last night," she said, "I was so upset and angry about all this I couldn't sleep and finally got up and rubbed myself all over with aconite and Noxema hand cream, with just a little bit of that fine gray ash you get after you put the oven on automatic cleaner, and flew to the Lenox place. It was wonderful! The spring peepers are all out, and the higher you get in the air the better you can hear them for some reason. At Darryl's, they were all still downstairs, though it was after midnight. There was this kind of Caribbean music that they make on oil drums pouring full blast out of the stereo, and some cars in the driveway I didn't recognize. I found a bedroom window open a couple of inches and slid it up, ever so carefully—"

"Jane, this is so thrilling!" Sukie cried. "Suppose Needlenose had smelled you! Or Thumbkin!"

For Thumbkin, Van Horne had solemnly assured them, beneath her fluffy shape was the incarnate soul of an eighteenth-century Newport barrister who had embezzled from his firm to feed his opium habit (he had been hooked during spells of the terrible toothaches and abscesses common to all ages before ours) and, to save himself from prison and his family from disgrace, had pledged his spirit after death to the dark powers. The little cat could assume at will the form of a panther, a ferret, or a hippogriff.

"A dab of Ivory detergent in the ointment quite kills the scent, I find," Jane said, displeased by the interruption.

"Go on, go on," Sukie begged. "You opened the window—do you think they sleep in the same bed? How can she stand it? That body so cold and clammy under the fur. He was like opening the door of a refrigerator with something spoiling in it."

"Let Jane tell her story," Alexandra said, a mother to them both. The last time she had attempted flight, her astral body had lifted off and her material body had been left behind in the bed, looking so small and pathetic she had felt a terrible rush of shame in midair, and had fled back into her heavy shell.

"I could hear the party downstairs," Jane said. "I think I heard Ray Neff's voice, trying to lead some singing. I found a bathroom, the one that *she* uses."

"How could you be sure?" Sukie asked.

"I know her style by now. Prim on the outside, messy on the inside. Lipsticky Kleenexes everywhere, one of those cardboard circles that hold the Pill so you don't forget the right day lying around all punched out, combs full of long hair. She dyes it, by the way. A whole bottle of pale Clairol right there on the sink. And pancake make-up and blusher, things I'd *die* before ever using. I'm a hag and I know it and a hag is what I want to look like."

"Baby, you're beautiful," Sukie told her. "You have raven hair. And naturally tortoiseshell eyes. And you take a tan. I wish I did. Nobody can take a freckled person quite seriously, for some reason. People think I'm being funny even when I feel lousy."

"What did you bring back in that sweetly folded towel?" Alexandra asked Jane.

"That's *his* towel. I stole it," Jane told them. Yet the delicate script monogram seemed to be a *P* or a *Q*. "Look. I went through the wastebasket under the bathroom sink." Carefully Jane unfolded the rose-colored hand towel upon a spidery jumble of discarded intimate matter: long hairs pulled in billowing snarls from a comb, a Kleenex bearing a tawny stain in its crumpled center, a square of toilet paper holding the vulval image of freshly lipsticked lips being blotted, a tail of cotton from a pill bottle, the scarlet pull thread of a Band-Aid, strands of used dental floss. "Best of all," Jane said, "these little specks—can you see them? Look close. Those were in the bathtub, on the bottom and stuck in the ring—she doesn't even have the decency to wash out a tub when she uses it. I dampened the towel and wiped them up. They're leg hairs. She shaved her legs in the bath."

"Oh that's nice," Sukie said. "You're scary, Jane. You've taught me now to always wash out the tub."

"Do you think this is enough?" Jane asked Alexandra. The eyes that Sukie had called tortoiseshell in truth looked paler, with the unsteady glow of embers.

"Enough for what?" But Alexandra already knew, she had read Jane's mind; knowing chafed that sore place in Alexandra's abdomen, the sore place that had begun the other night, with too much reality to digest.

"Enough to make the charm," Jane answered.

"Why ask me? Make the charm yourself and see how it goes."

"Oh no, dearie. I've already said. We don't have your— how can I put it?—access. To the deep currents. Sukie and I are like pins and needles, we can prick and scratch and that's about it."

Alexandra turned to Sukie. "Where do you stand on this?"

Sukie tried, high on whiskey as she was, to make a thoughtful mouth; her upper lip bunched adorably over her slightly protruding teeth. "Jane and I have talked about it on the phone, a little. We *do* want you to do it with us. We do. It should be unanimous, like a vote. You know, by myself last fall I cast a little spell to bring you and Darryl together, and it worked up to a point. But only up to a point. To be honest, honey, I think my powers are lessening all the time. Everything seems drab. I looked at Darryl the other night and he looked all slapped together somehow—I think he's running scared."

"Then why not let Jenny have him?"

"*No*," Jane interposed. "She mustn't. She stole him. She made fools of us." Her *s*'s lingered like a smoky odor in the long ugly scarred room. Beyond the little flights of stairs that went down to the kitchen area and up to the bedrooms, a distant, sizzling, murmuring sound signified that Jane's children were engrossed in television. There had been another assassination, somewhere. The President was giving speeches only at military installations. The body count was up but so was enemy infiltration.

Alexandra still turned to Sukie, hoping to be relieved of this looming necessity. "You cast a spell to bring me and Darryl together that day of the high tide? He wasn't attracted to me by himself?"

"Oh I'm sure he was, baby," Sukie said, but shruggingly. "Anyway who can tell? I used that green gardener's twine to tie the two of you together and I checked under the bed the other day and rats or something had nibbled it through, maybe for the salt that rubbed off from my hands."

"That wasn't very nice," Jane told Sukie, "when you knew I wanted him myself."

This was the moment for Sukie to tell Jane that she liked Alexandra better; instead she said, "We *all* wanted him, but I figured you could get what you wanted by yourself. And you did. You were over there all the time, fiddling away, if that's what you want to call it."

Alexandra's vanity had been stung. She said, "Oh hell. Let's do it." It seemed simplest, a way of cleaning up another tiny pocket of the world's endless dirt.

Taking care not to touch any of it with their hands, lest their own essences—the salt and oil from their skins, their multitudinous personal bacteria—become involved, the three of them shook the Kleenexes and the long blond hairs and the red Band-Aid thread and, most important, the fine specks of leg bristle, that jumped in the weave of the towel like live mites, into a ceramic ashtray Jane had stolen from the Bronze Barrel in the days when she would go there after rehearsal with the Neffs. She added the staring sugar head she had saved in her mouth and lit the little pyre with a paper match. The Kleenexes blazed orange, the hairs crackled blue and emitted the stink of singeing, the marzipan reduced itself to a bubbling black curdle. The smoke lifted to the ceiling and hung like a cobweb on the artificial surface, papery plasterboard roughed with a coat of sand-impregnated paint to feign real plaster.

"Now," Alexandra said to Jane Smart. "Do you have an old candle stump? Or some birthday candles in a drawer? The ashes must be crushed and mixed into about a half-cup of melted wax. Use a saucepan and butter it thoroughly first, bottom and sides; if any wax sticks, the spell is flawed."

While Jane carried out this order in the kitchen, Sukie laid a hand on the other woman's forearm. "Sweetie, I know you don't want to do this," she said.

Caressing the delicate tendony offered hand, Alexandra noticed how the freckles, thickly strewn on the back and the first knuckles, thinned toward the fingernails, as if this mixture had been insufficiently stirred. "Oh but I do," she said. "It gives me a lot of pleasure. It's artistry. And I love the way you two believe in me so." And without forethought she leaned and kissed Sukie on the complicated cushions of her lips.

Sukie stared. Her pupils contracted as the shadow of Alexandra's head moved off her green irises. "But you had liked Jenny."

"Only her body. The way I liked my children's bodies. Remember how they smelled as babies?"

"Oh Lexa: do you think any of us will ever have any more babies?"

It was Alexandra's turn to shrug. The question seemed sentimental, unhelpful. She asked Sukie, "You know what witches used to make candles out of? Baby fat!" She stood, not altogether steadily. She had been drinking vodka, which does not stain the breath or transport too many calories but which also does not pass like a stream of neutrinos through the system altogether without effect. "We must go help Jane in the kitchen."

Jane had found an old box of birthday candles at the back

of a drawer, pink and blue mixed. Melted together in the buttered saucepan, and the ashes from their tiny pyre stirred in with an egg whisk, the wax came out a pearly, flecked lavender-gray.

"Now what do you have for a mold?" Alexandra asked. They rummaged for cookie cutters, rejected a pâté mold as much too big, considered demitasse cups and liqueur glasses, and settled on the underside of an old-fashioned heavy glass orange-juice squeezer, the kind shaped like a sombrero with a spout on the rim. Alexandra turned it upside down and deftly poured; the hot wax sizzled within the ridged cone but the glass didn't crack. She held the top side under running cold water and tapped on the edge of the sink until the convex cone of wax, still warm, fell into her hand. She gave it a squeeze to make it oblong. The incipient human form gazed up at her from her palm, dented four times by her fingers. "Damn," she said. "We should have saved out a few strands of her hair."

Jane said, "I'll check to see if any is still clinging to the towel."

"And do you have any orangesticks by any chance?" Alexandra asked her. "Or a long nail file. To carve with. I could even make do with a hairpin." Off Jane flew. She was used to taking orders—from Bach, from Popper, from a host of dead men. In her absence Alexandra explained to Sukie, "The trick is not to take away more than you must. Every crumb has some magic in it now."

She selected from the knives hanging on a magnetic bar a dull paring knife with a wooden handle bleached and softened by many trips through the dishwasher. She whittled in to make a neck, a waist. The crumbs fell on a ScotTowel spread on the Formica countertop. Balancing the crumbs on the tip of the knife, and with the other hand holding a lighted match under this tip, she dripped the wax back onto the emerging figurine to form breasts. The subtler convexities of belly and thighs Alexandra also built up in this way. The legs she pared down to tiny feet in her style. The crumbs left over from this became—heated, dripped, and smoothed—the buttocks. All the time she held in her mind the image of the girl, how she had glowed at their baths. The arms were unimportant and were sculpted in low relief at the sides. The sex she firmly indicated with the tip of the knife held inverted and vertical. Other creases and contours she refined with the bevelled oval edge of the orangestick Jane had fetched. Jane had found one more long hair clinging to the threads of the towel. She held it up to the window light and, though a single hair scarcely has color, it appeared neither black nor red in the tint of its filament, and paler, finer, purer than a strand from Alexandra's head would have been. "I'm quite certain it's Jenny's," she said.

"It better be," Alexandra said, her voice grown husky through concentration upon the figure she was making. With the edge of the soft fragrant stick that pushed cuticles she pressed the single hair into the yielding lavender scalp.

"She has a head but no face," Jane complained over her shoulder. Her voice jarred the sacred cone of concentration.

"We provide the face" was Alexandra's whispered answer. "We know who it is and project it."

"It feels like Jenny to me already," said Sukie, who had attended so closely to the manufacture that Alexandra had felt the other woman's breath flitting across her hands.

"Smoother," Alexandra crooned to herself, using the rounded underside of a teaspoon. "Jenny is smooooth."

Jane criticized again: 'It won't stand up."

"Her little women never do," Sukie intervened

"Shhh," Alexandra said, protecting her incantatory tone. "She must take this lying down. That's how we ladies do it. We take our medicine lying down."

With the magic knife, the *Athame*, she incised grooves in imitation of Jenny's prim new Eva Perón hairdo on the little simulacrum's head. Jane's complaint about the face nagged, so with the edge of the orangestick she attempted the curved dents of eye sockets. The effect, of sudden sight out of the gray lump, was alarming. The hollow in Alexandra's abdomen turned leaden. In attempting creation we take on creation's burden of guilt, of murder and irreversibility. With the tine of a fork she pricked a navel into the figure's glossy abdomen: born, not made; tied like all of us to mother Eve. "Enough," Alexandra announced, dropping her tools with a clatter into the sink. "Quickly, while the wax has a little warmth in it still. Sukie. Do you believe this is Jenny?"

"Why . . . sure, Alexandra, if you say so."

"It's important that *you* believe. Hold her in your hands. Both hands."

She did. Her thin freckled hands were trembling.

"Say to it—don't smile—say to it, 'You are Jenny. You must die.' "

"You are Jenny. You must die."

"You too, Jane. Do it. Say it."

Jane's hands were different from Sukie's, and from each other: the bow hand thick and soft, the fingering hand overdeveloped and with golden glazed calluses on the cruelly used tips.

Jane said the words, but in such a dead determined tone, just reading the notes as it were, that Alexandra warned, "You must believe them. *This is Jenny.*"

It did not surprise Alexandra that for all her spite Jane should be the weak sister when it came to casting the spell; for magic is fueled by love, not hate: hate wields scissors only and is impotent to weave the threads of sympathy whereby the mind and spirit do move matter.

Jane repeated the formula, there in this ranch-house kitchen, with its picture window, spattered by hardened bird droppings, giving on a scrappy yard nevertheless graced at this moment of the year with the glory of two dogwoods in bloom. The day's last sunlight gleamed like a background of precious metal worked in fine leaf between the drifting twists of the dark branches and the sprays, at the branches' ends, of four-petalled blossoms. A yellow plastic wading tub, exposed to the weather all winter and forever outgrown by Jane's children, rested at a slight tilt beneath one of the trees, holding a crescent of filthy water that had been ice. The lawn was brown and tummocky yet misted by fresh green. The earth was still alive.

The voices of the other two recalled Alexandra to herself. "You too, sweetie," Jane told her harshly, handing her bubby back to her. "Say the words."

They were hateful, but on the other hand factual; Alexandra said them with calm conviction and hastily directed the spell to its close. "Pins," she told Jane. "Needles. Even thumbtacks—are there some in your kids' rooms?"

"I hate to go in there, they'll start yammering for dinner."

Alexandra said, "Tell them five more minutes. We must finish up or it could—"

"It could what?" Sukie asked, frightened.

"It could backfire. It may yet. Like Ed's bomb. Those little round-headed map pins would be nice. Even paper clips, if we straighten them. But one good-sized needle is essential." She did not explain, *To pierce the heart.* "Also, Jane. A mirror." For the magic did not occur in the three dimensions of matter but within the image matter generated in a mirror, the astral identity of mere mute things, an existence added onto existence.

"Sam left a shaving mirror I sometimes use to do my eyes."

"Perfect. Hurry. I have to keep my mood or the elementals will dissipate."

Off Jane flew again; Sukie at Alexandra's side tempted her, "How about one more splash? I'm having just one more weak bourbon myself, before I face reality."

"This is reality, I'm sorry to say. A half-splash, honey. A thimble of vodka and fill the rest up with tonic or 7 Up or faucet water or anything. Poor little Jenny." As she carried the wax image up the six battered steps from the kitchen into the living room, imperfections and asymmetries in her work cried out to her—one leg smaller than the other, the anatomy where hips and thighs and abdomen come together not really understood, the wax breasts too heavy. Whoever had made her think she was a sculptress? Darryl: it had been wicked of him.

Jane's hideous Doberman, released by some door she had opened along the upstairs hall, bounded into the living room, the claws of his feet scrabbling on the naked wood. His coat was an oily black, close and rippling and tricked out like some military uniform with orange boots and patches of the same color on his chest and muzzle and, in two round spots, above his eyes. Drooling, he stared up at Alexandra's cupped hands, thinking something to be eaten was held there. Even Randolph's nostrils were watering with appetite, and the folded insides of his aroused erect ears seemed extensions of ravenous intestines. "Not for you," Alexandra told him sternly, and the dog's glassy black eyes looked polished, they were trying so hard to understand.

Sukie followed with the drinks; Jane hurried in with a two-sided shaving mirror on a wire stand, an ashtray full of multicolored tacks, and a pincushion in the form of a little cloth apple. The time was a few minutes to seven; at seven the television programs changed and the children would be demanding to be fed. The three women set the mirror up on Jane's coffee table, an imitation cobbler's bench abandoned by the mechanical engineer as he cleared out for Texas. Within the mirror's silver circle everything was magnified, stretched and out of focus at the edges, vivid and huge at the center. In turn the women held the doll before it, as at the hungry round mouth of another world, and stuck in pins and thumbtacks. "Aurai, Hanlii, Thamcii, Tilınos, Athamas, Zianor, Auonail," Alexandra recited.

"Tzabaoth, Messiach, Emanuel, Elchim, Eibor, Yod, He, Vou, He!" Jane chanted in crisp sacrilege.

"Astachoth, Adonai, Agla, On, El, Tetragrammaton, Shema," Sukie said, "Ariston, Anaphaxeton, and then I forget what's next."

Breasts and head, hips and belly, in the points went. Distant indistinct shots and cries drifted into their ears as the television program's violence climaxed. The simulacrum had taken on a festive encrusted look—the bristle of a campaign map, the fey gaudiness of a Pop Art hand grenade, a voodoo glitter. The shaving mirror swam with reflected color. Jane held up the long needle, of a size to work thick thread through suede. "Who wants to poke this through the heart?"

"You may," Alexandra said, gazing down to place a yellow-headed thumbtack symmetrical with another, as if this art were abstract. Though the neck and cheeks had been pierced, no one had dared thrust a pin into the eyes, which gazed expressionless or full of mournful spirit, depending on how the shadows fell.

"Oh no, you don't shove it off on me," Jane Smart said. "It should be all of us, we should all three put a finger on it."

Left hands intertwining like a nest of snakes, they pushed the needle through. The wax resisted, as if a lump of thicker substance were at its center. "*Die*," said one red mouth, and another, "*Take that!*" before giggling overtook them. The needle eased through. Alexandra's index finger showed a blue mark about to bleed. "Should have worn a thimble," she said.

"Lexa, now what?" Sukie asked. She was panting, slightly.

A little hiss arose from Jane as she contemplated their strange achievement.

"We must seal the malignancy in," Alexandra said. "Jane, do you have Reynolds Wrap?"

The other two giggled again. They were scared, Alexandra

realized. Why? Nature kills constantly, and we call her beautiful. Alexandra felt drugged, immobilized, huge like a queen ant or bee; the things of the world were pouring through her and re-emerging tinged with her spirit, her will.

Jane fetched too large a sheet of aluminum foil, torn off raggedly in panic. It crackled and shivered in the speed of her walk. Children's footsteps were pounding down the hall. "Each spit," Alexandra quickly commanded, having bedded Jenny upon the trembling sheet. "Spit so the seed of death will grow," she insisted, and led the way.

Jane spitting was like a cat sneezing; Sukie hawked a bit like a man. Alexandra folded the foil, bright side in, around and around the charm, softly so as not to dislodge the pins or stab herself. The result looked like a potato wrapped to be baked.

Two of Jane's children, an obese boy and a gaunt little girl with a dirty face, crowded around curiously. "What's *that*?" the girl demanded to know. Her nose wrinkled at the smell of evil. Both her upper and lower teeth were trussed in a glittering fretwork of braces. She had been eating something sweet and greenish.

Jane told her, "A project of Mrs. Spofford's that she's been showing us. It's very delicate and I know she doesn't want to undo it again so please don't ask her."

"I'm *star*ving," the boy said. "And we *don't* want hamburgers from Nemo's again, we want a home-cooked meal like other kids get."

The girl was studying Jane closely. In embryo she had Jane's hatchet profile. "Mother, are you drunk?"

Jane slapped the child with a magical quickness, as if the two of them, mother and daughter, were parts of a single wooden toy that performed this action over and over. Sukie and Alexandra, whose own starved children were howling out there in the dark, took this signal to leave. They paused on the brick walk outside the house, from whose wide lit windows spilled the spiralling tumult of a family quarrel.

Alexandra asked Sukie, "Want custody of this?"

The foil-wrapped weight in her hand felt warm.

Sukie's lean lovely nimble hand already rested on the door handle of her Corvair. "I would, sweetie, but I have these rats or mice or whatever they are that nibbled at the other. Don't they adore candle wax?"

Back at her own house, which was more sheltered from the noise of traffic on Orchard Road now that her hedge of lilacs was leafing in, Alexandra put the thing, wanting to forget it, on a high shelf in the kitchen, along with some flawed bubbies she hadn't had the heart to throw away and the sealed jar holding the polychrome dust that had once been dear old well-intentioned Ozzie.

"He goes everywhere with her," Sukie said to Jane over the phone. "The Historical Society, the conservation hearings. They make themselves ridiculous, trying to be so respectable. He's even joined the Unitarian choir."

"Darryl? But he has utterly no voice," Jane said sharply.

"Well, he has a little something, a kind of a baritone. He sounds just like an organ pipe."

"Who told you all this?"

"Rose Hallybread. They've joined at Brenda's too. Darryl apparently had the Hallybreads over to dinner and Arthur wound up telling him he wasn't as crazy as he had first thought. This was around two in the morning, they had all spent hours in the lab, boring Rose silly. As far as I could understand, Darryl's new idea is to breed a certain kind of microbe in some huge body of water like Great Salt Lake—the saltier the better, evidently—and this little bug just by breeding will turn the entire lake into a huge battery somehow. They'd put a fence around it, of course."

"Of course, my dear. Safety first."

A pause, while Sukie tried to puzzle through if this was

meant sarcastically and, if so, why. She was just giving the news. Now that they no longer met at Darryl's they saw each other less frequently. They had not officially abandoned their Thursdays, but in the month since they had put the spell on Jenny one of the three had always had an excuse not to come. "So how *are* you?" Sukie asked.

"Keeping busy," Jane said.

"I keep running into Bob Osgood downtown."

Jane didn't bite. "Actually," she said, "I'm unhappy. I was standing in the back yard and this black wave came over me and I realized it had something to do with summer, everything green and all the flowers breaking out, and it hit me what I hate about summer: the children will be home all day."

"Aren't you wicked?" Sukie asked. "I rather enjoy mine, now that they're old enough to talk adult talk. Watching television all the time they're much better informed on world affairs than I ever was; they want to move to France. They say our name is French and they think France is a civilized country that never fights wars and where nobody kills anybody."

"Tell them about Gilles de Rais," Jane said.

"I never thought of him; I did say, though, that it was the French made the mess in Vietnam in the first place and that we were trying to clean it up. They wouldn't buy that. They said we were trying to create more markets for Coca-Cola."

There was another pause. "Well," Jane said. "Have you seen her?"

"Who?"

"*Her.* Jeanne d'Arc. Madame Curie. How does she look?"

"Jane, you're amazing. How did you know? That I saw her downtown."

"Sweetie, it's obvious from your voice. And why else would you be calling me? How was the little pet?"

"Very pleasant, actually. It was rather embarrassing. She said she and Darryl have been missing us *so* much and wish we'd just drop around some time informally, they don't like to think they have to extend a formal invitation, which they *will* do soon, she promised; it's just they've been terribly busy lately, what with some very hopeful developments in the lab and some legal affairs that keep taking Darryl to New York. Then she went on about how much she loves New York, compared to Chicago, which is windy and tough and where she never felt safe, even right in the hospital. Whereas New York is just a set of cozy little villages, all heaped one on top of the other. Et cetera, et cetera.'"

"I'll never set foot in that house again," Jane Smart vehemently, needlessly vowed.

"She really did seem unaware," Sukie said, "that we might be offended by her stealing Darryl right out from under our noses that way."

"Once you've established in your own mind that you're innocent," Jane said, "you can get away with anything. How did she look?"

Now the pause was on Sukie's side. In the old days their conversations had bubbled along, their sentences braiding, flowing one on top of the other, each anticipating what the other was going to say and delighting in it nonetheless, as confirmation of a pooled identity. "Not great," Sukie pronounced at last. "Her skin seemed . . . transparent, some-how."

"She was always pale," Jane said.

"But this wasn't just pale. Anyway, baby, it's May. Everybody should have a little color by now. We went down to Moonstone last Sunday and just soaked in the dunes. My nose looks like a strawberry; Toby kids me about it."

"Toby?"

"You know, Toby Bergman: he took over at the *Word* after poor Clyde and broke his leg on the ice this winter? His leg is all healed now, though it's smaller than the other. He never does these exercises with a lead shoe you're supposed to do."

"I thought you hated him."

"That was before I got to know him, when I was still all hysterical about Clyde. Toby's a lot of fun, actually. He makes me laugh."

"Isn't he a lot . . . younger?"

"We talk about that. He'll be two whole years out of Brown this June. He says I'm the youngest person at heart he's ever met, he kids me about how I'm always eating junk food and wanting to do crazy things like stay up all night listening to talk shows. I guess he's very typical of his generation, they don't have all the hangups about age and race and all that that we were brought up on. Believe me, darling, he's a big improvement on Ed and Clyde in a number of ways, including some I won't go into. It's not complicated, we just have fun."

"Super," Jane said in dismissal, dropping the *r*. "Did her . . . spirit seem the same?"

"She came on a little less shy," Sukie said thoughtfully. "You know, the married woman and all. Pale, like I said, but maybe it was the time of day. We had a cup of coffee in Nemo's, only she had cocoa because she hasn't been sleeping well and is trying to do without caffeine. Rebecca was all over her, insisted we try their blueberry muffins that are part of Nemo's campaign to get some of the nice-people luncheon business back from the Bakery. She hardly gave *me* the time of day. Rebecca. She just took one bite of hers, Jenny this is, and asked if I could finish it for her, she didn't want to hurt Rebecca's feelings. Actually, I was happy to, I've been *rav*enous lately, I can't imagine what it is, I can't be pregnant, can I? These Jews are real potent. She said she didn't know why, but she just hadn't had much of an appetite lately. Jenny. I wondered if she was fishing, to see if I knew why by any chance. She may know in her bones about the . . . the thing we did, I don't know. I felt sorry for her, the way she seemed so apologetic, about not having an appetite."

"It really is true, isn't it?" Jane observed. "You pay for every sin."

There were so many sins in the world it took Sukie a second to figure out that Jane meant Jenny's sin of marrying Darryl.

Joe had been there that morning and they had had their worst scene yet. Gina was in her fourth month by now and it was starting to show; the whole town could see. And Alexandra's children were about to be let out of school and would make these weekday trysts in her home impossible. Which was a relief to her; it would be a great relief, frankly, for her not to have to listen any more to his irresponsible and really rather presumptuous talk of leaving Gina. She was sick of hearing it, it meant nothing, and she wouldn't want it to mean anything, the whole idea upset and insulted her. He was her lover, wasn't that enough? *Had* been her lover, after today. Things end. Things begin, and things end. All grown-ups know that, why didn't he? Caught as he was so severely, rotated on the point of her tongue as on a spit, Joe became hot, and walloped her shoulder a few times with a fist kept loose enough not to hurt, and ran around the room naked, his body stocky and white with two dark swirls of hair on his back suggesting to her eyes butterfly wings (his spine its body) or a veneer of thin marble slices set so the molten splash of grain within made a symmetrical pattern. There was something delicate and organic about the hair on Joe's body, whereas Darryl's had been a rough mat. Joe wept; he took off his hat to beat his head on a doorframe: it was parody and yet real grief, actual loss. The room, the Williamsburg-green of its old woodwork and the big peonies of its curtains with their concealed clown faces and the cracked ceiling that had mutely and conspiratorially watched over their naked couplings, was part of their grief, for little is more precious in an affair for a man than being welcomed into a house he has done nothing to support, or more momentous for the woman than this welcoming, this considered largesse, her house his, his on the strength of his cock alone, his cock and company, the smell and amusement and weight of him—no buying you with mortgage payments, no blackmailing you with shared children, but welcomed simply, into the walls of yourself, an admission dignified by freedom and equality. Joe couldn't stop thinking of teams and marriage; he wanted his own penates to preside. He had demeaned with "good" intentions her gracious gift. In his anguish he surprised Alexandra by getting erect again, and since his time was short now, their morning wasted in words, she let him take her his favourite way, from behind, she on her knees. What a force of nature his pounding was! How he convulsed, shooting off! The whole episode left her feeling tumbled and cleansed, like a towel from the dryer needing to be folded and stacked on some airy shelf of her sunny, empty home.

The house, too, seemed happier for his visit, in this interval before the eternity of their parting sank in. The beams and floorboards of this windy, moistening time of the year chatted among themselves, creaking, and a window sash when her back was turned would give a swift rattle like a sudden bird cry.

She lunched on last night's salad, the lettuce limp in its chilled bath of oil. She must lose weight or she couldn't wear a bathing suit all summer. Another failing of Joe's was his forgivingness of her fat—like those primitive men who turn their wives into captives of obesity, mountains of black flesh waiting in their thatched huts. Already Alexandra felt slimmer, lightened of her lover. Her intuition told her the phone would ring. It did. It would be Jane or Sukie, lively with malice. But from the grid pressed against her ear emerged a younger, lighter voice, with a tension of timidity in it, a pocket of fear over which a membrane pulsed as at a frog's throat.

"Alexandra, you're all avoiding me." It was the voice Alexandra least in the world wanted to hear.

"Well, Jenny, we want to give you and Darryl privacy. Also we hear you have other friends."

"Yes, we do, Darryl loves what he calls input. But it's not like . . . we were."

"Nothing's ever quite the same," Alexandra told her. "The stream flows; the little bird hatches and breaks the egg. Anyway. You're doing fine."

"But I'm not, Lexa. Something's very wrong."

Her voice in the older woman's mind's eye lifted toward her like a face holding itself up to be scrubbed, a grit of hoarseness upon its cheeks. "What's very wrong?" Her own voice was like a tarpaulin or great dropcloth which in being spread out on the earth catches some air under it and lifts in a bubble, a soft wave of hollowness.

"I'm tired all the time," Jenny said, "and not much appetite. I'm subconsciously so hungry I keep having these dreams of food, but when I sit down to the reality I can't make myself eat. And other things. Pains in the night that come and go. My nose runs all the time. It's embarrassing; Darryl says I snore at night, which I never did before in my whole life. Remember those lumps I tried to show you and you couldn't find?"

"Yes. Vaguely." The sensations of that casual hunt rushed horribly into her fingertips.

"Well, there are more. In the, in the groin, and up under my ears. Isn't that where the lymph nodes are?"

Jenny's ears had never been pierced, and she was always losing little childish clip-on earrings in the tub room, on the black slates, among the cushions. "I really don't know, honey. You should see a doctor if you're worried."

"Oh I did. Doc Pat. He sent me to the Westwick Hospital to have tests."

"And did the tests show anything?"

"They said not really; but then they want me to have more tests. They're all so cagey and grave and talk in this funny voice, as though I'm a naughty child who might pee on their shoes if they don't keep me at a distance. They're scared of me. By being sick at all I'm showing them up somehow. They say things like my white-cell count is 'just a bit out of the high normal range.' They know I worked at a big city hospital and that puts them on the defensive, but I don't know anything about systemic disorders, I saw fractures and gallstones mostly. It would all be silly except at night when I lie down I can *feel* something's not right, something's working at me. They keep asking me if I'd been exposed to much radiation. Well of course I'd worked with it at Micheal Reese but they're *so* careful, draping you in lead and putting you in this thick glass booth when you throw the switch, all I could think of was, in my early teens just before we moved to Eastwick and were still in Warwick, I had an awful lot of dental X-rays when they were straightening my teeth; my mouth was a mess as a girl."

"Your teeth look lovely now."

"Thank you. It cost Daddy money he didn't really have, but he was determined to have me beautiful. He *loved* me, Lexa."

"I'm sure he did, darling," Alexandra said, pressing down on her voice; the air caught under the tarpaulin was growing, struggling like a wild animal made of wind.

"He loved me so much," Jenny was blurting. "How could he do that to me, hang himself? How could he leave me and Chris so alone? Even if he were in jail for murder, it would be better than this. They wouldn't have given him too much, the awful way he did it couldn't have been premeditated."

"You have Darryl," Alexandra told her.

"I do and I don't. You know how he is. You know him better than I do; I should have talked to you before I went ahead with it. You might have been better for him, I don't know. He's courteous and attentive and all that but he's not there for me somehow. His mind is always elsewhere, with his projects I guess. Alexandra, *please* let me come and see you. I won't stay long, I really won't. I just need to be . . . touched," she concluded, her voice retracted, curling under almost sardonically while voicing this last, naked plea.

"My dear, I don't know what you want from me," Alexandra lied flatly, needing to flatten all this, to erase the smeared face rising in her mind's eye, rising so close she could see flecks of grit, "but I don't have it to give. Honestly. You made your choice and I wasn't part of it. That's fine. No reason I should have been part of it. But I can't be part of your life now. I just can't. There isn't that much of me."

"Sukie and Jane wouldn't like it, your seeing me," Jenny suggested, to give Alexandra's hard-heartedness a rationale.

"I'm speaking for myself. I don't want to get reinvolved with you and Darryl now. I wish you both well but for my sake I don't want to see you. It would just be too painful, frankly. As to this illness, it sounds to me as if you're letting your imagination torment you. At any rate you're in the hands of doctors who can do more for you than I can."

"Oh." The distant voice had shrunk itself to the size of a dot, to something mechanical like a dial tone. "I'm not sure that's true."

When she hung up, Alexandra's hands were trembling. All the familiar angles and furniture of her house looked askew, as if wrenched by the disparity between their moral distance from her—things, immune from sin—and their physical closeness. She went into her workroom and took one of the chairs there, an old arrow-back Windsor whose seat was spattered with paint and dried plaster and paste, and brought it into the kitchen. She set it below the high kitchen shelf and stood on it and reached up to retrieve the foil-wrapped object she had hidden up there on returning from Jane's house this April. The thing startled her by feeling warm to her fingers: warm air collects up near a ceiling, she thought to herself in vague explanation. Hearing her stirring about, Coal padded out from his nap corner, and she had to lock him in the kitchen behind her, lest he follow her outdoors and think what she was about to do was a game of toss and fetch.

Passing through her workroom, Alexandra stepped around an overweening armature of pine two-by-fours and one-by-twos and twisted coathangers and chicken wire, for she had taken it into her head to attempt a giant sculpture, big enough for a public space like Kazmierczak Square. Past the workroom lay, in the rambling layout of this house lived in by eight generations of farmers, a dirt-floored transitional area used formerly as a potting shed and by Alexandra as a storage place, its walls thick with the handles of shovels and hoes and rakes, its stepping-space narrowed by tumbled stacks of old clay pots and by opened bags of peat moss and bone meal, its jerrybuilt shelves littered with rusted hand trowels and brown bottles of stale pesticide. She unlatched the crude door— parallel beaded boards held together by a Z of bracing lumber—and stepped into hot sunlight; she carried her little package, glittering and warm, across the lawn.

The frenzy of June growth was upon all the earth: the lawn needed mowing, the border beds of button mums needed weeding, the tomato plants and peonies needed propping. Insects chewed at the silence; sunlight pressed on Alexandra's face and she could feel the hair of her single thick braid heat up like an electric coil. The bog at the back of her property, beyond the tumbled fieldstone wall clothed in poison ivy and Virginia creeper, was in winter a transparent brown thicket floored, between tummocks of matted grass, with bubbled bluish ice; in summer it became a solid tangle of green leaf and black stalk, fern and burdock and wild raspberry, that the eye could not travel into for more than a few feet, and where no one would ever step, the thorns and the dampness underfoot being too forbidding. As a girl, until that age at about the sixth grade when boys become self-conscious about your playing games with them, she had been good at softball; now she reared back and threw the charm—mere wax and pins, so light it sailed as if she had flung a rock on the moon—as deep into this flourishing opacity as she could. Perhaps it would find a patch of slimy water and sink. Perhaps red-winged blackbirds would peck its tinfoil apart to adorn their nests. Alexandra willed it to be gone, swallowed up, dissolved, forgiven by nature's seethe.

The three at last arranged a Thursday when they could face one another again, at Sukie's tiny house on Hemlock Lane. "Isn't this cozy!" Jane Smart cried, coming in late, wearing almost nothing: plastic sandals and a gingham mini with the shoulder straps tied at the back of the neck so as not to mar her tan. She turned a smooth mocha color, but the aged skin under her eyes remained crêpey and white and her left leg showed a livid ripple of varicose vein, a little train of half-submerged bumps, like those murky photographs with which people try to demonstrate the existence of the Loch Ness monster. Still, Jane was vital, a thick-skinned sun hag in her element. "God, she looks terrible!" she crowed, and settled in one of Sukie's ratty armchairs with a martini. The martini was the slippery color of mercury and the green olive hung within it like a red-irised reptile eye.

"Who?" Alexandra asked, knowing full well who.

"The darling Mrs. Van Horne, of course," Jane answered. "Even in bright sunlight she looks like she's indoors, right there on Dock Street in the middle of July. She had the gall to come up to me, though I was trying to duck discreetly into the Yapping Fox."

"Poor thing," Sukie said, stuffing some salted pecan halves into her mouth and chewing with a smile. She wore a cooler shade of lipstick in the summer and the bridge of her little amorphous nose bore flakes of an old sunburn.

"Her hair I guess has fallen out with the chemotherapy so she wears a kerchief now," Jane said. "Rather dashing, actually."

"What did she say to you?" Alexandra asked.

"Oh, she was all isn't-this-nice and Darryl-and-I-never-see-you-any-more and do-come-over-we're-swimming-in-the-salt-marsh-these-days. I gave her back as good as I got. Really. What hypocrisy. She hates our guts, she must."

"Did she mention her disease?" Alexandra asked.

"Not a word. All smiles. 'What lovely weather!' 'Have you heard Arthur Hallybread has bought himself a darling little Herreshoff daysailer?' That's how she's decided to play it with us."

Alexandra thought of telling them about Jenny's call a month ago but hesitated to expose Jenny's plea to mockery. But then she thought that her true loyalty was to her sisters, to the coven. "She called me a month ago," she said, "about swollen glands she was imagining everywhere. She wanted to come see me. As if I could heal her."

"How very quaint," Jane said. "What did you tell her?"

"I told her no. I really don't want to see her, it would be too conflicting. What I *did* do, though, I confess, was take the damn charm and chuck it into that messy bog behind my place."

Sukie sat up, nearly nudging the dish of pecans off the arm of her chair but deftly catching it as it slipped. "Why, sugar, what an extraordinary thing to do, after working so hard on the wax and all! You're losing your witchiness!"

"I don't know, am I? Chucking it doesn't seem to have made any difference, not if she's gone on chemotherapy."

"Bob Osgood," Jane said smugly, "is good friends with Doc Pat, and Doc Pat says she's really riddled with it—liver, pancreas, bone marrow, earlobes, you name it. *Entre nous* and all that, Bob said Doc Pat said if she lives two more months it'll be a miracle. She knows it, too. The chemotherapy is just to placate Darryl: he's frantic, evidently."

Now that Jane had taken this bald little banker Bob Osgood as her lover, two vertical dents between her eyebrows had smoothed a little and there was a cheerful surge to her utterances, as though she were bowing them upon her own vibrant vocal cords. Alexandra had never met Jane's Brahmin mother but supposed this was how voices were pushed into the air above the teacups of the Back Bay.

"There are remissions," Alexandra protested, without conviction; strength had flowed out of her and now was diffused into nature and moving on the astral currents beyond this room.

"You great big huggable sweet thing you," Jane Smart said, leaning toward her so the line where the tan on her breasts ended showed within the neck of loose gingham, "whatever has come over our Alexandra? If it weren't for this creature you'd be over there now; *you'd* be the mistress of Toad Hall. He came to Eastwick looking for a wife and it should have been you."

"We *want*ed it to be you," Sukie said.

"Piffle," Alexandra said. "I think either one of you would have grabbed at the chance. Especially you, Jane. You did an awful lot of cocksucking in some noble cause or other."

"Babies, let's not bicker," Sukie pleaded. "Let's have our cozy time. Speaking of seeing people downtown, you'll never guess who I saw last night hanging around in front of the Superette!"

"Andy Warhol," Alexandra idly guessed.

"Dawn Polanski!"

"Ed's little slut?" Jane asked. "She was blown up by that explosion in New Jersey."

"They never found any parts of her, just some clothes," Sukie reminded the others. "Evidently she had moved out of this pad they all shared in Hoboken to Manhattan, where the real cell was. The revolutionaries never really trusted Ed, he was too old and too square, and that's why they put him on this bomb detail, to test his sincerity."

Jane laughed unkindly, but with that toney vibrato to her cackle now. "The one quality I never doubted in Ed. He was sincerely an ass."

Sukie's upper lip crinkled in unspoken reproval; she went on, "Apparently there was no sincerity problem with Dawn and she was taken right in with the bigwigs, tripping out every night somewhere in the East Village while Ed was blowing himself up in Hoboken. Her guess is, his hands trembled connecting two wires; the diet and funny hours underground had been getting to him. He wasn't so hot in bed either, I guess she realized."

"It dawned on her," Jane said, and improved this to "Uncame the Dawn."

"Who told you all this?" Alexandra asked Sukie, irritated by Jane's manner. "Did you go up and talk to the girl at the Superette?"

"Oh no, that bunch scares me, they even have some blacks in it now, I don't know where they come from, the south Providence ghetto I guess. I walk on the other side of the street usually. The Hallybreads told me. The girl is back in town and doesn't want to stay with her stepfather in the trailer in Coddington Junction any more, so she's living over the Armenians' store and cleaning houses for cigarette or whatever money, and the Hallybreads use her twice a week. I guess she's made Rose into a mother confessor. Rose has this awful back and can't even pick up a broom without wanting to scream."

"How come," Alexandra asked, "you know so much about the Hallybreads?"

"Oh," said Sukie, gazing upward toward the ceiling, which was tinkling and rumbling with the muffled sounds of television, "I go over there now and then for R and R since Toby and I broke up. The Hallybreads are quite amusing, when she's not in one of her moods."

"What happened between you and Toby?" Jane asked. "You seemed so . . . satisfied."

"He got fired. This Providence syndicate that owns the *Word* thought the paper wasn't sexy enough under his management. And I must say, he did do a lackadaisical job; these Jewish mothers, they really spoil their boys. I'm thinking of applying for editor. If people like Brenda Parsley can take over these men's jobs I don't see why I can't."

"Your boyfriends," Alexandra observed, "don't have very good luck."

"I wouldn't call Arthur a boyfriend," Sukie said. "To me being with him is just like reading a book, he knows so much."

"I wasn't thinking of Arthur. Is he a boyfriend?"

"Is he having any bad luck?" Jane asked.

Sukie's eyes went round; she had assumed everybody knew. "Oh nothing, just these fibrillations. Doc Pat tells him people can live with them years and years, if they keep the digitalis handy. But he hates the fibrillating; like a bird is caught in his chest, he says."

Both her friends, with their veiled boasting of new lovers, were in Alexandra's eyes pictures of health—sleek and tan, growing strong on Jenny's death, pulling strength from it as from a man's body. Jane svelte and brown in her sandals and mini, and Sukie too wearing that summer glow Eastwick women got: terrycloth shorts that made her bottom look high and puffbally, and a peacocky shimmering dashiki her breasts twitched in a way that indicated no bra. Imagine being Sukie's age, thirty-three, and daring to wear no bra! Ever since she was thirteen Alexandra had envied these pert-chested naturally slender girls, blithely eating and eating while her own spirit was saddled with stacks of flesh ready to topple into fat any time she took a second helping. Envious tears rose itching in her sinuses. Why was she mired so in life when a witch should dance, should skim? "We *can't* go on with it," she blurted out through the vodka as it tugged at the odd angles of the spindly little room. "We *must* undo the spell."

"But how, dear?" Jane asked, flicking an ash from a red-filtered cigarette into the paisley-patterned dish from which Sukie had eaten all the pecans and then (Jane) sighing smokily, impatiently, through her nose, as if, having read Alexandra's mind, she had foreseen this tiresome outburst.

"We *can't* just kill her like this," Alexandra went on, rather enjoying now the impression she must be making, of a blubbery troublesome big sister.

"Why not?" Jane dryly asked. "We kill people in our minds all the time. We erase mistakes. We rearrange priorities."

"Maybe it's not our spell at all," Sukie offered. "Maybe we're being conceited. After all, she's in the hands of hospitals and doctors and they have all these instruments and counters and whatnot that don't lie."

"They *do* lie," Alexandra said. "All those scientific things lie. There *must* be a form we can follow to undo it," she pleaded. "If we all three *con*centrated."

"Count me out," Jane said. "Ceremonial magic really bores me, I've decided. It's too much like kindergarten. My whisk is still a mess from all that wax. And my children keep asking me what that thing in tinfoil was; they picked right up on it and I'm afraid are telling their friends. Don't forget, you two, I'm still hoping to get a church of my own, and a lot of gossip does *not* impress the good folk in a position to hire choirmasters."

"How can you be so callous?" Alexandra cried, deliciously feeling her emotions wash up against Sukie's slender antiques—the oval tilt-top table, the rush-seat three-legged Shaker chair—like a tidal wave carrying sticks of debris to the beach. "Don't you see how horrible it is? All she ever did was he asked her and she said yes, what else could she say?"

"I think it's rather amusing," Jane said, shaping her cigarette ash to a sharp point on the paisley saucer's brass edge. " 'Jenny died the other day,' " she added, as if quoting.

"Honey," Sukie said to Alexandra, "I'm honestly afraid it's out of our hands."

" 'Never was there such a lay,' " Jane was going on.

"You didn't do it, at worst you were the conduit. We all were."

" 'Youths and maidens, let us pray,' " quoted Jane, evidently concluding.

"We were just being *used* by the universe."

A certain pride of craft infected Alexandra. "You two couldn't have done it without me; I was *so* energetic, such a good organizer! It felt *won*derful, administering that horrible power!" Now it felt wonderful, her grief battering these walls and faces and things—the sea chest, the needlepoint stool, the thick lozenge panes—as if with massive pillows, the clouds of her agitation and remorse.

"Really, Alexandra," Jane said. "You don't seem yourself."

"I know I don't. I've felt terrible for days. I don't know what it is. My left ovary, before every other period, it really hurts. And at night, the small of my back, such pain I wake up and have to lie curled on my side."

"Oh you poor big sad yummy thing," Sukie said, getting up and taking a step so the tips of her breasts jiggled the shimmering dashiki. "You need a back rub."

"Yes I do," Alexandra pouted.

"Come on. Stretch out on the sofa. Jane, move over."

"I'm so scared." Sniffles spiced Alexandra's words, stinging high in her nostrils. "Why would it be just the ovary, unless . . ."

"You need a new lover," Jane told her, dropping the *r* in her curt fashion. How did she know? Alexandra had told Joe she didn't want to see him any more but this time he had not called back, and the days of his silence had become weeks.

"Hitch up your pretty blouse," Sukie said, though it was not a pretty blouse but one of Oz's old shirts, with collar points that refused to lie down, because the plastic stays were lost, and an indelible food stain near the second button. Sukie bared the bra strap, the snaps were undone, a pang of expansion flooded Alexandra's chest cavity. Sukie's narrow fingers began to work in circles. The rough cushion Alexandra's nose was against smelled comfortingly of damp dog. She closed her eyes.

"And maybe a nice thigh rub," Jane's voice declared. Clinks and a rustle described how she set down her glass and crushed out her cigarette. "Our lumbar tension builds up at the backs of our thighs and needs to be released." Her fingers with their hardened tips tried to release it, pinching, caressing, trailing the nails back and forth for a *pianissimo* effect.

"Jenny—" Alexandra began, remembering that girl's silky massages.

"We're not hurting Jenny," Sukie crooned.

"DNA is hurting Jenny," Jane said. "D'naughty DNA."

In a few minutes Alexandra had been tranced nearly to sleep. Sukie's awful-looking Weimaraner, Hank, trotted into the room with his lolling lilac-colored tongue and they played this game: Jane set a row of Wheat Thins along the backs of Alexandra's legs and Hank licked them off. Then they placed some on Alexandra's back, where her shirt had been tugged up. His tongue was rough and wet and warm and slightly adhesive, like a huge snail's foot; back and forth it flipflopped on the repeatedly set table of Alexandra's skin. The dog, like his mistress, loved starchy snacks but, surfeited at last, he looked at the women wonderingly and begged them with his eyes—balls of topaz, with a violet cloud at each center—to desist.

Though the other churches in Eastwick suffered a decided falling-off in attendance during the summer rebirth of sun worship, Unitarian services, never crowded, held their own; indeed they were augmented by vacationers from the metropolises, comfortably fixed religious liberals in red slacks and linen jackets, splashy-patterned cotton smocks and beribboned garden hats. These and the regulars—the Neffs, the Richard Smiths, Herbie Prinz, Alma Sifton, Homer and Franny Lovecraft, the young Mrs. Van Horne, and a relative newcomer in town, Rose Hallybread, without her agnostic husband but with her protégée, Dawn Polanski—were surprised, once "Through the Night of Doubt and Sorrow" had been wanly sung (Darryl Van Horne's baritone contributing scratchy harmony in the balcony choir), to hear the word "evil" emerge from Brenda Parsley's mouth. It was not a word often heard in this chaste nave.

Brenda looked splendid in her open black robe and pleated jabot and white silk cravat, her sun-bleached hair pulled tightly back from her high and shining forehead. "There is evil in the world and there is evil in this town," she pronounced ringingly, then dropped her voice to a lower, confiding register that yet carried to every corner of the neoclassic old sanctuary. Pink hollyhocks nodded in the lower panes of the tall clear windows; in the higher panes a cloudless July day called to those penned in the white box pews to get out, out into their boats, onto the beach and the golf courses and tennis courts, to go have a Bloody Mary on someone's new redwood deck with a view of the Bay and Conanicut Island. The Bay would be crackling with sunshine, the island would appear as purely verdant as when the Narragansett Indians lived there. "It is not a word we like to use," Brenda explained, in the diffident tone of a psychiatrist who after years of mute listening has begun to be directive at last. "We prefer to say 'unfortunate' or 'lacking' or 'misguided' or 'disadvantaged.' We prefer to think of evil as the absence of good, a momentary relenting of its sunshine, a shadow, a weakening. For the world *is* good: Emerson and Whitman, Buddha and Jesus have taught us that. Our own dear valiant Anne Hutchinson believed in a covenant of grace, as opposed to a covenant of works, and defied—this mother of fifteen and gentle midwife to sisters uncounted and uncountable—the sexist world-hating clergy of Boston in behalf of her belief, a belief for which she was eventually to die."

For the last time, thought Jenny Van Horne, *the exact blue of such a July day falls into my eyes. My lids lift, my corneas admit the light, my lenses focus it, my retinas and optic nerve report it to the brain. Tomorrow the Earth's poles will tilt a day more toward August and autumn, and a slightly different tincture of light and vapor will be distilled.* All year, without knowing it, she had been saying good-bye to each season, each subseason and turn of weather, each graduated moment of fall's blaze and shedding, of winter's freeze, of daylight gaining on the hardening ice, and of that vernal moment when the snowdrops and croci are warmed into bloom out of matted brown grass in that intimate area on the sunward side of stone walls, as when lovers cup their breath against the beloved's neck; she had been saying good-bye, for the seasons would not wheel around again for her. Days one spends so freely in haste and preoccupation, in adolescent self-concern and in childhood's joyous boredom, *there really is an end to them, a closing of the sky like the shutter of a vast camera.* These thoughts made Jenny giddy where she sat; Greta Neff, sensing her thoughts, reached into her lap and squeezed her hand.

"As we have turned outward to the evil in the world at large," Brenda was splendidly saying, gazing upward toward the back balcony with its disused pipe organ, its tiny choir, "turned our indignation outward toward evil wrought in Southeast Asia by fascist politicians and an oppressive capitalism seeking to secure and enlarge its markets for anti-ecological luxuries, while we have been so turned we have been guilty—yes, guilty, for guilt attaches to omissions as well as commissions—guilty of overlooking evil brewing in these very homes of Eastwick, our tranquil, solid-appearing homes. Private discontent and personal frustration have brewed mischief out of superstitions which our ancestors pronounced heinous and which indeed"—Brenda's voice dropped beautifully, into a kind of calm soft surprise, a teacher soothing a pair of parents without gainsaying a dreadful report card, a female efficiency-expert apologetically threatening a blustering executive with dismissal—"*are* heinous."

Yet behind that shutter must be an eye, the eye of a great Being, and in a premonition not unlike her father's some months before Jenny had come to repose a faith in that Being's custody of her even while her new friends, and those humanoid machines at the Westwick Hospital, fought for her life. Having herself worked in a hospital those years, Jenny knew how bleakly statistical in the end were the results obtained by all that so amiably and expensively administered mercy. What she minded most was the nausea, the nausea that went with the drugs and now with the radiation directed into her semiweekly as she lay strapped and swathed upon that giant turntable of chrome and cold steel, which lifted her this way and that until she felt seasick. The clicked-off seconds of its radioactive humming could not be cleansed from her ears and persisted even in sleep.

"There is a brand of evil," Brenda was saying, "we must fight. It must not be tolerated, it must not be explained, it must not be excused. Sociology, psychology, anthropology: in this one instance all these creations of the modern·mind must be denied their mitigations."

I will never see icicles dripping from the eaves again, Jenny thought, *or a sugar maple catching fire. Or that moment in late winter when the snow is all dirty and eaten by thaw into rotten, undercut shapes.* These realizations were like a child's finger rubbing a hole in a befogged windowpane above a radiator on a bitterly cold day; through the clear spot Jenny looked into a bottomless never.

Brenda, her hair shimmering down to her shoulders—had it been like that at the beginning of the service, or had it come unpinned in her ardor?—was rallying invisible forces. "For these women—and let us not in our love of our sex and pride in our sex deny that they *are* women—have long exerted a malign influence in this community. They have been promiscuous. They have neglected at best and at worst abused their children, nurturing them in blasphemy. With their foul acts and unspeakable charms they have driven some men to deranged acts. They have driven some men—I firmly believe this—have driven some men to their deaths. And now their demon has alighted—now their venom has descended—their wrath hath—" As from the bell of a hollyhock a bumblebee sleepily emerged from between Brenda's plump painted lips and dipped on its questing course over the heads of the congregation.

Jenny tittered, to herself. Greta's hand gave another squeeze. On her far side Ray Neff snorted. Both the Neffs wore glasses: oval steel-rimmed grannies for Greta, squarish rimless on Ray. Each Neff seemed a single big lens, *and I sit between them*, Jenny thought, *like a nose*. An aghast silence focused upon Brenda, erect in her pulpit. Above her head hung not the tarnished brass cross that had been suspended there for years in irrelevant symbolism but a solid new brass circle, symbol of perfect unity and peace. The circle had been Brenda's idea. She took a shallow breath and tried to speak out through the something else gathering in her mouth.

"Their wrath has tainted the very air we breathe," she proclaimed, and a pale blue moth, and then its little tan sister, emerged; the second fell to the lectern, which was miked, with an amplified thud, then found its wings and beat its way toward the sky locked high behind the tall window.

"Their jealouthy hath poithoned uth all—" Brenda bent her head, and her mouth gave birth to an especially vivid, furry, foul-tasting monarch butterfly, its orange wings rimmed thickly in black, its flickering flight casual and indolent beneath the white-painted rafters.

Jenny felt a tense swelling within her poor wasting body, as if it were a chrysalis.

"Help me," Brenda brokenly uttered down toward the lectern, where the crisp pages of her sermon had been speckled with saliva and insect slime. She seemed to be gagging. Her long platinum-blond hair swung and the brass O shone in the shafts of sunlight. The congregation broke its stunned silence; voices were raised. Franny Lovecraft, in the loud tones of the deaf, suggested that the police be called. Raymond Neff took it upon himself to leap up and shake his fist in the sun-riddled air; his jowls shook. Jenny giggled; the hilarity pressing within her could no longer be stifled. It was, somehow, the animation of it all that was so funny, the irrepressible cartoon cat that rises from being flattened to resume the chase. She burst into laughter—high-voiced, pure, a butterfly of sorts—and yanked her hand from Greta's sympathetic, squeezing grasp. She wondered who was doing it: Sukie, everybody knew, would be in bed with that sly Arthur Hallybread while his wife was at church; sly old elegant Arthur had been fucking his physics students for thirty years in Kingston. Jane Smart had gone all the way up to Warwick to play the Hammond organ for a cell of Moonies starting up in an abandoned Quaker meeting-house; the ambience (Jane had told Mavis Jessup, who had told Rose Hallybread, who had told Jenny) was depressing, all these brainwashed upper-middle-class kids with Marine haircuts, but the money was good. Alexandra would be making her bubbies or weeding her mums. Perhaps none of the three was willing this, it was something they had loosed on the air, like those nuclear scientists cooking up the atomic bomb to beat Hitler and Tojo and now so remorseful, like Eisenhower refusing to sign the truce with Ho Chi Minh that would have ended all the trouble, like the late-summer wildflowers, goldenrod and Queen Anne's lace, now loosed from dormant seeds upon the shaggy fallow fields where once black slaves had opened the gates for galloping squires in swallowtail coats and top hats of beaver and felt. At any rate it was all so *funny*. Herbie Prinz, his jowly greedy thin-skinned face liverish in agitation, pushed past Alma Sifton and beat his way down the aisle and nearly knocked over Mrs. Hallybread, who like the other women was instinctively covering her mouth as, stiff-backed, she rose to flee.

"Pray!" Brenda shouted, seeing she had lost control of the occasion. Something was pouring over her lower lip, making her chin shine. "Pray!" she shouted in a hollow man's voice, as if she were a ventriloquist's dummy.

Jenny, hysterical with laughter, had to be led outside, where the apparition of her staggering between the bespectacled Neffs nonplussed the God-fearing burghers washing their automobiles at this hour along Cocumscussoc Way.

Jane Smart retired when her children did, often going straight to bed after tucking the two littlest in and falling asleep while the older ones watched an illicit half-hour of *Mannix* or some other car-chase series set in southern California. Around two or two-thirty she would awaken as abruptly as if the telephone had rung once and then fallen silent, or as if an intruder had tested the front door or carefully broken a windowpane and was holding his breath. Jane would listen, then smile in the dark, remembering that this was her hour of rendezvous. Arising in a translucent nylon nightie, she would settle her little quilted satin bed jacket around her shoulders and put milk on the stove to heat for cocoa. Randolph, her avid young Doberman, would come rattling his claws into the kitchen and she would give him a Chew-Z, a rock-hard bone-shaped biscuit to gnaw on; he would take the bribe into his corner and make evil music upon it with his long teeth and serrated purplish lips. The milk would boil, she would take the cocoa up the six steps to the living-room level and release her cello from its case—its red wood lustrous and alive like a superior kind of flesh. "Good baby," Jane might say aloud, since the silence in the flat tracts of the development all around—no traffic, no children crying; Cove Homes rose and retired in virtual synchrony—was so absolute as to be frightening. She would scan her splintered floor for a hole to brace her pin in and, dragging music stand and three-way floorlamp and straight-backed chair into place, would play. Tonight she would tackle the Second of Bach's suites for unaccompanied cello. It was one of her favorites; certainly she preferred it to the rather stolid First and the dreadfully difficult Sixth, black with sixty-fourth notes and impossibly high, written as it had been for an instrument with five strings. But always, in even Bach's most clockworklike ringing of changes, there was something to discover, something to *hear*, a moment when a voice cried out amid the turning of the wheels. Bach had been happy at Köthen, but for his wife Maria's sudden death and the so *simpatico* and musical Prince Leopold's marriage to his young cousin, Henrietta of Anhalt; Bach called the little bride an "*amusa*," that is, a person opposed to the muses. Henrietta yawned during courtly concerts, and her demands deflected princely attention away from the *Kapellmeister*, a deflection that helped prompt his seeking the cantorship in Leipzig. He took the new post even though the unsympathetic princess herself surprisingly died before Bach had left Köthen. In the Second Suite, there was a theme—a melodic succession of rising thirds and a descent in whole tones—announced in the prelude and then given an affecting twist in the allemande, a momentary reversal (up a third) of the descent; thus a poignance was inserted in the onrolling (*moderato*) melody, which returned and returned, the matter under discussion coming to a head of dissonance in the *forte d♯-a* chord between a trilled *b* natural and a finger-stinging run, *piano*, of thirty-second notes. The matter under discussion, Jane Smart realized as she played on and the untasted cocoa grew a tepid scum, was death—the mourned death of Maria, who had been Bach's cousin, and the longed-for death of Princess Henrietta, which would indeed come. Death was the space these churning, tumbling notes were clearing, a superb polished inner space growing wider and wider. The last bar was marked *poco a poco ritardando* and involved intervals—the biggest a *D-d'*—which sent her fingers sliding with a muffled screech up and down the neck. The allemande ended on that same low tonic, enormously: the note would swallow the world.

Jane cheated; a repeat was called for (she *had* repeated the first half), but now, like a traveller who by the light of a risen moon at last believes that she is headed somewhere, she wanted to hurry on. Her fingers felt inspired. She was leaning out above the music; it was a cauldron bubbling with a meal cooked only for herself; she could make no mistakes. The courante unfolded swiftly, playing itself, twelve sixteenths to the measure, only twice in each section stricken to hesitation by a quarter-note chord, then resuming its tumbling flight, the little theme almost lost now. This theme, Jane felt, was female; but another voice was strengthening within the music, the male voice of death, arguing in slow decided syllables. For all its fluttering the courante slowed to six dotted notes, stressed to accent their descent by thirds, and then a fourth, and then a steep fifth to the same final note, the ineluctable tonic. The sarabande, *largo*, was magnificent, inarguable, its slow skipping marked by many trills, a ghost of that dainty theme reappearing after a huge incomplete dominant ninth had fallen across the music crushingly. Jane bowed it again and again—low *C#-Bb-g*—relishing its annihilatory force, admiring how the diminished seventh of its two lower notes sardonically echoed the leap of a diminished seventh (*C#-bb*) ın the line above. Moving on after this savoring to the first minuet, Jane most distinctly heard—it was not a question of hearing, she *embodied*—the war between chords and the single line that was always trying to escape them but could not. Her bow was carving out shapes within a substance, within a blankness, within a silence. The outside of things was sunshine and scatter; the inside of everything was death. Maria, the princess, Jenny: a procession. The unseen inside of the cello vibrated, the tip of her bow cut circles and arcs from a wedge of air, sounds fell from her bowing like wood shavings. Jenny tried to escape from the casket Jane was carving; the second minuet moved to the key of D major, and the female caught within the music raced in sliding steps of tied notes but then was returned, *Menuetto I da capo*, and swallowed by its darker colors and the fierce quartet of chords explicitly marked for bowing: *f-a aufstrich, B♭-f-d abstrich, G-g-e aufstrich; A-e-c♯*. Bow sharply, up, down, up, and then down for the three-beat *coup de grâce*, that fluttering spirit slashed across for good.

Before attempting the gigue, Jane sipped at her cocoa: the cold circle of skin stuck to her slightly hairy upper lip. Randolph, his Chew-Z consumed, had loped in and lain near, on the scarred floor, her tapping bare toes. But he was not asleep: his carnelian eyes stared directly at her in some kind of startlement; a hungry expression slightly rumpled his muzzle and perked up his ears, as pink within as whelk shells. These familiars, Jane thought, they remain dense—chips of brute matter. He knows he is witnessing something momentous but does not know what it is; he is deaf to music and blind to the scrolls and the glidings of the spirit. She picked up her bow. It felt miraculously light, a wand. The gigue was marked *allegro*. It began with some stabbing phrases—dit-*duh* (*a-d*), dit-*duh* (*b♭-c♯*), dit dodododo dit *duh*, dit . . . On she spun. Usually she had trouble with these gappy sharped and flatted runs but tonight she flew along them, deeper, higher, deeper, *spiccato*, *legato*. The two voices struck against each other, the last revival of that fluttering, that receding, returning theme, still to be quelled. So this was what men had been murmuring about, monopolizing, all these centuries, death; no wonder they had kept it to themselves, no wonder they had kept it from women, let the women do their nursing and hatching, keeping a bad thing going while they, *they*, men, distributed among themselves the true treasure, onyx and ebony and unalloyed gold, the substance of glory and release. Until now Jenny's death had been simply an erasure in Jane's mind, a nothing; now it had its tactile structure, a branched and sumptuous complexity, a sensuous downpulling fathoms more flirtatious than that tug upon our ankles the retreating waves on the beach give amid the tumbling pebbles, that wonderful weary weighty sigh the sea gives with each wave. It was as if Jenny's poor poisoned body had become intertwined, vein and vein and sinew and sinew, with Jane's own, like the body of a drowned woman with seaweed, and both were rising, the one eventually to be shed by the other but for now interlaced, one with the other, in those revolving luminescent depths. The gigue bristled and prickled under her fingers; the eighth-note thirds underlying the running sixteenths grew ominous; there was a hopeless churning, a pulling down, a grisly *fortissimo* flurry, and a last run down and then skippingly up the scale to the cry capping the crescendo, the thin curt cry of that terminal *d*.

Jane did both repeats, and scarcely fumbled anything, not even that tricky middle section where one was supposed to bring the quickly shifting dynamics through a thicket of dots and ties; who ever said her *legato* sounded *détaché*?

The Cove development lay outside in the black windows pure as a tract of antarctic ice. Sometimes a neighbor called to complain but tonight even the telephone was betranced. Only Randolph kept an eye open; as his heavy head lay on the floor one opaque eye, flecks of blood floating in its darkness, stared at the meat-colored hollow body between his mistress's legs, his strident rival for her affection. Jane herself was so exalted, so betranced, that she went on to play the first movement of the cello part for the Brahms E Minor, all those romantic languorous half-notes while the imaginary piano pranced away. What a softy Brahms was, for all his flourishes: a woman with a beard and cigar!

Jane rose from her chair. She had a killing pain between her shoulder blades and her face streamed with tears. It was twenty after four. The first gray stirrings of light were planting haggard shapes on the lawn outside her picture window, beyond the straggly bushes she never trimmed and that spread and mingled like the different tints of lichen on a tombstone, like bacterial growths in a culture dish. The children began to make noise early in the morning, and Bob Osgood, who had promised to try to meet her for "lunch" at a dreadful motel—an arc of plywood cottages set back in the woods—near Old Wick, would call to confirm from the bank; so she could not take the phone off the hook and sleep even if the children were quiet. Jane felt suddenly so exhausted she went to bed without putting her cello back in its case, leaving it leaning against the chair as if she were a symphony performer excused from the stage for intermission.

Alexandra was looking out the kitchen window, wondering how it had become so smeared and splotched with dust—could rain itself be dirty?—and therefore saw Sukie park and come in along the brick walk through the grape arbor, ducking her sleek orange head in avoidance of the empty birdfeeder and the low-hanging vines with their ripening green clusters. It had been a wet August so far and today looked like more rain. The women kissed inside the screen door. "You're *so* nice to come," Alexandra said. "I don't know why it should scare me to look for it alone. In my own bog."

"It *is* scary, sweet," Sukie said. "For it to have been so effective. She's back in the hospital."

'Of course we don't really know that it was it."

"We do, though," Sukie said, not smiling and her lips therefore looking strange, bunchy. "We know. It was it." She seemed subdued, a girl reporter again in her raincoat. She had been rehired at the *Word*. Selling real estate, she had told Alexandra more than once over the telephone, was just too chancy, too ulcer-producing, waiting for things to click, wondering if you might have said something more subliminally persuasive in that crucial moment when the clients first see the house, or when they're standing around in the basement with the husband trying to look sage about the pipes and the wife terrified of rats. And then when a deal does go through the fee usually has to be split three or four ways. It really was giving her ulcers: a little dry pain just under the ribs, higher than you'd imagine, and worst at night.

"Want a drink?"

"Afterwards. It's early. Arthur says I shouldn't drink a drop until my stomach gets back in shape. Have you ever tried Maalox? God, you taste chalk every time you burp. Anyway"—she smiled, a flash of her old self, the fat upper lip stretched so its unpainted inner side showed above her bright, big, outcurved teeth—"I'd feel guilty having a drink without Jane here."

"Poor Jane."

Sukie knew what she meant, though it had happened a week before. That dreadful Doberman pinscher had chewed Jane's cello to pieces one night when she didn't put it back in its case.

"Do they think it's for good this time?" Alexandra asked.

Sukie intuited that Alexandra meant Jenny in the hospital. "Oh, you know how they are, they would never say that. More tests is all they ever say. How're your own complaints?"

"I'm trying to stop complaining. They come and go Maybe it's premenopausal. Or post-Joe. You know about Joe?—he really *has* given up on me."

Sukie nodded, letting her smile sink down slowly over her teeth. "Jane blames *them*. For all our aches and pains. She even blames them for the cello tragedy. You'd think she could blame herself for that."

At the mention of *them*, Alexandra was momentarily distracted from the sore of guilt she carried sometimes in the left ovary, sometimes in the small of her back, and lately under her armpits, where Jenny had once asked her to investigate. Once it gets to the lymph glands, according to something Alexandra remembered reading or seeing on television, it's too late. "Who of them does she blame specifically?"

"Well for some reason she's fastened on that grubby little Dawn. I don't think myself a kid like that has it in her yet. Greta is pretty potent, and so would Brenda be if she could stop putting on airs. From what Arthur lets slip, for that matter, Rose is no bargain to tangle with: he finds her a very tough cookie, otherwise I guess they'd have been divorced long ago. She doesn't want it."

"I do hope he doesn't go after her with a poker."

"Listen, darling. That was never *my* idea of the way to solve the wife problem. I was once a wife myself, you know."

"Who wasn't? I wasn't thinking of you at all, dear heart, it was the house I'd blame if it happened again. Certain spiritual grooves get worn into a place, don't you believe?"

"I don't know. Mine needs paint."

"So does mine."

"Maybe we should go look for that thing before it rains."

"You *are* nice to help me."

"Well, I feel badly too. In a way. Up to a point. And I spend all my time chasing around in the Corvair on wild-goose chases anyway. It keeps skidding and getting out of control, I wonder if it's the car or me. Ralph Nader hates that model." They passed through the kitchen into Alexandra's workroom. "What on earth is *that?*"

"I wish I knew. It began as an enormous something for a

public square, visions of Calder and Moore I suppose. I thought if it came out wonderfully I could get it cast in bronze; after all the papier-mâché I want to do something permanent. And the carpentry and banging around are good for sexual deprivation. But the arms won't stay up. Pieces keep falling off in the night."

"They've hexed it."

"Maybe. I certainly cut myself a lot handling all the wire; don't you just hate the way wire coils and snarls? So I'm trying now to make it more life-size. Don't look so doubtful. It might take off. I'm not totally discouraged."

"How about your little ceramic bathing beauties, the bubbies?"

"I can't do them any more, after that. I get physically nauseated, thinking of her face melting, and the wax, and the tacks."

"You ought to try an ulcer some time. I never knew where the duodenum *was* before."

"Yes, but the bubbies were my bread and butter. I thought some fresh clay might inspire me so I drove over to Coventry last week and this house where I used to buy my lovely kaolin was all in this tacky new aluminum siding. Puke green. The widow who had owned it had died over the winter, of a heart attack hauling wood the woman of the family that has it now said, and her husband doesn't want to be bothered with selling clay; he wants a swimming pool and a patio in the back yard. So that ends that."

"You look great, though. I think you're losing weight."

"Isn't that another of the symptoms?"

They made their way through the old potting shed and stepped into the back yard, which needed a mowing. First the dandelions had been rampant, now the crabgrass. Fungi— blobs of brown loaded by nature with simples and banes and palliatives—had materialized in the low damp spots of this neglected lawn during this moist summer. Even now, the

mantle of clouds in the distance had developed those downward tails, travelling wisps, which mean rain is falling somewhere. The wild area beyond the tumbled stone wall was itself
a wall of weeds and wild raspberry canes. Alexandra knew
about the briars and had put on rugged men's jeans; Sukie
however was wearing under her raincoat a russet seersucker
skirt and frilly maroon blouse, and on her feet open-toed
heels oxblood in color.

"You're too pretty," Alexandra said. "Go back to the
potting shed and put on those muddy Wellingtons somewhere around where the pitchfork is. That'll save your shoes
and ankles at least. And bring the long-handled clippers, the
one with the extra hinge in the jaw. In fact, why don't you
just fetch the clippers and stay here in the yard? You've never
been that much into nature and your sweet seersucker skirt
will get torn."

"No, no," Sukie said loyally. "I'm curious now. It's like an
Easter-egg hunt."

When Sukie returned, Alexandra stood on the exact spot of
grass, as best she remembered, and demonstrated how she had
thrown the evil charm to be rid of it forever. The two friends
then waded, clipping and wincing as they went, out into this
little wilderness where a hundred species of plants were
competing for sunlight and water, carbon dioxide and nitrogen. The area seemed limited and homogeneous—a smear of
green—from the vantage of the back yard, but once they were
immersed in it it became a variegated jungle, a feverish clash
of styles of leaf and stem, an implacable festering of protein
chains as nature sought not only to thrust itself outward with
root and runner and shoot but to attract insects and birds to
its pollen and seeds. Some footsteps sank into mud; others
tripped over hummocks that grass had over time built up of
its own accumulated roots. Thorns threatened eyes and
hands; a thatch of dead leaves and stalks masked the earth.
Reaching the area where Alexandra guessed the tinfoil-

wrapped poppet had landed, she and Sukie stooped low into a strange vegetable heat. The space low to the ground swarmed with a prickliness, an air of congestion, as twigs and tendrils probed the shadows for crumbs of sun and space.

Sukie cried out with the pleasure of discovery; but what she gouged up from where it had long rested embedded in the earth was an ancient golf ball, stippled in an obsolete checkered pattern. Some chemical it had absorbed had turned the lower half rust color.

"Shit," Sukie said. "I wonder how it ever got out here, we're miles from any golf course." Monty Rougemont, of course, had been a devoted golfer, who had resented the presence of women, with their spontaneous laughter and pastel outfits, on the fairway in front of him or indeed anywhere in his clubby paradise; it was as if in discovering this ball Sukie had come upon a small segment of her former husband, a message from the other world. She slipped the remembrance into a pocket of her raincoat.

"Maybe dropped from an airplane," Alexandra suggested.

Gnats had discovered them, and pattered and nipped at their faces. Sukie flapped a hand back and forth in front of her mouth and protested, "Even if we do find it, baby, what makes you think we can undo anything?"

"There must be a form. I've been doing some reading. You do everything backwards. We'd take the pins out and remelt the wax and turn Jenny back into a candle. We'd try to remember what we said that night and say it backwards."

"All those sacred names, impossible. I can't remember half of what we said."

"At the crucial moment Jane said 'Die' and you said 'Take that' and giggled."

"Did we really? We must have got carried away."

Crouching low, guarding their eyes, they explored the tangle step by step, looking for a glitter of aluminum foil. Sukie was getting her legs scratched above the Wellingtons and her handsome new London Fog was being tugged and its tiny waterproofed threads torn. She said, "I bet it's caught halfway up some one of these fucking damn prickerbushes."

The more querulous Sukie sounded, the more maternal Alexandra became. "It could well be," she said. "It felt eerily light when I threw it. It sailed."

"Why'd you ever chuck it out here anyway? What a hysterical thing to do."

"I told you, I'd just had a phone conversation with Jenny in which she'd asked me to save her. I felt guilty. I was afraid."

"Afraid of what, honey?"

"You know. Death."

"But it isn't *your* death."

"Any death is your death, in a way. These last weeks I've been getting the same symptoms Jenny had."

"You've *al*ways been that way about cancer." In exasperation Sukie flailed with the long-handled clippers at the thorny round-leafed canes importuning her, pulling at her raincoat, raking her wrists. "Fuck. Here's a dead squirrel all shrivelled up. This is a real dump out here. Couldn't you have found the damn thing with second sight? Couldn't you have made it, what's the word, levitate?"

"I tried but couldn't get a signal. Maybe the aluminum foil bottled up the emanations."

"Maybe your powers aren't what they used to be."

"That could be. Several times lately I tried to will some sun, I was feeling like such a maggot with all this dampness; but it rained anyway."

Sukie's thrashing grew more and more irritable. "Jane levitated her whole self."

"That's Jane. She's getting very strong. But you heard her, she doesn't want any part of reversing this spell, she *likes* the way things are going."

"I wonder if you've overestimated how far you can throw. Monty used to complain about golfers looking for their balls, how they'd always walk miles past where it could possibly be."

"To me it feels like we've *under*estimated. As I said, it really flew."

"You work out that way then, and I'll retrace a little. God, these fucking prickers. They're *hate*ful. What *good* are they, anyway?"

"They feed the birds. And rodents and skunks."

"Oh, great."

"Some aren't raspberries, I was noticing, they're wild roses. When we first moved to Eastwick, Ozzie and me, every fall I'd make jelly out of the rose hips."

"You and Oz were just too dear."

"It was pathetic, I was such a housewife. You're a saint," she told Sukie, "to be doing this. I know you're bored. You can quit any time."

"Not such a saint, really. Maybe I'm scared too. Here it is, anyway." She sounded nowhere near as excited as when she had found the golf ball fifteen minutes earlier. Alexandra, scratched and impeded by (her sensation was) some essential and unappeasable rudeness in the universe, pushed her way to where the other woman stood. Sukie had not touched the thing. It lay in a relatively open spot, a brackish patch supporting on its edges some sea milkwort; a few frail white flowers put forth their attractions in the jungle shadows. Stooping to touch the crumpled Reynolds Wrap, not rusted but dulled by its months in the weather, Alexandra noticed the damp dark earth around it crawling with mites of some kind, reddish specks collected like filings around a magnet, scurrying in their tiny world several orders lower, on the terraces of life, than her own. She forced herself to touch the evil charm, this hellishly baked potato. When she picked it up, it weighed nothing, and rattled: the pins inside it. She gently pried open the hollow aluminum foil. The pins inside had rusted. The wax substance of the little imitation of Jenny had quite disappeared.

"Animal fat," Sukie at last said, having waited for Alexandra to speak first. "Some little bunch of jiggers out here thought it was yummy and ate it all up or fed it to their babies. Look: they left the little hairs. Remember those little hairs? You'd think they would have rotted or something. That's why hair clogs up sinks, it's indestructible. Like Clorox bottles. Some day, honey, there will be nothing in the world but hair and Clorox bottles."

Nothing. Jenny's tallow surrogate had become nothing.

Raindrops like pinpricks touched their faces, now that the two women were standing erect amid the brambles. Such dry microscopic first drops foretell a serious rain, a soaker. The sky was solid gray but for a thin bar of blue above the low horizon to the west, so far away it might be altogether out of Rhode Island, this fair sky. "Nature is a hungry old thing," Alexandra said, letting the foil and pins drop back into the weeds.

"And thirsty," Sukie said. "Didn't you promise me a drink?"

Sukie wanted to be consoling and flirtatious, sensing Alexandra's sick terror, and did look rather stunning, with her red hair and monkeyish lips, standing up to her breasts in brambles, in her smart raincoat. But Alexandra had a desolate sensation of distance, as if her dear friend, fetching yet jaded, were another receding image, an advertisement, say, on the rear of a truck pulling rapidly away from a stoplight.

One of Brenda's several innovations was to have members of the church give an occasional sermon; today Darryl Van Horne was preaching. The well-thumbed big book he opened upon the lectern was not the Bible but a red-jacketed *Webster's Collegiate Dictionary*. "Centipede," he read aloud in that strangely resonant, as it were pre-amplified voice of his. "Any of a class (Chilopoda) of long flattened many-segmented predaceous arthropods with each segment bearing one pair of legs of which the foremost pair is modified into poison fangs."

Darryl looked up; he was wearing a pair of half-moon reading glasses and these added to the slippage of his face, its appearance of having been assembled of parts, with the seams not quite smooth. "You didn't know that about the poisonous fangs, did you? You've never had to look a centipede right in the eye, have you? *Have* you, you lucky people!" He was boomingly addressing perhaps a dozen heads, scattered through the pews on this muggy day late in August, the sky in the tall windows the sullen no-color of recycled paper. "Think," Darryl entreated, "think of the evolution of those fangs over the aeons, the infinity—don't you hate that word, 'infinity,' it's like you're supposed to get down on your knees whenever some dumb bastard says it—the infinity—and I guess my saying it makes me one more dumb bastard, but what the hell else can you say?—*think* of all those little wriggling struggles behind the sink and down in the cellar and the jungle that ended in this predaceous arthropod's—isn't that a beautiful phrase?—this predaceous arthropod's mouth, if you want to call it a mouth, it isn't like any of our ruby lips, I tell you, before those two front legs somehow got the idea of being poisonous and the trusty old strings of DNA took up the theme and the centipedes kept humping away making more centipedes and finally they got modified into fangs. *Pois*onous fangs. Hoo boy." He wiped his lips with forefinger and thumb. "And they call this a Creation, this mess of torture." The sermon title announced in movable white letters on the signboard outside the church was "THIS IS A TERRIBLE CREATION."

The scattered listening heads were silent. Even the woodwork of the old structure failed to creak. Brenda herself sat mute in profile beside the lectern, half hidden by a giant spray of gladioli and ferns in a plaster urn, given in memory this

Sunday of a stillborn son Franny Lovecraft had once produced, fifty years ago. Brenda looked pale and listless; she had been indisposed off and on for much of the summer. It had been an unhealthy wet summer in Eastwick.

"You know what they used to do to witches in Germany?" Darryl asked loudly from the pulpit, but as though it had just occurred to him, which probably it had. "They used to sit them on an iron chair and light a fire underneath. They used to tear their flesh with red-hot pincers. Thumbscrews. The rack. The boot. Strappado. You name it, they did it. To simple-minded old ladies, mostly." Franny Lovecraft leaned toward Rose Hallybread and whispered something in a loud but unintelligible rasp. Van Horne sensed the disturbance and in his vulnerable shambling way went defensive. "O.K.," he shouted toward the congregation. "So what? Well, you're going to say, this is human nature. This is human history. What does this have to do with Creation? What's this crazy guy trying to tell me? We could go on and on till nightfall with tortures human beings have used against each other under the sacred flag of one form of faith or another. The Chinese used to tear the skin off a body inch by inch, in the Middle Ages they'd disembowel a guy in front of his own eyes and cut his cock off and stuff it in his mouth for good measure. Sorry to spell it out like that, I get excited. The point is, all this stacked end to end multiplied by a zillion doesn't amount to a hill of beans compared with the cruelty natural organic friendly Creation has inflicted on its creatures since the first poor befuddled set of amino acids struggled up out of the galvanized slime. Women never accused of being witches, pretty little blonde dollies who never laid an evil eye on even a centipede, die every day in pain probably just as bad as and certainly more prolonged than any inflicted by the good old *Hexestuhl*. It had big blunt studs all over it, I don't know what the thermodynamic principle was. I don't want to think about it any more and I bet you don't either. You get the idea.

It was terrible, terrible; Jesus it was terrible." His glasses fell forward on his nose and in readjusting them he seemed to press his whole face back together. His cheeks looked wet to some in the congregation.

Jenny was not here; she was back in the hospital, with uncontrollable internal bleeding. This was the sermon's undercurrent. Ray Neff was not here today either—he had accepted an invitation from Professor Hallybread to go sailing in Arthur's newly bought gaff-rigged Herreshoff 12½' across to Melville. Greta was here, though, sitting alone. It was hard to know about Greta—what she thought, what she wanted. Her being German, though her accent was never as bad as the people poking fun of it would have had you believe, put a kind of grid across her soul when you tried to look inside. Straight straw-dull hair, cut short, and amazing eyes the blue of dirty dishwater behind her granny glasses. She never missed a Sunday, but it may have been simply the unreflective thoroughness of her race, the German race, that admirable machine always waiting for a romantic demon to seize the levers.

Van Horne had been silent a while, pawing through the dictionary clumsily, as if his hands were gloves. Old Mrs. Lovecraft could now be heard as she leaned over to Mrs. Hallybread and distinctly asked, "Why is he using those filthy words?" Rose Hallybread looked exceedingly amused; she was a tall woman with a tiny head set in a nest of wiry gray and black hair frizzed way out. Her very small face was the color of a walnut, creased and recreased by decades of sun worship; what she whispered back was inaudible. On her other side sat Dawn Polanski; the girl had fascinating wide Mongolian cheekbones and smudged-looking skin and that impervious deadpan calm of the lawless. Between them she and Rose did pack a lot of psychic power.

Van Horne dimly heard the commotion and looked up, blinked, pushed his glasses higher on his nose, and apologetically pronounced, "I know this is taking plenty long enough but here, right on one page, I've just come across 'tapeworm' and 'tarantula.' 'Tarantula: any of various large hairy spiders that are typically rather sluggish and though capable of biting sharply are not significantly poisonous to man.' Thanks a lot. And his limp little buddy up here: 'Any of numerous cestode worms (as of the genus *Taenia*) parasitic when adult in the intestine of man or other vertebrates.' Numerous, mind you, not just one or two oddballs tucked back in some corner of Creation, anybody can make a mistake, but a lot of them, a lot of *kinds*, a terrific idea, Somebody must have thought. I don't know about the rest of you gathered here, wishing I'd pipe down and sit down probably, but I've always been fascinated by parasites. I mean fascinated in a negative way. They come in so many sizes, for one thing, from viruses and bacteria like your friendly syphilis spirochete to tapeworms thirty feet long and roundworms so big and fat they block up your big intestine. Intestines are where they're happiest, by and large. To sit around in the slushy muck inside somebody else's guts—that's their catbird seat. You doing all the digesting for 'em, they don't even need stomachs, just mouths and assholes, pardon my French. But boy, the ingenuity that old Great Designer spent with His lavish hand on these humble little devils. Here, I scribbled down some notes, out of the *En-cy-clo-pedia*, as Jiminy Cricket used to say, if I can read 'em in this lousy light up here; Brenda, I don't see how you do it; week after week. If I were you I'd go on strike. O.K Enough horsing around.

"Your average intestinal roundworm, about the size of a lead pencil, lays its eggs in the feces of the host; that's simple enough. Then, don't ask me how—there's a lot of unsanitary conditions in the world, once you get out of Eastwick—these eggs get up into your mouth and you swallow 'em, like it or not. They hatch in your duodenum, the little larvae worm through the gut wall, get into a blood vessel, and migrate to your lungs. But you don't think that's where they're gonna retire and live off their pension, do you? No sir, my dear friends, this little mother of a roundworm, he chews his way out of his cozy capillary there in the lungs and gets into an air sac and climbs what they call the respiratory tree to the epiglottis, where you go and swallow him again!—can you believe you'd be so stupid? Once he's had the second ride down he *does* settle in and become your average mature wage-earning roundworm.

"Or take—hold it, my notes are scrambled—take an appealing little number called the lung fluke. Its eggs get out in the world when people cough up sputum. "Van Horne hawked by way of illustration. "When they hatch in fresh water that's lying around in these crummy, sort of Third-World places, they move into certain snails they fancy, in the form now of larvae, these lung flukes, follow me? When they've had enough of living in snails they swim out and bore into the soft tissues of crayfish and crabs. And when the Japanese or whoever eat the crayfish or crabs raw or under-cooked the way they like it, in they go, these pesky flukes, and chew out through the intestines and diaphragm to get into good old lung and begin this sputum routine all over again. Another of these watery little jobbies, *Diphyllo-bothrium latum* if I can read it right, the little swimming embryos are eaten first by water fleas, and then fish eat the water fleas, and bigger fish eat *those* fish, and finally man bites the bullet, and all the while these itty-bitty monsters instead of being digested have been chewing their way out through the various stomach linings and are *thriv*ing. Hoo boy. There're a ton of these stories, but I don't want to bore anybody or, you know, overmake my point here. Wait, though. You got to hear this. I'm quoting. '*Echinococcus granulosus* is one of the few tapeworms parasitizing man in which the adult worm inhabits the intestine of the dog, while man is one of the several hosts for the larval stage. Moreover, the adult worm is minute, measuring only three to six millimeters. In contrast, the larva, known as a hydatid cyst, may be large as a football. Man acquires infection'—get this—'from contact with the feces of infected dogs.'

"So here you have, aside from a lot of feces and sputum, Man, allegedly made in the image of God, as far as little *Echinococcus* is concerned just a way station on the way to the intestines of a dog. Now you mustn't think parasites don't dig each other; they do. Here's a cutie pie called *Trichosomoides crassicauda*, of whom we read, quote, 'The female of this species lives as a parasite in the bladder of the rat, and the degenerate male lives inside the uterus of the female.' So degenerate, even the Encyclopedia thinks it's degenerate. And, hey, how about this?—'What might be termed sexual phoresis is seen in the blood fluke *Schistosoma haematobium*, in which the smaller female is carried in a ventral body-wall groove, the gynecophoric canal, of the male.' They had a drawing in the book I wish I could share with you good people, the mouth up at the tip of something like a finger and this big ventral sucker and the whole thing looking like a banana with its zipper coming undone. Trust me: it is *nasty*."

And to those who were sitting restless now (for the sky in the top panes of the windows was brightening as if a flashlight were shining behind the paper, and the hollyhock tops nodded and shuffled in a clearing breeze, a breeze that nearly capsized Arthur and Ray out in the East Passage, near Dyer Island: Arthur was unaccustomed to handling the lively little daysailer; his heart began to fibrillate; a bird beat its wings in his chest and his brain chanted rapidly, *Not yet, Lord, not yet*) it appeared that Van Horne's face, as it bobbed back and forth between his scrambled notes and a somehow blinded outward gaze toward the congregation, was dissolving, was thawing into nothingness. He tried to gather his thoughts toward the painful effort of conclusion. His voice sounded forced up from far underground.

"So to wind this thing up it's not just, you know, the nice clean pounce of a tiger or a friendly shaggy lion. That's what they sell us with all those stuffed toys. Put a kid to bed with a stuffed liver fluke or a hairy tarantula would be more like it. You all eat. The way you feel toward sunset of a beautiful summer day, the first g-and-t or rum-and-Coke or Bloody Mary beginning to do its work mellowing those synapses, and some nice mild cheese and crackers all laid out like a poker hand on the plate on the glass table out there on the sundeck or beside the pool, honest to God, good people, that's the way the roundworm feels when a big gobbety mess of half-digested steak or moo goo gai pan comes sloshing down to him. He's as real a creature as you and me. He's as noble a creature, designwise—really *lov*ingly designed. You got to picture that Big Visage leaning down and smiling through Its beard while those fabulous Fingers with Their angelic manicure fiddled with the last fine-tuning of old *Schistosoma*'s ventral sucker: that's Creation. Now I ask you, isn't that pretty terrible? Couldn't you have done better, given the resources? I sure as hell could have. So vote for me next time, O.K.? Amen."

In every congregation there has to be a stranger. The solitary uninvited today was Sukie Rougemont, sitting in the back wearing a wide-rimmed straw hat to hide her beautiful pale orange hair, and great round spectacles, so she could see to read the hymnal and to take notes on the margin of her mimeographed program. Her scurrilous column "Eastwick Eyes and Ears" had been reinstated, to make the *Word* more "sexy." She had gotten wind of Darryl's secular sermon and come to cover it. Brenda and Darryl, from their position on the altar dais, must have seen her slip in during the first hymn, but not Greta nor Dawn nor Rose Hallybread had been aware of her presence, and since she slipped out in the first stanza of "Father, Who on Man Doth Shower," no confrontation between the factions of witches occurred. Greta had begun to yawn unstoppably, and Dawn's lusterless eyes furiously to itch, and the buckles of Franny Lovecraft's shoes had come undone; but all of these developments might be laid to natural causes, as might Sukie's discovering, the next time she looked in the mirror, eight or ten more gray hairs.

"Well, she died," Sukie told Alexandra over the phone. "At about four this morning. Only Chris was with her, and he had dozed off. It was the night nurse coming in realized she had no pulse."

"Where was Darryl?"

"He'd gone home for some sleep. Poor guy, he really had tried to be a dutiful husband, night after night. It had been coming for weeks, and the doctors were surprised she had hung on so long. She was tougher than anybody thought."

"She was," Alexandra said, in simple salute. Her own heart with its burden of guilt had moved on, into an autumn mood, a calm of abdication. It was past Labor Day, and all along the edges of her yard spindly wild asters competed with goldenrod and the dark-leaved, burr-heavy thistles. The purple grapes in her arbor had ripened and what the grackles didn't get fell to form a pulp on the bricks; they were really too sour to eat, and this year Alexandra didn't feel up to making jelly: the steam, the straining, the little jars too hot to touch. As she groped for the next thing to say to Sukie, Alexandra was visited by a sensation more and more common to her: she felt outside her body, seeing it from not far away, in its pathetic specificity, its mortal length and breadth. Another March, and she would be forty. Her mysterious aches and itches continued in the night, though Doc Paterson had found nothing to diagnose. He was a plump bald man with hands that seemed inflated, they were so broad and soft, so pink and clean. "I feel rotten," she announced.

"Oh don't bother," Sukie sighed, herself sounding tired.

"People die all the time."

"I just want to be held," Alexandra surprisingly said.

"Honey, who doesn't?"

"That's all she wanted too."

"And that's what she got."

"You mean by Darryl."

"Yes. The worst thing is—"

"There's worse?"

"I really shouldn't be telling even you, I got it from Jane in absolute secrecy; you know she's been seeing Bob Osgood, who got it from Doc Pat—"

"She was pregnant," Alexandra told her.

"How did you know?"

"What else could the worst thing be? *So* sad," she said.

"Oh I don't know. I'd hate to have been that kid. I don't see Darryl as cut out for fatherhood somehow."

"What's he going to do?" The fetus hung disgustingly in Alexandra's mind's eye—a blunt-headed fish, curled over like an ornamental door knocker.

"Oh, I guess go on much as before. He has his new crowd now. I told you about church."

"I read your squib in 'Eyes and Ears' You made it sound like a biology lecture."

"It was. It was a wonderful spoof. The kind of thing he loves to do. Remember 'The A Nightingale Sang in Berkeley Square Boogie'? I couldn't put anything in about Rose and Dawn and Greta, but honestly, when they put their heads together the cone of power that goes up is absolutely electric, it's like the aurora borealis."

"I wonder what they look like skyclad," Alexandra said. When she had this immediate detached vision of her own body it was always clothed, though not always clothed in what she was wearing at the time.

"Awful," Sukie supplied. "Greta like one of those lumpy rumpled engravings by the German, you know the one—"

"Dürer."

"Right. And Rose skinny as a broom, and Dawn just a little smoochy waif with a big smooth baby tummy sticking out and no breasts. Brenda—Brenda I could go for," Sukie confessed. "I wonder now if Ed was just my way of communicating with Brenda."

"I went back to the spot," Alexandra confessed in turn, "and picked up all the rusty pins, and stuck them in myself at various points. It still didn't do any good. Doc Pat says he can't find even a benign tumor."

"Oh sweetie *pie*," Sukie exclaimed, and Alexandra realized she had frightened her, the other woman wanted to hang up. "You're really getting weird, aren't you?"

Some days later Jane Smart said over the phone, her voice piercing with its indignation, "You *can't* mean you haven't already heard!"

More and more, Alexandra had the sensation that Jane and Sukie talked and then one or the other of them called her out of duty, the next day or later. Maybe they flipped a coin over who got the chore.

"Not even from Joe Marino?" Jane was going on. "He's one of the principal creditors."

"Joe and I don't see each other any more. Really."

"What a shame," Jane said. "He was so dear. If you like Italian pixies."

"He loved me," Alexandra said, helplessly, knowing how stupid the other woman felt her to be. "But I couldn't let him leave Gina for me."

"Well," Jane said, "that's a rather face-saving way of putting it."

"Maybe so, Jane Pain. Anyway. Tell me your news."

"Not just *my* news, the whole *town's* news. He's left. He's skipped, sugar pie. *Il est disparu*." Her *s*'s hurt, but they seemed to be stinging that other body, which Alexandra could get back into only when she slept.

From the wrathfully personal way Jane was taking it Alexandra could only think, "Bob Osgood?"

"*Dar*ryl, darling. Please, wake up. Our dear Darryl. Our leader. Our redeemer from Eastwick *ennui*. And he's taken Chris Gabriel with him."

"Chris?"

"You were right in the first place. He was one of those."

"But he—"

"Some of them can. But it isn't real to them. They don't bring to it the illusions that normal men do."

Har, har, diable, diable, saute ici, saute là. There she had been, Alexandra remembered, a year ago, mooning over that mansion from a distance, then worrying about her thighs looking too fat and white when she had to wade. "Well," she said now. "Weren't we silly?"

" 'Naïve' is the way I'd rather put it. How could we *not* be, living in a ridiculous backwater like this? Why are we here, did you ever ask yourself that? Because our husbands planted us here, and we like dumb daisies just *stay*."

"So you think it was little Chris—"

"All along. Obviously. He married Jenny just to cinch his hold. I could kill them both, frankly."

"Oh Jane, don't even say it."

"And her money, of course. He needed that pathetic little money she got from the house to keep his creditors at bay. And now there's all the hospital bills. Bob says it's a terrible mess, the bank is hearing from everybody because they're stuck with the mortgage on the Lenox place. He did admit there may be just enough equity if they can find the right developers; the place would be ideal for condominiums, if they can get it by the Planning Board. Bob thinks Herbie Prinz might be persuadable; he takes these expensive winter vacations."

"But did he leave all his laboratory behind? The paint that would make solar energy—"

Guilt

"Lexa, don't you understand? There was never anything there. We *ima*gined him."

"But the pianos. And the art."

"We have no idea how much of that was paid for. Obviously there are *some* assets. But a lot of that art surely has depreciated dreadfully; I mean, stuffed penguins spattered with car paint—"

"He loved it," Alexandra said, still loyal. "He didn't fake that, I'm sure. He was an artist, and he wanted to give us all an artistic experience. And he did. Look at your music, all that Brahms you used to play with him until your awful Doberman ate your cello and you began to talk just like some unctuous *bank*er."

"You're being very stupid," Jane said sharply, and hung up. It was just as well, for words had begun to stick in Alexandra's throat, the croakiness of tears aching to flow.

Sukie called within the hour, the last gasp of their old solidarity. But all she could seem to say was "Oh my God. That little wimp Chris. I never heard him put two words together."

"I think he *wanted* to love us," Alexandra said, able to speak only of Darryl Van Horne, "but he just didn't have it in him."

"Do you think he wanted to love Jenny?"

"It could be, because she looked so much like Chris."

"He was a model husband."

"That could have been irony of a sort."

"I've been wondering, Lexa, he must have known what we were doing to Jenny, is it possible—"

"Go on. Say it."

"We were doing his *will* by, you know—"

"Killing her," Alexandra supplied.

"Yes," said Sukie. "Because he wanted her out of the way once he had her legally and everything was different."

Alexandra tried to think; it had been ages since she had felt

: 307 :

her mind stretch itself, a luxurious feeling, almost muscular, probing those impalpable tunnels of the possible and the probable. "I really doubt," she decided, "that Darryl was ever organized in that way. He had to improvise on situations others created, and couldn't look very far ahead." As Alexandra talked, she saw him clearer and clearer—felt him from the inside, his caverns and seams and empty places. She had projected her spirit into a place of echoing desolation. "He couldn't create, he had no powers of his own that way, all he could do was release what was already there in others. Even us: we had the coven before he came to town, and our powers such as they are. I think," she told Sukie, "he wanted to be a woman, like he said, but he wasn't even that."

"Even," Sukie echoed, critically.

"Well it *is* miserable a lot of the time. It honestly is." Again, those sticks in the throat, the gateway of tears. But this sensation, like that resistant one of trying to think again, was somehow hopeful, a stiff beginning. She was ceasing to drift.

"This might make you feel a little better," Sukie told her. "There's a good chance Jenny wasn't so sorry to die. Rebecca has been doing a lot of talking down at Nemo's, now that Fidel has run off with the other two, and she says some of the goings-on over there after we left would really curl your hair. Apparently it was no secret from Jenny what Chris and Darryl were up to, at least once she was safely married."

"Poor little soul," Alexandra said. "I guess she was one of those perfectly lovely people the world for some reason never finds any use for." Nature in her wisdom puts them to sleep.

"Even Fidel was offended, Rebecca says," Sukie was saying, "but when she begged him to stay and live with her he told her he didn't want to be a lobsterman or a floor boy over at Dataprobe, and there was nothing else people around here would let a spic like him do. Rebecca's heartbroken."

"Men," Alexandra eloquently said.

"Aren't they, though?"

"How have people like the Hallybreads taken all this?"

"Badly. Rose is nearly hysterical that Arthur is going to be involved financially in the terrible mess. Apparently he got rather interested in Darryl's selenium theories and even signed some sort of agreement making him a partner in exchange for his expertise; that was one of Darryl's things, getting people to sign pacts. Her back evidently is so bad now she sleeps on a mat on the floor and makes Arthur read aloud to her all day, these trashy historical novels. He can never get away any more."

"Really, what a boring terrible woman," Alexandra said.

"Vile," Sukie agreed. "Jane says her head looks like a dried apple packed in steel wool."

"How *is* Jane? Really. I fear she got rather impatient with me this morning."

"Well, she says Bob Osgood knows of a wonderful man in Providence, on Hope Street I think she said, who can replace the whole front plate of her Ceruti without changing the timbre, he's one of those sort of hippie Ph.D.'s who've gone to work in the crafts to spite their father or protest the System or something. But she's patched it with masking tape and plays it chewed and says she likes it, it sounds more human. I think she's in terrible shape. *Very* neurotic and paranoid. I asked her to meet me downtown and have a sandwich at the Bakery or even Nemo's now that Rebecca doesn't blame us for everything any more, but she said no, she was afraid of being seen by those *others*. Brenda and Dawn and Greta, I suppose. I see them all the time along Dock Street. I smile, they smile. There's nothing left to fight about. Her color"— back to Jane—"is frightening. White as a clenched fist, and it's not even October."

"Almost," Alexandra said. "The robins are gone, and you can hear the geese at night. I'm letting my tomatoes rot on the vine this year; every time I go into the cellar these jars and jars of last year's sauce reproach me. My awful children have absolutely rebelled against spaghetti, and, I must say, it does pack on the calories, which is scarcely what I need."

"Don't be silly. You *have* lost weight. I saw you coming out of the Superette the other day—I was stuck in the *Word*, interviewing this incredibly immature and pompous new harbormaster, he's just a kid with hair down to his shoulders, younger than Toby even, and just happened to look out the window—and thought to myself, 'Doesn't Lexa look *fabu*lous.' Your hair was up in that big pigtail and you had on that brocaded Iranian—"

"Algerian."

"—Algerian jacket you wear in the fall, and had Coal on a leash, a long rope."

"I had been at the beach," Alexandra volunteered. "It was lovely. Not a breath of wind." Though they talked on some minutes more, trying to rekindle the old coziness, that collusion which related to the yieldingness and vulnerability of their bodies, Alexandra and—her intuition suddenly, unmistakably told her—Sukie as well deadeningly felt that it had all been said before.

There comes a blessed moment in the year when we know we are mowing the lawn for the last time. Alexandra's elder son, Ben, was supposed to earn his allowance with yard work, but now he was back in high school and trying to be a fledgling Lance Alworth at football practice afterwards— sprinting, weaving, leaping to feel that sweet hit of leather on outstretched fingertips ten feet off the ground. Marcy had a part-time job waitressing at the Bakery Coffee Nook, which was serving evening meals now, and regrettably she had become involved with one of those shaggy sinister boys who hung out in front of the Superette. The two younger children, Linda and Eric, had entered the fifth and seventh grades respectively, and Alexandra had found cigarette butts in a paper cup of water beneath Eric's bed. Now she pushed her snarling, smoking Toro, which hadn't had its oil changed since the days of Oz's home maintenance, once more back and forth across her unkempt lawn, littered with long yellow featherlike willow leaves and all bumpy as the moles were digging in for the winter. She let the Toro run until it had burned up all its gas, so none would clog the carburetor next spring. She thought of draining the sludgy ancient oil but that seemed *too* good and workmanlike of her. On her way back to the kitchen from the gardening-tool shed she passed through her workroom and saw her stalled armature at last for what it was: a husband. The clumsily nailed and wired-together one-by-twos and two-by-fours had that lankiness she admired and that Ozzie had displayed before being a husband had worn his corners down. She remembered how his knees and elbows had jabbed her in bed those early years when nightmares twitched him; she had rather loved him for those nightmares, confessions as they were of his terror as life in all its length and responsibility loomed to his young manhood. Toward the end of their marriage he slept like a thing motionless and sunk, sweating and exuding oblivious little snuffles. She took his multicolored dust down from the shelf and sprinkled a little on the knotty piece of pine two-by-four that did for the armature's shoulders. She worried less about the head and face than the feet; it was the extremities, she realized, that mattered most to her about a man. Whatever went on in the middle, she had to have in her ideal man a gauntness and delicacy in the feet—Christ's feet as they looked overlapped and pegged on crucifixes, tendony and long-toed and limp as if in flight—and something hardened and work-broadened about the hands; Darryl's rubbery-looking hands had been his most repulsive feature. She worked her ideas up sketchily in clay, in the last of the pure white kaolin taken from the widow's back yard in Coventry. One foot and one hand were enough, and sketchiness didn't matter; what was important was not her finished product but the message etched on the air and sent to those powers that could form hands and fingers to the smallest phalange and fascia, those powers that spilled the marvels of all anatomies forth from Creation's berserk precise cornucopia. For the head she settled on a modest-sized pumpkin she bought at that roadside stand on Route 4, which for ten months of the year looks hopelessly dilapidated and abandoned but comes to life at harvest time. She hollowed out the pumpkin and put in some of Ozzie's dust, but not too much, for she wanted him duplicated only in his essential husbandliness. One crucial ingredient was almost impossible to find in Rhode Island: western soil, a handful of dry sandy sage-supporting earth. Moist eastern loam would not do. One day she happened to spot parked on Oak Street a pickup truck with Colorado plates; she reached inside the back fender and scraped some tawny dried mud down into her palm and took it home and put it in with Ozzie's dust. Also she needed a cowboy hat for the pumpkin, and had to go all the way to Providence in her Subaru to search for a costume store that would cater to Brown students with their theatricals and carnivals and protest demonstrations. While there, she thought to enroll herself as a part-time student in the Rhode Island School of Design; she had gone as far as she could as a sculptress with being merely primitive. The other students were scarcely older than her children, but one of the instructors, a ceramist from Taos, a leathery limping man well into his forties and weathered by the baths and blasts of life, took her eye, and she his, in her sturdy voluptuousness a little like that of cattle (which Joe Marino had hit upon in calling her, while rutting, his *vacca*). After several terms and turnings-away they did marry and Jim took her and his stepchildren back west, where the air was ecstatically thin and all the witchcraft belonged to the Hopi and Navajo shamans.

"My God," Sukie said to her over the phone before she left. "What was your secret?"

"It's not for print," Alexandra told her sternly. Sukie had risen to be editor of the *Word*, and in keeping with the shamelessly personal tone of the emerging postwar era had to run scandal or confession every week, squibs of trivial daily rumor that Clyde Gabriel would have fastidiously killed.

"You must imagine your life," Alexandra confided to the younger woman. "And then it happens."

Sukie relayed this piece of magic to Jane, and dear angry Jane, who was in danger of being an embittered and crabbed old maid, so that her piano students associated the black and white of the keys with bones and the darkness of the pit, with everything dead and strict and menacing, hissed her disbelief; she had long since disowned Alexandra as a trustworthy sister.

But in secrecy even from Sukie she had taken splinters of the cello-front replaced by the dedicated hippie restorer on Hope Street and wrapped them in her dead father's old soot-colored tuxedo and stuffed into one pocket of the jacket some crumbs of the dried herb Sam Smart had become, hanging in her ranch-house basement, and into the other pocket put the confetti of a torn-up twenty-dollar bill—for she was tired, boringly tired, of being poor—and sprinkled the still-shiny wide lapels of the tuxedo with her perfume and her urine and her menstrual blood and enclosed the whole odd-smelling charm in a plastic cleaner's bag and laid it between her mattress and her springs. Upon its subtle smothered hump she slept each night. One horrendously cold weekend in January, she was visiting her mother in the Back Bay, and a perfectly suitable little man in a tuxedo and patent-leather pumps as shiny as boiling tar dropped in for tea; he lived with his parents in Chestnut Hill and was on his way to a gala at the Tavern Club. He had heavy-lidded protruding eyes the pale questioning blue of a Siamese cat's; he did not drop by so briefly as to fail to notice—he who had never married and who had been written off by those he might have courted as hopelessly prissy, too sexless even to be called gay—something dark and sharp and dirty in Jane that might stir the long-dormant amorous part of his being. We wake at different times, and the gallantest flowers are those that bloom in the cold. His glance also detected in Jane a brisk and formidable potential administrator of the Chippendale and Duncan Phyfe antiques, the towering cabinets of Chinese lacquerwork, the deep-stored cases of vintage wine, the securities and silver he would one day inherit from his parents, though both were still alive, as were indeed two of his grandparents—ancient erect women changeless as crystal in their corners of Milton and Salem. This height of family, and the claims of the brokerage clients whose money he diffidently tended, and the requirements of his delicate allergic nature (milk, sugar, alcohol, and sodium were among the substances he must avoid) all suggested a manageress; he called Jane next morning before she had time to fly away in her battered Valiant and invited her for drinks that evening at the Copley bar. She refused; and then a picture-book blizzard collapsed on the brick precincts and held her fast. His call that evening proposed lunch upstairs at the snowbound Ritz. Jane resisted him all the way, scratching and singeing with her murderous tongue; but her accent spoke to him, and he made her finally his prisoner in a turreted ironstone fantasy in Brookline designed by a disciple of H. H. Richardson.

Sukie sprinkled powdered nutmeg on the circular glass of her hand mirror until there was nothing left of the image but the gold-freckled green eyes or, when she slightly moved her head, her monkeyish and overlipsticked lips. With these lips she recited in a solemn whisper seven times the obscene and sacred prayer to Cernunnos. Then she took the tired old plaid plastic place mats off the kitchen table and put them into the trash for Tuesday's collection. The very next day a jaunty sandy-haired man from Connecticut showed up at the *Word* office, to place an ad: he was looking for a pedigreed

Weimaraner to mate with his bitch. He was renting a cottage in Southwick with his small children (he was recently divorced; he had helped his wife go belatedly to law school and her first action had been to file for mental cruelty) and the poor creature had decided to come into heat; the bitch was in torment. This man had a long off-center nose, like Ed Parsley; an aura of regretful intelligence, like Clyde Gabriel· and something of Arthur Hallybread's professional starchiness. In his checked suit he looked excessively alert, like a gimcrack salesman from upstate New York or a song-and-dance man about to move sideways across a stage, strumming a banjo. Like Sukie, he wanted to be amusing. He was really from Stamford, where he worked in an infant industry, selling and servicing glamorized computers called word processors. On hers she now rapidly writes paperback romances, with a few taps of her fingertips transposing paragraphs, renaming characters, and glossarizing for re-use standard passions and crises.

Sukie was the last to leave Eastwick; the afterimage of her in her nappy suede skirt and orange hair, swinging her long legs and arms past the glinting shopfronts, lingered on Dock Street like the cool-colored ghost the eye retains after staring at something bright. This was years ago. The young harbor-master with whom she had her last affair has a paunch now, and three children; but he still remembers how she used to bite his shoulder and say she loved to taste the salt of the sea-mist condensed on his skin. Dock Street has been repaved and widened to accept more traffic, and from the old horse trough to Landing Square, as it tends to be called, all the slight zigzags in the line of the curb have been straightened. New people move to town; some of them live in the old Lenox mansion, which has indeed been turned into condominiums. The tennis court has been kept up, though the perilous experiment with the air-supported canvas canopy has not been repeated. An area has been dredged and a dock and small marina built, as tenant inducement. The egrets nest elsewhere. The causeway has been elevated, with culverts every fifty yards, so it never floods—or has only once so far, in the great February blizzard of '78. The weather seems generally tamer in these times; there are rarely any thunderstorms.

Jenny Gabriel lies with her parents under polished granite flush with the clipped grass in the new section of Cocum-scussoç Cemetery. Chris, her brother and their son, has been, with his angelic visage and love of comic books, swallowed by the Sodom of New York. Lawyers now think that Darryl Van Horne was an assumed name. Yet several patents under that name do exist. Residents at the condo have reported mysterious crackling noises from some of the painted window sills, and wasps dead of shock. The facts of the financial imbroglio lie buried in vaults and drawers of old paperwork, silted over in even this short a span of time and of no great interest. What is of interest is what our minds retain, what our lives have given to the air. The witches are gone, vanished; we were just an interval in their lives, and they in ours. But as Sukie's blue-green ghost continues to haunt the sunstruck pavement, and Jane's black shape to flit past the moon, so the rumors of the days when they were solid among us, gorgeous and doing evil, have flavored the name of the town in the mouths of others, and for those of us who live here have left something oblong and invisible and exciting we do not understand. We meet it turning the corner where Hemlock meets Oak; it is there when we walk the beach in off-season and the Atlantic in its blackness mirrors the dense packed gray of the clouds: a scandal, life like smoke rising twisted into legend.